# THE
# MIST

# CARLA NEGGERS

# THE
# MIST

MIRA®

Recycling programs
for this product may
not exist in your area.

ISBN-13: 978-0-7783-2624-3

THE MIST

www.MIRABooks.com

**Printed in U.S.A.**

To Jim and Maureen,
and to Todd and Martha

Family!

# Chapter 1

*Beara Peninsula, Southwest Ireland*
*4:45 p.m., IST*
*August 25*

Lizzie Rush tensed at her table by the fire, watching out of the corner of her eye as a tall, fair-haired man entered the small village pub, shutting the door firmly against the gale-force wind and steady rain that had been lashing the southwest Irish coast for hours. The man wore an expensive trench coat unbuttoned over a dark brown sweater neatly draped across a flat abdomen, dark brown trousers and leather shoes that, although suited to walking the isolated hills of the remote Beara Peninsula, looked to be free of mud and manure.

The half-dozen local fishermen and farmers Lizzie had seen arrive over the past hour had hung up wet, worn jackets and scraped off their shoes and wellies or shed them and set them by the door. The men were gathered now over pints of Guinness and mugs of coffee at rickety tables by the front window. They paid no attention to the newcomer, nor did the brown-and-white springer spaniel flopped on the stone hearth close to the peat fire. The dog belonged to the barman and presumably was accustomed to the comings and goings at the pub.

Lizzie drank the last of her strong coffee. The past day had been a whirlwind. A last-minute overnight flight from Boston to Dublin. A few hours to check in to her family's small hotel in Dublin and try to talk herself into abandoning her trip to the Beara Peninsula. No luck there. Then it was back to the airport for a short flight west across Ireland to the tiny Kerry County airport and, finally, the drive here, to this quiet village on Kenmare Bay, in the rain and wind.

She set down her mug and turned a page in the beautifully illustrated book of Irish folktales she was reading while enjoying coffee and warm blackberry crumble by the fire. As tempting as it was, she knew she couldn't give in to the lure of the cozy, romantic atmosphere of the pub and let down her guard. As the newcomer walked over to the bar, she reminded herself he could have a weapon—a gun, a knife—concealed under his trench coat or tucked next to an ankle.

Or he could be an ordinary, if well-dressed, tourist getting out of the gale.

The barman, a wiry, sandy-haired Irishman named Eddie O'Shea, filled a pint from the tap. He'd been eyeing Lizzie with a mix of suspicion and curiosity since she'd shed her own dripping jacket and hung it on a wooden peg by the door, but he gave the newcomer a warmer reception.

"Ah," he said with a smile and a little hoot of surprise and recognition, "if it isn't Lord Will himself."

*Lord Will.*

Lizzie forced herself to calmly turn another page in her book.

"Hello, Eddie," the newcomer said in an upper-class British accent.

Eddie set the pint on a tray on the gleaming, polished five-foot stretch of wood in front of him and sighed. "You wouldn't be in Ireland for a bit of golf, would you?"

"Not today, I'm afraid."

Lizzie stared at a lush watercolor of a quaint Irish farm, grazing sheep and trooping fairies. Of all the things she'd anticipated could go wrong on this trip, having William Arthur Davenport turn up in the same Irish village, the same Irish pub she was in, wasn't one of them.

She let her gaze settle on the details of the captivating water-color—the pink-and-lavender sunrise above the green hills, the purple thistle along a country lane, the mischievous smiles of the fairies. The book was the work of Keira Sullivan, a Boston-based illustrator and folklorist with deep Irish roots. Lizzie had yet to meet Keira, but she knew Simon Cahill, the FBI agent with whom Keira was romantically involved.

Simon, Lizzie reminded herself, was the reason she was in Ireland. She'd heard he was here with Keira on the Beara Penin-sula while she painted and researched an old Irish story. As much as Lizzie hated to disturb the new lovers, she felt she had no choice. She had to act now, before Norman Estabrook could make good on his threat to kill Simon and his boss, FBI director John March.

Norman would kill Lizzie, too, if he discovered the role she'd played in the FBI investigation into his illegal activities over the past year, culminating in his arrest two months ago on suspicion of money laundering and providing material support to transna-tional drug traffickers. He was a thrill-seeking billionaire with a long reach. There was no doubt in her mind that he would never go to trial, much less end up in prison. For Norman Estabrook, death was preferable to confinement. He was under arrest now—he'd given up his passport, posted a huge bond and agreed to stay on his Montana ranch under electronic surveillance. But it wouldn't last. There was talk he was about to cut a deal with federal prosecutors and walk.

And when that happened, Lizzie thought, he'd come after the people he believed had betrayed him. Simon Cahill, John March—and their anonymous source.

Her.

When she'd finally decided to come to Ireland and talk to Simon face-to-face, Lizzie had created a cover story that would explain her presence on the Beara Peninsula without giving herself away. If not the truth, it wasn't an outright lie, either.

She simply hadn't counted on Simon's handsome, dangerous British friend turning up in Ireland, too. She had no desire to pop onto Will Davenport's radar.

Lizzie decided she wouldn't mind being a tiny fairy right now. Or a shape-shifter. Then she could turn herself into an ant.

An ant could disappear into a crack in the floor and not be noticed by the man at the bar.

She'd done her research. Will Davenport was the younger son of a British peer, the marquess of something—she couldn't remember his exact title. Peter, Will's older brother, managed the family's five-hundred-year-old estate in the north of England, and Arabella, his younger sister, designed wedding dresses in London. At thirty-five, Will was the wealthy owner of various properties in England and Scotland, with offices in an ivy-covered London brownstone.

That wasn't all he did. Two years ago—supposedly—he had abruptly abandoned his career as an officer with the Special Air Service—the SAS—to make his fortune. Lizzie, however, strongly suspected he had merely shifted from the SAS to the SIS, the British Secret Intelligence Service, popularly known as MI6.

She did know her spies.

Surreptitiously she tucked a few strands of black hair back under her red bandanna. She hadn't tried to disguise herself so much as make it less easy for anyone to describe her later on. "Oh, yes, I saw a woman at the pub. She had on a red bandanna and hiking clothes."

If things went wrong for her in Ireland, which they seemed about to do, that wasn't much for anyone, including the FBI, the Irish Garda and MI6, to go on.

Lizzie picked up her fork and scooped up the last of her warm crumble, fat blackberries oozing out from under the simple crust of sugar, flour and butter. She sat with her back to the wall, facing out into the pub. "It's hard for someone to stab you in the back if you've got it to the wall," her father had explained on her thirteenth birthday. "At least you'll have a chance to defend yourself if someone tries to stab you in the heart. You can see the attack coming."

Harlan Rush didn't look at life through rose-colored glasses, and he'd taught Lizzie, his only child, to do the same.

She wanted rose-colored glasses. She wanted, even for a few minutes, to be someone who could settle into a quaint Irish pub on a windy, rainy afternoon without considering that a killer could walk through the door, looking for her.

Across the pub, in their thick West Cork accents, the local men kidded and argued. Alone at her table, alone in their country, Lizzie was struck by their ease with each other—one that spoke of a lifetime together. She was on her own, and, by choice, had been for much of the past year, at least when it came to her dealings with Norman Estabrook and the FBI.

"I was hoping Keira would be here," Will Davenport said, with just the slightest edge of concern in his voice.

Just Keira? Why not Simon, too?

Lizzie settled back in her chair and reached down to pat the dog, his fur warm from the fire.

Something was wrong.

Eddie set another frothy-topped pint on the bar. "Keira's gone to Allihies for the day to research that old story. The one about the three brothers and the stone angel. It got her in trouble once. It hasn't again, has it?"

"I stopped in Allihies before driving up here," Davenport said. "She wasn't there, but I haven't come because of the story."

"The grandfather of the woman who told it to Keira heard the story in the Allihies copper mines. The last of them shut down years ago. Keira planned to visit the museum that's opened in the old Cornish church there." The Irishman lifted the pints onto a tray and gave Davenport a pointed look. "The mansion the British owners built for themselves has been turned into a luxury hotel."

The Brit didn't rise to the bait. "Things change."

"That they do, and sometimes for the better. Other times, not."

"Did Keira say when she'd return?"

"You'd think she'd be back by now, with the gale. That story of hers has drawn curious tourists all summer." As he walked out from behind the bar with the tray, Eddie glanced toward Lizzie. "They're all wanting to find the stone angel themselves."

"Assuming it exists," Davenport said.

The Irishman shrugged, noncommittal, and carried the beers to his fellow villagers. Lizzie was aware that both he and Will Davenport had played a critical role in uncovering the identity of a serial killer who'd become obsessed with Keira's story. She and Simon had, from all Lizzie had heard, encountered true evil. That was two months ago, when Simon was supposed to be laying low ahead of Norman's arrest.

While Eddie delivered the drinks, Davenport walked over to the fire, his gaze settling on Lizzie. She was used to being around men. She worked as director of concierge services and excursions for her family's fifteen highly individual boutique hotels, and she'd grown up with her four male Rush cousins, who now ranged in age from twenty-two to thirty-four. They were all striking in appearance, but, even so, she felt herself getting hot under the Brit's scrutiny. He had the bearing and edgy good looks that could spark even the most independent woman to fantasize about having her own prince charming come to her rescue.

Lizzie quashed that thought. No Prince Charming for her. Not now, not ever.

He nodded to her book, still open at the mesmerizing illustration of the farm. "Is that the Ireland you've come here to find?" His eyes, Lizzie saw, were a rich hazel, with flecks of blue, green and gold that changed with the light. "Fairies, thatched roofs and pretty gardens?"

Lizzie smiled. "Maybe it's the Ireland I have found."

"Do you believe in the wee folk?"

"I'm keeping an open mind. Keira Sullivan's quite the artist, isn't she? I overheard you and the barman. I gather you know her."

"We met earlier this summer. Did you just purchase her book?"

"Yes. I bought it in Kenmare this afternoon." That wasn't true. Keira's young cousin in Boston, Fiona O'Reilly, a harp student, had given it to her, but that, Lizzie decided, was something Will Davenport didn't need to know. "I heard about the story that brought Keira here. Three brothers tussle with fairies over an ancient Celtic stone angel. The brothers believe the angel will bring them good fortune in one form or another, and the fairies believe it's one of their own turned to stone."

Davenport studied her with half-closed eyes.

"It's a wonderful story," Lizzie added.

"So it is." His tone gave away nothing.

Lizzie pushed her empty plate to the center of the table. She wanted more coffee, but she'd already drunk two cups and figured they'd give her enough of a caffeine jolt to counteract any jetlag. She was accustomed to changing time zones but had slept only fitfully on her flight from Boston.

She turned the book over to the full-color, back-cover photograph of Keira Sullivan in a dark green velvet dress. She had pretty cornflower-blue eyes, and her long blond hair was decorated with fresh flowers. "Keira could pass for a fairy princess herself, don't you think?"

"She could, indeed."

Lizzie doubted she'd ever pass for a fairy princess, even if she wore velvet and sprinkled flowers in her hair.

Not that she was bad looking, but her eyes, a light green, seemed to have perpetual dark circles under them lately. She'd had a rough few days.

A rough year, really.

"Do you know Keira?" Davenport asked.

"No, we've never met."

"But you're familiar with the story—"

"It was in all the papers," Lizzie said, not letting him finish. "Yes."

He was clearly suspicious now, but she didn't care. His presence and Simon's absence were unexpected and called for a revision of her plan. Whatever she might have ended up telling Simon, she had no intention of telling his friend Lord Davenport anything.

She needed more information about what was going on, where Simon was, where Keira was.

"What brings you to the Beara Peninsula?" Davenport asked.

"I'm hiking the Beara Way." She wasn't, and she didn't like to lie, but it was easier—and possibly safer for all concerned—than telling the truth. "Not start to finish. It's almost two hundred kilometers. I don't have that much time to spare."

"You're on your own?"

She gave him a bright smile. "Now, that's a bold question to ask a woman having coffee and crumble by herself."

His eyes darkened slightly. "I trust you've a room for the night. The weather's terrible." He gestured back toward the bar where Eddie had returned with his empty tray. "Perhaps Eddie could direct you to a local B and B."

"It's decent of you to be concerned." Lizzie doubted concern for her had anything to do with his motive. She'd sparked his interest by having Keira's book out, by being there alone by the fire. If she was staying nearby, he wanted to keep an eye on her. "I have a tent. I can always camp somewhere."

She saw the beginnings of a smile. He had a straight mouth, a strong jaw, a hint of a wave to his dark blond hair. As good-looking and expensively dressed as he was, he wasn't in any way pretty or soft.

"I wouldn't have taken you for a woman who likes to sleep in a tent," he said, with the barest hint of humor.

In fact, she thought, he was right. It would take more than a suspicious British spy to get her to sleep in a tent in any weather. Not that she hadn't, or couldn't, or wouldn't if she needed to—but she'd have to have good reason. Wind, rain, rocks, uneven ground, no indoor plumbing. She wasn't fussy, but she did like the basics.

She got to her feet. Her walking shoes, which she'd bought

before leaving Dublin that morning and scuffed up to make them look less new, had toes shaped like a duck's bill. They were ugly but comfortable and, supposedly, indestructible.

"The gale's dying down already." She tried her smile again on Davenport, but it had no visible effect. "I haven't heard the windows rattle in the last ten minutes."

"You're American. Where are you from?"

"Las Vegas." Arguably true, given her lifestyle. There was a Rush hotel in Las Vegas, and she'd spent a great deal of time there.

"Is this your first trip to Ireland?"

"No, but it's my first visit to the Beara Peninsula." Lizzie turned the book of folktales to the front-cover illustration of a lush, magical-looking glen with fairies frolicking in the green. "Keira Sullivan has a talent for painting places that people can believe, want to believe, are real. Do *you* believe in fairies, Lord Will?"

"It's just Will. I allow Eddie his fun. What's your name?"

She didn't want to get into names. "I should go," she said, slipping the book into her backpack and leaving enough euros on the table to cover her tab.

Will said nothing as she hoisted her pack onto one shoulder. The dog looked up at her with his big brown eyes, and she leaned over to him and whispered, *"Slán a fhágáil ag duine."* Which, if she remembered correctly, was Irish for some kind of goodbye. She liked to think it was a phrase her Irish-born mother would have taught her if she'd lived.

The local men watched her from their tables, Eddie O'Shea from behind the bar, all of them accustomed, she thought, to the routines of their lives. Farm, sea, village, church, family. They'd all come up in the talk Lizzie had overheard. Her own life had few such routines, and she doubted Will Davenport's did, either.

She grabbed her jacket off the peg by the door and pulled it on, zipping it up as the men at the tables roared with laughter at a story one was telling. Why not stay and sit by the fire for the evening and never mind why she'd come to Ireland and this tiny, out-of-the way village?

But that, of course, was impossible.

She headed outside. The wind and rain had eased, leaving behind a fine, persistent mist. She dug out her cell phone and saw she had two text messages from her cousin Jeremiah, the third-born of her Rush cousins. He worked at the Whitcomb, her family's hotel in Boston. He was tawny-haired, blue-eyed and good-looking and claimed, as his brothers did, that Lizzie had them wrapped around her little finger.

An exaggeration.

Jeremiah never used text shorthand. His first message read:

Cahill and March in Boston.
No Keira.

Lizzie read the message again to make sure she hadn't made a mistake. Simon Cahill, a special agent with the FBI, and John March, the director of the FBI, were in Boston?

Why?

She'd run into Simon a half dozen times over the past year. He was a handsome, broad-shouldered bruiser of a man, a black-haired, green-eyed natural charmer who had persuaded Norman Estabrook that he was an ex-FBI agent with an ax to grind against March, his former boss.

Such, however, was not the case.

Had Simon already been on his way to Boston when she'd left for Ireland last night? Lizzie almost laughed out loud. Talk about ironic. She'd come to Ireland to convince Simon to do all he could to keep Norman in custody and not to fall for his line about having stumbled into a network of violent criminals. He had meant every word of his threat against Simon and Director March. It wasn't just about vengeance, either. Norman was no longer willing to sit on the sidelines. He was itching to do something dramatic and violent himself.

Lizzie returned her phone to her jacket pocket and shivered in the chilly early evening air.

If Keira Sullivan hadn't gone to Boston with Simon, where was she now?

And why was Will Davenport here and so serious?

Lizzie smelled pipe smoke and noticed an old man in traditional farmer's clothes seated on the front bench of a wooden picnic table by the pub door. His face was deeply lined, his eyebrows bushy above steady eyes that were a clear, even fierce, blue. He held up his pipe, smoke curling into the mist. "You'll be wanting to go to the stone circle."

She eased her pack off her shoulder. "For what?"

"For what you're looking for, dearie."

"How do you know what I'm looking for?"

He pointed his pipe up the quiet street. "There. It's down the lane and up the hill. You'll find your way." His eyes, gleaming with intensity, fixed on her. "You always do, don't you, dearie?"

Steadying herself against a sudden gust of wind that blew up from the harbor at her back, Lizzie peered past the rows of brightly painted houses—fuchsia, blue, yellow, red, mustard, all a welcome antidote to the gray weather. She loved the unique light, the special feel of being back in Ireland.

But find her way to what?

When she turned to ask, the old man was gone.

# THE MIST

Eddie O'Shea's springer spaniel wandered out of the pub and trotted up the village street in the direction the old man had pointed.

There was no one else about. A basket of flowers hung from a lamppost, swinging in the breeze, and Lizzie could identify with its drooping and dripping pink geraniums, purple petunias and sprays of lavender.

The dog paused and looked back at her, his tail wagging.

Lizzie could no longer smell the old farmer's pipe smoke in the damp air. If she'd been drinking Guinness instead of coffee she'd have been sure she conjured him up. As it was…she had no idea.

"All right," she called to the spaniel. "I'll follow you."

# Chapter 2

*Beara Peninsula, Southwest Ireland*
*5:50 p.m., IST*
*August 25*

Will Davenport stabbed the toe of his shoe into the wet gravel in front of the small, traditional stone cottage where Keira was staying while Simon was in Boston. The cottage was situated on a narrow lane cut along an ancient wall that ran parallel to the bay and the mountains. A steady wind blew dark clouds across the rugged, barren hills that swept up from the harbor to the spine of the peninsula.

He had resisted the temptations of Eddie O'Shea's pub—a pint, a fire, camaraderie—and returned to his car, finding his way here. Rambling pink roses scented the damp, cool air as the remains of the storm pushed east across Ireland. To the north, across Kenmare Bay, he could see the jagged outlines of the McGillicuddy Reeks of the Iveragh Peninsula, another finger of land that jutted into the Atlantic.

Keira's car was parked in the drive by the roses, and a light glowed in the cottage kitchen, but she hadn't come to the door when he'd knocked.

Was she having a bath, perhaps?

She had arrived in Ireland in June to paint and look into the Beara Peninsula origins of the folktale she'd heard in a South Boston kitchen. The *Slieve Mikish*—the Mikish Mountains—at the tip of the peninsula held rich veins of copper that had drawn settlers to the region thousands of years ago. Will had driven along Bantry Bay on the southern side of the peninsula, the weather deteriorating the closer he came to the Atlantic and Allihies. He'd talked to Simon briefly and had hoped to find Keira poking around among the skeletal remains of the long-abandoned Industrial Age mines scattered across the remote, starkly beautiful landscape. When he hadn't found her, he'd headed to the pub on Kenmare Bay, discovering not his friend's new love but a hiker with striking light green eyes and one of Keira's books.

Pushing back a nagging sense of worry, Will checked his BlackBerry and saw he had a message from Josie Goodwin, his assistant in London, who had arranged for his flight into Cork and the car that had awaited him.

Josie's words were straight to the point:

Estabrook free 9 AM MDT.

With a grimace at the unpleasant, if not unexpected, news, Will dialed Josie's number.

"I was about to call you," she said without preamble when she picked up. "I have more. Apparently Estabrook couldn't wait to get off his ranch and left in his private plane immediately after signing his plea agreement. I gather he's never been one to sit still. He must be stir-crazy after two months."

"Did he go alone?"

"Yes."

"Then he kept his promise to provide authorities with all he knows about his drug-trafficking friends?"

"The Americans must be satisfied or they wouldn't have let him go free."

"Josie, the man threatened to kill Simon and Director March."

"He insists he was speaking metaphorically."

Someone who didn't know Josie well could miss her wry tone, but she and Will had worked together for the past three years. He didn't miss it. "Metaphorically," he said. "I'll have to remember that one."

"Ireland is a long way from Montana, Will. Estabrook has no history of violence, nor is he suspected of having been involved with his associates' violent crimes. Not that participating in the spread of the poison of illegal drugs isn't a kind of violence."

"I'm at Keira's cottage now," Will said. "Her car is here, but she's not. She must have gone for a walk."

"From what Simon's told me, she does love to walk. They're a remarkable pair, aren't they, Will? True love is a rare thing, but they've found it."

This time, Will heard wistfulness in Josie's voice. She was the thirty-eight-year-old single mother of a teenage son and a woman who had faced more than her share of heartbreak. She was also a capable, resourceful member of the British Secret Intelligence Service, and Will trusted her without hesitation. She understood, as he did, that their lives and work ran more smoothly, more easily, unencumbered by romantic entanglements. She'd learned her lesson the hard way through personal experience. He'd learned his by example.

Matters, he thought, for another day.

"Have you talked to Simon?" he asked.

"Briefly. He appreciates that you're in Ireland and Keira's not alone. He'd never have left her if he'd known Estabrook would be released. He and March had hoped they could keep him in custody."

Will resisted any comment on the FBI director. He and March had a history, not a good one. "A woman was at the pub just now, reading one of Keira's books. A hiker. Small, slim, light green eyes, black hair. American. Do you recognize the description?"

"Long hair, short hair?"

"I don't know. Long, I think. I only saw a few strands. The rest was under a red bandanna."

"Ah."

Will sighed. "She said she's from Las Vegas and is here hiking the Beara Way."

"Alone?"

"As far as I could tell, yes."

"Seems a lovely thing to do," Josie said. "But you don't believe her, do you, Will?"

He didn't hesitate. "No."

"You wouldn't be drawn to an Irish village where an ancient, magical stone angel was reportedly discovered in a ruin?"

"Josie…"

"I've jotted down the description and will see what I can learn. One never knows. Good luck finding Keira. Simon trusts you completely."

"I owe him, Josie."

"Yes, you do."

Will stared down through the gray mist and fog down toward

the harbor, remembering back two years to a tragic, violent eighteen hours in Afghanistan that ended with Simon Cahill saving his life. It was a debt they both understood could never be repaid—and yet Will kept trying. But it wasn't why he'd come to Ireland. He had come, simply, as a friend.

"Will," Josie added crisply, "Simon knows you're not some fop who spends all his time fishing and golfing. He's aware by now that you weren't in Afghanistan to catch butterflies."

She disconnected before Will could respond.

He shoved his BlackBerry into his coat pocket, but part of him was still back in Afghanistan, alone, dehydrated, bruised and bloodied, determined to stay alive for one reason: he owed the truth to the memory and the service of the two SAS soldiers—his friends—who had died at his side hours earlier on that long, violent night. At great risk to himself, with only an ax, a rope and his own brute strength at his disposal, Simon had come upon the bombed-out cave and freed Will. Together they then dug out the bodies of David Mears and Philip Billings, who had died because Will had trusted the wrong man.

Another friend.

*Myles Fletcher.*

Will made himself silently say the name of the man—the British military officer and intelligence agent—who had compromised their highly classified mission, only to be captured and dragged off by the very enemy fighters he had embraced as allies.

After reuniting Will with his SAS colleagues, Simon had returned to his own classified mission on behalf of the FBI. He had never asked for an explanation of Will's presence in the cave—or thanks for saving his life.

After two years, Myles Fletcher's remains had yet to be recovered. Presumably his terrorist allies had turned on him and killed him after he'd served his purpose. There wasn't a shred of evidence that he was still alive, but Will wouldn't be satisfied until he had definitive proof.

The FBI had been onto a drug-trafficking and terrorism connection that had evaporated due to Will's failed mission. John March considered Will ultimately responsible for Myles's treachery.

Simon didn't blame Will for anything, but Will had discovered in their two years of friendship that little fazed Simon Cahill.

Except being on one side of the Atlantic while the woman he loved was on the other.

Will buttoned his coat and locked the memories back into their own tight compartment as he walked out to the lane in search of Keira.

# Chapter 3

*Beara Peninsula, Southwest Ireland*
*6:20 p.m., IST*
*August 25*

Lizzie pulled off her bandanna, relishing the feel of the cool wind and mist in her hair. Eddie's dog had led her onto a narrow country lane that followed a stone wall between bay and mountains. She tried to enjoy her walk past rain-soaked roses, holly and wildflowers, fragrant on the wet summer evening. She smiled at lambs settling in for the night and stood for a moment in front of an old, abandoned stone cottage, a reminder of the long-ago famine and subsequent decades of mass emigration that had hit West Cork hard.

Up ahead, the spaniel paused and looked back, tail wagging. Lizzie laughed, dismissing any notion that he was trying to lead her somewhere or was connected to her strange encounter with the old farmer.

Too little sleep. Too many Irish fairy stories.

She came to a cheerful yellow-painted bungalow. A red-haired woman stood at the kitchen sink while a man, handsome and smiling, brought a stack of dishes to the counter and young children colored at a table behind them. Feeling an unexpected tug of emotion, Lizzie continued along the lane. If nothing else, the cool air and brisk walk were helping to clear her head so that she could figure out what to do now that Simon Cahill was in Boston.

She could hear the intermittent bleating of sheep, out to pasture as far up into the rock-strewn hills as she could see. Pale gray fog and mist swirled over the highest of the peaks, settling into rocky dips and crevices. Given her cover story, she'd stuffed her backpack with hiking gear, dry clothes, flashlight, trail food, even a tent. All she had to do now was get herself onto the Beara Way and keep going. Hike for real. She could leave her car in the village and follow the mix of roads, lanes and trails up the peninsula to Kenmare, or down to Allihies and Dursey Island.

How many times had she debated walking away from Norman Estabrook and all she knew about him? She'd met him when he'd been a guest at her family's Dublin hotel sixteen months ago. He was a brilliant, successful hedge-fund manager who had the resources to indulge his every whim, and as an adrenaline junkie, he had many whims. He was known as much for his death-defying adventures as his immense fortune. He wasn't reckless. Whether he was planning to circumnavigate the globe in a hot-air balloon, jump out of an airplane at high-altitude, or head off on a hike in extreme conditions, he would prepare for anything that could go wrong.

At first, Lizzie had believed he was hanging out with major drug traffickers because he was naïve, but she'd learned otherwise. She now suspected that, all along, Norman had calculated that if he were caught, prosecutors would want his friends in the drug cartels more than they wanted him, the financial genius who'd helped them with their money. He was rarely impulsive, and he knew how to leverage himself and manage risk.

Lizzie had been at his ranch in Montana in late June when he'd realized federal agents were about to arrest him. He was a portly, bland-looking forty-year-old man who'd never married, and never would marry. Shocked and livid, he'd turned to her. "I've been betrayed."

He'd meant Simon Cahill, not her. Norman had hired Simon the previous summer to help him plan and execute his high-risk adventures. He'd known Simon had just left the FBI and therefore might not be willing to look the other way if he discovered his client was involved in illegal activities, especially with major drug traffickers.

Turned out there was nothing "ex" FBI about Simon.

In those tense hours before his arrest, Norman hadn't looked at himself and acknowledged he'd at least been unwise to cozy up to criminals. Instead, he'd railed against those who had wronged *him*. Other than a few members of his household staff, Lizzie had been the only one with him. He had never had a serious romantic relationship that she knew of—and certainly not with her. The people in his life—family, friends, staff, colleagues—were planets circling his sun.

The rules just didn't apply to Norman Estabrook. He'd gone to Harvard on scholarship, started working at a respected, established hedge fund right after graduating, then launched his own fund at twenty-seven. By forty, he was worth several billion dollars and able to take a less active role in his funds.

Lizzie had paced with him in front of the tall windows overlooking his sprawling ranch and the big western sky and tried to talk him into calling his attorneys and cooperating with authorities. But if she'd learned anything about Norman in the past year, it was that he did what he wanted to do. Most people about to be handcuffed and read their rights wouldn't get on the phone and threaten an FBI agent and his boss, but Norman, as he'd often pointed out, wasn't most people.

She'd watched his hatred and determination mount as he'd confronted the reality that Simon—the man he'd entrusted with his life—was actually an undercover federal agent.

That John March had won.

Retreating from the magnificent view, he had picked up the phone.

"Don't, Norman," Lizzie had said.

She wasn't even sure he'd heard her. Spittle at the corners of his mouth, his eyes gleaming with rage, he'd called Simon in Boston and delivered his threat.

"You're dead. Dead, dead, dead. First I kill John March. Then I kill you."

Lizzie remembered staring out at the aspens, so green against the clear blue sky, and thinking she, too, would be dead, dead, dead if Norman figured out that for the better part of a year she'd been passing information about him anonymously to the FBI. Until his arrest, she hadn't known if the FBI was taking her information seriously and had Norman's activities under investigation. She certainly hadn't known they had an undercover agent in position.

They didn't know about her, either. *No one* did.

Even with FBI agents spilling onto Norman's ranch—even when they'd interviewed her—Lizzie had kept quiet about her role. When she decided to head to Ireland, she'd taken steps to maintain her secret. Hence, the backpack, walking shoes and tale about hiking the Beara Way. Let Simon think she was stopping in on him and Keira while she was in the area. Get him talking about Norman, their mutual ex-friend, and her belief that he already had people in position to help him when he'd called Simon from his ranch that day. That he was serious and had at least the beginnings of a plan in place, and the FBI should get it out of him. For the past two months, she'd expected "conspiracy to commit murder" to be added to the list of charges against him. The FBI had his threat against its director and one of its agents on tape. Surely they'd be investigating whether he could carry it out.

Maybe they were, but here she was, her jacket flapping in the stubborn Irish wind and Simon Cahill and John March across the Atlantic in Boston. Lizzie hoped they were consulting on how to keep Norman in custody.

She came to a track that wound up into the hills and noticed fresh paw prints in the soft, wet dirt. Assuming they belonged to the springer spaniel, she followed them up the steep track. She'd go a little ways, then head back to her car. She couldn't fly to Boston tonight. She could go back to Dublin or find a local bed-and-breakfast. She needed sleep, food and information on Norman in Montana and Simon and March in Boston.

The dirt track curved and leveled off briefly at a hand-painted Beware of Bull sign nailed to a gate post. Lizzie paused and gazed out across the open pasture, where the distinctive silhouette of a prehistoric stone circle was outlined against the dark clouds.

Eddie's dog leaped from behind a large boulder, startling her. "There you are," she called to him, laughing at her reaction. "Hold on. I'm coming."

Not waiting this time, the dog pivoted and bounded up past scrubby junipers and over clumps of gray rocks toward the circle.

He obviously knew he had her.

Lizzie climbed over the barbed-wire fence and dropped onto the wet grass on the other side, dodging a sodden cow patty. Carefully avoiding more cow manure, she made her way across the rough, uneven ground of the pasture. In a sudden blur, the dog streaked back toward the fence and the dirt track, deserting her. She shrugged and decided to continue on to the stone circle, one of more than a hundred of the megalithic monuments in West Cork and south Kerry alone. As she came closer, she jumped from one rock to another, skirting a patch of mud. She entered the circle between two of the tall, gray boulders that had occupied their spots for thousands of years.

A breeze whistled softly up from the bay.

Lizzie counted eight heavy standing stones of different heights that formed the outer edge of the circle. A ninth had toppled over, and there was a spot for a missing tenth stone. A low, flat-topped slab that looked as if it had been turned on its side—the axis stone—made a total of eleven.

Below her, past green, rolling fields, the harbor was gray and churning with the last of the storm. She stood very still, absorbing the atmosphere. She had never been to a place so eerie, so strangely quiet. The ancients had chosen an alluring location for their stone circle, whatever its original purpose.

"I can understand how people see fairies here," she whispered to herself.

A shuffling sound drew her attention, and she turned just as a fat, brown cow edged slowly along the thick junipers outside the circle.

She felt uneasy, nervous even, and didn't know why.

A presence, she decided.

Another cow? The dog?

Was the old farmer out there in the shadows and fog? She remembered his strange words.

*"You'll be wanting to go to the stone circle."*

*"For what?"*

*"For what you're looking for, dearie."*

Lizzie noticed a movement in a small cluster of trees and took a shallow breath, listening, squinting toward the hills as she eased her pack off her shoulder.

Something—someone—was out there.

She wasn't alone.

# Chapter 4

*Beara Peninsula, Southwest Ireland*
*7:10 p.m., IST*
*August 25*

As she eased back between the two tall boulders, Lizzie felt her right foot sink deep into a low spot. She ignored the shock of water and mud oozing into her socks and placed a palm on one of the cool, wet stones.

The wind gusted and howled over the exposed hills and rocks, bringing with it a fresh rush of rain.

She shivered. Maybe that was all it was—a last gasp from the storm.

She heard a sound behind her and turned sharply. Across from her, a slender woman entered the ancient circle, her long, blond hair whipping in the wind. She wore an oversize Irish fisherman's sweater that hung almost to her knees and, Lizzie suspected, belonged to Simon Cahill, because this had to be Keira Sullivan.

She slowed as she approached the low axis stone.

"It's okay—I'm a friend," Lizzie said quickly, not wanting to startle her. Maybe *friend* was a stretch, but she could explain later. "I know Simon. Simon Cahill. You're Keira, aren't you?"

The other woman's eyes narrowed, her skin pale in the soft gray light. "I walked up here from my cottage. I came across the pasture—I've been restless. I was down at the old copper mines today and tried to blame the ghosts there, and the gale." She frowned without any obvious fear or panic. "What was that?"

Lizzie had heard it, too—rustling sounds toward the cluster of trees on the hillside. It wasn't the storm. Someone else was out there.

"It's not ghosts or the gale," she said, letting her backpack slip farther down her arm, ready to drop it and run, use it as a weapon—a shield. "We have to go."

Black clouds surged down the mountains. Rain, hissing and cold, pelted Lizzie's jacket and her bare head, soaked Keira's hair and wool sweater. But Keira didn't seem to notice the suddenly worsening conditions. "Who do you think is out there?"

"I don't know." Lizzie noticed the cow break into a run away from the trees. "We should hurry."

Keira pointed in the same direction. "There."

Lizzie had no time to answer. A man—compact, wearing a black ski cap—burst out into the open and charged through the gap in the circle.

"He's after you," Lizzie said. "Run, Keira. Run!"

"I can't leave you—"

"I can fight. Go. Please."

The man lunged for Keira, but she darted away from him, diving behind one of the standing stones.

He swore and pivoted after her. He had an assault knife in his right hand. Lizzie leaped into his path and swung her backpack hard against the knife blade, using her own momentum to add force to the blow. With a grunt of surprise, he lost his balance and stumbled backward over a protruding rock. Before he could regain his footing, she hit his knife again with her pack, following up with a sharp, low side kick to his left knee.

He yelped in pain and dropped the knife. Lizzie knew she had to press her advantage and quickly got in another low kick, scraping her foot down his shin. She stomped on his instep, not thinking, relying on her instincts and training. She'd practiced these moves a thousand times.

The attacker went down onto his back, writhing in the mud, manure and wet grass. Lizzie snatched up his knife before he could get to it and dropped onto her knees, putting the blade to his throat as he rolled onto his side and tried to get up.

"Keep your hands where I can see them," she said, "and don't move."

He complied immediately, his breathing shallow, as if he were afraid she'd cut him with the knife if he gulped or panted. One side of his face was pressed into the mud.

Lizzie turned the edge of the blade so that he could feel it against the thin skin over his carotid artery. "Do as I say or you're dead. Do you understand?"

"Aye. I understand."

He spoke with an Irish accent. A local hire, maybe. He could be faking the accent. Lizzie could manage a decent Irish brogue herself, and she was born in Boston. He was in his early to midthirties, with a jagged scar along his outer jaw that looked as if he'd earned it in a previous knife fight gone bad.

"You've broken my damn knee," he said.

"I doubt that."

Despite his pain, he spoke without fear, as if he knew it was only a matter of time before he'd get his knife back and complete his assignment.

Kill Keira Sullivan.

Lizzie had never killed anyone herself and hoped she never had to, but she knew how to do it. Her father had seen to that.

"I'll check him for more weapons," Keira said.

Lizzie nodded, breathing hard.

Keira knelt in the muck and patted the man down from head to toe with a steadiness and efficiency that didn't surprise Lizzie. Keira's uncle was a homicide detective in Boston, and Keira herself had stood up to a killer in June.

She produced another assault knife in her search but no other weapons.

Lizzie controlled her reaction even as her thoughts raced. Norman wasn't waiting. He was acting now. Had he specified what he wanted done to the woman Simon loved? How he wanted her killed?

Undoubtedly, Lizzie thought. Norman would relish such details and control.

Was he going after Simon in Boston? John March?

Who else?

She maintained her grip on the knife. "The man who hired you isn't just after Keira. Who's next?"

He hardly breathed. "I don't know anything."

"My friend, you need to be straight with me." She paused before asking again, "Who's next?"

He tried to swallow against the sharp edge of the knife. "It doesn't matter. You're too late. I can't stop what's going to happen. Neither can you."

"That's not what I asked."

He carefully spat bits of grass and dirt from his mouth. "Go to hell. I'll not answer a single question you put to me."

He was calling her bluff. Lizzie didn't know if she should cut him—if it would do any good in getting him to talk.

She heard a dog growl just outside the stone circle, a low, fierce sound that wasn't from Eddie's springer spaniel.

With her would-be attacker's spare knife in one hand, Keira stood back as a large black dog bounded into the circle and onto the prostrate axis stone next to her, directly in the Irishman's line of sight. He nervously eyed the hound. A knife to the throat didn't impress him, but a snarling black dog appearing out of nowhere obviously did.

Keira addressed the thug calmly. "Tell this woman what she wants to know. It'll ease the dog. He senses the danger you pose to us."

The man licked his lips. "I don't like dogs."

"Then answer me," Lizzie said. "Who's next?"

He hesitated a half beat. "The daughter of the FBI director."

"Abigail," Keira breathed, her blue eyes steady but filled with fear as she looked at Lizzie. "Abigail Browning. She's a homicide detective in Boston."

Lizzie knew all about Abigail Browning, John March's widowed daughter, but kept her attention focused on the Irishman. "What's the plan?" The rain had subsided to a misting drizzle, but she could feel mud and water soaking into her hiking pants. "Tell me."

"I can't. I'll be killed."

The dog gave a menacing growl and leaned forward on the ancient stone, lowering his head as if at any moment he might pounce on the man below.

"There's a bomb," the Irishman whispered, shutting his eyes, then quickly opening them again. He obviously didn't dare lose sight of the black dog.

"Where?" Lizzie asked.

"Back porch."

"It's a triple-decker. Whose back porch?"

Keira gasped, but Lizzie couldn't take the time to explain how she knew that Abigail Browning lived on the first-floor of a Jamaica Plain triple-decker she co-owned with two other Boston Police Department detectives, including Bob O'Reilly, Keira's uncle.

Their attacker didn't answer.

"Tell me now," Lizzie said.

The dog bared his teeth, thick white drool dripping from the sides of his mouth, and the Irishman responded with a visceral shudder.

Definitely not a dog lover.

He bit his lower lip. "First floor. Browning's place."

"When?" Lizzie asked.

He turned his gaze from the dog and fixed his eyes on her. "Now."

She stifled a jolt of panic. He wasn't lying. Between the thought of the dog ripping out his intestines and her cutting his throat, he wasn't willing to risk a lie. Her father had told her at around age fourteen there was nothing like the fear of bleeding out to motivate a man.

"We need to call Boston," Keira said.

Lizzie nodded in agreement, but her heart jumped when she saw a tall man crossing the pasture toward the stone circle.

Will Davenport.

Keira saw him, too, and cried out to him as he entered the circle. "Will! There's a bomb—I have to warn Abigail."

He sized up the situation with a quick glance. "All right. I'll call." He spoke with complete control. "Tell me the number."

"I don't have Abigail's number memorized. It's at the cottage."

"What about your uncle?"

She nodded. "It's easier if I dial." He passed her his BlackBerry. Keira had tears in her eyes, but her hands didn't shake as she hit buttons. "If they're all there…if Abigail's on her porch…" She continued to dial.

Will crouched next to Lizzie and placed his hand over hers on the knife. His hand was steady, warm. His eyes, the flecks of gold gleaming, leveled on hers. "Let me take care of him. You help Keira."

Lizzie didn't budge. "How do I know you're not going to take the knife and kill us both?"

"Because I don't need the knife."

There was that. Lizzie loosened her grip on the handle. "I have bungee cords in my pack. We can use them to handcuff him."

"It would seem you think of everything," Will said as she eased her hand out from under his and he held the knife at the Irishman's throat.

Rainwater streamed from Keira's hair down her face as she spoke to her uncle in Boston. "Bob. Thank God…"

She faltered, and Lizzie stood up. "The people in danger are your family and friends. Please. Let me do this." She put out a hand, and Keira gave her the phone. Lizzie forcefully addressed Keira's uncle on the other end. "Listen to me. Take cover. Take cover *now*."

"Who the hell is this?" O'Reilly demanded.

"A bomb's about to go off on Abigail's back porch."

He was already yelling. "Take cover, take cover! Scoop, Abigail, Fiona!"

The phone crackled.

Lizzie heard a loud booming sound.

An explosion.

"Lieutenant!"

The connection went dead.

# Chapter 5

*Boston, Massachusetts*
*2:37 p.m., EDT*
*August 25*

Two almost simultaneous explosions shook the triple-decker and knocked Bob O'Reilly off his feet. He landed on his left side, more or less in a sprawl, his cell phone clutched in his hand. He'd banged the hell out of his elbow but otherwise was all right.

He rolled onto one knee and jumped up, his ears ringing, his heart racing. He yanked open his back door and ran out onto the open porch of his top-floor apartment.

He could hear glass cracking, metal popping and what he swore was the hiss of flames.

"Fiona!" he yelled. "Scoop!"

Scoop Wisdom, another detective, had the second-floor apartment, but he and Fiona were picking tomatoes in Scoop's garden in the postage-stamp of a backyard.

Fiona was the eldest of Bob's three daughters.

Had they heard him yell for them to take cover?

"Dad! Daddy!"

*Fiona.*

She was screaming, but it meant she could talk.

His baby was alive.

Bob gripped the railing and leaned over, trying to see through the black smoke billowing up from below. "Hang on, Fi." He sounded as if he were being strangled. "I'm coming."

"Scoop. *Scoop!*" She was shrieking now. "Oh, my God!"

Her next words were unintelligible.

Bob tried not to react to her panic and fear. He saw flames now, licking up the support posts of the two porches under him.

He'd never make it down the back steps. He'd burn up.

He retreated into his kitchen and grabbed the small fire extinguisher by the stove, a Christmas present from Jayne, his youngest, who'd printed off a checklist of what to do to prepare for a disaster—power outages, floods, earthquakes, hurricanes.

Bombs going off.

Keira was in Ireland. How had she known about a bomb on Abigail's porch?

Who was the other woman with her?

Bob forced his thoughts back and tucked the fire extinguisher under his arm as he ran through his living room and out into the main hall.

There was no smoke in the stairwell. That was one good thing.

Was another bomb ready to go off?

Using his thumb, he hit 911 on his cell phone as he charged down the two flights of stairs. The dispatcher came on, and he identified himself as an off-duty police officer and gave his address, stated the nature of the emergency.

An explosion. A fire. Possible injuries.

"I think an off-duty officer is hurt," Bob said. "Detective Sergeant Cyrus 'Scoop' Wisdom. He's out back with my daughter, Fiona O'Reilly, age nineteen."

"Where are you?"

"First floor. Inside. I'm checking on a second off-duty officer, Abigail Browning."

The interior door to the apartment she shared with her fiancé, Owen Garrison, and the main door into the building were both ajar, which Bob took as a positive sign that she'd gotten out. He burst outside and ran down the front steps, expecting to find Abigail out on the sidewalk. Owen had left earlier. Bob had heard them laughing down on the street.

Her car was there, but she wasn't.

He said to the dispatcher, "She could have gone out back to help Scoop and Fi. That's where the fire is."

"You need to find a safe place and stay there."

"I'm a police officer. I know what I need to do. Stay on with me. I'll let you know what I find out."

"Lieutenant, you need to wait for help."

"I am the help."

"There could be another explosion. If there's a gas grill, the propane tank—"

"That's it," Bob said. "The second blast must have been the propane tank to Abigail's grill."

"Then you understand the need to stay where you are."

True, but Bob yanked open the unlatched gate to the narrow passage between his triple-decker and the one next door. Smoke blackened the still, late-summer air and burned his nostrils. He coughed, tasting fire.

"Daddy! Help me!"

Fiona was sobbing now as she cried out for him. She hadn't called him Daddy since she was ten. She was due to start her sophomore year as a classical harp major at Boston University, and now she'd been caught in a bomb going off at her father's house.

She deserved better.

Bob shoved his phone into his pants pocket and shouted to her. "Keep talking to me, kid. Where are you?"

He felt the wall of heat before he saw the orange and red flames engulfing Abigail's porch, a duplicate of his except neater—and now mostly obliterated by the blast. One structural beam was gone, another was burning, flames working their way up to Scoop's second-floor porch as if the devil himself were spewing them.

Anyone out back when the bomb had gone off and sent shrapnel flying everywhere would be in serious trouble, but Bob saw only flames, charred wood, debris.

He didn't see Abigail fighting her way through the fire, or Scoop or Fiona in the thick smoke blackening the small yard.

"Fiona, where are you?"

His throat was raw, burning, tight with fear. The fire extinguisher would be useless against the main fire, but he held on to it in case of smaller fires or secondary explosions. He pulled his polo shirt over his mouth and nose and pushed through the smoke, past the outdoor table where they all spent as much time as possible during Boston's too-short summer. The concussive wave from the explosion had knocked over the cheap plastic chairs, but the two Adirondack chairs had stayed put.

"Fiona! Scoop! Abigail! Someone talk to me."

"Here." Fiona's voice, slightly less hysterical now. "We're behind the compost bin. I can't move."

"Why can't you move?"

"Scoop…"

Bob jumped over a tidy row of green beans into Scoop's vegetable garden, his pride and joy. He'd kept them in salads all summer and shared whatever was ripe—first the peas and spinach, then the beans and summer squash. Now he was unloading tomatoes on his housemates. He'd been talking about freezing and canning some of next summer's harvest.

*Next summer.*

He'd be there. He had to be. Scoop wasn't meant to die this way.

Not in front of Fiona.

A moan, a sob came from behind the compost bin on the other side of the garden. Bob thrashed through tomato and cauliflower plants. Scoop had made the bin himself out of chicken wire and wood slats. He'd bought a book on composting. Now, at summer's end, the bin was full of what he referred to as "organic matter."

And earthworms. He'd ordered them from a catalog and told Bob not to tell Fiona because she was into the romance of composting and didn't need to know about the worms. He'd explained what they did to help speed the process of turning garbage into dirt. Bob's eyes had glazed over while he'd listened.

He stepped over a cauliflower plant, letting his shirt drop from his mouth as he saw Scoop's foot peeking out from the edge of the compost bin, toe down inside his beat-up running shoe.

No movement.

"Daddy. I can't…Dad…" Just out of sight behind the bin, Fiona was hyperventilating. "Scoop can't be dead!"

"He's not dead."

Bob blurted the words without knowing if they were true, something he tried never to do. But they had to be. Scoop was all muscle. He was a boxer, a wrestler, a top-notch cop.

Steeling himself for what he might see, Bob took a quick breath, sucking in smoke, and stepped behind the compost bin.

Scoop was sprawled facedown on Fiona's lap. She'd wriggled partway out from under him and was half sitting, pinned between him and the bin. Her thin, bare arms were wrapped around him, smeared with blood and blackened bits of shrapnel.

Bob could see that most of the blood wasn't hers.

She looked up at him with those wide, blue eyes he'd first noticed when she was a tot. Tears streamed down her pale cheeks, creating little rivers of blood and soot.

"Fi," he said, forcing himself not to choke up. "You okay? You hurt?"

"Just a little shaken up. I—Dad." She gulped in a breath, shivering uncontrollably, teeth chattering, lips a purplish-blue and bleeding from where she'd bitten down on them. "Scoop. He saved me. He saved my life."

Shrapnel from the bomb or something on Abigail's porch—a propane tank, a grill, a bucket, the railing—had ripped into Scoop, cutting his back, his arms, his legs. His shirt was shredded, the white fabric soaked in blood. A hunk of metal stuck out of the back of his neck, just below his hairline. Several other pieces were embedded in the meat of his upper left arm.

A single jagged piece of metal was stuck in his leg below the hem of his khaki shorts.

Bob knelt on one knee and checked Scoop's wrist for a pulse, getting one almost immediately. "He's alive, Fi."

She tightened her grip on him, blood seeping between her fingers. "What happened?"

"There was an explosion. Firefighters and paramedics are on the way. Just don't move, okay?" Bob tried to give her a reassuring smile. "Don't move."

Scoop moaned and shifted position, maybe a quarter inch.

Bob said, "Don't you move, either, Scoop."

Most of the blood seemed to be from superficial cuts, and the blast could have just knocked the wind out of him, but Bob wasn't taking any chances. With his shaved head and thick muscles, Scoop was a ferocious-looking cop even bloodied and sinking into shock. If he wasn't feeling pain now, he would soon.

Bob hesitated, but he knew he had to ask. "Before the blast— did you see Abigail?"

Fiona paled even more. "The phone rang. She…"

"Easy, Fi. Just take it slow." But Bob could feel his own urgency mounting, dread crawling over him, sucking the breath out of him. He had to concentrate to keep it out of his expression, his voice. "Okay?"

"She went to answer the phone."

"When?"

"Just before the explosion." Fiona squeezed her eyes shut, fresh tears leaking out the corners and joining up with the rest of the mess on her cheeks. "Not long before. I can't remember. Minutes?" She opened her eyes, sniffled. "I…*Dad*. I'm going to be sick."

Bob shook his head. "Nah. You're not going to puke on Scoop."

Had he misinterpreted the partially open doors? What if Abigail hadn't been fleeing the fire but, instead, someone had gone in after her?

*Why?*

What was he missing?

He placed his palm on his daughter's cheek, noted with a jolt how cold it was. "Help will be here soon." He spoke softly, trying to stay calm, to be assertive and clear without scaring her more. "We can't move Scoop. It's too dangerous."

"I'll stay with him."

Bob nodded. "Okay. The fire won't get here. Do what you can to keep Scoop still, so he doesn't dislodge a piece of shrapnel and make the bleeding worse. You be still, too. You could be hurt and not feel it."

"I'm not hurt, Dad, and I know first aid."

He lowered his hand from her cheek. She'd always been stubborn—and strong. "Hang in there, kid. I won't let anything happen to you." But hadn't he already?

Her lower lip trembled. "You're going to find Abigail, aren't you?"

*Abigail.* He pushed back his fear and nodded. "Yeah."

"It's okay, Dad." Fiona gave him a ragged smile. "You can count on me."

His heart nearly broke. He hated to leave her, but she and Scoop would be better off staying put than having him try to get them out to the street.

And he had to find Abigail.

Bob leaned his fire extinguisher next to the compost bin and pulled his cell phone out of his pocket. "I don't know what all you heard," he said to the dispatcher, "but you can talk to my daughter."

Fiona's fingers closed around the phone. They were callused from endless hours of harp practice. She should be practicing now, but here she was, the victim of some dirtbag.

He couldn't think about that now. "The 911 dispatcher is on the line. He'll help you. Do what he says."

She nodded.

Bob looked back toward the house. Scoop's porch was on fire now, too. The triple-decker was a hundred years old. Bob had seen others like it burn. Firefighters would have to get there fast if they stood a chance of saving it.

Didn't matter to him one way or the other.

He ran back through Scoop's vegetables and across the yard. The heat was brutal. Sweat poured down his face and soaked his armpits and chest, plastered his undershorts to his behind. Gunk burned in his eyes.

He could hear sirens blaring maybe a block away, but he couldn't wait. When he reached the street, he took the front steps two at a time.

Black smoke drifted out from Abigail's apartment.

Pulling his shirt back up over his face, he dived into her living room, but he didn't see her passed out on the floor.

No sign of her in the dining room, either.

The smoke was thick, dangerous. The fire was close.

He took another couple of steps, but he couldn't get to the kitchen or the bedroom in back, closer to the fire.

He was coughing up soot. He felt his knees crumbling under him but stiffened and made sure he didn't collapse. He was fifty and in decent shape. It wasn't exertion that had him out of breath as much as emotion, but he locked the fear into its own dark compartment and focused on what had to be done.

Get Scoop and Fiona out of the backyard and to the E.R.

Find Abigail.

Find the bastards who'd set off a bomb on her porch.

No question the fire wasn't an accident. Keira and the other woman in Ireland had been right that it was a bomb.

Two hulking firefighters materialized on either side of him and got him by the arms and led him back outside. He shook them off when they reached the sidewalk. "An off-duty police officer is out back with my daughter. He's hurt bad. She isn't." His eyes felt seared as he pointed toward the gate. "They're behind the compost bin. Scoop. Fiona. Those are their names."

The firefighters took off without a word. More firefighters

poured off trucks, heading inside and out back. Paramedics arrived. Two police cruisers. Bob looked back at the triple-decker. He and Scoop and Abigail had just put on new siding. A new roof.

Tom Yarborough, Abigail's partner, a straight-backed son of a bitch if there ever was one, got out of an unmarked car and approached the house. Bob forced himself to think. The FBI, ATF, bomb squad, arson squad—the damn world would be on this one.

Neighbors drifted out of houses up and down the street to check out the commotion, see if they could help. Find out if the fire would spread and if they should get out of there. Yarborough, already taking charge, addressed two uniformed officers. "Keep them back." He looked at Bob. "You okay?"

"I'm fine." Bob spat and filled him in on Scoop and Fiona. "Firefighters are back there now."

"How'd the fire start?" Yarborough asked.

"Bomb on Abigail's back porch."

Yarborough had no visible reaction. "Where is she?"

"Missing."

"What about Owen?"

Bob shook his head. "He wasn't here."

"Is he a potential target? What—"

"Hell," Bob interrupted. "I have to warn him. Give me your cell phone."

Yarborough flipped him an expensive-looking phone that Bob immediately smudged with soot, sweat and blood. *Scoop's blood.*

"Bob," Yarborough said. "Lieutenant, I can dial—"

"I don't know his number. You'd think…" He opened up the phone and stared at it. "I should have all Abigail and Owen's numbers memorized. They have enough of them. Cell, here,

Beacon Street, Texas, Maine. The way they live. Their luck. I should know their numbers."

"Owen's cell phone is in my address book."

Bob squinted at him. "In what?"

"Let me, Bob," Yarborough said. He took the phone, hit a couple of buttons, handed it back to Bob. "It's dialing."

Owen picked up on the first ring. "Hey, Tom."

"It's Bob." A thousand bad calls he'd made in his nearly thirty years as a cop, and he could feel his damn voice crack. "Where are you?"

"Beacon Street." A wariness, a hint of fear, had come into Owen's voice. "What's going on? Where's Abigail?"

"Are you safe?"

"Talk to me, Bob. What's happened?"

"I don't know. I'm at the house. She's not here. There's been a fire." No point getting into the details. "Listen to me. I'm sending Yarborough over there. He'll check things out. Right now, you need to get everyone out of the building."

"The fire was set," Owen said.

"It was a bomb, Owen. Move now. Abigail's one of our own. We'll find her." But Owen was ex-military and one of the world's foremost experts in search-and-rescue. He was head of Fast Rescue, a renowned rapid response organization. He'd think he could find her, too. "You know this is different. It's not what you do—"

"I'll be in touch."

He disconnected.

Bob didn't bother trying him again. Owen wouldn't answer. He'd get everyone out of the Federal Period house on Beacon Street owned by his family and used as the offices for their charitable foundation. Then he'd go after Abigail.

"I'll get over there," Yarborough said.

"There could be bombs at Fast Rescue headquarters in Austin and their field academy on Mount Desert Island. If people are there—"

Yarborough gave a curt nod and ran back to his car.

A self-starter. That was one good thing about him.

Bob noticed his hands were steady as he hit more buttons on Yarborough's phone to see if Abigail's cell number popped up. It did, and he hit another button to dial it.

One ring and he was put through to her voice mail.

He waited impatiently for the tone, then said, "It's Bob. Call me."

A young uniformed officer, a thin rookie with close-cropped blond hair, approached him with obvious concern. "Sir, you need to take it easy. Maybe you should sit down."

"Maybe?"

He grimaced and rephrased, "You should."

"That's better. No maybes. Now go do something. I have to get back to my daughter. Keep the firefighters from tackling me to the ground."

"Sir, I think you should get off your feet."

"You think? Are you arguing with me?"

The kid turned green. He'd need to get some spine if he was going to make it in the BPD. "No, sir, I'm not arguing with you. I'm telling you to stay back and let the firefighters do their job."

Bob stared at the kid and felt nerves or craziness or something well up in him. He broke into a barking laugh, then covered it with a cough. He bent over, hawking up a giant black gob and spitting it on the sidewalk. When he stood up straight, he had the awful sensation that he was about to cry. Then he'd have to retire and buy a house next to his folks in Florida, because he'd be finished.

The rookie was looking worried. "Lieutenant?"

Bob went very still and pointed to a dark, still-moist substance on the curb about a yard up from where he'd spit. "There. Check that out. Looks like blood, doesn't it?"

"I'll cordon off the area," the rookie said with a sharp breath.

Bob bent over to get a closer look at the spot. It had to be blood. "Abigail didn't just step out for a walk," he said half to himself.

"I don't think so, either, sir."

He stood up straight. "What do you think, rookie?"

The cop flushed but held his ground. "Everything suggests that Detective Browning has been kidnapped."

"Yeah." Bob wiped the back of his hand across his face, the weight of what had just happened hitting him. The stark, stinking reality of it. "I think so, too."

A line of shiny black SUVs rolled onto the residential street.

"The feds," the rookie cop said. "How did they get here so fast?"

"Abigail's father is in town."

"The FBI director? Just what we need."

The SUVs stopped well back of the fire trucks. Bob realized he didn't have enough of a head start to outrun the FBI.

Nowhere to go, either.

"The spot," Bob said to the rookie.

The kid jumped into action and bolted for his cruiser, shouting to his partner, a woman who looked just as young, just as inexperienced.

Down the street, Simon Cahill leaped out of the back of the middle SUV. He was a man who could dance an Irish jig and was in love with Bob's niece, Keira, but right now what Bob saw coming at him was pure FBI special agent.

The SUV started moving, but stopped again. This time, John March got out. His iron-gray hair and dark gray suit were still perfect despite the heat and the awful scene in front of him.

March had been a hotshot young detective when Bob was a rookie. Now he had about a million G-men behind him, but his eyes, as black as his daughter's, were filled with pain.

Bob understood.

March hadn't jumped out of the SUV because he was the head of the FBI, but because he was Abigail's father.

Simon got to the sidewalk first. "Bob," he said, "what's going on?"

Bob's mouth was dry, his eyes and throat burning. He looked up at the hazy sky and collected himself as March joined. There was just no way out of it, and Bob told Simon and March about the blast. "We're looking for Abigail now." He kept his tone as coplike as he could. "Firefighters are still checking her apartment, but I was in there and didn't find her. Her front door and the main front door were both standing open right after the blast."

"Her car's here," March said.

"We're cordoning off the area, checking vehicles. If she was shaken up in the blast, she could have wandered into someone's backyard."

Simon stepped out of the way of more firefighters. "What about Owen?"

Bob's head throbbed. "He's on Beacon Street. Yarborough's heading there now. What are you two doing here?"

Simon answered, his voice steady. "Abigail called about an hour ago and asked us to meet her. She didn't say why."

Bob didn't know why, either, but he had an idea. Earlier that summer, she'd learned that her father had a tight, almost father-son relationship with Simon Cahill that had started twenty years ago after the execution-style murder of Simon's father, a DEA agent. She'd been trying to wrap her head around that one for weeks and could have asked them both over to talk about it.

And just before they arrive, a bomb goes off?

There was also Norman Estabrook's threat against Simon and her father, and the serial killer Simon and Keira had taken into custody in June, as well as dozens of other ugly cases Abigail had been involved in. Before Bob could follow up, the rookie cop came back up to him, white-faced now. "Lieutenant…I just…"

The kid was standing next to March, who said quietly, "Easy, Officer. Just say what you have to say."

The rookie didn't meet the FBI director's eyes, as if he thought he might go up in a puff of smoke if he did. "I just spoke to Detective Yarborough. Owen Garrison wanted to come over here and headed to his car after evacuating the Garrison house. He checked it first, and…"

"And what?" Bob asked. "He found a bomb?"

The rookie nodded. "Yes, sir. The bomb squad's on the way, but Mr. Garrison has already disarmed the device himself."

"Himself," Bob said, sighing.

Simon and March didn't speak, but they were well aware, as Bob was, that Owen would know how to disarm a wide variety of bombs. The one in his car opened up a second crime scene.

How many more bombs would they find? Who'd planted them? How? When?

*Why?*

It was going to be a long day. Right now, Bob just wanted to see Scoop and his daughter, but he had to get one more bit of black news over with.

He turned to Simon. "Keira called from Ireland."

The color drained from Simon's face. "Why, Bob?"

"She and another woman called to warn me there was a bomb on Abigail's back porch."

# Chapter 6

Lizzie had used the bungee cords in her pack to tie the Irishman's wrists behind his back. He was sullen now as they headed back to the village, she on his right, Will on his left. Keira walked quietly behind them. The black dog skulked in the shadows above the ancient wall along the lane.

"Keep up," Lizzie said to the Irishman, "or we'll leave you to the dog."

He turned his gaze to her, his eyes flat. "I'll keep up."

When they reached the village, the dog bounded off suddenly, disappearing into the hills.

Lizzie glanced back at Keira, her hair hanging in wet tangles. She'd tried calling her uncle in Boston again but was unable to get through to him. "There's still hope," Lizzie said. "Don't give up."

Keira smiled faintly. "You're an optimist."

"Most days."

"Most days I am, too."

But she obviously knew, as Lizzie did, that hope and optimism wouldn't dictate whether Bob O'Reilly and whoever else was at the triple-decker in Boston had survived the blast. It would depend on luck, skill, training and timing.

Unless fairies showed up. For all Lizzie knew, they'd had a hand in what had just happened up at the stone circle. She and Keira had dealt with the Irishman and kept him from killing them, but the mysterious black dog had persuaded him to tell them about the bomb.

It was all very strange.

There was no question in Lizzie's mind that Norman Estabrook was responsible for the attack on Keira Sullivan and the bomb in Boston. He'd gone after Simon's new love and John March's daughter.

And it was just the beginning.

Eddie O'Shea and two other small, wiry men, all in wool caps, materialized out of the shadows and jumped lightly off the stone wall onto the lane. Lizzie had had no idea they were there. The barman fell in next to her. "My brothers, Aidan and Patrick," Eddie said by way of introduction as the other two men dropped back to Keira.

Will greeted the brothers with a nod. He'd said little since the connection to Keira's uncle in Boston went dead. He was a man, Lizzie thought, of supreme self-control. He'd briefly questioned the Irishman, who insisted he'd come to the Beara Peninsula alone and had no partners waiting in the village. Lizzie believed him, if only because of his deep, palpable fear of the black hound.

Aidan pulled off his jacket and draped it over Keira's shoulders, and she managed a smile, thanking him. When they came to the pub, Eddie's dog was at the door to greet them.

The pub was empty, the local farmers and fishermen gone home for the night. The springer spaniel collapsed lazily in front of the fire.

Will shoved their would-be killer onto a chair at the table Lizzie had vacated earlier. His ski cap had come off in his scuffle with her. He had sparse, dark hair and blue eyes, and she saw now, in the light and relative safety of the pub, that he was muscular and fit. She realized she'd done well to best him.

She also realized Will would have had no trouble if he'd arrived in the stone circle a bit sooner. Lizzie reminded herself not to be fooled into thinking his expensive clothes and aristocratic background meant he couldn't fight as well as any other SAS officer and spy.

"I'll ring the guards," Patrick, the youngest O'Shea, said.

"Patrick and I'll watch for them," Aidan, the eldest, added, and the two brothers headed down a short hall to the back of the pub.

Keira shrugged off Aidan's coat and hung it on a peg, then joined Lizzie and the dog by the fire, all of them muddy and wet. The pub was toasty warm, but Lizzie had to fight to keep herself from shivering. She slipped the thug's spare assault knife into her jacket pocket and held her hands toward the flames, spreading out her fingers. She noticed bloody scrapes on her knuckles and wrists, but she couldn't remember any pain and felt none now.

"I'll have Patrick and Aidan fetch some ice and bandages," Eddie said.

"Thank you, but there's no need, really." She gave him a quick smile. "What I'd truly love is a sip of brandy."

He nodded, but gave his bound fellow Irishman a hard glare.

"Move a muscle, and I'll have a knife to your throat before your next breath."

The thug glowered but said nothing.

Eddie went behind his bar and got down three glasses and placed them on a tray. Keeping an eye on his customers, he uncapped a bottle of brandy and splashed some into each glass.

Keira took a breath, containing her emotion. "Why are you here?" she asked Will. "Have you talked to Simon?"

"Earlier. Not in the past few hours. I spoke to Josie at your cottage and again on my way to the stone circle." He studied her carefully, obviously debating how much to tell her about what he knew. "Norman Estabrook's no longer in U.S. federal custody."

Lizzie concentrated on the flames. She knew Will would be watching for her reaction.

Keira stayed steady. "Simon was right, then. Estabrook cut a deal with prosecutors in exchange for his cooperation."

"They can re-file charges at any time if he doesn't hold up his end," Will said, then added, "There's more, I'm afraid. He left his Montana ranch this morning on a solo flight in his private plane."

"Then no one really knows where he is." Water dripped from the ends of Keira's hair, mingling with the dog's muddy prints on the warm hearth. "Will, Norman Estabrook threatened to kill both Simon and John March."

"I know, Keira. He has no history of violence, and apparently he and his attorneys were able to persuade prosecutors that he spoke in the heat of the moment."

"I don't believe that," Keira said.

Neither did Lizzie, but she was staying quiet.

Will glanced at the bound Irishman, then at Lizzie, then shifted back to Keira, his expression giving away nothing of what he was thinking. "Is there anything I can do for you?"

"I'm fine, thanks to—" Keira turned to Lizzie with a look of embarrassment. "You just saved my life and I don't even know your name."

After what had happened at the stone circle and in Boston, with a possible British spy with them in the pub, Lizzie was even more determined not to get into names. Simon would recognize her, but he wasn't here—and the attack on Keira and the bomb in Boston changed everything.

She needed a new plan.

She moved away from the fire, out of Will's immediate line of sight. He was handy in a fight, but she had to get her bearings before she dared giving up her anonymity.

Eddie brought the tray of brandy over to the fire and handed a glass each to her, Keira and Will. For a split second, Lizzie thought the barman's suspicion of her had eased, but as he stood back with his empty tray, he tilted his head and frowned at her.

Still didn't trust her.

He turned to Will. "I told Patrick and Aidan I'd wager our black-haired stranger here knew how to knock together a head or two." He sniffed at the bungee-corded thug. "I see I was right."

Keira warmed her hands over the peat fire. "I wasn't much help." She glanced at Lizzie. "You certainly do know how to handle yourself in a fight."

"Adrenaline," she said.

"It was more than adrenaline."

"I've taken a few self-defense classes." Starting with her father when she was two. "Luck helps. I had surprise on my side. Our friend here had size, strength and experience."

"And two knives," Keira said.

"If he'd managed one good punch, he'd have knocked me clear across the bay to the Ring of Kerry."

Keira smiled, but Will didn't react at all to Lizzie's attempt at light-heartedness. The glow of the fire reflected in his eyes, deepening the gold flecks. His control was not, she knew, to be mistaken for nonchalance. He was a very capable, dangerous man on high alert.

"Why didn't you run when you had the chance?" Keira asked.

"Story of my life," Lizzie said with a smile.

Will sipped his brandy. "You fought with real skill."

"A maniac coming at you with a knife'll do that."

Keira pushed up the sleeves of her oversize sweater, the hem of her skirt soaked and muddy. She was clearly worried about her family and friends in Boston—about Simon—but she had a kind of inner serenity that Lizzie admired. Serenity wasn't her long suit.

She took one small sip of her brandy and set the glass on the table. As tempted as she was, she wasn't about to settle in for the evening with a bottle of brandy and a chat with the Irish police, who would arrive soon.

She moved in front of the man who'd attacked her. He was outnumbered and unlikely to kick her. Nonetheless, she knew how to fight from a bound, seated position and, assuming he did, too, stayed clear of his feet. "You didn't decide to attack Keira on your own, out of the blue," she said. "Who hired you?"

He turned his head from her. Even if he didn't respond, his body language would be instructive and perhaps give her—and Will Davenport—answers. Will undoubtedly had far more experience with interrogations than she did, but her father had taught her basic techniques.

"You didn't sneak off to the stone circle on a whim," Lizzie said. "Who sent you?"

The Irishman shifted back to her, cockier and less fearful now that the black dog had gone on his way. "D'you have someone in mind?" he asked sarcastically.

An unexpected coolness eased up Lizzie's spine and made her catch her breath as she remembered a night in Las Vegas in June, in the last days before the FBI arrived at Norman's Montana ranch with a warrant for his arrest.

"I do." She spoke in a near whisper. She'd come to believe Norman wanted to bloody his own hands, but now she realized he'd also wanted the drama of this multipronged attack. He'd needed help to pull it off. "I do have someone in mind. He's British. Maybe forty, with medium brown hair, gray eyes. About your height. Noticeably fit."

"How would I remember him?"

She put her palms on her thighs and leaned forward, eye to eye with him. "He's dangerous and charming and very focused. You'd remember."

"No one I know," the Irishman said.

Lizzie had no idea whether or not he was telling the truth, but she was aware of Will studying her, assessing her in steely silence. Her description of his countryman had clearly struck a nerve.

Maybe he was the one she should be questioning.

She tried not to let him distract her. "Why attack Keira with a knife? Why not shoot her? Why not poison her blackberry crumble?"

"Because of the serial killer," Keira said suddenly, quietly from the fire. "That's why, isn't it?"

The Irishman averted his eyes, giving his answer.

Lizzie saw now what he'd planned. "A copycat killing. You wanted to throw the guards off your trail by making it look as if someone was imitating the serial killer who was here earlier this summer."

He breathed in through his nostrils. "I've hurt no one."

"Not for lack of trying, my friend." She ran a fingertip along the rim of her glass on the table. "Eddie and his brothers would recognize you if you were a local. Where are you from? Dublin? Cork? Limerick?"

He didn't react to any of the cities she named.

Will stepped forward and unzipped the Irishman's right jacket pocket. "Let's have a look," he said, withdrawing a battered leather wallet. He opened it up and slid out a bank card with his thumb. "Michael James Murphy. Is that your real name? I expect it is. You thought you had an easy job tonight, didn't you, Mr. Murphy?"

"I tried to save her. That one," Murphy said, nodding toward Keira, his tone slightly less sullen. "I saw this black-haired witch meant to do her harm. It's lucky I happened on when I did."

Lizzie rolled her eyes. "Such a liar."

He glared at her. "You can fool them, maybe, but you don't fool me. I'll explain myself to the guards."

"Great. You do that. In the meantime, you're alone out here on the Irish coast with all of us."

He smirked at her, unimpressed.

Keira turned from the fire, her cheeks red now from the heat, a stark contrast to the rest of her deathly pale face. "He must have been watching for me on the lane and saw me walk up to the stone circle." She drank more of her brandy, holding the glass with both hands. "I thought the rain had stopped for good and a walk would ease my restlessness. I was missing Simon. Afraid for him."

Keira's love for a man Lizzie had kept at arm's length for the past year felt as natural and honest as the Irish night.

Michael Murphy—or whatever his name was—snorted at Lizzie. "You almost broke my poor knee. It hurts like the devil."

She was unrepentant. "What did you expect me to do when you came after me with your knife?"

"I was scared out of my wits, trying to save Keira. Untie me. I've done nothing to deserve being trussed up like a Christmas turkey."

"Nothing?" Lizzie raised her eyebrows, almost amused at his brazenness. "That's rich, my friend."

She took her brandy glass to the bar and set it on the smooth wood, resisting a sudden surge of loneliness. She had friends. Family. Why was she doing this on her own? She glanced at Will, his quiet control as he dialed his BlackBerry more unnerving than if he'd been in a frenzy. He would be focused on first things first. He'd see to Keira's safety.

Then he'd deal with Lizzie.

Her trip to Ireland wasn't going at all as she'd hoped it would. Instead of disrupting Norman's plans for violent revenge, she'd landed in the middle of their execution. She could no longer pretend she'd just stopped by the little Irish village to see Simon Cahill while she was walking the Beara Way. Simon and his friend Lord Davenport had only to put their heads together and, with their resources inside and outside of government, they'd figure out who she was. In the meantime, she had room to maneuver.

Will held his BlackBerry out to Keira. "It's Simon. He and Director March weren't present when the bomb went off. Your uncle and cousin are unhurt." He hesitated for a fraction of a second. "Detective Wisdom is seriously injured."

"What about Abigail?"

"She wasn't in the blast."

Keira took the phone. "Simon," she said in a raw whisper, "I'm fine. I love you."

Lizzie's throat tightened as Keira spoke to the man she loved. She'd found her soulmate, and Simon had found his.

Every instinct Lizzie had told her she had to get out of there now or she wouldn't be able to leave. She didn't want to end up under the thumb of Irish law enforcement. They'd call the FBI and the Boston police, and then where would she be?

In cuffs herself as a material witness, or even a suspect.

If Scoop Wisdom was able to talk, he'd tell the FBI and his BPD colleagues about the black-haired woman he'd caught lingering in front of the triple-decker yesterday afternoon. He'd walked out from the backyard with a colander of green beans that, somehow, made him look more intimidating.

"Can I help you?" he'd asked her.

Hesitating, debating with herself, Lizzie had opted not to tell him the truth. "No. Sorry. I'm just catching my breath." She'd smiled. "Shin splints."

He hadn't bothered hiding his skepticism, but he hadn't stopped her as she'd gone on her way, boarding her flight to Ireland that evening. She'd decided to talk to Simon Cahill instead of John March's detective daughter, Abigail, or her detective friends.

And now, twenty-four hours later, a bomb had exploded on Abigail's back porch, severely injuring Detective Wisdom.

Lizzie reached for her backpack on the hearth. Had she screwed up by not talking to him yesterday? If she had, would he and his detective housemates have found the bomb?

Her father would tell her not to look back with regret but to learn and to help her figure out what she needed to do next.

She felt the sting of her cuts and scrapes now. "Norman isn't flying off to a resort to celebrate his freedom," she said, addressing Simon's British friend. "He'll be furious that his plan didn't work. He'll try again."

Will eased closer to her, his eyes changeable and intense in the heat of the fire. He was taking in everything, studying her, seeing, she was sure, more than she wanted to reveal. An image came, unbidden, unwanted, of them together in a pretty Irish inn, with no worries beyond which book to read or which bath salts to choose.

"You obviously know Estabrook," he said quietly. "Are you a friend?"

"Norman doesn't have real friends."

"He's very wealthy. Some people are drawn to wealth."

"Yes. Some people are." Lizzie saw clearly now what she needed to do. If she was to be of any help now that Norman was acting on his intentions, she had to remain anonymous for as long as possible. She couldn't explain her association with him and his entourage of wealthy investors, adventurers, staff, hangers-on and drug traffickers. "I imagine by now most everyone knows Norman Estabrook's not your basic mild-mannered billionaire adventurer. If you'll excuse me—"

"You've had an ordeal tonight." Will brushed a fingertip across her hand, just above her split knuckles. "You're hurt."

She gave a dismissive shrug. "Nothing a nice hot bath and a lot more brandy won't cure." She lifted her pack onto her shoulder, feeling her jetlag, too. "Please don't stop me. I'm no good to anyone sitting in a garda interview room."

His eyes stayed on her. "I'll find out who you are."

"You could take my backpack from me and find out now, but you won't. We're both in a foreign country." She tilted her head back and challenged him with a cool smile. "You don't want to get into a tussle with me just as the guards arrive and risk getting yourself arrested. You and Keira have enough to explain as it is."

The change in his expression was subtle, but something about it instantly had her conjuring images of fighting him, sparring with him, blocking, counterattacking. Going all out, no-holds-barred.

It was sexy, the idea of getting physical with her very own James Bond.

Further proof, Lizzie decided, of the deleterious effects of jetlag, adrenaline, a knife fight in an Irish stone circle and two sips of brandy on an otherwise perfectly normal brain.

It was time to go.

She lifted Murphy's assault knife out of her pocket and handed it to Eddie O'Shea. "Thank you for the brandy and for your help tonight. Your brothers, too."

He took the knife, his suspicion, if anything, even more acute now. "Just here walking the Beara Way, you say."

But the barman didn't stop her, either, as she headed back out into the quiet, pretty village.

She heard a dog barking in the distance and, high up in the hills, the bleating of sheep. The wind had died to a gentle breeze, and the rain had stopped, the air cool, scented with roses and lavender.

The picnic table was empty. There was no old farmer with a pipe and strange talk.

Lizzie walked past the brightly painted houses and the lampposts with their hanging flower baskets to her little rented car.

No one followed her.

She got behind the wheel but warned herself not to let down her guard just yet, even for a few seconds. As she started the engine, she felt the ache in her muscles from the bruises she'd incurred doing battle in the Beara hills, and she acknowledged a desire to go back to the pub and believe she had allies there, people she could trust.

Instead she pulled out onto the street and found her way back to the main road, the sky slowly darkening over Kenmare Bay.

She wondered how long she had before the Irish Garda, the Boston police, the FBI and one handsome British spy came after her.

Probably not long.

# Chapter 7

*Boston, Massachusetts*
*3:40 p.m., EDT*
*August 25*

A phone call...

Abigail Browning remembered teasing Scoop and Fiona from her back porch about tomatoes. She'd been laughing when she'd gone inside to answer the phone.

She was between the two men who'd grabbed her off the street a few minutes later and was walking with them now on what felt like a marina dock. They'd thrown a smelly car blanket over her head and shoved guns in her ribs. They were pure, brazen, hired thugs who obviously would prefer to shoot her and dump her body—or not to have kidnapped her in the first place.

They'd have just let her burn up in the fire.

She smelled saltwater and the fishiness of low tide. The sounds of boats in front of her and traffic behind her suggested a marina in busy Boston Harbor.

She suppressed her anger and fear and concentrated on what was in her control right now, at this moment.

She could listen, assess, stay alert.

Conserve her energy and try to survive.

"You should take the blanket off my head. It'll draw attention."

"Anyone asks, we'll say you're seasick, and the bright light makes it worse," the man on her right side said in a South Boston accent. "You go along with us."

"How? Turn green on command?"

He inhaled sharply, telling her he didn't like her answer.

Didn't like her.

She'd debated staying out on the porch and not answering the phone. Owen would call her on her cell phone. Tom Yarborough, her partner, would page her or try her cell first. But her father and Simon were on their way, and they would call her home phone if something came up.

It was hot outside, and Abigail had figured she'd scoot into the kitchen, take the call and fill a pitcher of iced tea and bring it out.

Her front doorbell had rung as she'd answered her phone.

Or was she imagining that part?

No. She was sure.

The voice on the other end of the line had been very clear and precise. It hadn't been the man with the South Boston accent. Probably the driver of the van waiting in the street. "In five seconds," he'd said, "a bomb will go off on your back porch. Five...four..."

By three, Abigail was in the living room.

At zero, as promised, came the explosion, thrusting her to the floor and sucking the wind out of her. She'd crawled to her feet, her ears ringing as she'd pulled open her front door.

Scoop...Fiona...Bob...she remembered thinking she had to get to them.

She'd run into the main entry and opened that door. As she'd leaped down the steps, two men swooped in on her in a coordinated maneuver and dragged her to the van. Disoriented from the blast, she'd clawed one of them—the one with the Southie accent—enough to draw blood, but she'd been unable to do more to defend herself.

They stuffed her in the back of the van, dived in with her and sped off, a third man at the wheel.

Three armed men against her. Not good odds. When they finally came to a stop, the driver had muttered something about going on ahead to get things ready and left Abigail with the two men in the back of the van.

"Careful," the man to her left said now. "We don't want to lose you to the sharks, do we?"

"Sharks," she said through the blanket. "Funny."

Half lifting, half shoving, they got her onto what was obviously a boat. A decent size one, too. They forced her down narrow steps before pulling the blanket off her head and taking her into a small, dark stateroom, where they pushed her onto a metal chair.

Working quickly, they blindfolded her with some kind of scarf, tying it so tightly, it pulled even her short hair enough that her eyes teared up. Using what felt like rope, they tied her hands and ankles to the chair back and legs.

Abigail knew she had to control panic and claustrophobia before they could get started and spiral, taking on a life of their own. She breathed in through her mouth to the count of eight. She held her breath for eight. She exhaled through her nose for eight.

Finally she said, "I hope you didn't bleed on me."

Her sarcasm was met with a backhand smack to the left side of her face, striking her cheekbone. The pain was immediate and searing, but she bit it back.

"Ouch," she said without inflection.

"It'll be a pleasure to kill you when the time comes," the man with the Southie accent said.

She did her breathing exercise again.

In for eight. Hold for eight. Out for eight.

"Estabrook and his Brit friend can deal with her," the man added "This whole business stinks. I'm going up for a drink."

"They'll be here in a few hours," the second man said.

"Then they can have a drink with me."

Abigail heard a door shut, the click of a lock turning. She listened, but heard no one breathing nearby, no footsteps.

She was alone.

*Estabrook.*

So. Norman Estabrook was free. He was the reason Abigail's father and Simon were in Boston. The reason, ultimately, that she'd called them that morning and asked to talk to them.

Had Estabrook just tried to carry out his threat to kill the men he claimed had betrayed him?

Abigail did three more sets of her breathing exercises and pictured Owen on his deck at his summer house on Mount Desert Island, smiling at her. He was rugged, hard-edged, a sexy mix of Boston and Texas, a search-and-rescue expert and a man of action who wouldn't take to having his fiancée kidnapped.

But what if he'd been targeted, too?

And Simon and her father. What about them? Had the men who'd grabbed her known they were en route to see her?

Did they know why?

She stopped the thoughts in their tracks. Even if she was alone, there could be a surveillance camera in the room. She didn't need to spool up if she were being watched for signs of distress.

In for eight. Hold. Out for eight.

The boat got underway. The marine patrol would be on the lookout for her. She hoped her captors made a mistake—that they'd already made one and the yacht was under watch now, SWAT planning her rescue.

*Owen...*

Abigail saw him coming to her on a moonlit Maine night and felt him making love to her, imagined every touch, every murmur of his love and passion. She heard the waves crashing on the rocks outside their window and the cries of the seagulls in the distance.

He was with her.

Whatever happened, Owen was with her.

# Chapter 8

Farther up the peninsula, Lizzie turned off the main road onto a sparsely populated lane that crawled over the twilit hills and would take her to the market village of Kenmare at the head of the bay. It wasn't a shortcut, but she hoped she'd be less likely to run into the *An Garda Síochána*—the Guardians of the Peace.

In other words, the police.

Once in Kenmare, she would go on to the small Kerry County airport and fly to Dublin.

At least she had the start of a new plan.

She pulled over to the side of the road—it wasn't much more than a sheep track—and got out, welcoming the brisk wind in her face. The physical effects of her first real fight with an opponent determined to kill her and the thought of what had happened in Boston had left her drained.

And encountering Will Davenport had left her thoroughly rattled.

She looked out across the hills that plunged sharply to the bay, its water gray under the clearing, darkening sky. She walked along a barbed-wire fence. She hadn't passed another car since leaving the main road. The only evidence of other people were the lights of a solitary farmhouse far down on the steep hillside.

A trio of fat sheep meandered across the rock-strewn pasture toward her. Even in the dark, she could see the splotches of blue paint on their white wool that served as brands. She could put aside her distaste for camping and pitch her tent right here among the rocks and sheep and forget everything she had on her mind, including the good-looking Brit who, she suspected, would have her name before the clock struck midnight Irish Summer Time.

Will Davenport could become a very big problem. As she watched the sheep nudge closer to the fence, she wondered how Will knew the Brit she'd run into in Las Vegas. Because she was sure he did…

Yes. He definitely could become a problem.

She'd arrived in Las Vegas in late June after a few days on her own at her house in Maine and a quick stop in Boston to make an appearance at the family hotels' main offices. Her uncle, Bradley, her father's younger brother, ran the company and had been losing patience with her erratic schedule. He'd even begun making noises about finding another role for her. She was very good at getting a lot accomplished in a short time and had managed to placate him. Traveling from one Rush hotel to another had allowed her the flexibility to dip in and out of Norman's world as well as to breathe new life into her ideas about the concierge services and excursions the hotels offered. Her uncle, however, liked to see her at meetings and behind a desk once in a while. Since his older brother lived in Las Vegas, Bradley hadn't objected to Lizzie's heading there. He'd given up seeing her father at meetings or behind a desk a long time ago.

She'd enjoyed being back in the hot, dry, sunny, vibrant town her father called home, but Norman had arrived unexpectedly that same morning for a high-stakes poker game. Lizzie hadn't been able to bring herself to smile at him. Still unaware of Simon's undercover mission at that point, she'd been trying to figure out what else she could do to fire up the FBI to go after Norman. But none of his drug-cartel friends had been with him, and she'd made an effort to relax.

During a break in the game, a man with close-cropped brown hair had approached Norman and spoke to him briefly out of Lizzie's earshot. Whatever they discussed, it had seemed important. She'd retreated to the hotel bar, and ten minutes later, the Brit joined her. She did her best to look bored as she simultaneously nursed a bottle of water and a martini.

He'd eased onto the stool next to her. Unlike Norman, he'd struck her as being very fit. "More of that water in your bag, love?"

"Sure." She'd reached into her tote bag and handed him a bottle. It was Vegas. She knew to stay hydrated. "I'm Lizzie Rush. Who're you?"

He'd taken the water and uncapped it. "You should behave, love." He'd winked at her, and she'd noticed he had gray eyes. "Sorry, I can't stay. I'm in a rush. No pun intended."

He'd left, chuckling to himself, and later that night, Lizzie had reluctantly flown to Montana with Norman. Simon had been scheduled to join them after visiting his friend Will Davenport in London. He and Norman were to work on plans for future high-risk adventures.

Three days later, Norman was under arrest.

Lizzie had provided the FBI with a description of the mysterious Brit in Las Vegas, anonymously, over the Internet, a trick she'd actually taught her father.

As far as she knew, nothing had come of it.

She'd asked her father about him before she'd left for Montana. "Who's the Brit?"

"No one I know."

He could have been telling the truth.

Or not.

And now here she was in Ireland with sheep nuzzling up to her. She got a disposable cell phone out of her jacket pocket and dialed her father's cell phone. "It's me, Dad. Are you in Las Vegas?"

"Losing at poker. How are you, Lizzie?"

She could hear the worry in his voice but sidestepped his question. "Do you remember the Brit who stopped to talk to Norman Estabrook in June?"

"Who?"

"You heard me. I asked you about him that night, and you said you didn't know him. I'm wondering if you've run into him since, or maybe done a little digging."

"I'm losing at five-card stud, sweetheart. Just dying here. Where are you?"

She pictured him at his poker table at the hotel, at just under two hundred rooms their largest. Harlan Rush was a tawny-haired, square-jawed man in his late fifties. He was handsome and rich, and he'd swept her Irish mother off her feet thirty-one years ago after she'd stayed at the Whitcomb Hotel in Boston on business. She had been in Irish tourism development.

Supposedly.

Lizzie didn't want to tell her father where she was. "Let's just say I'm jetlagged."

He sighed. "You're in Ireland. I told you not to go there. Years ago. I told you."

"Ireland isn't the problem."

"It's bad luck for us."

"I love it. Cousin Justin is doing great at the Dublin hotel, which, I might add, is a huge success. Maybe Ireland was bad luck for you and my mother."

"I remember you reaching for her as a baby. 'Mama' was your first word. She was gone, and it was still your first word."

"Don't, Dad."

"You're in trouble. I can hear it in your voice."

She looked up at the sky. There'd be stars tonight. She could stay here and watch them come out. "I think the Brit we saw in Las Vegas might know another Brit, Will Davenport, who is friends with Simon Cahill."

"Cahill? The FBI agent?" Her father groaned. "Lizzie."

"And I think Will is from your world," she said.

"*Will,* he is now? How well do you know him?"

"We just met over brandy in an Irish pub."

"You only drink brandy when you're in trouble."

"Not only," she said with a smile, hoping it relaxed her voice, "but it's the best time."

"Go back to Maine and watch the cormorants."

"Dad—"

"That bastard friend of yours, Estabrook, was turned loose this morning. He's not your problem. You understand that, don't you?"

"Sure. So, nothing on my Brit in June?"

He hesitated just a fraction of a second. "No name. No nothing. Forget him, Lizzie. If he and Lord Davenport are friends, forget him, too."

"I said his name was Will. I didn't say 'Lord.'"

"What, he *is* a lord? I was being sarcastic."

True or not, her father wasn't telling her everything, not because he was a liar, but because he never told her or anyone else all he knew about anything. He could have researched Simon Cahill's friends as easily as she had—before or after Norman's arrest. Her father had never particularly liked her hanging out with Norman and his entourage.

"Will *is* from your world, isn't he?"

"Just because I taught you a few things doesn't mean you should be jumping to conclusions about what I used to do for a living."

"Is that a yes or a no?"

"You're an amateur with the skills and the instincts of a pro, Lizzie, but you're still an amateur. You don't have anyone behind you. You stand alone."

"I have you."

"Lizzie." He took in a breath. "If you need me, I'll be there for you. You know that."

"I do, Dad."

"Your aunt Henrietta is in Paris buying linens."

"I adore Aunt Henrietta, but do you know what it's like to shop with her?"

"I do. Pure hell. Paris is closer to Ireland than Maine. Pop over and help her. Get drunk on expensive brandy. Have some fun, Lizzie." He hesitated before continuing. "The Davenports are a fine British family. A bunch of good-looking devils, too. If you have cause to drink brandy, having a sip or two with a Daven-port isn't a bad thing."

That was all the endorsement she needed. "Thanks. You can go back to your poker game. You're not bluffing on a pair of threes, are you?"

"I wish. Stay safe, my girl."

"I love you, Dad."

After she hung up, Lizzie smiled as more sheep joined her trio and crowded along the fence, the wind blowing their long, woolly coats. Because of her father, she could defend herself in a fistfight, spot a tail, disarm a rudimentary bomb. "The first step, Lizzie," he'd told her, "is knowing the bomb is there."

She returned to her car and dug a change of clothes out of her pack, just as prosaic as the ones she had on, but clean, and put them on right there at the side of the road, in front of the sheep. She kicked off her mud-and-manure-encrusted shoes and tossed them in the trunk in exchange for a pair of pricey little flats she'd picked up at Brown Thomas in Dublin. Her father had hated and avoided Dublin for as long as she could remember. It was where Shauna Morrigan Rush, his wife, Lizzie's mother, had died.

An accident, according to Irish authorities and John March, the young Boston detective who'd looked into her death, later to join the FBI and become its director.

Lizzie shut the car trunk, questions coming at her all at once.

"Resist speculating," her father had told her time and time again. "Discipline your mind. Focus on what you can do."

Easier said than done when knives, bombs, FBI agents and spies were involved, but she would do her best.

A horned sheep baaed at her, and she baaed back.

"There," she said with a laugh. "I could just stay here and talk to the sheep."

She remembered having formal tea with her grandmother, Edna Whitcomb Rush, a stern but kind woman who had never expected to help her older son raise a daughter. She'd tried to explain why Lizzie's father had to be away for long periods. "He's a scout for new locations and ideas for our hotels."

Ha. A scout.

Harlan Rush was a spy, and he'd taught his daughter everything he knew.

Lizzie abandoned the sheep and climbed back into her car, started the engine and continued along the dark, isolated road. She glanced in her rearview mirror.

Still no sign of the garda or Will Davenport on her tail.

At least not yet.

# Chapter 9

*Boston, Massachusetts*
*4:25 p.m., EDT*
*August 25*

Simon ran his fingertips over a colored pencil sketch Keira had done of the ancient Celtic stone angel she still swore she'd seen on the hearth of a ruin in the southwest Irish hills.

There'd been a black dog that night, too.

She and that village were quite the combo.

She'd given the sketch to Fiona O'Reilly, who'd taped it onto the far wall of the chandeliered drawing room where she and her friends often gathered to play Irish music, courtesy of Owen Garrison, whose family had owned the elegant Beacon Hill house for more than a century. The sparsely furnished first-floor room was used for meetings and functions. The offices of the Dorothy Garrison Foundation, established in memory of Owen's sister, were on the second floor. Owen was just eleven and

Dorothy Garrison just fourteen when she'd drowned near their family summer home off the coast of Maine. Their distraught parents had relocated from Boston to Austin, Texas. After a stint in the army, Owen founded Fast Rescue, a highly respected nongovernmental organization that provided rapid response to disasters, natural or manmade, anywhere in the world.

Simon, a search-and-rescue expert himself, had volunteered for Fast Rescue eighteen months ago after he and Owen had become friends through John March. Owen knew March because of their ties to Maine, where Owen had discovered the body of March's son-in-law, Christopher Browning, an FBI agent murdered four days into his Mount Desert Island honeymoon. Last summer—seven years later—his widow and Owen had fallen for each other and finally uncovered the identity of Chris's killer.

At the same time, Simon had begun working a deep under-cover assignment for the FBI, insinuating himself into Norman Estabrook's world of high stakes adventure, finance and criminal activity. A year later, just before Norman's arrest in late June, Simon had met Keira Sullivan…and a few hours ago, because of him, she'd almost been killed for a second time that summer.

A second simple sketch depicted a Dublin windowbox at Christmas. The box was filled with pinecones, evergreen boughs and baubles and draped with sparkling gold ribbon. As always, Keira had captured more than just a scene…a mood, a wish, a dream.

Simon's own mood was dark. His sole commitment was to finding and stopping Norman. It wasn't a wish or a dream—it was his damn job.

The small foundation staff had been sent home, but the bomb squad had gone through the building and given the all clear. Law enforcement was still everywhere, especially in the alley where

Owen had discovered the bomb in his parked car. Bob O'Reilly had been by, in a focused and formidable rage at the day's events. Two bombs in his city. A friend and fellow police officer in stable but critical condition. Another friend and officer missing. A daughter traumatized.

A niece attacked in Ireland.

*Keira.*

But she was unhurt and in the care of the Irish police. The over-riding priority now was the safe return of Abigail Browning. Every available law enforcement resource was deployed in the search for her.

BPD officers and FBI agents were posted at the Garrison house, hovering in the foyer. Simon had first laid eyes on Keira there in June, just days before she'd discovered her stone angel in an Irish ruin. He could see her standing in the doorway that night with her fairy-princess blue eyes and long, flaxen hair. Maybe it had been love at first sight. Maybe it hadn't, but love her he did. He'd joined her in Ireland in early August. While Keira sketched and painted, Simon did what he could to aid the ongoing inves-tigation into Estabrook and his drug-trafficking friends.

He walked across the bare wood floor to the middle of the drawing room, where Owen was silently staring up at an unlit chandelier as if somehow it could offer him hope, if not answers. Simon recognized his friend's stillness and pensiveness as his way of containing his emotions—the gut-wrenching fear they all had for Abigail.

"I'd trade places with her in a heartbeat," Owen said, his gaze still on the chandelier.

"She knows. She'll latch onto your feelings for her and use them to give her strength. You've seen it before with people in tough situations."

Before coming to Boston in June—before meeting Keira—

Simon had joined Owen and Fast Rescue in responding to a major earthquake in Armenia. They'd pulled dozens of children from the rubble of their collapsed school. Many were seriously injured. Some came out unscathed. More hadn't survived. Owen had never flinched from doing, getting others to do, what had to be done.

How many children had said they knew that someone would come, that they wouldn't be left there alone? How many had drawn strength from thoughts of their mothers and fathers—of the people who loved them—as they'd waited for help?

Owen was impatient and action-oriented by nature, and his reserve now was an indication of just how deeply worried he was. "Bob says the blood on the sidewalk isn't hers."

Simon nodded. A haemostatic test had confirmed it was human blood—but it wasn't Abigail's type. "I'm guessing that means she was in good enough shape to fight back when she was grabbed."

"I hope so. What's the update on Scoop?"

"He's stitched up and sedated. A hunk of shrapnel that hit the base of his skull is causing problems, but doctors are more optimistic than they were at first."

Owen shut his eyes briefly. He knew how to stay focused in a crisis given his years in the military and his experience responding to horrific disasters all over the world. Earthquakes, tsunamis, mudslides, floods. Terrorist attacks. But this was personal.

"I don't want to be here standing under a chandelier." He shifted to look at Simon, the strain showing now in his angular face. "I hate feeling helpless."

Simon tried to smile. "A man who just disarmed a car bomb isn't helpless. It's been a while, hasn't it?"

"Not long enough."

"Amen to that."

"It was a simple device."

"Still would have blown you to Kingdom Come."

Owen remained tense, serious. "Thanks to Keira, I had warning. The bomb at the triple-decker was exploded by remote control. The one in my car was designed to go off when the key in the ignition was turned. There was enough C4 to blow up the entire car and kill anyone inside or in close proximity."

"No one had to watch for you to get in," Simon said.

Owen looked back up at the chandelier. "Why kill me and kidnap Abigail?"

"That's a good question."

"Tom Yarborough interviewed me himself—I told him everything I could think of. I left Abigail in bed early this morning and headed out to my car. I didn't see anyone on the street there or here who didn't belong. I parked in the alley where I always park and got to work."

"Fast Rescue work?"

He nodded. "We're moving the headquarters to Boston."

"Since when?"

"We made the decision in early August. I haven't told Abigail." His voice caught, almost imperceptibly. "I was keeping it as a surprise. The move will help cut down on travel. We're..." He let his voice trail off. "It doesn't matter now."

"It does matter. Ab will be thrilled, but she'll also slice you to ribbons for keeping secrets."

Owen's smile didn't reach his eyes. "I would argue there's a difference between a surprise and a secret."

"Go ahead. Argue that when Ab's back."

"You know she hates being called Ab, which, of course, is why you do it." He turned to Simon with a faint, grim smile. "The chandelier needs dusting."

"I'm sorry about all this, Owen."

"It's not your fault. Don't even go there. Any word on Estabrook?"

"Still no sign of him or his plane. There's a search underway, but he flew into remote country. It could be days, weeks or even months before we find him. We might never find him."

"Especially if he doesn't want to be found."

Simon understood where Owen was headed. "Norman gave up damning details on some very violent people who can't be happy with him. Today's festivities could be their work. They could be responsible for the bombs, the attack on Keira. They could have lured Norman up in his plane, or he knew they were after him and decided to disappear. He could be a target, too."

"Is that what you believe, Simon?"

He didn't hesitate. "No, but we have to keep an open mind."

"Law enforcement has to consider every angle," Owen said. "I don't."

"It's also possible that Norman will return from his flight by nightfall and what happened here and in Ireland is the work of someone involved with one of Abigail's cases, old or new—or one of Scoop's or Bob's. It could have something to do with you or her father. Belief only gets us so far," Simon added. "We can't jump the gun and miss the real bad guys because of wrong assumptions."

"But it's Estabrook," Owen said.

Simon was silent a moment, then nodded.

"He obviously had help. Pulling off three simultaneous attacks within hours of his release means he must have had at least the barebones of a plan in place, probably before he was arrested. What's the purpose, Simon? What does he want?" Owen broke off, shook his head. "You should get out of here. Go to Ireland and be with Keira."

There wasn't anywhere in the world Simon would rather be right now than with Keira. He thought of her in the stone circle above her cottage, a killer coming at her with a knife, and couldn't push back a wave of regret. "If I'd gone fishing with Will Davenport in Scotland in June instead of coming here to Boston, none of you would be in the middle of this mess. Keira would be safe."

"Or dead," John March said bluntly, entering the room. More FBI agents crowded into the foyer but kept a reasonable distance. "That serial killer was already interested in her Irish story and would have had free rein if you hadn't been in her life. Who's to say what would have happened? And Keira's safe now."

But Abigail, his daughter, wasn't. Genuinely shaken, Simon wished he could melt into the cracks in the floor. "I have no right when you and Owen..." He didn't finish his thought.

"You have every right," March said. "Estabrook's gone after the people closest to us. He doesn't want them."

Simon nodded. "I know. He wants us."

"And he doesn't just want us dead. I could handle straightforward revenge, but he wants us to suffer first." March looked at his future son-in-law. "Owen, I don't know what to say."

"I want to go after her, John."

"No. It's too risky. We don't know enough. Work with us. Maybe you saw something, or Abigail said something..." March stopped abruptly, his expression tight, controlled, a reminder that he'd worked in law enforcement for almost forty years. "Abigail wouldn't want you to go solo, either."

"Then let me go to Montana and help look for this bastard. I can find his plane. I have search-and-rescue teams ready to go."

March sighed. "Someone—undoubtedly the man you want to

fly to Montana and find—tried to kill you today. You do know that, don't you?"

"I was warned in time. I found the bomb. I'm alive." Owen walked over to the tall windows that looked out on Beacon Street and across to Boston Common. "I'm not dwelling on what might have happened."

"Crews are searching for Estabrook now."

Owen glanced back at March. "Not my crews."

Neither Simon nor March responded.

Simon joined his friend at the windows. Pedestrians passed by on the street—tourists, students, state workers, business people. "I've been trying to understand Norman's thinking for a year. He faces death to feel alive." Simon hesitated, then said, looking back at March, "He thwarts authority to feel alive."

"Why me, Simon?" March asked quietly.

It was Owen who answered. "He sees you as an equal. Equals are rare in his universe. Everyone else is a lesser mortal to him, but you…" He shrugged. "You're the head of the most powerful law enforcement agency in the world."

The FBI director, who'd been a surrogate father to Simon since his own father had died twenty years ago, joined them at the windows. As March stared outside, Simon could feel the older man's pain, his fear for his daughter. His emotion was almost unbearable to witness.

"I'm not wealthy," March said finally. "I don't go on high-risk adventures. I'm just a cop. That's it. Whether I'm on a beat here in Boston or in an office in Washington, I'm still just a cop doing a job."

Simon shook his head. "Not in Norman's eyes. You're a challenge. He wants you as an enemy. Going up against you and the entire FBI is another way for him to face death."

Owen turned from the windows. "He'd rather die in action than wither away in a prison cell."

"That works for me," March said. "My wife's under protection in Washington. You two should be, too. Turn yourselves over to agents. Let us see to your safety."

"I'll work with the FBI and help in any way I can," Owen said stiffly, "but I'll see to my own safety."

Simon's eyebrows went up. "You're kidding, John, right? I spent a year with Norman and his drug-trafficking pals without a net. *Now* you're worried?"

"Simon..."

"Forget it. I'm working this investigation now that Keira's in safe hands."

He didn't go into more detail. Will Davenport was in Ireland, and he and March had a history, not a good one. Simon didn't know the specifics but suspected their animosity went back to Afghanistan and how and why Will had ended up trapped in a cave with two of his men dead, a third dragged off by enemy fighters. Simon had been there himself on assignment for the FBI. He suspected his reasons for being near the cave were at least marginally related to Will's reasons, but the Brits had clammed up after the tragic loss of three of their own—or at least had clammed up to him. Maybe not to March.

Simon saw that March was scrutinizing him with an expression that was more cop than friend or father figure, and he knew his comment had sparked the FBI director's interest.

Time to make his exit.

He clapped a hand on Owen's shoulder, nodded to March and left without saying anything else. What more was there to say? He headed into the foyer and down the front steps onto the wide sidewalk. A half-dozen fellow FBI agents and BPD officers watched him, and he wondered if they had orders to make sure he didn't go off on his own.

Too bad if they did.

The air was warm, even hot, in the fading afternoon. He thought of Will's description of the woman who'd intercepted the man sent to attack Keira in Ireland. "Long, straight black hair and light green eyes," Will had said. "She's small, but very fast and self-assured. I saw her tackle Murphy from a distance. She had him on the ground, his own knife to his throat, before I'd cleared the fence. Who do you suppose she is, Simon?"

He'd said he had no idea, which was true.

Now, he wasn't so sure. A woman did come to mind, but it made no sense at all.

Lizzie Rush, kicking ass in an Irish stone circle?

She was one of the many high-end members of Norman's entourage who'd claimed to be shocked by his illegal activities.

The FBI agent who'd interviewed Lizzie after Norman's arrest had described her to Simon. "Clueless. A little annoyed. Very eager to get back to her reprobate daddy in Las Vegas."

The last time Simon had run into her, she was wearing a slim, expensive black dress with a bottle of water and a martini at her elbow as she'd amused herself at a cocktail party at Norman's Cabo San Lucas estate. Afterward, she, Norman and Simon had discussed preliminary plans for a Costa Rican adventure. She obviously knew her business, if not what her financial-genius friend was up to.

So what was she doing in the same Irish village as Keira?

"I'd have managed on my own somehow," Keira had said, not with bravado but a calm certainty that Simon had learned over the past two months not to doubt. "But I was glad to have help."

Regardless of who'd saved whom, someone had sent a killer after her.

Simon crossed Beacon Street and took the steep, stone stairs down to Boston Common. A breeze stirred through the tall trees, and he glanced back at the Garrison house to see if anyone had followed him.

Not yet, but his fellow law enforcement officers were still watching him. In their place, he'd be doing the same.

He dialed a London number on his cell phone. "Money-penny," he said when Josie Goodwin, Will's assistant, answered. "Dare I ask where you are?"

"Special Agent Cahill," Josie said. "I suspected I might hear from you tonight."

"I have a name for you."

"I'm ready."

"Lizzie Rush. If she's our black-haired mystery woman, you can have Will tell her to back off and mind her own business."

"Perhaps she knows more than you realize."

"Then she can call me and tell me. She's bored, rich and very pretty, Josie. She can't interfere—" But he stopped abruptly. He'd been thinking about Lizzie Rush ever since he'd spoken to Will and Keira, when and where he'd seen her, her relationship with Norman. What if she *did* know more than he'd realized? He sighed. "Hell, Josie."

"Indeed, Simon," she said. "Suppose this woman has been a quiet player right from the start? Is it possible Director March had an anonymous source funnel him information?"

It wasn't just possible. He did have one. A dozen times over the past year, March himself had handed Simon critical pieces of information—photographs, names, account numbers—that could only have been obtained by someone close to Norman Estabrook. March never confirmed or denied the existence of a source and instructed Simon not to speculate. Just take the information and do his job.

Of course, Simon had speculated, especially in the weeks since Norman's arrest. Various names came to mind—accountants, bookkeepers, hedge-fund staffers, household help…

But Lizzie Rush?

"Leave her to Will," Josie said.

Simon heard something in her voice. "Moneypenny," he said, "you wouldn't be holding back on me, would you?"

"Why, Simon, what a thing to say."

She disconnected in mock horror.

Which told Simon she *was* holding back. Josie Goodwin was a force unto herself, but she would only go so far with Simon, friend of her boss or no friend. Will was a lone wolf who lived a dangerous life and tried to protect those around him from that life.

It wasn't always possible, Simon thought as he dialed Owen's cell number. "March still breathing down your neck?"

"Right here."

"I'll help you get to Montana."

Owen was silent a moment. "Thank you."

"Like you aren't already plotting how to get there on your own. At least my way will keep you from getting arrested." But Simon couldn't maintain his normal good cheer. "I've done search missions with you, Owen. If anyone can find Norman's plane, it's you."

"I'm ready to leave now."

Simon managed a smile. "I thought you might be."

Seeing how his Boston residence had just been totaled by fire, smoke and water damage, Owen had nothing to pack. He could always stop at a Wal-Mart on his way to Montana.

As he shut his phone, Simon looked east toward Boston Harbor, squinting as if it would help him see past the tall buildings and the Atlantic and connect with Keira in Ireland. He concentrated on his love for her. Will wouldn't leave her until he was satisfied that the garda, her fairies and the O'Shea brothers would keep her safe.

Keira had objected, but she also understood.

This one wasn't her fight.

# Chapter 10

*Beara Peninsula, Southwest Ireland*
*10:15 p.m., IST*
*August 25*

Keira stood at the pine table in her cottage on the lane below the stone circle, shoving art supplies—paints, pencils, brushes, sketch pads—into a wooden case. "The woman who helped me tonight knew what to ask. She knew names. Bob, Scoop, Abigail. Simon. Owen." Keira paused, raising her eyes to Will. "She knew everything. Who is she?"

"I don't know," Will said, shrugging on his coat.

Garda detectives had inspected Keira's cottage for explosive devices and were waiting outside to take her to a safe place. Will had arrived in the stone circle too late to be of any real use. Simon would hate himself for not being there. But it didn't matter, did it? Their mysterious black-haired woman had dispatched Murphy and questioned him like a professional, then boldly went on her way ahead of the guards' arrival.

They were looking for her now.

But she'd been right: Will could have stopped her.

Why hadn't he?

He already knew the answer. He hadn't stopped her for the same reason he hadn't interrupted her when she'd asked Michael Murphy about the Brit she'd believed had sent him to kill Keira.

*"He's dangerous and charming and very focused."*

Keira paused a moment in her packing. "You're going to find out who she is, though, aren't you?"

"Yes."

"You didn't stop her from leaving."

"No, I didn't."

Keira's cornflower-blue eyes leveled on him, but she said nothing further as she flipped through a stack of small sketch pads, choosing two to take with her.

The scent of the rambling pink roses out front sweetened the breeze that floated through the open windows, gentler now that the gale had died down. Keira's hair was tangled, her clothes and shoes muddy from her ordeal in the stone circle. The Irish detectives had told her she could shower later at the safe house where they were taking her.

Keira had made it plain she didn't want to go anywhere except to Simon and her family and friends in Boston. She could refuse protection, but she didn't. Garda teams had kicked into immediate action upon their arrival in the village, taking away Michael Murphy, cordoning off the stone circle and searching the pub, Keira's cottage and the boat she and Simon had shared for much of the past month for explosive devices and hidden thugs.

"Bombs, Will," she said suddenly, reaching for a nub of an eraser. "I keep thinking about Scoop. He's a great guy. He adopted two stray cats—the firefighters got them out safely." She dropped the eraser into her box and wiped the back of her hand across tear-stained cheeks. "He's in critical but stable condition. Will…"

He touched her slender shoulder. "Keira, I'm sorry. I know how difficult this is for you."

"Scoop's strong. He'll pull through." She picked up the brush she'd dropped. "He has to. And Abigail. I can't—if I think about her, where she could be, what she's going through, I'll fall apart, and that won't help anyone."

Will had learned from Simon that his newfound love had moved from city to city for years, at home everywhere and nowhere. Finally she'd returned to Boston to be near her mother, who had withdrawn from the world to live as a religious ascetic in a cabin she'd built herself in the woods of southern New Hampshire. Keira had developed a closer relationship with her uncle, Bob O'Reilly, and younger cousins in Boston, and she, Abigail Browning and Scoop Wisdom had become friends.

Then Simon Cahill had entered her life.

"It's not Simon's fault." Keira again fastened her gaze on Will. "He's a target just like the rest of us."

"What has Simon told you about Norman Estabrook?"

"We haven't talked about him that much. He's petulant, vindictive and brilliant. He courts danger to feel alive." She reached for more art supplies as she continued. "He trusted Simon with his life."

"It wasn't misplaced trust," Will said. "Simon never did anything to deliberately endanger Estabrook."

"From what I gather, he's obsessive about safety measures and backup plans. Whatever happened today—whatever went wrong or right—he'll have various courses of action from which to choose."

"That won't make him easier to find."

She nodded grimly. "Simon and I have only just found each other. I can hear him singing Irish songs now. He and my uncle have beautiful voices. I can't sing a note. My mother, either. A few months ago, she was living a quiet, solitary life of prayer in the woods, and now she's back in the city with all this…" Keira snapped her art case shut. "I wouldn't blame her if she gives up on us and goes back to her cabin."

"Your mother's safe, Keira," Will said. "The Boston police and the FBI won't let any harm come to her."

He read her expression, saw that she was as stubborn and independent as Simon had promised she was, and also as brave. Wherever the garda tucked her for her own safety, she'd do what she could to help the investigation. She wasn't one to sit back.

There was a light knock on the kitchen door, and an officer poked his head in. "Two minutes, and we have to go."

Keira took a breath. "I don't even know what I've packed, but I suppose I can always ask someone to make a supply run for me if it comes to that." She raised her eyes again to Will. "You'll have to come meet the gang one day. We're supposed to do Christmas in Ireland this year. My uncle, my cousins, my mother and me."

"It'll be cold, dark and wet."

She smiled. "I hope so. I promised to take my cousin Fiona to pubs to hear Irish music. She has her own Irish band. I want to talk to her, see her—Scoop saved her today. Simon didn't say so outright, but there must have been a lot of blood." Keira sniffled back more tears, as much from anger and frustration as worry and grief. "I don't want to run and hide, Will."

"That's not what you're doing."

"Isn't it?"

She didn't wait for an answer and retreated to the cottage's sole bedroom, emerging in less than a minute with a brocade satchel, her hair brushed and pulled back into a ponytail. She was lovely, creative and unexpectedly pragmatic. Will wouldn't be surprised if the garda had found a safe house in the village. She seemed protected there.

"I'll do whatever I need to do," she said quietly. "You know that, don't you?"

"And Simon knows." Will smiled at her. "You and your fairy prince will soon be reunited."

Keira took his hand, squeezing it as she leaned forward and kissed him on the cheek. "Whatever debt you think you owe Simon, he says you don't owe him anything. You never did."

"This isn't about debts owed, Keira."

"No. I suppose it isn't." Her eyes steadied on him with just a hint of a spark. "If you end up in Boston, beware of sneaking around under the noses of the police there. You've never met my uncle, but he'll be on a tear after what's happened."

"He's Boston Irish, isn't he?"

"Yes."

Will winked at her. "Then I don't need to meet him."

She let go of his hand and whispered, "Be safe."

He left before the guards could change their mind and take him into custody for additional questioning. He'd parked on the lane, his car spotted with bits of pink rose petals flung there in the wind and rain, a tangible reminder, somehow, of Keira's ordeal.

As he drove toward the village, he looked up at the wild hills silhouetted against the dark Irish night. He hated to leave Keira, but she would be safe here.

And he had a job to do.

★ ★ ★

A light shone in the window of the pub, and the door was unlocked. Will found Eddie O'Shea behind his bar, cleaning up for the night. The guards had gone, their investigative work completed, at least for now.

When he saw Will, Eddie said, "A bomb sweep is a fine way to scare off paying customers. Will you be wanting a drink, Lord Will?"

"Coffee, please, if you have it."

"I've water still hot in the kettle." He set a coffee press on the bar and scooped in fresh grounds. "Next time, ring me when you feel an urge to come to Ireland. I'll be on my toes for trouble."

"The trouble started before I arrived."

"True enough. It was the same earlier this summer with Keira and her stone angel and that other bloody killer." The barman shuddered. "I've pictures that'll never leave my head from those terrible days."

"I wish it could have been otherwise, Eddie."

"As do I." He poured water over the grounds, replaced the top on the press and set it in front of Will to steep. He got out a mug and a pitcher of cream, his movements automatic, routine. "The guards talked to our friend Michael Murphy. It's his real name. He's too dim-witted to make one up. He's a known thug in Limerick."

"Good at his work?"

"Not good enough...fortunately for Keira and her black-haired friend." O'Shea pushed the coffee paraphernalia in front of Will and looked thoughtfully at him. "The guards wish we'd stopped her from leaving the scene."

Will knew they did. "You saw her for yourself—her torn

knuckles, her muddy clothes, the way she handled Mr. Murphy. Would you have wanted to take her on?"

"She wasn't too quick to give up his knife."

And she'd disarmed him, weaponless herself. Murphy hadn't expected her, and even when he saw her, he'd obviously discounted her as a threat, especially a lethal one. He was strong and capable, a veteran fighter, but she'd had his face in the mud and manure before he'd had a chance to land a single blow.

Eddie showed not the slightest edge of fatigue despite the night's events. "I expect the guards will have to sort through layers of tawdry criminals to get to whoever hired Murphy. Man, woman or animal."

"I expect so," Will agreed, pouring his coffee. It was very hot and very strong, and suddenly he hoped he'd have reason to sit here one evening, chatting with the amiable Irish barman over matters that didn't involve violence.

"You don't know where the guards have taken Keira, I suppose?" Eddie asked.

Will shook his head. "I'm sorry, no."

"I'd be wasting air asking them. As long as she's safe." He nodded to the coffee. "What else can I get you? I've a bit of blackberry crumble left. There's soup, but Patrick made it, and it's not fit for the pigs."

"No food. Thanks."

"You're gloomy."

He was, and he knew why. The evening had launched him back two years, to the cave in Afghanistan and the deaths of men who'd trusted him.

For their sakes, he had to focus on the task at hand.

He drank some of his coffee and addressed the barman. "Did

you see Michael Murphy in the village earlier today?" He paused. "Before today?"

Eddie emptied the stainless-steel kettle into a small sink. "I don't remember seeing him before tonight. I told the guards as much."

"He could have a partner. I understand that strangers come in here on a regular basis—particularly this time of year, particularly this summer with the publicity over Keira's stone angel. Did anyone strike you as not belonging? Someone who wasn't a typical tourist, perhaps?" Will set his mug on the bar and kept his gaze on the Irishman. "Think, my friend. Who stood out to you in recent days?"

Eddie took the still-hot coffee press and dumped the grounds, then rinsed the glass container in the sink and set it to drain. Finally he said, "A Brit like the one our black-haired friend described was here a week ago, maybe more."

Will got very still. "Tell me about him."

"He had soup and left."

"Were Keira and Simon here?"

Eddie shook his head. "Not yet. They arrived from the north five days ago on the boat you loaned them. This man was here before then."

"Did he ask about them?"

"No. I'd recall if he did. Given his manner, I'd wager he was a military man. He had a self-control that reminded me of you, Lord Will." Eddie slopped an overly wet cloth onto the bar. "Not that I know about military men."

Will kept his hands steady even as his heartbeat quickened. So much for self-control. He envisioned Myles, arms crossed on his chest as he lay on his back and gazed up at the starlit Afghan sky and said, quite sincerely, he was as comfortable sleeping there, on the rocks in the open, as he'd have been at Buckingham Palace.

In the eight years Will had known and trusted him, Myles Fletcher had never shown a hint of a grasping nature. He'd never shown himself to be a man who could betray his country—his mates.

"What else can you remember?" Will asked, keeping his tone even. "The smallest detail could be significant."

"He paid with euros and sat alone, kept to himself. He asked for water—no coffee or alcohol. When he left, he walked down to the harbor, then down the lane. Aidan, Patrick and I took turns following him. He knew it and didn't care."

"Did he stay overnight in the village?"

"I don't know where he stayed. We lost him eventually. He brought up Keira's story about the stone angel when he was in here, but only for a moment, and he wasn't the first nor the last. It's been happening all summer."

"What did you tell him?"

A spark of mischief flared in the Irishman's eyes. "I told him to find a rainbow and follow it to a pot of gold."

Will smiled in spite of his tension. Eddie O'Shea enjoyed keeping his pub, but he wasn't one to suffer fools or intruders gladly. And he liked Keira and Simon. But who didn't?

Eddie continued mopping the bar with his wet cloth. "Did we do the right thing after all, Will, in letting our black-haired woman go?"

"You're worried about her," Will said.

"What if she's in over her head and a danger to herself? To others? We could have stopped her, Lord Will." The barman stood back and dropped the cleaning cloth into the sink, then got a dry one and soaked up the excess water on the gleaming bar. "Not without a fight, I'll wager, one I'm not sure we'd have won. She knows how to put her foot to the right spot on a man, I'll say that. I could see it when she came in here." He motioned toward the pegs by the front door. "The way she took off her jacket and hung it… Never mind the rest."

"From what I witnessed," Will said, "I'd guess she's received training."

"Of your sort?"

He let Eddie's question slide unanswered.

"Is that why you let her go?" Eddie's eyes shone with both amusement and suspicion. "A strapping Brit like yourself, worrying a tiny woman would best you."

"She'd just bested an armed, hired killer."

"Ah. You wouldn't stand a chance, would you?"

Will pictured her at the fire with Keira's book of folktales and smiled. "I didn't say that." He passed a business card that Josie had made up for him in London across the bar. "Call me anytime. For any reason."

"And the same, Lord Will. You call me anytime. I'll do whatever I can to help." Eddie took Will's empty mug and set it in the sink. "Who's the Brit you're thinking I saw?"

Will knew he couldn't answer. A lie, the truth—neither was acceptable, and so he said nothing.

Eddie seemed to understand the line his question had crossed. "If I see him again?"

"If you see him again," Will said carefully, "treat him like a shopkeeper who's here on holiday."

"Or he'll kill me in my sleep?"

Josie Goodwin answered from the door. "It won't matter if you're asleep," she said as she unzipped her coat, its style more suited to London than a quiet Irish village. She walked over to the bar, steady if visibly shaken. "I came as soon as I could. I'll be of more use here than in London should Keira need a hand,

and perhaps I can persuade our garda friends to share information. I miss the city already. It's bloody dark out there."

A strongly built, attractive woman in her late thirties, she was as pale as Will had ever seen her. He'd been aware of her presence in the door, but he didn't know how much she'd overheard. He started to introduce her to Eddie, but the Irishman put up a hand to stop him. "I'll leave you two to your chat. I can see I won't be wanting to hear what you have to say."

As he retreated, Will felt Josie's emotions, checked, under control but there. "Josie," he said, "we don't know—"

She cut him off neatly. "Let me just say my piece and get it done. You should go back to London, Will. Leave this mess to the Americans and the Irish to sort out."

"You've more on our mystery woman?"

"Her name is Lizzie Rush." Josie eased onto the tall bar stool next to Will. "She's one of the hotelier Rushes. She's in charge of their concierge and excursion services and leads quite an adventurous life."

"What's her connection to Simon?"

"She was with Norman Estabrook in Montana the day he was arrested. The FBI questioned her but didn't detain her."

"Are she and Estabrook romantically involved?"

"No. Absolutely not, according to what little I have managed to learn. He liked having attractive, successful people around him. She was one of them."

"Does she have a connection to John March?"

Josie sighed. "I'm still digging."

"March would use anyone to get what he wants."

"He's a suffering father right now, Will."

"I know. The man's in an impossible position."

"He often is." Obviously restless, she jumped down from the

stool and went around to the other side of the bar, where she helped herself to a glass and a bottle of Midleton Rare Whiskey. "You can't let your dislike of Director March interfere with your judgment."

"It's mutual dislike, but also impersonal on a certain level since we've never met face-to-face. I'm convinced he's known more about Myles than he's ever been willing to tell us. He doesn't believe I can be fully trusted." Which was more than Will had ever admitted to Josie about his attitude toward the current FBI director and was all he planned to say. "Is Lizzie Rush a rich woman meddling in affairs of no concern to her because she's bored and has a zest for adventure, or does she have her own quarrel with Norman Estabrook?"

"She could also be on his side in a peculiar way," Josie said as she splashed whiskey into her glass, adding without sympathy, "If she's sticking her nose where it doesn't belong, she could get it cut off."

"Instead of fleeing, she stopped Keira from being killed."

"Which by itself means nothing, Will. You know that. What you saw tonight could have been staged, cooked up by her and Murphy to mislead us. This woman could have her own agenda and not give a damn about Keira, Estabrook, Simon or anyone else."

There was no one on the planet more clear-eyed or more unlikely to let emotion cloud her judgment than Josie Goodwin. Will recognized how much he'd come to rely on her not just for her efficiency, but as a sounding board. "I suppose theoretically she could have her own plans that could get mucked up if Keira and the people in Boston were killed."

"What about Abigail Browning?" Josie asked, taking a swallow of her whiskey even before she set down the bottle. She choked a little and gave her chest a pound with her fist. "Sorry. I haven't had a drop of alcohol in months. I was crying over my sorrows too many nights and…" She waved a hand. "Never mind. Perhaps our Lizzie Rush, regardless of why she was here, can help find Detective Browning."

Will narrowed his eyes. "You've more information?"

"Not much. I spoke to Simon." She got a pained look. "It's not good. There are no witnesses or substantial leads, and so far, there have been no calls for ransom."

"But no body, either, I gather."

"Correct. No body." Josie made a face as she swallowed more of her Midleton's. "You know I don't care for whiskey, don't you?"

Will smiled. "Yes, Josie, I know."

She coughed, took a smaller swallow this time. Her eyes, a dark blue, were hard and unforgiving, a contrast to the vulnerability her pale skin suggested.

A woman of contrasts, Josie Goodwin.

"You're a wealth of information, as always," Will said. "What would I do without you?"

"Live a lovely life in Scotland, I've no doubt." She returned the whiskey bottle to its place in Eddie's lineup. "Do you believe Miss Rush could help us find Myles Fletcher, that bloody traitor?"

"Josie…"

"It's a serious, professional question, Will."

"We've no reliable evidence that he's alive."

Josie polished off her whiskey, giving a final shudder of distaste as she turned back to him. "The barman's description, Will. It fits."

"It fits other British men, too, I'm sure. It isn't definitive by itself."

Josie gave him a long, cool look as she rinsed her glass. "You're trying to spare me."

He attempted a smile. "You? Never."

"All right, then. We'll do this your way. There's no good answer here, is there? Either Myles Fletcher was a traitor killed two years ago, or he survived and is now a cold-blooded mercenary."

Myles Fletcher was a name Will knew Josie didn't want to utter and certainly wasn't one he wanted to hear. "I should have worked harder to find him."

"We all did everything possible. Everything, Will."

"What if he's not—"

"Don't." Her voice was hoarse, her eyes dark and intense. "Don't, Will. Please."

He acceded to her wish with a reluctant nod and didn't continue.

"If Estabrook has hired Myles or allied himself with him in any way, it means he has someone on his payroll who can help him realize any violent impulses he has." Josie fell silent a moment. "I hope that's not the case."

"I do, too."

She didn't look at Will. "If Myles is alive, I hope he's lost his memory and has opened a tea shop in Liverpool. If not…" She glanced up, her cheeks less pale now. "I had the chance to smother him to death."

"Josie."

"All right, then. On we go. I'll investigate possible connections between Myles and Lizzie Rush, between him and her family." Josie hesitated, then said, "Perhaps she's in love with him. Myles does have a way with women."

"From her questioning of Michael Murphy, I would say Lizzie doesn't know him at all—"

"Which could be what she wants you to think." Josie came around to the other side of the bar. "I needn't remind you that

Myles is a capable, ruthless killer. If he's alive, Will, don't think you can reason with him."

"Josie, I'm sorry his name's come up."

But she wasn't finished. "If you see him, put a bullet in his head. Find a way to do it. He's a predator. He hovers in the bush, waiting for the right moment, the right prey. Then he springs. I know, Simon. I was his prey once."

"He manipulated both of us, in different ways," Will said softly. "We owe his service, what he once was, an open mind."

Josie zipped up her coat, her eyes bitter now as well as hard. "Myles knows how to make people see what they want to see in him." She went on briskly, before Will could respond. "Interestingly the Rush family doesn't own a hotel in the U.K. They do, however, own what I understand is a charming hotel in Dublin."

"And how is this relevant?" Will asked.

"Because I reserved a room for you there for tonight. It should be quite lovely. You can see for yourself and let me know. They're expecting you for a very late arrival."

"Do you believe that's where Lizzie went, or do you know?"

"An educated guess, and either way, it's a good place to start. You *are* going after her, aren't you?"

Will thought of Lizzie Rush's green eyes, black-lashed and bold, yet, he was sure, hiding secrets, fears. But didn't everyone?

"Yes," he said, "I'm going after her."

"Excellent. I approve." At last, a glint of humor. "Give my best to Simon when you see him. And Keira?" Josie asked, more subdued, speaking as if she knew the woman Simon Cahill had fallen for earlier that summer, although the two of them had yet to meet. "She's all right?"

Will nodded. "Impatient to be with Simon."

"Ah, yes. One can imagine. Well," she added, "you should leave. Dublin's over three hundred kilometers, but you'll manage. You're accustomed to odd hours, long days—" she gave him a wicked smile "—and longer nights."

Will sighed and gave no comment.

"In any event," Josie said, "you've much to keep you wide-awake and on your toes."

"I see that plans have been made and announced, and I have only to comply."

"Finally he sees the light."

But their cheerfulness was momentary. "What about you, Josie?" Will asked her.

"I've booked a room at a five-star hotel in Kenmare, but perhaps I would be wise not to make the drive over these dark roads after gulping whiskey. Imagine the international row if I'm picked up by the Irish authorities. Much better to work with them discreetly."

Eddie O'Shea wandered back in behind his bar, nothing in his demeanor indicating he'd eavesdropped. "My brother Aidan has a room at his farm down the lane," he said to Josie. "You'd be welcome to stay."

Josie smiled, looking genuinely delighted. "A night on an Irish farm. A perfect ending to a difficult day."

# Chapter 11

*Boston, Massachusetts*
*6:25 p.m., EDT*
*August 25*

The late afternoon sun beat down on the sidewalk in front of the triple-decker where Bob had lived for the past three years. There was no shade and no breeze. Sweat trickled down his temples and stuck his shirt to the small of his back. The firefighters had put out the fire and torn up and hosed down what they needed to, creating a big mess but saving the building, at least structurally. Abigail's and Scoop's back porches were cinders. Her apartment would have to be gutted to the studs. Hard to say yet about the other two places. They'd have to get the insurance people out here.

At least no one found any other bombs.

Ever since the ambulance had left with Scoop, bloodied, in rough shape, Bob had made it clear he was in charge of the investigation. He'd gotten through the major briefing with city, state and federal law enforcement personnel held on the street outside the crime scene tape. He had detectives canvassing the neighborhood for witnesses, processing the scene, putting together rudimentary timelines.

The working theory had dirtbag, or dirtbags, slipping into the backyard of the triple-decker and placing an explosive device under the small gas grill on Abigail's first-floor porch. Since she and Owen rarely used the grill and, given their busy lives, spent little time sitting out on the porch, the bomb could have been there for a few days, a few hours. It had been detonated by a remote-controlled switching device.

The bomb in Owen's car had to have been placed there after he'd arrived on Beacon Hill. Otherwise he'd have blown up when he turned the key leaving Abigail's apartment that morning.

According to Fiona, Bob's warning had given Scoop a split second to grab her and dive behind the compost bin.

Saved by dirt and kitchen scraps.

Only Scoop.

They'd all done the drills. What happens if police officers are targeted by a series of bombs?

This, Bob thought. This is what happens.

He was satisfied that people were doing what they were supposed to, except the idiot who'd thought it would be okay to tell his ex-wife, the mother of their three daughters, where to find him.

Tight-lipped and drawn, Theresa O'Reilly glared at him under the hot sun. "Never again." She pointed a blunt-nailed finger at him in that way she had. "Do you understand me? *Never* again."

Bob let her anger bounce off him. Getting into it with her never worked. "Fiona doesn't want to go home with you and the girls."

"I don't care what she wants. She's not going back to her apartment."

"Whoa. I'm with you, Ter."

Without consulting either parent, their eldest daughter had decided to sublet an apartment for the summer with three of her musician friends. The bomb squad had been through their place in Brighton but hadn't found anything. They'd also checked the South Boston waterfront apartment where his sister, Eileen, Keira's mother, was house-sitting after giving up her crazy life in the woods. She'd left Bob a message on his cell phone saying she was praying for everyone's safety. That was good. He'd surprised himself by saying a prayer himself.

For Abigail, he thought. For her safe return.

Theresa's eyes filled with tears. "I'm sorry." She was shaking, her teeth chattering. "It's awful. This whole thing."

Bob felt terrible. "Yeah. I know. I'm sorry, too."

She was chief of operations at a high-tech firm in suburban Lexington. They'd met when he was a patrol officer and she was an office temp with big dreams. They'd stuck together until Jayne, their youngest, was four. That was seven years ago. He'd tried marriage again two years later, for about three seconds. Theresa hadn't remarried, but she had a boyfriend. Another executive. She'd sworn off cops after Bob.

He couldn't stand his ex-wife's fear. "Dyeing your hair these days, Ter?"

"Go to hell. And don't call me 'Ter.' It's Theresa."

"Okay. It's Theresa."

She sighed, dropping her arms to her sides. Her hair was a honey-blond—total dye job, he was sure—and she had lines at the corners of her eyes and around her mouth, but she looked good. The years hadn't been so kind to him. He needed to take off a few pounds, and there were brown spots on his arms and face that hadn't been there before. He was a redhead. His doctor was always on him about sunscreen.

Yeah. How about burning his face off in a fire? What would sunscreen do for that?

"Bob?"

"I'm tuned in, Ter. Just waiting for your next shot."

She shook her head at him. "Bastard." She touched his arm, briefly. "Are you all right?"

"Never better."

He glanced at the black FBI SUV where BPD detectives were reinterviewing Fiona. She'd had a break and sat in the air-conditioning for a while, had something to eat and drink. Now she was slumped against the SUV and back at it.

Enough already.

"Wait here," Bob told his ex-wife. "I'll spring Fi as soon as I can. It'll be a few minutes."

"I'm not going anywhere."

He knew she was true to her word. For all the ways they irritated each other, she was a devoted mother. His legs felt wobbly as he headed for the SUV. Adrenaline dump. Nothing a couple of shots of Jameson's wouldn't cure. They'd help the guilt, too. Theresa had wanted him to go to night school and become a lawyer like John March. All those years ago, begging him. She'd never liked police work. She'd never gotten used to the anxiety or believed the statistics. "You carry a gun to work, Bob," she'd told him. "What more do I need to know?"

No answer to a question like that. What more *did* Theresa need to know?

He saw Tom Yarborough make his way over to her. Yarborough had been a rock since the explosion, professional, focused, but not unemotional. He and Abigail had worked together for eight months and were always butting heads. Bob had straightened out a few disagreements between them, but they both were top-notch homicide detectives who respected each other. Abigail was just easier to get along with.

Theresa was dabbing a tissue at her eyes now. Bob couldn't take tears and turned his attention to his daughter.

Fiona had gone through her ordeal first with him, in the initial hysteria as the paramedics were working on Scoop, and then in more detail, with more control, with Yarborough and Lucas Jones. Lucas was Abigail's former partner. He'd been promoted to lieutenant last fall and moved over to narcotics. Since Norman Estabrook was in cahoots with drug traffickers, Lucas said he should be in on the investigation. He was still with Fiona as she slumped against the side of the SUV. He'd left a picnic with his young family in Roxbury to head to the scene. He was built like a sparkplug and relished being a professional more than a tough guy. But he could be both.

"How you holding up, kid?" Bob asked his daughter.

She gnawed on her lower lip. "Okay."

"She's wrung out," Lucas said, "but she's doing great."

If Bob had to pick someone to interview his daughter, it'd be Lucas. The guy was a peach as well as one of BPD's finest detectives. But Bob didn't want Fiona talking to cops. He wanted her back with her friends, playing Irish drinking songs.

Down the street, Simon Cahill arrived and showed his FBI credentials to a uniformed BPD officer. He had two FBI suits with him who'd obviously been assigned to keep him alive, but he split off from them and walked over to the SUV. He looked cool, unfazed by the action around him, but that, Bob had learned, was Simon. Even so, he wasn't the affable man who'd danced and sung to Irish tunes with Keira in the triple-decker's backyard two months ago. A yard that was now charred, wet, bloody and filled with crime scene investigators.

"Bob…" Simon took a moment to clear his throat. "I'm sorry."

"For what? Did you set the bombs?"

"I should have seen this through before I got involved with Keira. Estabrook was already obsessed with John March, but—"

"Stop. You know regrets won't help now."

"You're right." He blew out a breath, recovering his composure. "I'd like to take Fiona through what happened."

Lucas heard him and stepped away from her, protective. "You can see my notes."

Simon ignored him, his eyes on Bob.

Bob sighed. "One fed talks to her. You. That's it."

"I'll see to it."

"And I stay," Bob added.

Lucas didn't look happy, but he moved off without argument. Simon opened up the back door to the SUV, reached inside and got out a bottle of water. He flipped open the top, shut the door and handed the water to Fiona. She mumbled her thanks.

"Feeling okay?" Simon asked.

She nodded. The paramedics had checked her over, but, except for a few cuts, scrapes and bruises, she was fine. She'd cleaned up as best she could, and Bob had bullied his way upstairs to his place and fetched her a fresh shirt. It didn't smell that bad of smoke and it was in better shape than the shirt she'd worn over there that morning, now soaked in Scoop's blood.

Staring at the sidewalk, sipping her water, Fiona said that she was picking tomatoes with Scoop and humming Irish tunes, and next thing, he flung her behind the compost pile and there was smoke and fire and debris—and blood.

"Did you see anyone before the blast?" Simon asked.

She shook her head.

"What time did you arrive?"

"Around two. I wanted to talk to my dad about our Christmas trip to Ireland. You know Keira's going with us, right? Our grandmother was born in Ireland, and my dad and her mom are of Irish descent on both sides."

Simon smiled gently. "I'm familiar with your Irish family roots."

"I had some information I printed off the Internet about where to have tea in Dublin on Christmas Eve. Doesn't that sound like fun, having tea in Ireland on Christmas Eve?"

Bob worked harder on his gum. He'd already been through two packs. Simon wouldn't care about tea in Dublin or anywhere else, but he said, "I can see your dad at high tea, can't you?"

"He'll love it."

"Probably will. So, you got your print-outs together and headed to your dad's place. Where were you?"

"The Garrison house on Beacon Street. I was practicing harp."

"Any of your friends there?"

"No, I was alone. Well, except for Owen, but he was upstairs at the foundation offices. He was there when I arrived at ten." She'd obviously already gone through the timeline. "Mostly I just practiced."

"Did you take the T over here," Simon said, "or did you drive?"

"The T. Then I walked. It was a beautiful day. *Is.*" She sucked in a breath and took a gulp of water. "I feel sick."

Simon ignored her. Bob would have, too. "Where'd you get on the T?"

"Downtown Crossing. The Orange Line."

"Anyone get on with you?"

"I think so. I didn't pay attention. No one stuck out to me."

"Anyone get off the T with you?"

"No, and no one followed me. I always check. It's habit." Her eyes lifted to her father. "My dad taught me to notice things."

Simon didn't even glance sideways at Bob, just stayed focused on Fiona. "So, you're walking toward your dad's place…"

"I didn't notice anything unusual then, either. Cars, people. When I got here, I went out back. I didn't knock or ring the doorbell or anything."

"Your dad was expecting you?"

She nodded. "I'd called him on my cell phone when I got off the T. I went out back and yelled up to let him know I was here."

"Gate to the backyard was unlocked?"

"Yes. I just walked right in. I told Dad I'd pick tomatoes and bring them up to him. Scoop had plenty. *Has* plenty." She shot an angry look at Simon and then Bob as if she expected them to argue with her, but it didn't last. She continued, less combative. "The firefighters and paramedics stomped on the tomatoes getting to us, but I think some of them are still okay. Scoop will be back in his garden soon."

"All right." Simon leaned against the SUV, not looking hot, tense or remotely exhausted, despite the guilt and tension he had to be experiencing. "You're in the backyard. You give your dad a shout. Was he outside?"

Fiona shook her head. "He came onto his back porch when he heard me. He said hi, then went back inside."

"And Scoop was in the garden?"

"That's right."

"Did he invite you to join him, or did you invite yourself?"

"I invited myself. I love tomatoes."

"So you join him. Then what?"

She drank more water before she answered. "Abigail said hello."

"Where was she, do you remember?"

"Her porch. I thought at first she was in her kitchen, but I…" Fiona's hands trembled visibly. This was where her story took a turn from picking tomatoes in the summer sun to hell. "I was wrong. She was on her porch."

"What exactly did she say?" Simon asked.

Fiona thought a moment. "She said, 'Hey, Fiona, don't let Scoop pawn off wormy tomatoes on you.'"

Simon smiled. "Scoop have anything to say about that?"

"He held up a gorgeous, round, red tomato and said, 'See that, Browning? You can't buy tomatoes that pretty.'"

"And she said?"

Fiona's lower lip trembled in a way that reminded Bob of her as a baby. "Nothing. Not that I heard." She scrunched up her face, concentrating. "A phone rang. I didn't think of it until now. That must have been—that's why she went inside."

"To answer the phone," Simon said.

"Then Dad yelled, and Scoop grabbed me."

"So first the phone, then your dad, then Scoop."

"Yes."

"Then what?"

"Scoop hurled me behind the compost bin."

"Did he say anything?" Simon asked.

"Not a word. He knocked the breath out of me. I had just enough time to notice I couldn't breathe when the bomb exploded. I had no idea what was going on. Then Scoop…" She was taking rapid, shallow breaths now, off in her own world of memory, fear. "Everything felt like it happened at once. The explosion, the concussion—it felt like the air was being sucked out of me, the whole backyard. Scoop grunted and then—there was so much blood."

"It was pieces of the grill and the propane tank that hit him," Bob interjected. "Scoop's injuries had nothing to do with saving you. If he'd jumped behind the compost bin by himself, he still—"

"If I'd protected him instead of him protecting me, he'd be fine," Fiona said stubbornly, adamant. "Just like I am now."

Before Bob could respond, Simon stood up from the SUV. "That's not the way it works. You're a nineteen-year-old college student. Scoop's a cop. He did what he's trained to do."

"He's a hero," she said.

Bob didn't speak. He couldn't now. He'd lose it, and that wouldn't help his daughter.

And it wouldn't help Abigail.

Fiona handed Simon her water bottle, her hands steadier. "I didn't see anyone on the street or at the houses next door. I didn't hear anyone. Nothing. Not even a dog barking or a television. It was all background noise to me. White noise. I remember humming 'Irish Rover' as I came into the yard."

Bob had heard her, his sweet daughter humming one of her Irish tunes. He hadn't remembered until now.

She smiled suddenly at Simon. "You and my dad both can sing. You should sing with my ensemble sometime."

Fiona always said "ensemble," Bob thought, never band.

Simon winked at her. "We can dance an Irish jig, too."

"That's right, yes! I had no idea until this summer. Dad kept his talents bottled up inside him for years." She turned to Bob, strands of blond hair stuck to her pallid cheeks. "Because of Deirdre McCarthy and what happened to her."

Bob grimaced at the mention of the girl who'd lived on his street when he was growing up and was brutally murdered at nineteen, changing his life forever. He said, "Deirdre had the voice of an angel. Mine's nothing in comparison."

"I keep thinking about her," Fiona said. "I never knew her. She died—she was murdered—long before I was born, but it's like her spirit's been a part of our lives and I didn't even know it."

Bob didn't want her thinking about Deirdre, but what could he do? By not talking about Deirdre McCarthy for thirty years, he'd kept the tragedy and horror of her death out of his daughters' minds, out of their consciousness, and yet her long-ago murder had inspired the devil-obsessed serial killer who'd come after Keira in June.

Would his daughters and niece have been more prepared if they'd known about Deirdre, if he hadn't tried to protect them?

He jerked himself back to the matter at hand.

Simon opened the back door of the SUV and tossed in the empty water bottle, then shut the door again, hard—just, Bob knew, to break some of the tension and refocus Fiona. He returned to his position against the SUV. "You said earlier you heard Abigail scream after the explosion."

"I know that's what I told you." Fiona stared again at her hands. "But I didn't hear her scream. I thought I did, but I didn't. I don't know what I heard. Everything really didn't happen all at once. It was the phone ringing and then Dad yelling and then Scoop grabbing me and *then* the explosion. In that order. It was all so fast. I know people say that, but it was."

"You've done well to break it down for us," Simon said.

But she looked up at her father. "Did you see something, Dad? How did you know to warn us?"

He hadn't told her about the call from Ireland. About Keira. The other woman on the line. He hadn't told Lucas Jones or Tom Yarborough, either. They hadn't asked him the question Fiona had just asked. They weren't being patient or negligent. They were just taking things in order.

Simon knew, but he said nothing.

"Dad," Fiona said, "if you warned us, someone must have warned *you*, right? Who?"

"You and your dad can talk in a bit," Simon said. "Let's go back to your practicing this morning at the Garrison house. Did you notice anyone there—"

"Who could have planted the bomb in Owen's car? I don't know. I don't think so." She was clearly fading, getting impatient, frazzled. "I can't...I don't know."

"I have just a few more questions, okay? We'll go through them without your dad."

Bob didn't protest. He kissed his daughter on the head and started back toward Theresa, but the ATF and FBI and state detectives and the whole damn lot pounced and dragged him down the street for another briefing.

The ATF guy, who was Bob's age, was pontificating. "It was C4," he said. "It's ideal for this kind of bomb. Just a quarter pound will destroy a propane tank and the surrounding structure."

The BPD bomb squad guy agreed. The fire department's arson squad guy threw in his opinion.

Bob chewed a fresh piece of gum. "The bombs didn't place themselves under Abigail's grill or in Owen's car, and she didn't just evaporate." He worked the gum harder. "Someone grabbed her and stuffed her into some kind of vehicle and got her out of here. Under my damn nose."

No one said anything.

He continued, all eyes on him. "The phone call got her inside off the porch. These bastards didn't want to kill her. Scoop, Fiona—didn't matter if they died. Me. Who cares? The blast could have thrown Abigail off her feet. Stunned her, knocked her out. Whatever, the bad guys were ready and hauled her out to a waiting vehicle." Bob nodded to the spot on the sidewalk on the other side of the crime scene tape where he'd noticed the blood earlier. "She got a piece of one of them."

He paused, but still no one spoke. He knew what they were thinking. With one colleague in serious condition and another missing, he was slipping into posttraumatic stress syndrome.

He could feel his pulse tripping along. "I was focused on the blast. The diversion worked. I didn't see a thing. The vehicle—nothing."

"How'd they get to her porch and plant the bomb?" the ATF guy asked.

Bob wanted to strangle him. "Gee. I guess I probably let them in and showed them Abigail's grill and said, Hey, there's a good spot. No one'll notice a bomb there."

"Any telephone repairs, cable repairs, electricians, carpenters—"

"I gave my statement. Scoop'd give his, except he's unconscious. And Abigail's not here, in case you haven't noticed."

The ATF guy winced. "Sorry, Lieutenant."

The arson investigator said, "Anything we can do for you, Bob? For your family?"

Bob had a half-dozen retorts ready, none of them nice, but he saw the earnest look on the guy's face. Everyone wanted to help. Everyone felt lousy for him.

He had to get out of there.

He found refuge in the passenger seat of his heap of a car and scraped gunk off his cell phone, then dialed Eddie O'Shea at his little village pub on the southwest Irish coast. Bob had already talked to Keira and an Irish detective about the attack on her. Now he wanted to talk to the bartender. They'd met earlier in August, when Bob had ventured to the land of his ancestors for the first time. He went with his sister in the days after she'd finally given up on her solitary life in the woods and rejoined civilization, such as it was. Keira had already fallen for Simon.

Bob hoped Simon would be on the trip to Ireland at Christmas with Keira, his daughters and his sister. They could sneak off for a beer or two. Christmas seemed far away now. Out of reach and impossible.

O'Shea answered after a couple of rings.

"Irish cops still there?" Bob asked.

"They've gone. They searched my pub for bombs, Bobby."

O'Shea insisted on calling him Bobby. Drove him nuts. "Find any?"

"Just Patrick's cooking."

It was a valiant attempt at humor. Eddie O'Shea had lived a quiet life before June when Keira had wandered into his pretty village on Kenmare Bay. "Trust no one," Bob said. "The guards. Your Irish fairies. No one, O'Shea. Do you hear me?"

"Are you well, Bobby?"

"Burned off my eyebrows."

"Simon?"

"A man with a mission." Bob felt his throat constrict. He'd developed a liking for Simon Cahill, and no question Simon believed he'd brought Norman Estabrook down on them all. Bob wasn't so sure. It was like Estabrook was a deadly virus lying dormant in their lives, just waiting for a chance to spread and do its damage. "I want to hear about this Irishman who tried to kill my niece."

"He knew about the bomb."

"The one in my house. There was another one in a car."

"Ah. He didn't mention that one. He's a hired man."

"Why did he tell Keira?"

"He didn't. He told that black-haired firebrand."

Keira had described her to Bob. "Any word on who she is?"

"Not that anyone's told me. She knows what she's doing, Bobby, I'll say that."

"But she's not law enforcement?"

"Ah, Bobby…I don't want to think about who she might be."

"Like what? A spy?" Bob's head pounded. "Never mind. You're a bartender. You love conspiracies. Was she alone?"

"Yes. She said she was walking the Beara Way, but she knew about Norman Estabrook, the billionaire Yank—"

"I know who he is."

"That's not a surprise." Eddie hesitated, then said in a near whisper, "Lord Will was here, Bobby."

"Simon's friend?"

"We can trust him. I'm sure of it. And Keira. She'll be safe here, Bobby. She has more spine than most."

"That she does." Bob didn't want to hang up. He hated the idea of Keira being across the ocean, alone, worried about Simon, targeted by a killer. She'd always been like another daughter to him. "Crazy artist. Tell her to cool her heels and paint pictures of Irish fairies and thistle, and I'll be in touch when I can."

Bob disconnected and got out of the car. The ATF guy came over. "Who were you talking to just now, Lieutenant?"

His open suspicion and arrogance went up one side of Bob and down the other, and he decided he just wasn't doing anymore right now. "A bartender in Ireland," he said. "I asked him for his recipe for rhubarb crumble."

Bob headed back to his ex-wife and his daughter before the ATF guy could rip his head off.

# Chapter 12

*Off the coast of Massachusetts*
*7:45 p.m., EDT*
*August 25*

Abigail rode out another wave of nausea, forcing herself not to give in to seasickness. What would Owen say? He'd never been seasick in his life. Thinking about him gave her strength. He'd tell her to sleep while she could. Bob, Scoop, Yarborough, Lucas—her father. They'd all tell her the same thing. Simon would, too, but she didn't know him as well as the others.

Although some days she wondered if she knew her father at all.

She squeezed her eyes shut and fought back tears. They would only make her blindfold wet and worsen her discomfort. She ached, and she itched, and she wanted to fight these bastards but couldn't. They'd taken turns checking on her, providing a sip of water, threatening her if she tried to escape.

Two men whose voices she didn't recognize were arguing on

the other side of the door. One man was clearly American—petulant, arrogant. The other was British—fearless, angry.

"You promised you'd be there for me," the American said.

The Brit snorted. "Not like this, you bloody fool."

"*Don't* talk to me that way."

"I'll talk to you any way I choose. I agreed to do a job, and you went behind my back and hired these utter morons to indulge your petty desire for vengeance."

"There's nothing petty about anything I do. I don't care what your credentials are, you're a mercenary who works for me. You're to do as I say."

"I will, but in my professional judgment—"

"You've made your opinion clear," the American said, less irritated. "Let's go forward from where we are now and not worry about the past. Agreed?"

A moment's hesitation. "Agreed."

The door creaked, opening abruptly. Abigail straightened as best she could. Her shoulders and thighs were painfully stiff, and her fingers and toes, despite her efforts to wiggle them, had gone numb.

She heard footsteps circling her chair. "My, my. You have had a difficult day, haven't you?" It was the American, smug, yet also, underneath, clearly agitated. "I have, too. I had a long, hard journey from Montana."

*Norman Estabrook.*

Abigail forced herself not to react.

"The risks I've taken today and the aggravation I've experienced are worth it, Detective Browning, just to see you here, at my mercy." He was in front of her now. "Your daddy and your friends in law enforcement have no idea where you are or where I am. None whatsoever."

"Enjoy your role as kidnapper in chief while you can,

Norman." Abigail hated the raspiness of her voice, but at least it was strong. "It's not going to last. You screwed up today, didn't you? Everything didn't go as planned, did it?"

She felt his breath hot against her face. "I have you. I have Abigail March Browning, John March's daughter. Tell me, Detective. Don't you think your father needs his own personal devil to fight?"

"We can call and ask him."

"He needs me. He needs an enemy who is his equal. You learned about good and evil this summer, didn't you? The serial killer who came after your friend Keira was fascinated with the devil. You investigated him. He understood that God needs Lucifer."

Abigail suppressed a shiver of fear. She'd learned more about the nature of evil in June than she'd ever wanted to know. In her eight years as a detective, she had never come across such flat-out evil—the conscious, deliberate choice to commit vile acts of gratuitous violence on innocent people.

"I don't know about God and Lucifer," she said. "My father's an ordinary human being. So are you."

"There's nothing ordinary about me. Prosecutors and even my lawyers made the mistake of thinking I was like other men. I have resources and connections the FBI can't touch."

"You won't when you're in prison."

Estabrook gave a low chuckle. "Your father must be in torment right now, knowing that I have you and he's responsible. Knowing he had me, and he let me go."

"It wasn't his idea. He objected to your deal. He's not all powerful."

"He didn't believe I was capable of violence. He wanted my friends more than he did me. Imagine the possibilities going forward, Detective. I challenge the most powerful law enforcement officer in the world every day for the rest of his life, until he finally dies a bitter, broken old man."

"You're just not that special," Abigail said.

This time, Estabrook's laugh wasn't right in her ear, and she realized he must have stood up straight. His voice was congenial when he spoke. "At first I just wanted John March dead. Now, I want him to suffer. I want him to suffer and suffer and suffer." Estabrook was silent a moment, then added, "There are others I want to kill with my own hands."

Abigail concentrated on her breathing before fear could take hold, as her captor obviously hoped it would.

In for eight. Hold for eight. Out for eight.

She heard a door click shut but continued with her breathing exercise. She did three sets before she stopped and focused again on her surroundings.

"You have relentless friends." It was the man with the British accent, speaking softly, close to her. "They're looking for you now."

"Estabrook's gone?" she asked, calmer now.

"For the moment."

She swallowed, her mouth and throat dry from lack of water—and from tension, from fighting panic, nausea and claustrophobia. "It'll go better for you if you set me free now, before my friends find me."

"I take your point."

He sounded pragmatic, neither relishing nor concerned about the prospect of going up against various arms of the law enforcement community.

"What time is it?" she asked.

"Around eight o'clock. Are you injured?"

"I'm fine. Let me go before—"

"You're in a tough spot, Detective. I suggest you not waste your energy arguing for something that can't happen."

"Then tell me about my friends who were home when your bomb went off. Scoop, Bob, Fiona." She used their first names to humanize them, to make them real to this man. "What's their condition? Are they all right?"

"There were no deaths, and Detective O'Reilly and his daughter are uninjured."

She steeled herself against any emotion. "Scoop?"

"Detective Wisdom was cut by flying shrapnel. He'll survive, but he'll have a rough go for a while."

"Owen," Abigail whispered. "What about him?"

"A handy sort, your man Owen."

She sank into her chair, her arms aching from being tied behind her back. How could she have brought this down on her friends? "You have baggage," Bob had told her when she was a rookie determined to make detective, a grief-stricken widow who had quit law school and wanted to help other people get answers. He hadn't minced words. "Husband an FBI agent killed on your honeymoon in an unsolved homicide. Daddy set to become the next FBI director. I should send you packing back to law school."

At first, Bob had considered Owen more baggage, with his wealthy family, his constant travel with Fast Rescue. These were distractions as far as Bob was concerned, reasons she couldn't dedicate herself to the job, reasons she didn't fit in with the department and never would. But she had proved herself.

She heard footsteps as the Brit approached her in her chair. "All of you are remarkably lucky," he said.

"That's what I feel right now. Lucky. Did you try to kill Owen, or did you mean to kidnap him, too?"

"Kill."

Her stomach lurched, but she refused to throw up. "Another bomb." She kept her tone unemotional, professional. "Where? His family's house on Beacon Street?"

"His car."

"Bastards."

"He was warned in time. So, love," the Brit said, closer to her now, "how do you suppose that happened?"

Abigail wriggled in her chair to distract him from any hint in her expression that she had even the remotest theory.

"You're meant to respond," he said mildly.

"I have no idea how it happened. I was stuffed in the back of a van. But your plan hasn't worked the way it was meant to, has it?"

"Did I say it was my plan?"

She realized he was in front of her, perhaps a few inches away, and she warned herself not to be misled by his quiet, almost wry tone. This was a disciplined, controlled and very dangerous man.

"What do you want with me?" she asked.

"Nothing at the moment, love. You and your friends are formidable foes. Your dad as well."

"That's the fun of it for Norman, isn't it? You're a pro. You know he's taking unnecessary risks for his own amusement."

"Perhaps in our own way, love, we all do."

Abigail tried to relax her jaw muscles and ease the tension in her neck and shoulders. "I've heard a small boat pull up to this one several times. What did you do, fly Estabrook into a private airport, then bring him here?"

"That doesn't matter now, does it?"

"That's true. You can walk away. Help me. Let me go back home and plan my wedding."

The Brit gave a short laugh. "And what would I get by walking away? Hold still, love. I'm going to cut the ropes on your wrists and ankles."

"What's your name? What should I call you?"

"Fletcher."

"First name or last name?"

"Either."

It might be real, or it might not. "You're British?"

"Long live the Queen."

He had a sense of humor, anyway.

"Wrists first," he said. "You'll feel the knife. Don't panic, although I can see you're not the type."

He slid the cool blade of a knife between Abigail's skin and the rope. He was too efficient—too professional—to indulge in unnecessary cruelty. If he decided to kill her, he'd be quick about it, at least.

"Easy, love," he said as she felt the bonds give way. "Go slow. You'll be stiff. You've been in the same position for a while. I'm freeing your ankles next."

As she eased her arms over the back of the chair and onto her lap, Abigail winced at the flush of pain and barely noticed him tackling the ropes on her ankles. She slowly pushed one foot forward, biting back tears. Blood rushed into her toes and fingers, and, against her will, she moaned out loud. He untied her blindfold, carefully peeling it from her eyes. She blinked a few times, unkinked her arms and legs, and finally focused on her surroundings. There was a light on now, and she could see a pool table in the middle of the stateroom, next to her chair, and a low sectional sofa on the length of an interior wall.

Her captor leaned back against the pool table, giving her a moment. He was a clean-shaved, exceptionally fit-looking white male, approximately forty years old, skimming six feet, with close-cropped, medium brown hair and gray eyes. No visible scars or tattoos or other distinguishing features. Not that any were needed for Abigail to remember him.

He smiled. "Take a good look, love. You'll want to describe me accurately to your sketch artists." He gestured to the left side of her face. "The men hit you?"

She resisted a wisecrack. "The one with the South Boston accent did."

"He's a bit of a hothead. Care to take a moment while I'm here and freshen up?"

She nodded. "Yes."

He stood up from the pool table and gently took her by the elbow. "On your feet, then."

He started to help her up, but she shook him off and rose on her own. She was stiff and sore, but steady. He led her to a door in the back of the stateroom, next to a wet bar.

"Knock when you've finished. You have two minutes."

"I can't—"

"You can, love."

He opened the door and shut it softly behind her when she went in, leaving her in the pitch-dark. She banged up against something—a sink, she thought—and righted herself, feeling on the wall for a light switch. She found one and flipped it on. She saw she was in a small, tidy head equipped with a shower, sink and toilet. There were dispensers of liquid soap and hand cream, a basket of potpourri, a stack of neatly folded hand towels. Touches of comfort and elegance for the prisoner.

Abigail locked the door and turned on the water in the sink while she did her business.

She washed up with soap and water as best she could, skipped the hand cream and buried her face in a fluffy, expensive white towel, indulging in a few seconds of self-pity and fatigue. But there was no time. She dropped the towel on the floor and stuck her mouth under the faucet and drank as much water as she dared. She didn't want to be sick, but she couldn't count on when she'd be allowed to drink again. Or eat. She was starving.

Finally she inspected herself for injuries that adrenaline and the numbness from sitting in one position for so long could have kept her from feeling. Her wrists and ankles were rope-burned but not bleeding. She had bruises here and there from struggling to get free on the ride to the marina, but nothing she needed to worry about.

"Thirty seconds," Fletcher said from the other side of the door.

She looked in the mirror at the swelling on her cheek. She'd have a shiner.

When she unlocked the door, Fletcher took her by the elbow and led her back to her chair. "I won't tie you up again," he said, sitting her down, "but not because I trust you not to attempt escape. Because I know you won't succeed."

"Where are you taking me?"

"For a little boat ride." He straightened, looked at her without expression. "Do you play pool?"

"Not really."

"Your chance to practice, then, love."

"Why did you stay with me if you weren't going to tie me back up?"

"I wanted to be here in case you passed out once you got on your feet." He nodded to the wet bar. "There's ice, food and drink. Help yourself."

"Thank you."

He left without another word.

# Chapter 13

*Dublin, Ireland*
*1:05 a.m., IST*
*August 26*

Lizzie welcomed the lights and activity of Dublin late at night. Her cab dropped her in front of her family's boutique hotel, located on a side street off St. Stephen's Square. Two uniformed bellmen, one of them her twenty-two-year-old cousin Justin, greeted her at the brass-trimmed main door with a bow that always made her feel like a princess, which she decidedly was not, especially tonight. She was too stiff, too scraped and felt too hunted to be anything but what she was—a woman who needed a hot bath and a friendly face. Although the flight from Kerry to Dublin was less than an hour, she finally felt her fatigue, dragging down her spirits, making her even more aware of her isolation—of what she'd done.

Fresh out of college, Justin was the youngest of the Rush

brothers, working in Dublin for at least the next six months. His sensitive mouth and dreamy navy-blue eyes were from his mother, but his tawny-hair and square jaw were all Rush.

He eyed Lizzie's backpack, her walking shoes tied to the strap by their laces. She'd brushed the mud and dung off them as best she could, but he wasn't impressed. "Those shoes, Lizzie. Do you want me to toss them?"

He hadn't had Rush frugality drilled into him by their Whitcomb-Rush grandmother the way she had. "You don't think they can be salvaged?"

He peered at them. "What did you do, tramp through a pasture? They're filthy inside and out, and, no, I don't think they can be salvaged." He shifted his gaze to her. "Where have you been?"

"A stone circle in West Cork."

"In a gale?"

"The best time."

She smiled and started up the half-dozen steps to the lobby, but he grabbed her muddy pack from her. "Excuse me, ma'am, but carrying luggage, even luggage that smells like a barn, is my job."

"You're not supposed to comment on whether a guest's luggage is old, ripped, cheap—"

"Covered in sheep manure?"

"I think it's cow manure."

"Terrific," he said without enthusiasm.

When they reached the lobby, quiet and softly lit this late, Lizzie felt herself start to relax. She was back on familiar ground and just wanted to sink into one of the comfortable chairs angled in front of the fireplace.

Justin was staring at her bloodied knuckles now. "What did you do, get into a brawl in your stone circle?"

"I discovered that Beware of Bull signs are posted for a reason."

Technically it wasn't a lie. Her cousin looked skeptical, but there was no need to involve him or anyone at the hotel in her problems, or to give them any information that the garda or the FBI might decide they wanted.

She retrieved her room key from the front desk and turned to Justin. "I'll take my bag upstairs myself. If anyone asks about me, say I'm in Las Vegas. No. Not Vegas. My father's there. Rome. Tell them I'm in Rome."

"How is Uncle Harlan?"

"Losing at poker last I spoke with him."

"He wouldn't know what to do with a winning hand," Justin said. "I can have your shoes cleaned overnight. Try, anyway."

"Thanks, Justin, but I'll hang on to them." Lizzie pushed a hand through her hair, still tangled from the wind and her fight with Michael Murphy. "Do you happen to know if a Brit named Will Davenport is scheduled for a late check-in?"

"Lizzie…"

She could see from her cousin's expression she'd guessed right. Justin would be on top of all guest arrivals. "When he gets here, call me, okay? He's British. Tall, blond."

"We're talking about Lord Davenport, right?"

"You know him?"

"We've never met. His younger sister's a wedding dress designer in London. Lady Arabella Davenport."

"How do you know these things?"

He grinned. "I'm the bellman. I know everything. Lady Davenport designed the dresses for a wedding here this summer. Mum was visiting then, and you know how she is."

Lizzie did, indeed. Her aunt loved anything connected with fabrics and design, especially if it involved hotels or weddings. Preferably both. "She put you through an analysis of every stitch?"

Justin gave a long-suffering nod. "It would help if you'd hang out with her once in a while and let her talk to you about these things."

"I adore Aunt Henrietta, but talking wedding dresses—"

"Better than taking on an Irish bull."

Lizzie pictured Arabella Davenport's older brother walking into the quiet pub before her fight in the stone circle. Whatever his sister's talents, Lizzie was certain that his didn't involve weddings. As controlled and polite as he'd been, he'd clearly arrived in the little village on Kenmare Bay prepared to do battle. But she suspected he arrived everywhere prepared to do battle.

She shook off the image. "I'm wiped out, Justin. I'll see you in the morning."

She got two steps before her cousin spoke again. "Did Lord Davenport have a role in muddying your shoes?"

She glanced back at him. Perhaps because he was the youngest, or so much his mother's son, Justin had a tendency to see more than most people in a similar position would see. "It's a long story."

"With you, Lizzie, it always is." He sighed. "I'll call when your Brit gets here."

Should her circumstances call for a quick exit, Lizzie's one-bedroom suite was conveniently located on the second floor near the stairs. She brought her backpack into the bathroom and set it on the tile floor, where any crusts of dried mud and manure that fell off would do the least damage. As she stripped to her skin, she fought back images of whipping her pack against Michael Murphy's assault knife…of the drooling, snarling black dog…of the swirling fog and mist.

Instinct and training had taken over the moment she'd realized she wasn't alone in the stone circle, but now, in the familiar surroundings of her favorite hotel, she could finally let down her guard—at least until Lord Davenport arrived. But she and Keira Sullivan had come close to being killed a few hours ago. Would Will have arrived in time to save them if she'd failed?

A moot question, Lizzie told herself as she pulled on a cuddly hotel robe and tied it tightly around her waist.

She went into the beautifully appointed living room of the suite and ordered a full Irish breakfast from room service. Her blackberry crumble was long gone, and she was starving. But she resisted ordering brandy, or a martini.

She sank onto the sofa and grabbed a deck of cards off the coffee table, an antique she and her aunt had bought two years ago at an estate sale in County Clare. Each of the hotel's thirty-seven rooms was individually decorated, as much as possible, with furnishings and objets d'art from Ireland.

Against her father's objections, Lizzie had spent eighteen months working at their Dublin hotel, loving every minute. She and her aunt had crawled through countless Irish galleries, choosing Irish paintings, pottery, sculpture, glasswork, throws and whatever else caught their fancy. Lizzie recognized a copper vase they'd found at a gallery in Kenmare. It was fashioned by a contemporary Irish metalworker but reminded her of the old mines where Keira's story of the stone angel had originated.

Lizzie moved the copper vase and a stack of books on Ireland aside, creating space on the table, and dealt the cards into four piles of thirteen each for a game of bridge. She sorted the hands and counted up the points, then silently bid each one as if she didn't know what was in the others. She produced an offense and defense and played the game. Flipping one card after another, keeping track of aces and kings and trump cards, scooping up winners and losers. The process anchored her mind while allowing it the freedom to roam.

She had to have her thoughts in order before she made the call she knew she had to make.

The offense won. She dealt another hand.

Her breakfast was delivered by a longtime employee of the hotel, an older woman who didn't ask why Lizzie was having breakfast at such an hour. She set the tray on the coffee table, and when she left, Lizzie debated eating her meal, taking her bath and going to bed. She could postpone her call and tell Justin to never mind and not to let her know after all when Will Davenport arrived.

Instead she buttered a chunk of brown bread and took a bite as she got out her disposable cell phone and dialed a number she'd received in a terse e-mail last summer. She'd called it only twice before, preferring to stick to e-mail whenever possible.

It was just after 9:00 p.m. on the U.S. East Coast, but John March picked up after the first ring. "Where are you?"

"Ireland." No reason not to tell him that much. "Norman didn't go on a joy ride this morning. He didn't crash into a mountain or run into mechanical problems and make an emergency landing somewhere. You know that, don't you?"

"Yes."

"I'm sorry about what happened today. I wish I'd known sooner. Are Scoop Wisdom and your daughter—"

"You're the one who needs to do the talking."

Lizzie's heart jumped painfully. "The bomb was a diversion, wasn't it?" Her father had taught her about bombs, diversionary tactics. "Norman had your daughter kidnapped, didn't he?"

"Talk."

She picked up her fork. If she let John March intimidate her now, she'd be of no help to him or anyone else—especially Abigail Browning. "I'm debating whether to try black pudding," she said, poking it on her plate. "What do you think?"

"It's made with pig's blood. Tastes like sausage."

She could hear anguish in his voice. "White pudding?"

"No pig's blood. Suet, oatmeal. This and that."

"Doesn't sound very appetizing. I guess some things I just don't want to know."

"That's true for any of us."

Under the strength and determination that had characterized the FBI director in her dealings with him, Lizzie now heard the terror of a father for his missing daughter.

"Are you still in Boston?" she asked.

"Yes."

"Simon?"

"He's still here, too."

Lizzie stared at the warm brown bread, butter, eggs, bacon, grilled tomatoes—the black and white pudding—on her simple white china plate, all a reminder of normalcy. She'd led a relatively normal life of family, work, travel and the occasional romance and adventure before she'd let her curiosity—her sense of duty—ask questions and see things others might ignore. Once she'd found herself in a room of violent drug traffickers, what was she supposed to have done? She'd started by e-mailing names and surreptitious photos to John March.

But hadn't she been looking for an excuse to contact the detective who'd looked into her mother's death thirty years ago?

It didn't matter. Instead of dropping out of Norman's circle of friends as she otherwise would have, Lizzie had dived in and hung on for the next year.

"Norman will never look at himself and understand he was

arrested because he did wrong." She spoke calmly, despite her own fatigue and fear. "He'll blame you and Simon. And me, if he ever finds out what I've done."

March didn't soften. "You're the woman who saved Keira Sullivan and warned Bob O'Reilly about the bomb."

"I'm not sure Keira needed my help. An Irish gale, an ancient stone circle, a black dog out of nowhere. Spooky." Not to mention an aristocratic British spy. Lizzie stabbed her fork into the black pudding and cut off a small piece. "For all the time I've spent in Ireland, I've never tried black or white pudding. I suppose you have Michael Murphy's file on your desk by now?"

"The Irish authorities are cooperating in the investigation."

An oblique response. "He's Norman's doing."

"No one's leaping to any conclusions."

"I am," Lizzie said.

"Estabrook has no reason to take this risk."

"Did he have any reason to circumnavigate the world in a hot-air balloon?"

"That's an adventure."

"You're articulating a professional point of view. I understand that, but you don't believe it. You know as well as I do that Norman is responsible for what happened today. Yesterday here in Ireland, actually. It's after midnight." She eyed the bit of pudding on the end of her fork. "Maybe you have to grow up eating black pudding to appreciate it."

"You're exhausted. I can hear it in your voice."

"Maybe a full Irish breakfast will help. I've been banged up before, but I was in my first real fight for my life tonight." She felt herself sinking deeper into the soft cushions of the sofa. "For someone else's life, too."

"You won," March said.

"I could have killed Murphy. I had his own knife at his throat."

"Did you want to kill him?"

Lizzie let her mind drift back to the moment in the stone circle when she'd first became aware of the shadows by the cluster of trees. "No. I didn't want to kill him."

"Why are you in Ireland?"

"I was reading about Irish fairies and decided—"

"You wanted to talk to Simon," March said.

"It doesn't matter now. I was almost too late to help Keira. I *was* too late to warn your daughter."

"Bob O'Reilly's daughter and Scoop Wisdom are alive because of you."

Lizzie felt no satisfaction at March's statement. "Norman has virtually limitless resources."

"The U.S. federal government can match them."

"He could be anywhere by now. Trust me. He has a plan. He's not anyone's victim. He's compulsive, and he's a thrill seeker. Be sure your profilers understand what that really means. Be sure you understand. I didn't see it myself at first, but Norman is a dangerous, violent man."

She heard March take in a sharp breath. "You let me believe you're a professional. You're not, are you?"

She didn't answer.

"I want to know who you are," he said.

"You'll find out on your own soon enough. Please listen to me, Director March. You can't tell a soul about me or what I've done. You can't come after me. You'll be risking my life and my ability to help find your daughter if you do."

"I can have an agent meet you tonight, wherever you are. Let me help you. I don't want you to endanger yourself or this investigation by taking unnecessary risks."

"There is one thing." Lizzie hesitated, wondering if she was going too far—if she'd gone too far already. But she didn't stop herself. "I have a tall, handsome, patrician Brit on my tail. Will Davenport. He and Simon are friends. He came to Ireland to see about Keira. Can I trust him?"

"Even if you can, would you? Do you trust anyone?"

It wasn't a question she wanted to answer tonight. "Norman doesn't know I've been helping you. I want to keep it that way." She tried a bite of the black pudding. "You didn't steer me wrong. Black pudding does take like sausage."

She shut her phone before he could respond.

Would March figure out who she was and have her hotel stormed by armed agents at sunrise? He could make it happen, even in Ireland.

But he wouldn't. John March was a hard man who often faced only bad choices, and right now, she was safe and his daughter wasn't. And he'd made his choice. He would let his anonymous source have room to maneuver and give her a chance to find Norman Estabrook—and save her own skin as well as his daughter's.

Lizzie ate a few more bites of her meal before she gave up and headed for the bathroom, turning on the water in the tub as hot as she could stand. She added a scoop of lavender bath salts and, as they melted, shed her robe and dipped slowly into the steaming water. The heat eased the ache and stiffness in her muscles and the scent of lavender soothed her soul. Images washed over her— Simon and Norman in Montana going over plans for a Patagonia hike...the enigmatic Brit winking at her in Las Vegas...Scoop Wisdom walking out to the street with his colander of beans... Keira Sullivan and the black dog in the stone circle.

Will Davenport eyeing her over his brandy.

Lowering herself deeper into the tub, an image came to her of John March at her family's hotel in Boston last August. It was the anniversary of her mother's death, and he was drinking Irish whiskey alone at a table in the pub named in her honor. Lizzie had been in Boston, making one of her strategic appearances at the hotel offices, and had stopped at the Whitcomb.

She hadn't approached the FBI director and former Boston detective and doubted he'd been aware of her presence. Now she couldn't help but wonder where they'd all be if she'd identified herself as the anonymous source who'd been supplying him information on Norman Estabrook and his drug-trafficking friends.

But she hadn't.

She got out of the tub, dried off with a giant towel and slipped back into her robe. She returned to the living room and, no longer in the mood for a chat, set her tray in the hall and called down for its removal. When she sat back on the sofa, she managed to deal another hand of bridge, but she didn't sort the cards and instead curled up under a throw made of soft Irish wool and gave in to her fatigue.

When the telephone rang, she bolted upright, instantly awake. She glanced at the clock as she answered. It was almost 4:00 a.m.

"He's here," Justin said. "What should I do now?"

"Send him up."

"Lizzie? Are you sure?"

"I'm sure."

"All right, I won't tell anyone."

She felt a surge of heat. "It's not like *that*." But she couldn't tell him the truth. "I'll explain one day, Justin, I promise."

"I imagine it'll be a tale."

"Let Davenport think he's checking into his own room and I'll take it from there."

"You lead a complicated life," her cousin said.

As Lizzie hung up, her bathrobe fell open, the cool night air hitting her exposed skin.

This won't do, she thought. She'd come to Ireland to talk to an FBI agent about a man she was convinced would commit murder, not to greet a British lord in nothing but a hotel bathrobe.

Best to jump into some clothes before Will Davenport got to the door.

# Chapter 14

*Dublin, Ireland*
*3:47 a.m., IST*
*August 26*

By the time she heard a key card slide into the slot in the door, Lizzie had on a long knit skirt and a T-shirt. She was still barefoot, but at least she wasn't naked under her bathrobe. She unchained the door and opened it. Will had his trench coat slung over one arm and a scarred leather bag in his hand, which at least meant she didn't have to worry about Justin turning up.

"I had a feeling you were good," she said.

Will gave her the slightest smile. "And I had a feeling you were on the other side of this door."

"We Rushes like to keep an eye on spies in our hotels."

"You're imaginative. May I assume I'm invited in?"

"You may."

Lizzie stood back, and he walked past her and set his bag on the floor next to the coffee table. As she shut the door, she noticed him glance at the scattered cards on the table. She ran a hand through her hair, remembered she hadn't combed it since her bath and wondered what had gotten into her, arranging for an MI6 agent to share her room.

She scooped up the cards. "Playing bridge by myself helps me think. My method of creative problem solving."

"What problems were you trying to solve tonight?"

"You. What to do when you showed up."

The soft light from a brass floor lamp created shadows that darkened his eyes and made them even more difficult to read. "And your answer was to have me sent up here to your room?"

"No, I'd already figured that one out. I knew I didn't want you wandering around on your own and eliciting secrets about me from the staff." Not to mention her cousin.

"You worked here yourself prior to becoming director of concierge services for all your family's hotels."

"Ah. You've been busy."

"I have an able assistant."

"I loved working here. I learned a lot. Ireland offers an incredible variety of opportunities—great restaurants, rich history, natural beauty."

"So it does."

"Most of what the staff could tell you about me is innocuous enough. I can speak a bit of Irish and have a fondness for Irish butter and fresh Irish seafood, especially mussels, and I love to walk." She tidied up the deck, using both hands, which, she noticed, were trembling slightly. An annoyance, but she blamed her interrupted sleep, not the man across from her. "But I decided I didn't want anyone telling you about my Grafton Street shopping sprees."

As far as she could tell, Will didn't respond to her attempt at humor or even notice it. "Has Norman Estabrook been to this hotel?"

"I met him here, actually. A year ago this past April." She set the cards back on the table. Interrogation time. "He hired Simon Cahill as a consultant a few months later."

Will laid his coat over the back of a chair. He looked every inch the British lord turned SAS officer and spy as his gaze held hers. "Perhaps you should tell me who you are."

"You're here. Obviously you already know."

"Lizzie Rush, hotelier and—what else?"

"I haven't had time for much else lately."

"Why did you come to Dublin tonight?"

"Would you believe I got tired of walking the Beara Way and had a hankering for nice sheets?"

His outright smile caught her off guard. "No."

"It's my favorite of our hotels. It opened twenty years ago— over my father's objections. He's not much on Ireland, but my aunt and uncle fell in love with Dublin. I was ten years old, and I wanted to come here so bad."

"Your father wouldn't allow it?"

"I never told him how much I wanted it." She spun over to a chest and pulled open a drawer. "My feet are cold," she said, grabbing a pair of wool socks. "I arrived in Dublin this morning and checked in here before I went off on my adventure. I always stay in this room. Cute, isn't it?"

"It's lovely." He obviously didn't care one way or the other about her suite. "Did your father visit you during your posting here?"

"No, he did not," she said, dropping onto a chair and slipping on her socks. It was an intimate thing to do in front of a man she'd known for mere hours, but cold feet were cold feet. "My father and I get along, in case you're wondering. We just have different views on Ireland."

"Lizzie…"

His sudden intensity mixed with the softness of his voice shot her up from her chair. This was *not* one of her Rush cousins. "I'm talking too much. You must be hell in an interrogation. You're so smooth and—" She stopped herself. How many of his interrogation subjects would be affected by the concern in his voice, the drape of his sweater on his broad shoulders? "Never mind. I dozed off, and now I'm in one of those crazy half-awake, half-asleep states."

"You're not accustomed to the intensity of the fighting you did earlier tonight, and you're jetlagged. Why did you fly from Boston?"

"I didn't say I did."

The slight smile again. "As I said, I have an able assistant."

"Does that mean I really do have MI6 on my case?"

"You have a flare for dramatics as well as an active imagination."

"It's been that kind of year. Our main offices are in Boston. I spent a lot of time there growing up." She didn't go into more detail. "How's Keira?"

"She's safe in garda hands."

"That's good. I assume you wouldn't be here otherwise. I wish I could have met her under better circumstances. What happened in the stone circle was…" Lizzie tried to find the right word and realized she couldn't. "It was different."

"Where did you learn defense tactics?"

She gave him a knowing smile. "I read the SAS handbook on self-defense."

"You've been doing research of your own, I see."

"You're not denying you're a British SAS officer?"

"Did Simon tell you about my background?"

He had her there. She'd given herself away. "I knew you and Simon were friends, and I'm a curious type—which is how I ended up in a knife fight in the Irish hills. What about you?"

"I was looking for Keira. Were you drawn to Estabrook because of his adventures? I gather you're something of a daredevil yourself."

"I wasn't drawn to Norman at all. I just hung out with him and his friends on and off. Long weekends, vacations, when he was at one of our hotels."

"You came a long way to find Simon."

This time, she was ready for the dodging and darting of his questions. "I came a long way to hike the Beara Way. I'd heard Keira's story about the stone angel and thought I might run into her and Simon."

With a glimmer of a smile, Will moved close to her, just inches from her, and before she could catch her breath, he touched his fingertips to her hair. "You're an adept fighter but not a particularly adept liar."

"Not tonight, maybe. Ordinarily I'm a very adept liar."

"You were concerned Estabrook would go free, and you arranged a cover story that would allow you to talk to Simon without his thinking you'd come to Ireland specifically for that reason."

"Norman's legal situation was added impetus for me to choose the Beara Peninsula for my hike." She licked her lips, dry now, sensitive. "I've wanted to walk the Beara Way for some time."

"You didn't last long, did you?"

"A gale and a knife attack took all the fun out of my adventure."

"You also started in the very village where you'd expected to find Simon. Do you always hike alone?"

Lizzie decided she was in over her head with this man and broke for the closet. She yanked open the door. "Call downstairs for whatever you need," she said, standing on her tiptoes to reach up to the shelf. "Help yourself to the tub. The lavender bath salts here are my favorite. My aunt Henrietta and I picked them out together. I soaked for thirty minutes earlier tonight. Almost fell asleep and drowned myself." But as she glanced back at him with a breezy smile, she realized she now had him picturing her in the tub.

*Definitely* in over her head.

She pulled a fluffy duvet and pillow down from the shelf. "You can have the bedroom. I'll take the sofa. That way," she said, carrying the bedding to the sofa, "I can hear you if you try to sneak out."

"Lizzie."

She unfurled the duvet. "If I'm wrong about you, I can defend myself. I don't care if you're SAS, MI6 or a bored British aristocrat."

Will slipped an arm over her shoulders and turned her gently to him, surprising her. "You're exactly what you seem to be, aren't you?"

"And that would be?"

"A hotelier who's more comfortable picking out bath salts and hiking the Beara Way than defending herself and a perfect stranger from a killer."

"Maybe I'm comfortable with picking out bath salts *and* taking on killers."

"I should have followed you from the pub. I could have spared you…" He seemed to shake off any regret. "Lizzie, you're not a professional. Whatever you're up to, you don't have to go about it alone."

He *was* good, she decided. Under the expensive clothes and polished manners, the upper-class bearing, were the quiet competence and self-assurance of a man who knew what he was doing—who, in fact, had real training and experience.

But Lizzie had held tight to her secrets for a long time. Once she let go of them, they wouldn't just be hers anymore. She'd be giving up the security they'd provided her for over a year. She'd be forced to trust whomever she confided in.

It was a big step. Too big.

"What I'm up to right now," she said lightly, "is falling asleep on my feet."

Will responded by easing his arm down her back to her hips, as if helping her to stay upright. "You're trying to keep yourself from telling me the truth."

No kidding. "What I've told you is the truth."

"It isn't everything."

"A two-way street, I'm afraid." She suddenly realized she still smelled of lavender and wondered if he noticed. "You're an attractive and dangerous man, Will Davenport, and you're wearing a very soft, warm sweater. That's a near-irresistible combination for a sleepy woman."

He kissed her forehead, so close now she could feel the warmth of his sweater. "Then I'll be noble and resist for both of us," he said, a slight roughness to his voice that suggested resisting wasn't that easy for him.

Lizzie's throat tightened, and part of her wanted just to sink into his arms and let him protect her, keep her safe. How much longer could she carry on alone? Norman had crossed a threshold in the past twenty-four hours. People had nearly died. A woman was missing. *He* was missing. But he still trusted her, Lizzie thought, and that gave her a certain leverage with him, perhaps the only leverage anyone had. If she let anyone—the director of the FBI, Simon, this Prince Charming of a stranger with her now—interfere, she risked losing the one advantage she had in helping to find Abigail Browning.

And, possibly, in staying safe herself.

Will touched a thumb to her upper cheekbone. "You've dark circles under your lovely eyes. You're exhausted." He let his thumb drift down to the corner of her mouth before his hand fell back to his side. "Good night, Lizzie."

"Why did you come here?" she asked, a little hoarse.

He winked at her. "The lure of a beautiful, mysterious woman."

"You're a very charming liar, Lord Davenport."

"Sweet dreams," he said.

He picked up his bag and ducked into the bedroom, shutting the door softly behind him.

Lizzie blew out a breath.

A *very* attractive, dangerous man.

She stretched out on the sofa in her skirt and T-shirt and pulled the duvet and her wool throw up to her chin.

Morning couldn't come soon enough.


Lizzie had left her robe on the bathroom floor.

Will picked it up and hung it on a hook on the back of the door, noting that the soft terry cloth was still damp from her bath.

A perilous observation, that one. He abandoned it before it could take hold and spawn images that would make for an even longer night ahead.

"Too late," he muttered, picturing small, green-eyed Lizzie Rush settling into her bath.

The bathroom smelled of lavender and, very faintly, of dried mud. He saw the rucksack she'd had with her on the Beara in a corner behind the door and immediately seized on the distraction. If he was too "noble" to take advantage of her fatigue and her own desire for distraction, he was perfectly at peace with having a look in her rucksack.

He got onto one knee and unzipped the main compartment.

It was packed with supplies anyone would take on a multiday hike. The garda had her bungee cords. After seeing how quickly she'd thought of them and the skill with which she'd used them on Michael Murphy, Will wouldn't be surprised to discover she'd packed them with tying up a prisoner in mind. He continued his search but found no weapons or any other items that would immediately undermine her story of how she'd happened upon Keira Sullivan and the man sent to kill her.

Feeling no guilt whatsoever at having invaded her privacy, Will showered and returned to the bedroom. It was small and tastefully decorated in neutral colors, but he found himself unable to relax. He stared at the closed door to the living room and debated going out there to argue sleeping arrangements.

He could also go out there and demand Lizzie tell him about the Brit she'd described to Michael Murphy and whom Eddie O'Shea in turn had described to Will.

If it *was* Myles…

Now, when Lizzie was about to fall asleep and would just be letting down her guard, was the perfect time to confront her. Why had she asked about that particular man? What did he have to do with Norman Estabrook and her relationship with the American billionaire? But not only had Will seen the dark circles under Lizzie's eyes and the tremor in her hands, he had to acknowledge an attraction to her that was both dangerous and compelling.

And perfectly natural, he thought with a small smile.

She needed sleep and time to recover from her ordeal, and he needed a few hours to chase back the ghosts and remember why he was here, now, in Lizzie Rush's suite in Dublin. His physical reaction to her only complicated matters.

He could have easily carried her in here and made love to her.

He could hear David Mears and Philip Billings teasing him about his love life. "You're a lone wolf, Will," David had said; he had been a stocky, hard-drinking man with a wicked sense of humor. "Heaven pity the poor woman who falls for you."

Philip, a formidable ladies' man but who had lately fallen for one of Arabella's friends back in London, had hooted in agreement. "And heaven pity you when you meet your match, because such a woman won't be like any you have in mind. She'll knock you on your arse, and we'll be there, Mears and me, saying we told you so."

Will pulled back the duvet on his bed and climbed in.

The sheets, too, smelled of lavender.

# Chapter 15

*Off the coast of Massachusetts*
*1 a.m., EDT*
*August 26*

Abigail had just started to play pool when Estabrook and the Brit—Fletcher—entered her stateroom. She'd slept fitfully before giving up, deciding she preferred to stay awake and alert. Estabrook wore a porkpie hat and yachting attire that might make a casual passerby less likely to recognize him, but he'd had his face plastered in the media for weeks while people speculated why a self-made billionaire would take up with ruthless criminals. Abigail had made a point of memorizing his face after he'd threatened to kill Simon and her father.

Fletcher calmly grasped the pool cue in her hands. She relinquished it without a struggle. "I'm not very good, anyway—at pool. You're right in thinking I could do some damage with the cue."

He said nothing as he set the cue aside.

Estabrook smirked at her. "I see your black eye's blossomed, Detective. Have you slept?"

She decided to answer. "A little."

"As much as I relish your father's suffering, I regret seeing you suffer. You're in pain, and you're frightened."

Abigail wanted to kill him. "You should let me go. Release me and give up the people who actually set the bombs. It wasn't you. You were in Montana."

Of course, since he'd hired the men who'd carried out the attacks, he was ultimately responsible. There'd be no deal. He hadn't beamed himself east. There'd be a trail, and her colleagues in law enforcement would pick it up and follow it to her. She trusted them. In the meantime, she had to stay alive and do what she could to throw Estabrook off balance and keep him there.

He thrived on risk and wouldn't rattle easily.

"Don't play me for a fool, Detective. May I call you Abigail?" He smiled, having fun with her.

"Sure. Why not?"

"Have a seat," he said.

She shrugged and started for the sectional on the wall.

"Not there." Estabrook smiled nastily and pointed to the metal chair his men had tied her to earlier. "There."

Abigail made herself keep her eyes on him. "Suit yourself."

Fletcher stood back, quiet, observant, and she passed him and sat down, stretching out her legs and crossing her ankles. During her hours alone, she'd done yoga to loosen up after having sat in one position for so long. "If you give yourself up," she said, addressing Estabrook, "I'll tell my friends you're not the one who smacked me in the face."

"Do you think I care?"

"You will when they catch up with you."

He leaned against the pool table and put his hands on either side of him, gripping the edge as he gazed down at her. "Your father put Simon up to betraying my trust and friendship, but they've failed. Here I am, a free man."

Abigail yawned. "Bugs you, doesn't it, that the feds used you to get to bigger fish? You're not happy being a little fish. You knew exactly what you were doing when you hooked up with drug traffickers, but it never occurred to you they were a bigger deal than you were."

Estabrook smiled, as if he was reading her mind and drawing strength from her fear.

Let him. She'd have her chance. "So what happened today?" She kept her voice matter-of-fact. "Your guys screwed up. Did they not know my father and Simon were in Boston?"

"I hired professionals," he said, an edge in his voice. "I gave them free rein to make decisions based on their best judgment. I operate that way in everything I do. Micromanaging is a sign of weakness."

"They were on their way to see me—Dad and Simon." She said "Dad" deliberately and saw Estabrook's reaction, the gleam of fury in his eyes, the thinning of his mouth. She didn't let herself react to his hatred. "If your guys had better intel and had just waited a few minutes…" She sighed. "But, no. They pulled the trigger on their bomb and grabbed me."

Estabrook breathed in through his nose. "I wish I could have been there when Simon and your father arrived to smoke, fire and blood."

"Your guy's blood. He dripped on the sidewalk."

Fletcher remained impassive, but she could see she'd gotten to Estabrook. He stood up from the pool table, his hat crooked on his head. "You're not half as clever as you think you are, Detective."

She ignored him. "I was home all morning, and Scoop went down to his garden early. He's trying to stay ahead of the harvest. I figure your guys planted the bomb sometime before this morning. Overnight? Yesterday? I guess it could have been anytime. There were two explosions. The second was my gas grill, right? Haven't used it in weeks."

"All moot now, my dear," Norman said.

"True, but I have to think about something besides my testimony at your trial. Your guys could have hit the trigger anytime, but they didn't. Why wait?"

"Synchronicity."

"Ah. You wanted to time everything with your release."

"Why were you meeting Simon and your father?"

"To discuss you," she said coolly.

Estabrook seemed to like her answer. He moved in front of her and leaned in close, his eyes puffy, bloodshot under the broad rim of his hat. "You bear a strong resemblance to your father. I see him in the shape of your mouth, your nose. It can't have been easy growing up with such a man. Do you blame him for your husband's death?"

"No."

"Christopher Browning was an FBI special agent. Your father wasn't director then, but he was very powerful. He's kept secrets from you, hasn't he?"

"Everyone has secrets. You, for instance. Your secret? You know you don't measure up. You've known since you were a scared little boy." Abigail swallowed, felt a twinge of nausea. She'd never done well being cooped up, never mind on a boat. "You're still that scared little kid inside. It's nothing to hide from. Let me go and stop this before you can't turn back. Before someone ends up really hurt."

She could see he'd tuned her out. He stood up straight and reached for a pool cue, a fresh one, not the one she'd used. "Until this summer, you had no idea your father was a surrogate father to Simon." Estabrook turned to her knowingly. "Did you, Detective?"

"No, I did not."

"Brendan Cahill and your father were friends. He was a DEA agent in Colombia. He was murdered when Simon was fourteen."

"I imagine you're real familiar with the DEA and FBI."

His grip on the pool cue tightened visibly. "Your father saw to Simon for twenty years, and you had no idea. So many secrets, Detective. So many secrets your father has."

"My father stayed in contact with a boy who'd lost his own father and tried to help out when he could. It wasn't a secret. I just didn't know about it. Simon's a great guy and a fine FBI agent. A lot of your criminal colleagues are being rounded up and arrested thanks to him—and you and your cooperation with the feds." Abigail gestured to her plush surroundings. "Is that what this is about? Are you getting away from them? Trying to convince whoever's left among your drug-cartel friends that you're dead? Are you afraid they'll come after you?"

Estabrook laid the cue on the pool table. "You shouldn't deliberately try my patience, Detective."

His tone—cool, remote—turned her stomach. He was, she thought, a man eager to commit violence. Keeping her own tone conversational, she changed the subject. "Where are we going? Do you own property on the New England coast? Are we heading to some place in particular—a friend's house maybe? Or are we just sailing in circles?"

He picked up the eight ball and cupped it in his fleshy palm. "What's a friend, Detective?"

There was a sudden sadness about him that Abigail wasn't about to fall for. She knew it had nothing to do with real fellow feeling but only with his narcissistic view of himself and his place in the world.

He set the ball back on the table and shifted to Fletcher. "You know what I want," he said, and abruptly left the stateroom.

Fletcher waited a few seconds after the door shut before he walked over to Abigail. "You can stand up if you'd like." He nodded back toward the pool table. "Go ahead and return to your game."

"Not afraid I'm going to shove a pool cue up your—"

"No," he said with an unexpected smile, "I'm not, and not because you're not capable of doing so but because you know you need me."

"And why do I need you, Mr. Fletcher?"

His gray eyes settled on her. "Because I can get you out of here alive." He took her by the hand and helped her to her feet. "Simon Cahill and your father had help from someone else with close ties to Mr. Estabrook."

"I wouldn't know." Abigail removed Estabrook's cue from the table, returned it to the rack and got hers. She kept her voice even. "They're FBI. I'm BPD. Two different things."

"Mr. Estabrook wants the identity of this person."

"What difference does it make now?"

"I get paid more if I deliver whoever it is to him." Fletcher gathered up the scattered balls and racked them. "You know, Abigail, or you know more than you realize."

She picked up the white cue ball. A name came to her. She pushed it back down deep. But it was there.

*Lizzie Rush.*

Lizzie was wealthy, elegant and attractive and would fit in with

Estabrook's friends and hangers-on, but her family was connected to Boston and she had a personal interest in Abigail's father.

In fact, Lizzie Rush was the main reason Abigail had asked Simon and her father to meet her that morning, before the bomb went off.

She set the ball on the table and lined up her pool cue, even as regret washed over her. She hadn't told Owen about her questions, her suspicions. She could rationalize her silence: she didn't know enough; she was acting as a police officer and not just out of personal curiosity.

The truth was, she'd learned to keep secrets at her father's knee.

Her father, who would be terrified for her now, was one of the best men she'd ever known. His secrets arose out of his sense of duty and commitment. They were a product of who he was— a man who could be trusted, who didn't speak out of turn and often faced tough choices.

Fletcher lifted the rack from the triangle of balls and stood back. Abigail shot the cue ball across the table. It smashed into the racked balls and sent them spinning everywhere. Three solid-colored balls went into pockets. Pure luck. She had no idea what she was doing.

"You were right," Fletcher said with a smile, "you're not very good."

She almost laughed as she lined up another shot. "You're connecting dots that can't be connected," she said. "I can't help you. I've been busy with my own job."

"Who can help me, then, love?"

Her stomach lurched.

*Fiona.*

Abigail tapped a solid red ball into a corner pocket and forced Bob's daughter out of her mind. Her name, her image, everything about her. But she could see Fiona just last night, playing a small harp with her Irish band at Morrigan's Pub at the Whitcomb, the Rush hotel in Boston.

*"This isn't a good idea, Fiona."*

*"Why not?"*

*"I can't explain. Who do you know here? Who have you met?"*

*"No one, really."*

Fiona had blushed, and Abigail had noticed a young, cute, male Rush standing in the door and wondered if she'd overreacted and Fiona wasn't about to stumble into one of John March's labyrinths. As much as Abigail loved her father, she was well aware that he had left a complex trail behind him in his near sixty years on the planet.

Fiona knew every Irish bar in town that offered live music, and Morrigan's would be one of the better paying and more prestigious. She could have found it on her own, but she hadn't. She'd found it because *her* father knew Abigail, who was head over heels in love with Owen Garrison. And Owen's family, with its strong ties to Beacon Hill, often stayed at the Whitcomb and put up friends there.

Abigail's father had known the Garrisons even before she'd met Chris Browning, who had grown up just down the rockbound shore from their summer home on Mount Desert Island. But her father's relationship with the Garrisons had nothing to do with her concerns about Fiona O'Reilly playing Irish music at Morrigan's.

Her concerns had everything to do with the woman in whose honor the bar had been named—Shauna Morrigan, Lizzie Rush's mother.

Even to think about any of them now, with Fletcher watching her, Abigail knew, was dangerous.

As she leaned forward, lining up another shot, she felt the strain of the last hours in her lower back. She was dehydrated and knew she needed to drink more water, but the thought nauseated her. "You'll have to speak up," she said. "My ears are still ringing from you bastards blowing up my apartment and smacking me in the face."

"We have time."

She concentrated on taking her shot, but she was too late. Fletcher had already seen that she'd lied.

"Enjoy your game," he said quietly, and left.

# Chapter 16

*Dublin, Ireland*
*7:23 a.m., IST*
*August 26*

The bedroom door was still shut when Lizzie awoke, the early morning sun finding its way through the sides of the room-darkening window shade. She slipped into comfortable slim black pants, a black top and her new flats and dabbed on just enough makeup to convince people she'd slept okay.

Making as little noise as possible, she went out into the hall and took the stairs down to the lobby. She smiled at the woman at the front desk, who was new, and headed for the hotel's small street-level restaurant, its tables covered in Irish lace. Lizzie chose one on the back wall that had a view of the door out to the lobby. She ordered coffee and scones and chatted a moment with her waiter, a college student from Lithuania. Last night on the Beara Peninsula suddenly seemed surreal, and she half expected her cousin to wander in and act as if she'd just arrived from Boston and none of it had happened. Her fight in the stone circle, the bomb, Abigail Browning, Norman's disappearance…the fair-haired Brit asleep in her suite.

Lizzie could blame her delusions on jetlag and go shopping.

But as she spread her scone with butter and raspberry jam, her handsome suitemate, dressed in another deliciously soft-looking sweater, joined her at her table.

Without waiting for an invitation, he sat across from her. "My sister loves Dublin. I'll have to ask her if she's stayed here."

"She's a wedding dress designer in London. Arabella. It's a pretty name. You have an older brother, too. Peter. He manages the family farm, that being a five-hundred-year-old estate in the north of England."

"All of which," Will said, marginally impressed, "you could find on the Internet."

"In fact, I did."

She'd also done a bit of spying on the Davenports herself when she was in London in early July, but she chose to keep that fact to herself. Will had sparked her interest after she'd learned Simon wasn't ex-FBI after all and remembered the two men were friends.

Will's pot of tea and a steaming scone arrived. For a man who had slept only a few hours, he looked remarkably alert. And serious, Lizzie thought.

He poured his tea. "You're playing a very dangerous game, Lizzie. It's time to stop."

She reached for more jam. She'd combed her hair and pinned it back, but she suspected there were still knots in it. It'd been a long night on the sofa. "If you were going to sic the FBI or the guards on me," she said, "you'd have done it by now."

As he set the teapot down, she noticed a thin, straight four-inch scar on his hand, perhaps from a knife fight that hadn't gone as well as hers had last night.

"You're not the dilettante you've pretended to be," he said, lifting his cup and taking a sip as he eyed her over the rim. "You didn't learn your fighting skills from reading a handbook. Who taught you?"

"I frequently travel on my own, and I decided it would be smart to take self-defense classes. But I do have the SAS handbook." She sat back. "You're not smiling, Will."

"I woke up worried about you."

"Ah. Maybe I should have given you the sofa instead. I slept just fine. Nothing to worry about." She slathered jam on a chunk of scone and indulged, relishing the sweet, rich taste. "It'll be back to mesclun soon. You and Simon are obviously good friends, but that's not why you followed me here."

"Do you have friends, Lizzie?"

"You mean in addition to my four cousins and Norman?"

Will still didn't smile. "Correct."

"Yes, I have friends, although I've neglected most of them lately." She leaned back and studied him as he placed his cup in its saucer and broke off a piece of his scone. "No jam, no butter? You're an ascetic."

"I wasn't the one who engaged in hand-to-hand combat last night."

"Combat? When you put it that way…" But Lizzie couldn't maintain her light mood, feigned as it was. "I'm not that hungry, having had a full Irish breakfast at midnight. How long have you known Simon?"

Will deliberated a moment. "Two years."

"Norman got very curious when he found out Simon was hanging out with you in London. Did you know he was working undercover, or did you think he was a former FBI agent with a grudge against Director March?"

"Simon and I didn't discuss Norman Estabrook."

"Then MI6 isn't interested in him?"

Will gave her a slight smile. "Very clever, Lizzie. What are your plans for today?"

"Defying jetlag. Past that, I don't know." She abandoned her scone for her coffee, not meeting his eye as she said, serious now, "I asked Michael Murphy about one of your countrymen last night. I saw your reaction, Will, and I think he's why you're here in Dublin. You know him, don't you?"

"As I indicated," he said, picking up his teacup again, "you're playing a dangerous game."

Lizzie didn't relent. "Who is he?"

"A ghost."

"Another spook?"

He sighed. "I never said…"

"You didn't have to. This man showed up in Las Vegas a few days before Norman's arrest. Is he SAS? Special Branch? A fugitive?"

"He's a killer. Eddie O'Shea ran into him on the Beara Peninsula last week. Simon and Keira weren't there."

Lizzie absorbed this new information and felt a sting of regret that Eddie and his brothers had had their quiet lives disrupted. But they seemed capable of handling anything. "Did this man arrange the attack on Keira?"

"Whatever he did, Lizzie, you must stay away from him. As capable as you are, you can't best him. If you know anything about him, tell me now."

"At least give me his name."

Will steadied his gaze on her, the blue, green and gold of his eyes melding into a gleam of black. "His name is Myles."

She stifled an involuntary gasp at the pain in his voice. "He's your friend," she said. "Will—"

"I haven't seen the man you and Eddie O'Shea described myself." His words were measured, everything about him under control. "I could be wrong."

"We only talked for a few minutes. He joined me at the hotel bar and asked me for a bottle of water and…" Lizzie paused, remembering that strange encounter in Las Vegas. "He told me to behave."

There was an edge of sadness to Will as he smiled. "That sounds like Myles. Had he and Estabrook already met?"

Lizzie nodded. "He—Myles, the Brit—went up to Norman in the middle of his poker game. No one else at the table seemed to know him. I couldn't hear what he and Norman said to each other, but it seemed important. That's one reason why I remember him."

"There's another reason?"

She didn't look away but instead met Will's gaze straight on. "I was trying to remember everything."

"Why, Lizzie? This was before Estabrook's arrest. Were you aware of his illegal activities?"

She smiled easily. "I should take the Fifth on that one. That's the Fifth Amendment. Bill of Rights. U.S. Constitution—"

"Lizzie. We're not discussing one of your hotel luxury excursions."

Didn't she know.

"I'm sorry," he said immediately. "That was patronizing."

"I shouldn't have gone vapid hotel heiress on you."

"Which you're not."

"No, I'm not. Will, if your friend Myles is helping Norman exact his revenge, Abigail Browning is in serious trouble, isn't she?"

"For the past two years, I've thought Myles was dead."

"Until you heard me describe him last night. That's why you let me leave, isn't it? You didn't want me stuck for hours with garda detectives. You wanted to talk to me yourself. Have you told the FBI?" But Will's expression startled her, and she almost knocked over her coffee. "I see now. Simon, you, Myles. Comrades in arms?"

"You see too much, Lizzie." Will lifted the teapot again and changed the subject as he refilled his cup. "What's your relationship with Estabrook?"

She decided to answer. "He thinks I understand him."

"Do you? Did he discuss his intentions for revenge with you?"

"Not specifically. I just happened to be with him in Montana when he threatened to kill Simon and Director March. I can't always tell what's bravado and fantasy with Norman and what he actually plans to do. He's grandiose and, at the same time, very smart and very calculating. I'd hoped his lawyers and a brush with incarceration would straighten him out, and he'd accept that violent revenge was a fantasy. But I also doubted that would happen. He's taken it on as his next death-defying challenge."

Will settled back in his chair. "Lizzie…"

But she'd gone far enough. She gave him a bright smile. "All of a sudden, Lord Davenport, you look very much like a man who never puts jam and butter on his scones." She noticed Justin in the doorway and waved to him. "You met my cousin Justin last night. I practically grew up with him and his three older brothers. My father traveled frequently. Still does."

"Your mother—"

"My mother died when I was a baby. Ripple effects, Will." Lizzie got to her feet, laid her napkin next her plate. "So much of life is about ripple effects. Drop a stone into a pond, and you don't always know what and who will be affected as the ripples make their way across the water. Take your time with your tea. Justin will help you with whatever you need. I have a flight to catch."

"Be careful, Lizzie."

She beamed a smile at him. "I'm always careful."

He didn't move to get up. "I suspect we have different ideas about what that means."

She was aware of him watching her as she walked across the restaurant to her cousin. "Run interference for me," she said to him. "I need a head start on our Lord Davenport. You won't be able to outmaneuver him, so don't try. Just buy me some time."

Justin straightened, obviously up to the job. "What if he's scheduled to take the same flight as you to Boston?"

"No worries," she said, heading for the lobby. "Lord Davenport will fly first-class. I'll be in coach."

Justin Rush, who bore a detectable resemblance to his cousin in the shape of his nose and eyes, sat across from Will and started telling family secrets.

A delaying tactic.

"Lizzie's a worry," the youngest Rush said. "From what my parents and older brothers tell me, she always has been. Whit's the eldest. He's named after our paternal grandmother, who was a Whitcomb. Then Harlan—Lizzie's dad is a Harlan, too, named after our grandfather Rush, who talked our grandmother into converting her family home on Charles Street in Boston into a hotel."

"Did it require much convincing?"

"Almost none. She'd discovered rats and roaches in the butler's pantry." Justin reddened. "There aren't any there today, of course."

"Of course," Will said. "So it's Whit, Harlan—then Lizzie?"

"That's right. Then Jeremiah. I'm last." He smiled, a charmer. "The baby."

"I see."

"Lizzie spent a lot of time with us and our grandmother Rush growing up, but she traveled with her father, too. Do you know she's as good at five-card stud as she is at ordering wine in a five-star restaurant?"

"And she plays bridge," Will said.

"By herself. She tell you it anchors her mind? Personally, a pint of Guinness does the job for me. How well do you know her?"

"We only met last night."

"Where? Not Dublin, not from the state of her shoes, at least. Were you tramping through stone circles and fighting Irish bulls with her in West Cork?"

Will wondered when word of the attack on Keira would reach Justin Rush in Dublin, or if it had and he was just more adept at dissembling than his cousin. "I ran into her in a West Cork pub."

Justin looked momentarily awkward and glanced toward the door, as if he hoped Lizzie would be there to take him off the hook. He turned back to Will. "Lizzie's a free spirit, but she's a hard worker, too. She's worked at every one of our hotels just like the rest of us. She's very good at her job. My dad would fire her if she wasn't."

"But she's been on a bit of a hiatus this past year, hasn't she?"

"Sort of." The red spread to her young cousin's neck. "She got mixed up with that cretin Norman Estabrook. I know it's wrong of me, but I hope his plane—never mind. I won't say it out loud."

"Where does Lizzie's father live? Boston?"

"Uncle Harlan avoids Boston whenever possible."

"And Ireland, too, I gather," Will said.

He noticed a wince of genuine discomfort as Justin's expression softened. "It's because of the memories."

"Lizzie's mother?"

Justin feigned great interest in a pepper grinder.

Will persisted. "What happened to her?"

"She died in a freak accident when Lizzie was a baby—here in Dublin, as a matter of fact. She was Irish herself. She was here to visit her family."

"She came without Lizzie?"

He nodded.

"And without her husband?"

Another awkward nod. "It was eight years before I was born. She flew to Dublin for a five-day visit and tripped on a cobblestone on Temple Bar. She hit her head. They say she died instantly." Justin cleared his throat and lifted his gaze from the pepper grinder. "Just one of those things."

It didn't sound like just one of those things, but Will could see Justin had said all he planned to say on the matter, and possibly all he knew. "Where does your uncle Harlan live, then, if not Boston?"

"His official residence is Las Vegas, but I doubt he's there half the year. He's on the board of the family biz, but he doesn't have an active role these days. He spends most of his time traveling and gambling."

"I understand Lizzie travels a great deal. Does she also gamble?"

"Not with money. She's a risk-taker, but she's tight with a buck. She's debating whether to rent or tear down the old Rush family place in Maine. No one else wanted it, but she loves it— the location, anyway. The house itself is a wreck." Justin Rush shrugged, clearly reluctant to share so much information about his cousin, but he had his marching orders and needed to hold Will's interest and stall him. "Lizzie says it's unpretentious."

Will smiled, imagining Lizzie wringing costs out of a renovation project with carpenters and architects. She'd have her way. But he steered Justin back to the more immediate concerns at hand. "Do you know Norman Estabrook yourself?"

"I've met him. I carried his bags."

"When he stayed here a year ago this past April," Will said.

"What, do you know *everything* already?"

"Not at all. How did Mr. Estabrook strike you?"

"I didn't really notice him. I was here on spring break. I had my hands full not to drop bags on the toes of hotel guests. I've improved since then. Mr. Estabrook had some adventure in the works—I think he hiked the Skelligs, but I'm not sure. He had quite an entourage with him. Ran me ragged."

"Do you consider Lizzie part of his entourage?"

Justin looked slightly annoyed as well as protective. "Lizzie would never be part of anyone's entourage."

"But she was here then, in Dublin," Will said.

"Yes. On her own—not with him. That's when they met." Justin picked up a crumb of his cousin's abandoned scone. "They were never more than just friends. And if you're going to ask if she has a boyfriend, I'm not going to tell you."

His tone suggested she didn't, which pleased Will more, undoubtedly, than was smart. "Do you remember anyone else from Mr. Estabrook's entourage?"

"Nope."

"Did he stay here again after that April visit?"

"Not that I know of." Justin glanced down at his crumb, then up again, his eyes showing more maturity. "Is Lizzie in trouble?"

"I don't know. I hope not."

"She can kick butt with the best of them. She's practiced on all of us. She bloodied my brother Jeremiah's nose last New Year's."

"Your family was gathered for New Year's? Where?"

"Vegas. All of us, including Uncle Harlan."

"Your hotel's very comfortable," Will said, rising, "and you did your job. You delayed me."

Justin got to his feet. "You wanted to learn more about Lizzie."

Will saw the unease in the young Rush's expression. "Justin, is your family worried about her?"

"Doesn't much matter, does it? Lizzie thinks she's on her own."

Will had his own experience with worried family members left behind, but he was a professional officer. Lizzie Rush, clearly, was not. He said quietly, "I'm not going to hurt her."

"But will you help her?"

"If I can. If she'll let me."

"Sometimes I think she likes living dangerously."

"Perhaps she's merely trying to do what she can to help with a difficult situation and leave her family out of it." Will didn't wait for a reply. "You've given your cousin sufficient time to get to the airport. It's a pleasure to meet you, Justin. If you're ever in London, look me up."

He frowned, scrutinizing Will a moment, then sighed. "I don't start work until later. Come on, I'll drive you to the airport myself. You're chasing Lizzie to Boston, right?"

"I already have a flight arranged."

"Your own plane?"

Will didn't answer.

"Oh, that's good—you flying a private jet across the Atlantic and Lizzie stuck in coach with her deck of cards." Justin laughed. "That'll teach her to sneak off."

En route to the airport, Will learned a few more tidbits. Lizzie's full name was Elizabeth Brigid Rush. Her mother was born Shauna Morrigan. "There are family rumors about Aunt

Shauna," Justin said. "My brother Jeremiah is convinced she spied on the Boston Irish mob."

"This was before she married your uncle?"

"Jeremiah thinks so. Who knows? There are family rumors about Uncle Harlan, too." Justin grinned as he pulled into the airport. "*Now* I've gone too far. For all I know, you're a British spy."

Indeed, Will thought, deciding he liked Justin Rush.

# Chapter 17

*Boston, Massachusetts*
*8 a.m., EDT*
*August 26*

Bob felt the metal bars under the thin mattress as he rolled onto his back, reminding him that he'd spent the night on the pullout sofa in his niece's attic apartment in the Garrison house. Sunlight streamed through lace curtains Keira had bought in Ireland. He draped an arm over his eyes to block out the sun and slumped deeper into what passed for a bed. His feet hung off the end. He hadn't wanted to sleep. He'd still be at BPD headquarters now if Tom Yarborough hadn't all but put a gun to his head and dragged him to Beacon Hill.

Yarborough had probably gone right back to work.

Bob adjusted his position and got another poke in the back. Everyone had offered him a place to stay. Theresa, Lucas Jones, even Yarborough. Hell, the mayor and the commissioner would have put him up for the night if he'd asked. Easier to stay in his niece's vacant apartment with her pictures of Irish fairies and cottages, her books of folktales and poetry.

Simon and March had an FBI detail looking after their safety. Neither liked it or had wanted to sleep any more than Bob had. Simon, in particular, wanted to chase Estabrook on his own, but not only did he have a giant target painted on his back, he would be more help to Abigail working the investigation than going solo. He knew Estabrook, his contacts, how he thought, places he liked, places he'd been or had talked about. If he could hide millions for drug traffickers, he could hide himself.

Someone would have paged or called or shouted up the stairs if Estabrook or his plane had turned up, but Bob checked his messages, anyway.

Nothing.

He walked to the window in his undershorts and pulled back the Irish lace curtains, grimacing when he saw that the protective detail the commissioner insisted be put on his chief homicide detective was still down there. Waste of manpower as far as Bob was concerned. He'd rather have them out looking for Abigail and the bombers, but he didn't have a choice.

He headed for the bathroom and took a shower, using Keira's almond soap, which wasn't as girlie as he'd feared. He'd managed to grab a couple changes of clothes out of his apartment. They didn't smell too sooty to him, but they might to someone else. Not his problem.

Yarborough met him downstairs. He was as straight-backed as ever but looked raw around the edges. He'd never say the tension was getting to him, but Bob wouldn't, either. "Morning, Lieutenant. You sleep?"

"Like a baby. You?"

"Some."

Bob squinted across Beacon at the Common, all dappled shade on a sunny summer morning. It'd be another hot day. "Did you find Abigail and just not want to wake me?"

"No. Sorry."

The guy had no sense of irony. Bob turned back to him. "What's going on? Why are you here?"

Yarborough rubbed the back of his neck. He was a cool, controlled type, but right now, he looked miserable. "Fiona refused police protection this morning and cleared out of her mother's house. She's over eighteen. We can't force her."

"I can. Where is she?"

Yarborough didn't answer.

"You don't know, or you don't want to tell me?"

"ATF wants to put her under surveillance."

"My daughter?"

"Yeah."

"Why?"

"They think she could have seen something here yesterday morning and she just doesn't realize it."

"Big difference between protection and surveillance," Bob said, stony. "The feds don't call the shots when it comes to my family. Where's Fi now?"

"I don't know. In my opinion—" Yarborough abandoned his thought. "Never mind."

Bob glared at him. "In your opinion, what?"

Yarborough sighed and looked out at the Common. "I got the feeling when we interviewed her that she's holding back."

"What do you mean, holding back? Holding back what?"

The younger detective didn't flinch at Bob's tone. "I don't know. Lucas thought so, too." Like Bob wouldn't kill him if Lucas agreed. "We think she's got something on her mind, but she's not sure it's relevant. She's afraid of getting someone into trouble or wasting our time."

Bob didn't respond as he considered what Yarborough was saying.

Yarborough rubbed the side of his mouth with one finger. "I'm not criticizing her."

"Yeah. It's okay. I'm not armed. Not yet." Bob fished out his cell phone and tried Fiona's number, but he got her voice mail. He left a message and tried texting her. "I hate these damn buttons. My fingers are too big. I can't see the screen." He messed up and had to start over. "Fi's fast, but little Jayne—she's a whiz. Her teacher has the students leave their cell phones in a box when they come to class. Eleven years old, and they all have cell phones. Where's the money coming from? When I was a kid, we had one phone in the house. It was a big deal when the first family on the street got an extension."

"It's called progress, Lieutenant," Yarborough said.

"It's called kids texting their friends spelling words and the capital of Wisconsin. Or don't kids take tests anymore?" Bob managed to type in "call me" and hit some other damn button to send the thing. "I'm going to the hospital to visit Scoop. Ten to one Fiona's there. Any update on his condition?"

Yarborough was expressionless. "He's alive." He looked at Bob in the uncompromising way he had. "I'll drive you over there."

No way of talking him out of it. Bob gestured to the uniformed officers. "Tell them to go to work."

"Lieutenant—"

"Never mind. I'll do it."

Yarborough raised a hand, stopping him. He walked over to the cruiser, said a few words, then rejoined Bob. "Let's go," he said tightly.

"So, if someone jumps out of the bushes with a gun and tries to shoot me, you're diving in front of the bullet?"

"I'm shooting the bastard first. You're on PTSD watch, you know."

"Posttraumatic stress disorder doesn't happen in a day. It's normal to have the yips right after a crisis."

"The yips, Lieutenant?"

"Sleeplessness, flashbacks, startle response. Not that I have any of that. I told you, I slept like a baby—"

"Bob. Stop, okay? I know."

He grinned at the younger detective. "Is that the first time you've called me by my first name? Honest, Yarborough, we might make a human being out of you yet."

Yarborough clamped his mouth shut, a muscle working in his jaw as he got out his keys and walked to his car. He unlocked the passenger door. "I keep wondering where Abigail spent the night."

"No point going down that road."

"She's good, but…" Yarborough yanked open the door and stood to one side for Bob to get in. "It's okay. I checked for bombs already."

"You're a ray of sunshine, Yarborough."

"Always aim to please the boss."

Bob got rid of him when they arrived at the hospital. There were enough cops there for him to get a ride to BPD headquarters if he needed one, and Yarborough was clearly itching to do something besides escort him around town.

And Bob was right. He found his eldest daughter shivering in the corridor outside Scoop's hospital room. Scoop had been moved out of ICU to a regular room, another positive sign. It wasn't the air-conditioning that had Fiona shivering. If anything, the temperature was on the warm side. She was on edge. Bob wasn't thrilled with her for refusing police protection, but he melted when he saw her. Uniformed officers were posted outside Scoop's room and drifting past her while she mustered courage to go in and see him.

Scoop's family was there. His colleagues from internal affairs. Bob wasn't going to embarrass Fiona—or himself—by treating her like a two-year-old, but she had to go back under police protection. Just because she was over eighteen didn't mean she didn't have to listen to his common sense advice.

She tried to smile. "This is worse than any performance anxiety I've experienced," she said, her arms crossed tight on her chest. "Performing is nothing compared to facing a man who nearly died saving your life."

"Scoop won't look at it that way," Bob said.

"I don't care how he looks at it. It's what happened."

"I know, Fi."

A white-coated doctor who didn't look much older than Fiona came out of Scoop's room. "You can go in now," she said. "He's awake."

Fiona nodded without speaking.

The doctor headed for the nurses' station. When his daughter still didn't move, Bob said, "Scoop will want to see you and know you're okay."

She blinked back tears. "He saved my life," she said again.

Bob had talked to Theresa last night, and she'd told him Fi had been repeating those words ever since they'd left his burned-up house.

"Maybe you saved his life, too. If you hadn't been there, he might have gone for the porch and Abigail when the bomb went off. Instead he grabbed you and dived for cover." Bob nodded to the doorway. "Go on in, Fi. Just talk to him a few minutes."

She nodded, and Bob gritted his teeth as he watched his daughter enter the small room and walk up to one side of Scoop's bed. Scoop was on his side, bandaged, bruised, stuck with IVs. He had his own clicker for pain medication.

"Hey, Scoop," Fiona said, her voice clear and strong now. "How're you feeling? Don't talk if it hurts."

"I'm getting there. You?"

Standing just outside in the hall, Bob could barely hear him.

"Just some bumps and bruises," Fiona said. "I'm fine. We're all fine."

Bob knew that Tom Yarborough and Lucas Jones would have asked her not to mention Abigail to anyone, even to Scoop, not just to keep him from worrying about her but to maintain tight control over the investigation.

"I just wanted to say hi and thank you," she added, her voice a little less strong.

"Don't thank me, Fi. I should have spotted the bomb." Scoop sounded weak, drugged, but lucid. "Before it went off. You got a detail on you?"

"I'm okay."

"Fiona."

Bob grinned to himself. Good for you, Scoop, he thought.

"I said no." She was defensive now. "I don't want a protective detail. I don't need one. The bomb wasn't meant for me."

"Abigail," Scoop said.

Bad move, Bob thought. She should have lied and told him she had a protective detail. Even drugged and fighting pain, Scoop would have his cop instincts. As an internal affairs detective, he was used to penetrating lies told by men and women trained to see through them. He was the best in the department at detecting any type of lie.

Fiona sniffled. "Sorry, Scoop, I didn't hear you. I should leave. You should be with your family. I'm taking it easy today. I'm heading over to the Garrison house to practice."

"Good. Play an Irish tune for me."

"I will. I'll play something fun. Something happy."

But Scoop didn't respond, and Bob saw he'd drifted off. Fiona withdrew, bursting into tears when she reached her father. He tried to hug her, but she jerked away. The officers watched her closely, and he could tell they knew she was his daughter. So could she, and it just irritated her more.

Better irritated than sobbing and shivering.

She ran down the hall. Bob didn't go after her. The foundation staff would be back to work at the Garrison house, and patrol cars would be making frequent checks.

He went in to see Scoop. "You awake?"

"No."

"You look like hell."

"Feel worse."

"They say you're going to live."

Scoop paid no attention. "While I have the energy." He licked dry, chapped lips. "Before I konk out again. There's a woman."

"There always is with you."

"That's not what I mean. Black hair. Long, straight. Little thing. Green eyes. She was on our street."

"Okay," Bob said, unimpressed.

Scoop seemed to try to focus, but his eyelids were swollen from the fluids being pumped into him. "Day before the bomb. She stopped in front of the house. Said she had shin splints."

"She got your attention?"

"Yeah. I wondered…" He licked his lips again, his movements sluggish as he struggled to stay alert.

The man needed rest. "I'll look into it," Bob said. "A small woman with black hair, green eyes and shin splints."

Bob didn't tell Scoop, but the description also fit the woman in Ireland who'd taken on the s.o.b. sent to kill Keira. Michael Murphy continued to deny he intended to hurt anyone, but the Irish police didn't believe him. Bob didn't, either.

"Abigail was on to something," Scoop said in a slurred whisper. "She…her father…ask her."

Bob wouldn't lie to Scoop about Abigail, but he didn't have to. Scoop was out.

On his way out of the hospital, Bob dialed Theresa's cell number. "You know Fiona was just here visiting Scoop?"

"I assumed as much. She went back to her apartment first thing this morning. One way to get her out of bed early, put a police detail on her."

"It's a thought," Bob said without humor. "At least her apartment's in BPD jurisdiction. We can keep an eye on her."

Theresa got all hot. "If you're implying I should have kept her here, I tried. She's as stubborn as you are."

"You're at work today?"

"What's that supposed to mean?"

"It's just a question. Yes or no answer. Easy."

"Yes."

Bob ignored her tight, irritated tone. He didn't even blame her for being testy.

"If you have vacation days left, take them. Go to the beach with the girls."

"Fiona won't go. She and her band have paying gigs. Classes start soon. She—"

"You can make her go."

"So could you. You've got a gun, because that's what it'll take.

She's nineteen, Bob. She makes her own decisions. It's time you respected that."

"I don't like her decisions."

"Well, you can't control what she does. Neither can I. We can influence but not control."

"You been to see a shrink or something?"

She swore at him, really irritated now.

"Take Maddie and Jayne to the beach, Ter. I'll deal with Fi."

"She may play harp, Bob, but she's just like you."

"Prettier."

"Thank God."

"Ter?" He sighed. "I'm sorry."

She disconnected without a word.

Yarborough appeared out of nowhere and fell in beside him. Bob frowned. "I thought you were doing something useful."

"I decided I didn't want to leave you alone," Yarborough said, almost kindly, and nodded toward his car. "Come on. I'll take you wherever you want to go."

"The crime scene."

"The—"

"That would be my house, Tom."

He looked uncomfortable for a half beat. "Okay. Let's go."

"Abigail ever mention a small, black-haired woman to you?"

"No, why?"

"You ever see one?"

"Like, two million every time I get on the subway."

"She's got green eyes, too. And shin splints."

Yarborough was staring at him as if he might have to make a detour to the psych ward, but he said, still kindly, "You can tell me about her on the way to Jamaica Plain."

Which was when Bob knew he looked as sick and worried as he felt. But it didn't matter. He had to stay focused and do his job.

"Abigail's strong," Yarborough said, all reassuring. "She'll—"

"I'm getting my gun."

The younger detective looked relieved. "Good idea."

# Chapter 18

*Off the New England coast*
*Mid-day*
*August 26*

Norman Estabrook entered the stateroom with Fletcher two steps behind him. The billionaire looked more rested, and he wasn't wearing his porkpie hat. His light brown hair needed a trim. Abigail sat up on the sectional. She was nauseated but so far had managed to keep her food down. The wet bar was well-stocked with gourmet items, but she'd have loved a plain piece of toast.

"You're pale," Estabrook said. "Are you getting enough to eat?"

"Plenty."

"Did you sleep?"

She nodded. Fitful sleep, pacing, jumping jacks, pool, a shower. She'd done what she could to maintain her energy and stay attuned to her surroundings, the voices outside her door, the comings and goings of the small boat. She'd tried to use her worsening seasickness to her advantage and let it remind her she was still alive and still wanted to feel good and enjoy life.

"Have you ever met Lizzie Rush?" Estabrook asked abruptly.

His question took Abigail by surprise, but she answered truthfully. "No, I haven't."

"But you've heard of her?"

"Her family. They own the Whitcomb Hotel in Boston."

"She stayed with me through my arrest and my discovery of Simon's betrayal. I haven't heard from her since the FBI took her away. I imagine your father got to her."

Abigail walked over to the pool table and rolled a solid blue ball into a trio of other balls. It knocked against a yellow one, bounced off the side of the table and stopped at the edge of a pocket. "I wouldn't know," she said without looking at either man. "Believe it or not, my father hasn't discussed your case with me."

"If you think referring to me as a 'case' will give you the upper hand, Detective, or irritate me, or make me feel bad, you're wrong. I know I matter to your father." Estabrook picked up the eight ball. "Lizzie grew up without a mother. Did you know that?"

"I'm not familiar with her background." That, Abigail thought, tapping in her blue ball with the tip of her finger, was an outright lie.

Estabrook massaged the eight ball. "She's just a few years younger than you. While you were growing up with a mother and father, Lizzie was being shuffled back and forth among various relatives. Her father traveled frequently for his work with the Rush hotels. She would stay with her uncle and aunt and their four sons in Boston, and her grandmother in Maine. Lizzie was a motherless little girl, Detective Browning."

"You seem to know a lot about her."

"I know a lot about everyone I have as a guest in my home."

But Simon had fooled him, and that grated. "What happened to Lizzie's mother?" Abigail asked, although she knew the answer to her question. Not the whole answer. Only her father would know the whole answer.

She was aware of Fletcher waiting by the door with his arms crossed on his chest. He managed somehow to look both bored and impatient.

Estabrook set the eight ball back on the table and gave it a sharp spin. "Lizzie's mother was Irish. Shauna Morrigan Rush. She died in Dublin when Lizzie was seven months old. Her death was ruled an accident—a freak fall—but who's to say? It's daunting to think about the little things that can have such an impact on our lives. One wrong move on an unfamiliar cobblestone street, and your daughter's an orphan."

Abigail subtly held on to the edge of the table as she tried to control another wave of her persistent nausea. "Do you have plans for Lizzie? Is she helping you?"

"All in good time."

Whatever her role, Lizzie Rush wasn't his equal, not in his eyes. Her father was. Simon? Estabrook, Abigail thought, would take special pleasure in exacting his revenge on Simon Cahill.

Estabrook turned abruptly to Fletcher. "Continue."

"I need you to leave," the Brit said.

"As you wish," he said coolly.

Fletcher lowered his arms to his sides and walked over to Abigail. He put his finger on her chin and tilted her bruised cheek toward the light. "The swelling's down a bit."

"I think so, too. How did you and Estabrook meet?"

"We had tea together at Buckingham Palace."

"For all I know you're telling the truth. You seem like a practical sort. What do you want out of this?"

"Money."

"I have access to money. We can work out our own deal."

"You're feeling sick," he said.

"I've turned green, have I?"

"More chartreuse."

"Ugly color, chartreuse, but to each his own. I hope being pregnant isn't this bad." She gave him a faltering smile. "I want kids. Do you have any?"

His eyes went flat. "No."

There was something there. A loss, a chance missed. "Give up Norman in exchange for cash and a safe exit back to whatever hole you crawled out of. There'll be a reward for my safe return."

"Mr. Estabrook has access to hundreds of millions of dollars. What do you suppose the FBI or Boston police would pay for you? Your fiancé comes from a wealthy family, but compared to Mr. Estabrook? I don't think so, love. Sorry."

"We can set you up with a new identity. He'd never find you. In your line of work, you must have enemies hunting you. You can make a fresh start."

"I've made my choices."

Abigail rolled a yellow ball from one end of the pool table to the other, without it hitting any other balls. "What does Estabrook want?"

Fletcher didn't hesitate. "To kill the people who tried to destroy him."

"It's not that simple, and I think you know it. And no one tried to destroy him. He broke the law." She stood up from the pool table. "He's become more and more obsessed with thwarting my father, hasn't he?"

"I'm afraid I'm not particularly interested in his motives."

"He appreciates an adversary as strong as he is. He sees himself as a special person, and he wants special adversaries—such as the director of the FBI."

Fletcher picked up a pool cue and examined the array of balls on the table.

"You're obviously not stupid," Abigail said. "Anyone taking the risks you've taken would want to be well paid."

"You're making assumptions that perhaps you shouldn't."

Without a doubt, but she said, "You should listen to me."

He got down low, sized up the array of balls on the table. "You're aching to shoot me and dump me overboard, aren't you, love? I can't say I blame you."

"I wouldn't dump you overboard. I'd let your body fall into the ocean if the bullets took you in that direction. Norman's, too." She walked to the end of the table, watching as Fletcher lined up his cue on a solid red ball. "I heard a smaller boat coming and going again. Have you kidnapped anyone else?"

He made his shot, crisp, clean, two solid-colored balls pivoting into pockets. But he didn't answer her.

"Is Lizzie Rush on board?" Abigail asked. "Are we on our way to meet her somewhere? Maine, maybe? Estabrook mentioned her grandmother had a house there."

Fletcher walked around the table, standing close to Abigail as he sized up another shot. "You know more about Miss Rush than you let on to Mr. Estabrook."

"Not much more. Simon Cahill met Estabrook at a Fast Rescue fund-raiser held at the Rush family's hotel in Boston last summer. My fiancé is the founder and director of Fast Rescue. But you know that already, don't you?"

Fletcher leaned far over the table and angled his cue sharply. "It's good that you didn't lie about that one, love," he said, making another perfect shot.

"I'm not the one with something to hide. For example, kid-napping a police officer." She fought more seasickness, bile rising in her throat. "Not going to tell me Estabrook's plan for me, are you?"

"There is one. Have no doubt of that."

"You don't sound very enthusiastic." Abigail stepped back away from the table, giving him room for another difficult shot. "You don't like this, do you? You're a professional, and Norman's a bril-liant, narcissistic, crazed amateur. He's off the reservation, isn't he?"

"Perhaps you should vomit and get it over with."

She ignored his remark. "If you had your way, what would you do, put a bullet in my head and dump me overboard?"

"No profit in that, love." He tapped a ball into a side pocket. "Does talking keep you from vomiting?"

She almost smiled. "So far, so good."

Eyeing the remaining balls on the table, he said, without looking at her, "There's a way you can help me. If you do, I'll help you when the time comes."

"What can I do for you?"

Fletcher positioned his cue for another shot. "You can tell me what you know about Will Davenport."

This was a surprise. "He's a friend?"

"Once upon a time."

Abigail considered her answer and decided there was little risk to the truth. "I'm sure I know less about him than you do. He and Simon were friends before Simon hooked up with Fast Rescue. I've never met Davenport, but I understand he's a wealthy British noble, a former military officer. I don't know the details, but I suspect he and Simon didn't meet over tea and crumpets."

"Correct. They did not."

"Simon worked in counterterrorism before he went undercover after Estabrook. I've wondered if he was on to some kind of drug-terrorism connection there. What about you, Fletcher? How do you know Davenport?"

He fired off another shot without answering.

"You were with the good guys?"

"I was with them. I wasn't one."

His hard, quick shot sent balls banging into each other, richocheting off the sides of the table.

Abigail maintained her composure. "Davenport provided assistance—voluntarily—with the Ireland end of a case we wrapped up earlier this summer involving a serial killer."

"Then Will hasn't been to Boston?"

"Not that I'm aware of."

"I believe you. Now," Fletcher said, moving around the table, his tone unchanged, "tell me about Fiona O'Reilly."

He caught Abigail totally off guard, which, she realized, had been his intention. She couldn't stop herself. The images of the previous day and her fear for Fiona were too much. Bile rose in her throat, and she stumbled. Fletcher moved fast, grabbing her, half carrying her to the bathroom, shoving her in front of the toilet. She vomited until she had nothing left inside her, then dry heaved for a few more minutes.

Finally, spent, eyes tearing and bloodshot, hands shaking, she splashed herself with cold water and looked at her reflection. She was bruised, ashen. "Owen," she whispered. "Give me strength. I love you so much."

When she turned, Fletcher was in the doorway. "I have to leave for a while," he said, impassive. "We can talk later. I'll let you get some sleep."

When she was alone again, Abigail lay down flat on the carpeted floor next to the pool table and closed her eyes.

In through the nose for eight.

Hold for eight.

Out through the mouth for eight.

"Again," she said, ignoring the tears trickling down her temples into the carpet.

In for eight. Hold for eight.

Out for eight.

# Chapter 19

*Boston, Massachusetts*
*4:15 p.m., EDT*
*August 26*

Fiona O'Reilly relaxed slightly when she entered the Whitcomb Hotel on Charles Street, her small lap harp in a soft case over one shoulder, and saw Jeremiah Rush in the lobby. The hotel was so elegant with its antiques and shining brass, but Jeremiah, she thought, was amazing.

And she desperately wanted to relax.

She'd practiced for hours in the drawing room at the Garrison house. Owen wasn't around, but the foundation's staff was back at work and police cars stopped by. Tom Yarborough, Abigail's partner, came into the drawing room at one point and asked her if she'd remembered anything else about yesterday. She'd said no and resumed practicing. Now she wondered if she shouldn't have. If she should have just told him. But what if she was wrong? What if she was just being stupid? *Hundreds* of people had been on Beacon Street yesterday who could have planted the bomb in Owen's car. The man she'd seen...

She lowered her harp off her shoulder. She was proud of herself for having screwed up the courage to visit Scoop. Seeing him so vulnerable was awful, but she'd done it. She hadn't chickened out. Turning down police protection hadn't made her afraid. The opposite. The prospect of bodyguards, even police bodyguards, scared her more than being on her own. She was an adult now and could decide for herself. She felt empowered.

She pulled herself out of her thoughts and greeted Jeremiah. "I'm here early. I hope you don't mind."

"Of course not." He got up from the dark wood desk, rumored to have belonged to his great-something-grandfather Whitcomb, and walked around to her. "I heard about the fire at your father's house yesterday. How is everyone? Are you okay? Were you there?"

"I was there but I wasn't hurt. It was pretty frightening. I didn't sleep much last night, but I practiced most of the day. That always helps. I've been working on a Mozart concerto for flute and harp." She gave Jeremiah what even felt like a strained smile. "Of course I slipped in a few Irish tunes."

He frowned at her. He wore a light tan suit that didn't have a single wrinkle. He was working reception right now, but he seemed willing to do a variety of jobs. Fiona had seen him running a vacuum last week. "I can tell you've been through an ordeal," he said. "I saw on the news one of the detectives was badly hurt—"

"Scoop. His real name's Cyrus Wisdom. He's doing much better today. I'm not supposed to talk about the fire while it's still under investigation." That was the response Lucas Jones had suggested she give to any questions. He'd strictly forbidden her from talking about Abigail. Fiona made herself smile again. "I came here to get away from everything for a while."

"Whatever we can do, let us know."

"Thanks." She changed the subject. "I thought I'd work some on planning our Ireland trip."

"My brother Justin's there now," Jeremiah said, heading back behind the desk. "He's a bellman at our Dublin hotel. He's a natural. I swear he'd stay a bellman if our dad would let him. Mum wouldn't care. She just wants us to be happy."

Fiona's mother had said that morning she just wanted Fiona and her sisters to be safe. Happy would be nice, too, she thought, suddenly feeling depressed.

Jeremiah opened a side drawer in the desk and pulled out a stack of brochures and an Ireland guidebook. "I've been collecting these for you. There's a brochure on our Dublin hotel."

"Does it serve tea on Christmas Eve?"

"Sure does." He came back around to Fiona and handed her the stack. "Are you sure you're okay? You look—"

"I'm fine," she said quickly, realizing she was about to cry. She brushed a stray tear and tried to smile. "Is your brother in Dublin cute?"

"He thinks so."

Fiona laughed, but more tears escaped, and she thanked Jeremiah and took the steps down to Morrigan's. It was at ground level, with full-size windows looking out on Charles Street. She found herself eye-to-eye with a dirty-faced toddler in a stroller. He waved at her, and she waved back, instantly feeling better.

She set her harp on the small stage. She and her friends had performed at Morrigan's a half-dozen times over the summer. Her father didn't know. She thought he'd object. Scoop and now Abigail knew, but Fiona hadn't asked them not to tell her dad.

Then it'd seem like she was keeping it a secret instead of just not having gotten around to telling him.

She sat at a table under a window with her brochures and ordered a Coke Zero. She wasn't sure which friends would show up, but it didn't matter. They all could play more than one instrument and would manage with whatever they had. Morrigan's patrons always seemed to enjoy her ensemble's performances.

She opened up one of the brochures to a photograph of a country lane that reminded her of her cousin Keira's paintings. Fiona knew something terrible had happened in Ireland, too, but no one would tell her anything except that Keira was safe.

Keira was as excited as Fiona was about their trip to Ireland and had said she couldn't wait to take her younger cousin to Irish pubs for live music. "You can join in, and we can get your dad and Simon to sing—just not my mum and me." Keira's mother, Fiona's aunt Eileen, had come home from studying in Ireland in college pregnant with Keira. She'd had some kind of mad, mysterious affair in the same ruin, apparently, where Keira had found her Celtic stone angel. The angel had disappeared, but Fiona had no doubt her cousin had seen it. Keira believed that whatever had happened to it, it was where it was meant to be.

As Fiona finished her Coke, a man she didn't recognize walked over to the stage area and pointed to her harp. "It looks like an angel's harp," he said in a British accent.

Fiona felt a shiver in her back. She'd just been thinking about Keira's stone angel. "There are several different kinds of harps," she said.

"And can you play all of them, Miss O'Reilly?"

Now the hairs on her arms and the back of her neck stood on end, and her breathing got shallow and her mouth went dry. But she didn't move.

The man pulled out the chair across from her and sat down. "It's all right, love. I'm a friend."

"I've never met you. I'll scream if you try anything."

He smiled, winked at her. "You do that, love. Scream loud. How was your harp practice at the Garrison house?"

"How—"

"It's a beautiful day for a stroll, isn't it?"

Fiona thought she'd pass out. To calm herself, she looked up at a poster of the brightly painted Georgian doors of Dublin. They were already on her list of sights to see at Christmas.

"Have a sip of your drink," the Brit said.

"It's not alcoholic. I'm under twenty-one."

There were several people in the bar. Jeremiah was just up the stairs. Fiona reminded herself she wasn't alone. Feeling more in control, she focused on the man across from her. "You followed me?"

"Yes, love. I can follow you anytime, anywhere. You'll never know if I'm there or not there." He leaned back in his chair. "When and where did you last see Simon Cahill?"

"Why do you want to know?"

"He's an old friend."

"I don't believe you. Did you have anything to do with the fire at my dad's?"

His eyes narrowed on her, and he leaned toward her. "I asked you a question, love. Best you answer."

"Yesterday. At my dad's." Fiona wanted to sound strong and defiant but thought she sounded weak, afraid. She cleared her throat. "It was after the fire. Late. That's when I saw Simon last."

The Brit had gray eyes that seemed to see right through her. "You're telling the truth," he said, satisfied. "That's smart. What about Director March?"

"I just got a glimpse of him yesterday. I didn't talk to him."

"And your friend Lizzie Rush?" He paused, watching Fiona. "When did you see her last?"

"She's not—I barely know her."

"When, love?"

She didn't want to tell him anything more.

"I can ask someone else. Her cousin up—"

"No, don't," Fiona broke in. "Leave Jeremiah alone. It was a few days ago. I don't remember the exact day."

"Here?"

"Yes." Fiona gulped in a breath, sweating now. "I have no idea where she is now. My friends and I perform here on occasion. I don't know the Rushes at all, really."

The Brit smiled. "Like your Irish music, do you? Well, Miss O'Reilly, I have a different sort of job for you." He pointed up at the window behind her, toward the street. "I want you to go back to the Garrison house. Call no one. Tell no one. Do you understand?"

Fiona nodded, her heart pounding.

"There's an alley off a side street just before you reach the house. Don't go into it. Stop and call your copper dad and tell him to come and have a look. Will you do that for me, love?"

"Yes."

Fight to escape. That was what her dad had taught her. He'd also taught her not to leave one crime scene for another. "It almost never works out," he'd said, "but use your fear as your guide. Let it help you."

The Brit reached across the table and tucked a finger under her chin, forcing her to meet his eye. "A man is in grave danger. Only you can get him help in time."

"Who is it?"

He ignored her. "When you speak with your dad, tell him Abigail is alive and unharmed. Will you do that for me, too, love?"

"Abigail," Fiona said. "Where—"

He tapped her chin with one finger. "Now, don't start. Just listen and do as I say. Tell your dad that he and his colleagues in law enforcement have an imaginative and dangerous enemy."

"You."

"I'm no one's enemy." He sat back again, his eyes hard. "No one's friend, either. Can you remember what I just said, love?"

"Yes. Yes, I can remember."

"There you go. Don't follow me. Don't have anyone else follow me." He nodded toward the street. "Lizzie Rush will be arriving very soon from Ireland. If you see her in time, she can go with you."

"How do you know she—"

He winked. "You'd be surprised what I know."

"I didn't see you yesterday. No one did."

"I know. Now you have seen me, but it's all right. I'm not going to hurt you. I especially enjoyed your Irish music. Special quality it has, doesn't it? Even for a Londoner like myself."

"What do you want with Abigail?"

"Nothing. I'm her only hope. I must leave now. If you do anything to interfere, she'll be dead before nightfall. You need to stay calm and do as I ask." The Brit stood up, looming over Fiona as he reached a hand out to her. "On your feet on three. Count with me. It'll help you focus. One. Two. Three."

She got up without his assistance. Should she scream? Kick him? Create a scene? If a man was dying...

She raised her chin to the Brit. "My sisters are under police protection."

He smiled. "You will be now, too. Alley. Your dad. Abigail. You can remember?"

"Why are you doing this?"

"It's important not to leave loose ends."

Fiona didn't breathe or speak as he trotted lightly up the steps and back out to Charles Street.

A cab pulled up to the hotel and a small, black-haired woman got out.

Lizzie Rush. As promised.

# Chapter 20

*Boston, Massachusetts*
*5:35 p.m., EDT*
*August 26*

Lizzie headed toward the Whitcomb lobby, shaking off the pummeled feeling she always had after the long flight across the Atlantic. It was late afternoon in Boston, late evening in Ireland, but she wasn't quite on either clock. She figured she'd need the five hours she'd gained heading west from Dublin. She didn't know how long she'd have before Will turned up. Based on the text message she'd received from Justin when she landed, probably not long: Brit to Boston. Right behind you.

Justin wasn't one to waste words.

Spending the night in the same suite as a British intelligence agent was one thing. Having him following her was another, but Lizzie had an advantage in Boston. She knew the city and had family there, and Will didn't. She'd contemplated him, her situation and her options while playing one solo game of bridge after another on her little tray table.

How did Will Davenport fit into whatever was going on, and where was he now?

Was he trouble?

"*Everyone's* trouble," she muttered, quoting her father, even as she welcomed the familiar surroundings of the Whitcomb's classically appointed lobby.

A dour-looking Sam Whitcomb, in actuality a firebrand privateer during the American Revolution, stared down at her from his oil portrait above the unlit marble fireplace. Henrietta wanted to replace him with one of Keira Sullivan's wildflower watercolors.

Lizzie focused on the situation at hand, smiling at her cousin Jeremiah as he stood up from his desk. "I cut my trip to Ireland short," she said.

"Justin's already filled me in," Jeremiah said, shaking his head. "Lizzie. What's going on? All hell's broken loose in Boston. I've never seen so many cops on the streets."

"I noticed. What do you know?"

"Nothing. Fiona O'Reilly's here. Cops are mum on the details about the fire at her father's place and the evacuation at the Garrison house. Your friend Norman Estabrook's disappeared, too. You know that, right?"

"Yes, but I'm not in contact with him."

"The FBI hasn't been in touch?"

Lizzie shook her head. No need to mention that she'd been in touch with John March herself. "I haven't spoken to Norman since his arrest."

Jeremiah seemed faintly reassured. "But you're back here because Simon Cahill and FBI Director March are in town, aren't you?" Her cousin narrowed his eyes on her. "Lizzie..."

Of all her cousins, Jeremiah was the one most tuned in to the history between March and her mother, but Lizzie dodged his question. "I'm not involved in Norman's legal case, Jeremiah. I wish I'd never had anything to do with him."

"I don't blame you. I imagine most of his friends feel the same way. What are you going to do now?"

"Pick up my car and head to Maine."

Go to Maine, she'd decided on her flight across the Atlantic. Figure out what she could do to help find Norman and leave the rest of her family out of it. John March might give her time, but if Scoop Wisdom had provided her description to his BPD colleagues, they could already be after her. Best, she'd reasoned, to stick to her cover story and go about her business as if she had nothing to hide. She'd gone to Ireland to hike the Beara Way and pop in on Simon Cahill, only to end up in the middle of a knife fight. It made perfect sense that she'd come straight home and head to her house in Maine.

Whether or not Norman thought she was an ally—believed she hated John March as much as he did—Lizzie had no doubt he would expect her to head to Maine.

Jeremiah touched her shoulder and looked past her. "Fiona…"

Lizzie turned as Fiona O'Reilly stumbled on the steps up from Morrigan's and hesitated, very pale, barely breathing. She stared at Lizzie a split second before bolting down the main steps and out to Charles Street.

"I wonder what just happened," Jeremiah said. "A man joined her downstairs. I've never seen him here before. He just left."

"What did he look like?" Lizzie asked.

"Brown hair, fit—not that he did push-ups on the floor, but I wouldn't want to take him on in a bar fight."

Lizzie felt the same shiver of coolness she'd experienced last night questioning Michael Murphy. "Was he British?"

"I didn't hear him myself. Lizzie, we're not talking about Lord Davenport, are we?"

She shook her head. "For one thing, Will's blond. Put hotel security on alert. I'll go after Fiona."

Her cousin took a sharp breath. "Should we call the police? Fiona's father—"

"Yes. Call Lieutenant O'Reilly and tell him something's up with her." Lizzie thought quickly. She didn't like keeping Jeremiah in the dark, but there was no time. "I owe you an explanation, but right now I need to go after Fiona. Keep her here if she returns."

"*I* should go."

She managed a smile. "My father taught me the tricks of the trade, not you." But her smile faded. "If the man who was with Fiona shows up again, don't confront him. Don't go near him. He's dangerous, Jeremiah."

"Who is he?"

"My guess? A British spy."

Her cousin rolled his eyes. "You think my golden retriever's a spy."

"He *is,* but of a different sort."

The humor helped break the tension, just enough to give her energy. Wishing she had on the shoes she'd worn last night in the stone circle instead of her flats, Lizzie headed out to Charles Street and up past a knot of college students and tourists to the intersection at Beacon Street. She spotted Fiona running in the direction of the Garrison house in what appeared to be blind panic.

Cursing her shoes, Lizzie took off after her on the uneven sidewalk. "Fiona, hold on," she called as she closed in on the teenager.

Fiona didn't break her stride. "I have to hurry."

"Why? Jeremiah told me a man joined you just now." Lizzie kept her voice calm. "Fiona, what did he say to you?"

"Did you see him? He thinks we're friends. I told him I hardly know you. It's true. He said not to follow him." She slowed slightly, clearly terrified. "You didn't try—you didn't send Jeremiah—"

"No one's following him."

"He knew you'd come. He told me a man's in danger and I should go to the alley by the Garrison house and—and—" Already close to hyperventilating, she gulped in more air as they continued up Beacon Street. "And then call my dad."

"Did this man threaten you?"

"He implied Abigail's life depends on my cooperation. There's a man dying. What if it's someone I know—one of Dad's detectives, one of my friends? We practice at the Garrison house. We—"

"Don't speculate." Lizzie tried to penetrate Fiona's mounting panic. "Let's just figure out what to do."

Fiona was marginally calmer as she glanced at Lizzie. "He said you could go with me."

"All right. Let's do this together."

Fiona slowed her pace and walking now, still breathing hard, turned onto a side street that led up onto Beacon Hill. She stopped at the entrance to a narrow alley that ran behind two elegant brick mansions.

"This must be it." She had her cell phone clutched in one hand. "He told me to call my dad and not go in the alley."

Lizzie peered into the alley. "He didn't say I couldn't go in, did he?"

Fiona shook her head, already dialing her cell phone.

"I'll stay in sight. I'm not leaving you, Fiona."

"I'll be okay."

Lizzie stepped into the alley, which dead-ended at a tall stockade fence. She expected to hear a moan, ragged breathing, a cry for help, but there was nothing. She glanced back at Fiona, who was holding herself together as she talked on her phone, and took another two steps. A car was parked along the fence. She walked around it, past a stack of empty flower pots. The sounds of Beacon Street traffic fell away, blocked by the two big houses.

She stopped abruptly, hearing flies. Placing a hand on the car's hood, cool in the shade, she leaned forward and saw a man was on the ground, slumped against the fence.

Even from a distance of a few yards, Lizzie could see he was dead.

Fiona, off the phone now, started into the alley. Lizzie shook her head at her. "Don't, Fiona. You don't need to see this."

But Fiona covered her mouth with her wrist and kept coming. Mindful that she was in what was now a crime scene, Lizzie edged closer to the dead man. She had to be sure she hadn't made a mistake and he was alive.

No mistake. He'd been shot—obviously—in the left temple. He was middle-aged and slightly overweight, dressed in dark chinos and a dark polo shirt, with a gash on his right forearm, as if someone had fingernail-clawed him.

Fiona gasped, "Is he—"

"He's dead, Fiona."

She dropped her wrist from her mouth. She'd stopped shaking, but her face was ashen. Her blue eyes were fixed on the dead man.

Lizzie felt her heart jump. "Fiona, do you know who this is?"

"No—I mean, I don't know his name. We never..." She motioned back toward Beacon Street. "I saw him on the street when I arrived at the Garrison house yesterday morning. He was walking across from the Common. I didn't talk to him."

"Was he alone?"

She nodded. "He said hi to me. He—" She squinted, as if digging deep to remember more. "He had a messenger bag with him. I remember thinking it looked heavy. It...he..."

"You couldn't have known what would happen," Lizzie said quietly.

"He must have had the bomb in the bag. I could have stopped him. If Owen hadn't been warned, he'd have—the bomb would have gone off." Fiona stopped suddenly, focusing on Lizzie. "I wasn't supposed to say that. About the bomb."

"It's okay," Lizzie said. "I already figured it out."

"The man...the Brit...he..."

Fiona broke off, turned and fled, tripping, gagging, back out to the street. Lizzie ran after her, slowing when she saw that Will Davenport had intercepted Fiona. He had an arm wrapped around her waist as she covered her mouth with both hands and cried.

"It's all right." He spoke firmly, but his tone was reassuring. "You're safe."

Fiona took a step back, and Will let her go. "The man who..." She was hyperventilating again. "He had an English accent. I think it was English. He said I..." She gulped in a breath and mumbled, "My dad will be here any second."

Lizzie understood Fiona's fear and tried to reassure her. "This is Will Davenport. He and Simon Cahill are friends."

"I'm sorry I frightened you," Will said gently.

"There's a man dead in the alley," Lizzie told him. She heard sirens. The police would be there soon. "The Brit I ran into in Las Vegas and Eddie O'Shea ran into at his pub is in Boston. He told Fiona to come here. He knew I was headed back from Ireland." Lizzie gave Will a hard look. "Did you tell him?"

"No, Lizzie." He didn't look tired or even rumpled after his long flight, but his expression had taken on a studied control, a certain distance. "I told you this morning. For the past two years, I've believed Myles to be dead."

"Then you haven't been lying to me?"

"I have not."

"Who is he? Who is this Myles?"

"You've just seen for yourself." Will's eyes were flinty. "Myles Fletcher is a killer."

Fiona, listening to every word, cried out in shock but didn't move.

Lizzie glanced back toward the alley. "Yes. I did just see for myself. Are you going after him?"

Fiona gasped and grabbed Will's wrist. "No! You can't! He said—he said not to follow him. He said he's Abigail's only hope." She was close to hysteria. "Please."

"All right, then." Will gently extricated himself from her hold. "I won't go after him."

Lizzie's head was spinning, and she felt ragged from jetlag, adrenaline, fear, being cooped up on a plane for hours with nothing to do but play cards and think. She turned to Will. "Now that Myles Fletcher has surfaced, I imagine you and your MI6 and SAS friends will want to figure out what he's up to."

Will ignored her and addressed Fiona. "How long ago did you see this man?"

"A few minutes. Ten, fifteen. Please, you can't..."

"I'll do as you ask and not go after him. We'll wait here together for your father."

"He called me 'love,'" Fiona whispered.

Will's eyes shut briefly, but Lizzie saw the pain in them. She was touched by his gentleness with Fiona but knew what she had to do. "I haven't witnessed anything." She looked once again down the alley, as if part of her expected the dead man to walk out and say it was all a joke, a bit of makeup and sheer nerve. But she knew it wasn't. "I'm no good to anyone if I'm stuck here explaining myself to the police."

Will didn't respond immediately. Lizzie gave him a moment. Finally he said, "You work for John March."

She skimmed the back of her hand along his jaw, rough with stubble. Sexy. A reminder he wasn't a Prince Charming out of a fairy tale. "Find me," she said, her voice hoarse, then shifted her attention to Fiona. "I have to go. You're safe with Will."

The sirens blared closer now. Lizzie bolted up the side street. Will didn't follow her. She cut down pretty residential Chestnut Street, running past classic Beacon Hill homes with their black iron fences, brass-fitted doors and wreaths of summer flowers. She came to Charles Street at the bottom of Chestnut, and fighting tears of her own, ducked into the Whitcomb. Without saying a word, she headed straight through the lobby past Jeremiah and down a half-dozen steps to the rear exit.

Her cousin reached her before she could get the back door open. With Whit and Harlan Rush as older brothers, Jeremiah had learned to stay cool in a crisis. "Lizzie, what's going on?"

She knew she had to give him the basic facts. She owed him that much. "Fiona and I just found a man shot to death up by the Garrison house. The Brit who was with her earlier told her where to find him."

"What can I do?"

"The police will be here any minute. I have to go, Jeremiah. I can't stay." She raked a hand through her hair as she consid-

ered her options. "You can find me a car. I can't take mine—
or yours. The police…" She didn't finish.

"Take Martha's. Martha Prescott. She's Mum's new assistant." He unlocked a drawer to a small cupboard, pulled a set
of keys from a series of hooks and handed them to Lizzie without hesitation. "Gray Honda on Mount Vernon. The only free
space will be the driver's seat." He smiled through his obvious
worry. "Martha's a slob."

Lizzie started to thank him, but he just shoved her out the door
into the narrow alley behind the hotel. The Rushes might not
get everything right, she thought, but they could be counted on
in a pinch.

She ran between parked cars and a Dumpster out to Mount
Vernon Street, finding the gray Honda halfway up to Louisburg
Square. It had a Beacon Hill resident's sticker in the back wind-
shield, and every available space beyond the driver's seat was
loaded with fabric samples, empty soda cans, CDs, paperbacks,
magazines, torn envelopes. Martha Prescott, indeed, was a slob,
but apparently also incredibly creative and good at her job. Anyone who worked for Henrietta Rush would have to be.

The car had a full tank of gas, and Lizzie was quickly on her way.

As she pulled onto Storrow Drive, her cell phone rang. She
checked the screen, recognized her father's Las Vegas number and
almost didn't answer. "Don't distract me," she said as cheerfully
as she could manage. "I'm in traffic."

"Dublin?"

"Boston. Storrow Drive."

Her father sighed. "I just got off the phone with a Boston detective named Yarborough. A real s.o.b. He's threatening to fly
out here. Lizzie, tell me what's going on?"

"It's complicated."

"So? I'm playing solitaire. Clock. Ever play clock? My eyes are bleeding it's so boring. I've got time. Take me through it. Start to finish."

"There is no finish. Not yet."

"All right. Start to where we are now."

"The two Brits. Will Davenport and the one I asked you about who was in Las Vegas in June—I think they're both from your world."

"What world would that be?"

"Dad, I can't...I have a name for the one we saw in Vegas. Myles Fletcher."

"I'll see what I can do."

She hesitated. "John March is in town."

Her father sighed again. "Terrific. Have you seen him?"

"No. I'm trying to get out of here." She squeezed into the left lane, heading for I-93 North. "Dad, I just found a dead man."

"Damn, Lizzie."

"I think he planted at least one bomb yesterday." Was it only yesterday? "John March's daughter is missing." She slowed in the crush of traffic. "Dad, I can help."

"Lizzie. Oh, Lizzie."

"Norman's obsessed with March. I didn't see it at first. I only saw it in the last days before his arrest."

"Lizzie."

"I know March investigated my mother's death." She fought back more tears. "I haven't wanted to tell you. I understand how painful—"

Her father cut her off. "Does Estabrook know about March and your mother?"

"He never said so, but—yes." She eased onto the interstate, speeding up as she escaped the twists and turns of Storrow Drive.

"I'm sure he knows. I didn't realize it at the time, but I think that's why he made the call threatening Simon and Director March in front of me. He assumes I hate March."

"So will the cops. Once they put the pieces together, you'll look as obsessed with John March as this bastard Estabrook is."

"That's why I'm not sticking around."

Silence. "That's not why."

Lizzie pictured her handsome father moving a card to the six o'clock position, a glass of Scotch at his side. He never drank Irish whiskey.

"You're in deep, Lizzie," he said. "You have been all along, haven't you?"

She didn't answer.

Another sigh. "I'm heading to Boston as soon as I finish my game of clock. I'll run interference with the feds. I'll stay as long as you need me."

"You hate Boston."

"Not as much as I hate Ireland."

She managed a smile. "Thanks, Dad."

But he was serious. "You're hoping Estabrook comes after you, aren't you?"

"If I knew what he was going to do, where he was, I'd tell the FBI."

"You're an amateur, Lizzie."

"So is Norman. He'll use Abigail Browning to get what he wants. Then he'll throw her away."

"I could call Detective Yarborough and have him stop you."

"You won't."

"No." Her father didn't speak for a moment. "I have a picture of my mother as a little girl playing dress-up in the drawing room at the hotel in Boston. She has on an Edwardian gown she found in the attic. She's standing on a chair, giggling in front of a mirror. Imagine your grandmother giggling."

"Dad…"

"She did her best, Lizzie. We all did."

"You did great. All of you. I miss Gran, too." Lizzie tried to concentrate on her driving. "If you don't get cold feet and actually do head out here, I should warn you that cousin Jeremiah has put his wild youth behind him. He's a tough taskmaster these days. He'll throw you out if you don't behave."

Her father laughed. "Sounds like a challenge."

She sobbed out loud when she hung up, but her hand was steady as she dialed the number John March had given her over a year ago.

He answered immediately. "Where are you?"

"My name's Lizzie," she said, her voice cracking as she finally told him the truth. "Lizzie Rush. But you know that now, don't you?"

"You misled me. I thought you were a professional."

"Was I even on your list of suspects?"

"No."

"You could have hesitated," she said, making an attempt at levity.

"I want you to come in. Now. Help us." He took in a breath. "Lizzie, let me help you."

"I was with Norman in June when he called Simon and threatened to kill the two of you. I knew he meant it. I knew he would turn violent." The late afternoon sun beat down hard on the busy road. "I should have found a way to stop him. He has your daughter because I didn't."

"You work for a chain of luxury boutique hotels. It's not your job—"

"Don't ever let my aunt and uncle hear you call our hotels a chain."

"Lizzie. Stop. Come in."

She stayed in the middle lane of I-93. "Did you try to stop my mother? She was your informant, too, wasn't she?"

"You're operating on assumptions and suppositions." His tone was more mystified and worried than harsh. "You've done your part. More than you should have. Your efforts helped us arrest major, dangerous drug traffickers."

"Norman's free."

"Not because of you. Stand down."

"Thirty years ago, you let my mother go to her death, didn't you? You regret it now."

"I regretted it then."

"Did you warn her of the danger she was in? Did she ignore you? Did you ignore—" Lizzie took a breath, gripping the steering wheel of her borrowed car. "Never mind."

"You are not to endanger yourself. You are not to interfere with this investigation. I'll sit down with you when this is over and answer every question you have about your mother." March paused, then added, "Every question I can answer."

Lizzie knew what she had to do. She'd figured out on the flight from Dublin, before Fiona and Myles Fletcher and the dead man in the alley—before Will had turned up.

Her eyes were dry now. "I'd love to sit down with you and talk about my mother. Until then, Director March, the rules are the same. Norman can't know I've been helping you. He can't know I'm not on his side. He won't just kill me if he finds out what I've done. He'll kill your daughter."

"This isn't your fight," March said.

"It is now. Keep your guys and the BPD off my case."

"Let me help you, Lizzie. Not the FBI. Me. Abigail's father."

His anguish brought fresh tears to her eyes. "You know that

won't work. I'm not doing anything crazy. I'm just going about my business the same way I have for the past year."

"I was your age when your mother died. Looking back, I know now how young I was. How young she was. And your father."

"Then she didn't trip on a wet cobblestone, did she?"

"I've made mistakes. Don't become one of them."

"There's one thing you can do for me. If Norman finds out what I've done and comes after my family—"

"We'll protect them, Lizzie. You have my word."

"You know you don't need to protect my father, don't you?"

March didn't answer.

"He's mad right now as it is. If he sees a bunch of FBI agents coming at him—" Lizzie didn't finish her thought. "He's not retired. He just pretends to be. He's the reason I was able to lead you to believe I was a professional."

"We can protect you, too."

"I hope you find your daughter. More than anything."

"Thank you," he said, his voice strangled now. "Lizzie—"

But she hung up on the director of the FBI, moved to the far right-hand lane and tossed her cell phone out the window. It was an inconvenience, but she didn't want the feds, the BPD or a bunch of spies pinging the number and finding her.

# Chapter 21

*Boston, Massachusetts*
*6:02 p.m., EDT*
*August 26*

Will kept his emotions in check, as much for his own sake as Fiona O'Reilly's, but there was no longer any question. Myles Fletcher was alive. Near. In Boston. Perhaps watching the police arrive at the murder scene.

Will had asked Fiona to repeat everything Myles had said to her. "It's important," he'd told her. "I can help in a way the police can't."

Fiona had complied. She was calmer now, hugging her arms to her chest as police cruisers descended on Beacon Street. "Your friend killed the man in the alley, didn't he?"

"Your father and his detectives will determine who is responsible. What you must do now is to be sure you've told me all you know."

She stared down at the pavement as if looking for ants.

Will knew he couldn't let her off the hook. "You've had a terrible scare, Fiona. It's understandable you don't want to do anything to distract investigators and send them in the wrong direction."

"Abigail's missing. Every minute…" She squinted up at him. "Every *second* counts."

On his cab ride into Boston from the airport, Will had called both Simon and Josie for updates, but there was still no sign of Abigail Browning, Norman Estabrook or his plane. He couldn't give Fiona false comfort. She was the daughter of an experienced detective and would see right through it.

"Good detectives prefer to have as much information as possible," he said. "They want to rely on their own experience and training to decide what's worthwhile and what isn't."

"I know," Fiona said, not combative, just stating the facts. As traumatized as she was, Will could see a similar inner strength he had observed in her cousin, Keira.

"What are you holding back?"

"Abigail…" Fiona curled her fingers into tight fists. "She stopped by the pub at the Whitcomb Hotel the night before last. Morrigan's. My friends and I were performing. We were wrapping up our final set. I could see she was uptight about something. She pulled me aside after we finished and told me it wasn't a good idea for me to be there."

"At the hotel?"

Fiona nodded. "She said she'd explain later but I should just…" The teenager sucked in a breath, fighting her own emotions. "She said I should trust her."

"What did you say to her?"

"Nothing. I didn't argue with her. I ignored her. I thought

she didn't want me there because Morrigan's is a bar and I'm under twenty-one and a cop's daughter. When I saw her—" Fiona again stared down at the pavement. "I avoided her yesterday. Before the bomb went off. I was snotty. I didn't want to talk to her. Now…"

"You feel guilty," Will said.

Tears spilled down her cheeks, and she sobbed silently as two police cruisers screeched to a halt at the alley, followed immediately by an unmarked police car. A redheaded man who had to be Fiona's father leaped out and trotted straight for her.

"Dad," Fiona whispered, using both hands now to wipe her tears.

A stiff, serious younger man got out from behind the wheel, joined uniformed officers and headed into the alley.

Bob O'Reilly was apoplectic when he reached his daughter. "I thought you played the damn harp so you wouldn't get yourself mixed up in a murder investigation." He sighed, his blue eyes— the same shade as Fiona's, as Keira's—filled with fear and guilt. "Fi…hell. You okay?"

She brushed her tears with the back of her wrist and nodded.

O'Reilly turned to Will. "Lord Davenport, I presume."

"Yes, Lieutenant. I'm sorry we're meeting under such difficult circumstances."

"Yeah, so am I. Simon's on his way." O'Reilly shifted back to his daughter. "Tell me what happened."

Fiona repeated her story. Will listened for additional details but heard nothing that made him doubt it was Myles who'd sat across from a nineteen-year-old musician and told her how to find a man he knew to be dead, presumably whom he'd killed himself. Possibly he was in fact Abigail Browning's only hope, but that didn't mean he was on her side.

Will let the questions come at him. Why was Myles Fletcher

involved with Norman Estabrook? Had the man Will had once
trusted and considered a friend become a cutthroat mercenary?
Was Myles now on no one's side but his own?

Had he never been on anyone's side but his own?

When Fiona finished, Bob O'Reilly had the look of the
veteran detective he was. "Where's Lizzie Rush now?"

"She left." Fiona gave Will a sideways glance before turning
back to her father. "She stayed cool. The whole time, Dad. She
tried to keep me from seeing…the man."

"She a friend of yours?"

"I only…no."

He narrowed his eyes on his daughter. "What were you doing
at the Whitcomb Hotel, Fi?"

"My ensemble performs there. I didn't tell you—" A touch
of combativeness sparked in her blue eyes. "I knew you
wouldn't approve."

"I don't," her father said bluntly. He nodded to the unmarked
car. "Go sit in the air-conditioning. Get off your feet."

"Dad—"

"Go on, kid." He touched a thumb to a stray tear on her cheek.
"I'll be right here. I'm not going anywhere."

"That man…the one who was killed…"

"We'll figure out what happened to him. Go." O'Reilly struggled for a smile. "See if you can find some harp music on the
radio."

Will noticed her reluctance as she headed for the unmarked
car, but he decided it had more to do with her desire not to miss
anything than to remain with her father.

O'Reilly took a pack of gum from his pocket and tapped out a
piece. He unwrapped it, balled up the paper in one hand and shoved
it into his pocket with the rest of the pack. A ritual, Will realized.

The detective chewed the gum as he studied Will. "You know this guy, our killer Brit?"

"I didn't see him, Lieutenant O'Reilly."

"That's not what I asked."

Will said nothing. He wasn't in a position to explain his history with Myles Fletcher to this American detective. At the same time, Will didn't want to do anything that would impede the investigation into the murder in the alley and any connection the dead man or Myles had to Abigail Browning's disappearance.

"Here's the thing," O'Reilly said. "After thirty years as a cop, I often know when someone's lying or not telling me everything—unless it's one of my daughters. Want me to ask again?"

Will shook his head. "There's no need. Your daughter described a man I thought I knew."

"But now that he's put a bullet in some guy's brain, you're thinking maybe you didn't know him after all. His name?"

Will looked back at the car where Fiona sat alone in the back seat, the door still open. "Myles Fletcher."

"Who is he?"

"I told you—"

"No, you didn't. What's he do for a living? Is he a British noble? Does he go fishing a lot in Scotland? Does he know Simon Cahill?" O'Reilly worked hard on his gum. "I can rattle off a dozen other questions if you want or you can just tell me."

Will thought of Lizzie going into the alley on her own and finding a man shot to death by someone he should have dealt with himself two years ago.

He knew now what he had to do. "My assistant, Josie Goodwin, can help you." He kept his tone professional, without emotion. "Simon knows how to reach her. She'll be more precise and thorough than I can be."

"She in London?"

Will met the detective's eye. "Ireland. With your niece."

"Great," O'Reilly said sarcastically. "Just great. Did this Fletcher character send that thug after Keira?"

"I don't know."

"Another nonanswer. Does Fletcher know Abigail Browning, John March or Simon Cahill?"

"Lieutenant…"

"Norman Estabrook?"

"If you'll allow me, Lieutenant O'Reilly, I suggest you speak with Director March."

"All right. I'll do that." The detective's tone was cool, suspicious—and careful. As if he knew he didn't want to go too far and end up having his hands tied. "What do you know about the black-haired woman who helped my niece in the wilds of Ireland last night?"

He waited, but Will didn't fill the silence. He had anticipated that Boston law enforcement would have Lizzie's description by now. Undoubtedly, she had, too.

"I talked to Eddie O'Shea," O'Reilly continued. "He described her. American. Small, fast, black hair, green eyes. Knows how to fight—she took on an armed killer. The Irish cops are trying to find out who she is, where she went."

"Again—"

"Talk to March. Talk to anyone but you." O'Reilly pointed a thick finger at Will. "Eddie says you were there, and you let this woman go."

"Your niece is safe, Lieutenant, thanks to her."

"And a big black dog and no doubt fairies, too. I'm glad for that."

Fiona slipped out of the car and stood by the open door.

Her father didn't stop. "I saw Scoop Wisdom in the hospital.

He's all cut up. A mess. He managed to describe a suspicious woman he saw on our street the day before our house blew up. Small, green eyes, black hair. Even with all the pain dope in him, Scoop remembered her. Who is she?"

Will maintained a steady gaze on the senior law enforcement officer. "Again, you'll want to speak with Director March."

Before O'Reilly could respond, Fiona approached him. "Dad." She remained calm, but she was very pale. "Dad...I..."

Her father stared at her. "You know?"

"The woman—she—"

The detective groaned half to himself. "Ah, hell. Are we talking about Lizzie Rush? The woman who just helped you—"

"Her family owns the hotel on Charles Street."

"The Whitcomb. Yeah, I know. Why—"

"I told you, my ensemble plays there. We've been playing there all summer. The Rushes are nice people."

"The Rushes are..." O'Reilly glared at his daughter. "How well do you know them?"

Fiona looked miserable. "I didn't meet Lizzie until a few weeks ago. Her cousin Jeremiah has been helping me plan our trip to Ireland. He said Lizzie had worked there. Dad, I know she's not responsible for the bombs. She can't be."

"What did you two talk about besides Ireland?"

"I told her everything. I told her about Keira and Simon, and you and Aunt Eileen and the serial killer, and Ireland—the story about the stone angel. I told her that Keira and Simon borrowed a boat from Simon's friend, a British lord, and...Dad, I'm sorry."

O'Reilly looked as if he couldn't decide between hitting something or grabbing his daughter and running. "Relax, Fi." His tone softened as he unwrapped another piece of gum. "You didn't tell Lizzie Rush anything she couldn't have found out on her own."

"I feel like a blabber."

"Lizzie's easy to talk to," Will said quietly. More police cars descended on the scene. Yellow tape was going up. Onlookers were arriving. He knew he had to make his stand now. "I can find her, Detective, but not if I'm caught up with your people."

Bob O'Reilly was clearly a man under monumental strain, but he remained focused. "This Fletcher character?"

"I can find him, as well."

"Does Simon go way back with him?"

"No, he doesn't. Lieutenant, you know if I don't leave now, I won't be able to without a lot of time and fuss."

The detective put the fresh piece of gum in his mouth. "Go."

The Whitcomb was smaller, narrower and more traditionally furnished than the Rush hotel in Dublin, but equally high-end and individual. A man who bore a striking resemblance to Justin Rush walked into the lobby from a side door. This would be Jeremiah, Will remembered. The third-born of the four Rush brothers and Lizzie's cousin.

"Lord Davenport, right?" Jeremiah nodded to a door behind him. "Through there. Down the steps. Out back."

"Thank you," Will said.

He followed Jeremiah's instructions and found himself in an alley with broken pavement, parked cars and Simon Cahill standing in front of a large Dumpster. Unlike his fellow FBI agents who'd begun to arrive farther up Beacon Street as Will had left, Simon wore jeans and a polo shirt.

Will descended the steps. "I wondered if you might find your way here. Has Lizzie—"

"She took off before I got here. Abigail's partner called me. Tom Yarborough. You'll meet him—he'll see to it."

"He's the detective who was with Lieutenant O'Reilly just now?"

Simon gave a curt nod. "He said you let Lizzie go."

"I did," Will admitted.

"Yarborough's ready to take her, you and me into custody. Her father, too."

"Is the tension getting to him?"

"Not a chance. He's just that way." Simon's expression was more that of an FBI agent than a friend as he eyed Will. "Myles Fletcher is alive?"

"Apparently so. He killed that man in the alley and arranged for Fiona O'Reilly to find him. I've been trying to think how he could have become involved with Estabrook."

"He could have figured out you and I were friends, discovered I was working for Estabrook and watched and waited for his chance."

"His chance for what? Money? Action? To get back at us, perhaps? Me for damaging his relationship with his friends in Afghanistan. You for saving my life."

"I could believe money and action," Simon said. "Not revenge. The Myles Fletcher you described to me is too pragmatic to indulge in revenge."

Will felt the humid heat of the afternoon and smelled asphalt, gasoline fumes and, faintly, garbage. As immaculate as the Whitcomb was, he and Simon were nevertheless in an alley. Will shut his eyes, launching himself back two years. He saw Philip and David fighting for their lives. For his life. For the life of the man who'd betrayed them.

And yet…none of what had happened had ever made sense

to him. Will had fought alongside Myles Fletcher. They'd trained together, gone drinking together. They'd tracked enemy fighters together, disrupted ambushes, cleaned out caches of weapons, called in close-air support—whatever their various missions had required.

"Will…"

He opened his eyes, focusing again on Simon. "You're right. Myles is too much a professional to take the risks he did today purely for revenge. He's doing a job."

Simon walked toward the hotel. There were terra cotta pots of red geraniums on each step up to the back door. "The Lizzie Rush I know is elegant, personable, attractive and smart, but she's not anyone I'd remotely imagine taking on a knife-wielding thug." He turned to Will. "Or you. She's under your skin, isn't she?"

He sidestepped the question. "How did you see her role with Estabrook?"

"They were friendly, not in a romantic way. She wasn't involved in his riskier adventures. She'd organize a hike in the Grand Canyon, a whale-watching trip, a kayaking tour of the Maine coast—the normal stuff people want to do."

"And all the while, she was gathering information on Estabrook and his friends and passing it on to John March."

Simon leaned over and straightened one of the flowerpots. "I knew we had an anonymous source. An important one. But Lizzie…" He shook his head. "She never was on my radar."

Will stared at the geraniums. How had he let his life become so complicated? He could see his mother walking in his garden in Scotland, not far from her home village. She'd never imagined herself marrying his father. What had Lizzie thought as a little girl, playing out here in this alley? Had she ever imagined finding a man murdered up the street?

"Lizzie's father is an intelligence officer who taught her his tradecraft," Will said. "She knew how to keep you and Director March from discovering her identity. When did you first meet her?"

"Last summer, here at the Whitcomb. That's when Norman hired me. I was in Boston for a Fast Rescue dinner, and he was a guest at the hotel. He and Lizzie were already friends."

"With your search-and-rescue expertise, you were in the perfect position to go undercover." Will toed a bit of broken asphalt. "As we've seen in the past two days, Lizzie is brazen and resourceful. Does she know March?"

Simon looked uncomfortable.

"This isn't about my own history with Director March," Will said. "I'm trying to ascertain the facts. When did you become aware March had a source?"

"Last summer. We didn't want to endanger whoever it was by getting too close. We both assumed we were dealing with a professional. Of the possibilities—Lizzie Rush wasn't even on the list."

"*Could* she be affiliated with an intelligence agency?"

Simon sighed. "I think she is exactly what she appears to be."

"She's playing with fire," Will said. "But she could also be the one who can lead us to March's daughter."

"I'd trade myself for Abigail in a heartbeat." Simon's guilt was palpable as he continued. "So would her father. She got caught in the middle. This isn't her fight."

"Why kidnap her but try to kill Keira?"

"Norman's making us suffer. That's all I know. We have to find him, Will. His plane didn't evaporate into thin air. Owen Garrison will find it." Simon plucked a dried, brown leaf from a geranium and smiled sadly as he looked at Will. "Scoop's influence."

"Simon...I'm sorry. But you must understand. You are not responsible for Norman Estabrook's actions."

"Could we have this wrong, Will? What if Fletcher is working for the drug cartels and not for Norman?"

"Regardless who is paying him, Myles is working for himself."

Simon crumpled up the dead leaf. "According to Tom Yarborough, the dead man Lizzie and Fiona found had a deep scratch on one arm. We know Abigail got a piece of whoever kidnapped her yesterday. There was blood at the scene. If he was the one who grabbed her and Fletcher killed him—"

"Fiona had seen him. She'd have remembered eventually. It's not the sort of risk Myles would take. He could simply have handled a problem and tried to mislead us at the same time."

"So he shot a man in the head for a reason instead of just because he could?"

"Fair enough, Simon. Nonetheless, I doubt Myles would get in the middle of a scheme for violent revenge, even a well-paying one. If he's working for Estabrook, there's likely another reason." Will regretted he hadn't arrived in Boston in time to deal with Myles himself, but hadn't that been his old friend's plan? Myles had known Lizzie had left Dublin that morning—and undoubtedly knew that Will had, too. He pushed back his fatigue and worry, forcing himself to continue. "Simon, Myles and Estabrook can't discover Lizzie is an FBI informant."

"I know. If they do, she goes onto Norman's hit list right up there with March and me."

Will pictured Lizzie sitting across from him at their lace-covered table in Dublin. He could see the intensity and the light green color of her eyes, the shape of her mouth as she'd tried to put her fight in the stone circle behind her and decide what to do about him.

He'd checked on her during the night, her duvet half off, her skirt and T-shirt askew as she'd slept on the sofa.

"Will? I'm losing you again."

He heard the concern in his friend's voice. "I need to leave now, Simon. I trust you, and I trust Josie. I'll keep an open mind when it comes to everyone else."

"Right, Will," Simon said, skeptical, but he managed a quick smile. "You've always wanted a woman who could put a knife to your throat."

The back door to the hotel opened, and Jeremiah Rush jumped down the half-dozen steps in a single bound. "Two detectives are here to interview the staff and anyone who might have seen the Brit who scared the hell out of Fiona O'Reilly. I thought you'd want to know. My dad's on his way. He's not wild about a killer showing up here."

Simon eyed the younger Rush. "Do you know where your cousin went?"

"Lizzie?" Jeremiah instantly looked uncomfortable.

"That would be the one, yes."

"She's like a sister to my brothers and me. Her father's a great guy, but he was on the road so much..." Jeremiah shoved a hand through his tawny hair and gave a quick laugh, obviously trying to divert the FBI agent in front of him. "We all think he's a spy."

Will almost smiled. "So your brother Justin said this morning in Dublin."

Jeremiah's hand fell to the back of his neck, then his side, as if he was feeling cornered, torn by what he knew and what he feared. "You two..." He motioned first to Will, then to Simon. "Lord Davenport, Special Agent Cahill. How do I know I can trust you?"

"We're not a danger to your cousin," Will said.

"The people you hang out with are."

"What about the people she hangs out with?" Simon asked sharply.

A ferocity came into Jeremiah's eyes, one that Will had seen in his cousin. "I hope Norman Estabrook ends up dead or in a holding cell by nightfall."

Simon didn't react to Jeremiah's emotion. "Your family has resources, contacts. Are you looking for Estabrook yourselves? What about your uncle? What's he up to?"

"Uncle Harlan? I have no idea. We all want to do whatever we can to help." Jeremiah was clearly worried—and angry. "I thought Lizzie had hooked up with a rich eccentric and was having a little fun for herself. Estabrook held a New Year's Eve bash for his friends at our hotel in Las Vegas. Lizzie didn't want me to go, but we were having our own family party and I dropped in on him and his friends."

"I remember," Simon said.

Jeremiah fastened his gaze on the FBI agent. "I should have thrown him off the roof that night. Uncle Harlan would have helped me make it look like an accident."

Simon's brow went up, obviously as uncertain as Will whether Jeremiah Rush was serious. The entire Rush family defied stereotype, and not one of them was to be underestimated.

Will didn't want to come under the scrutiny of the Boston detectives now on-site. They might not be as amenable to letting him go about his business as Bob O'Reilly had been. They could easily conclude the lieutenant had been under duress, considering his daughter had just encountered a killer and a murder victim, and wasn't thinking straight. Even with Simon, an FBI agent, at his side, Will could find himself with a long night of explaining ahead.

He turned again to Jeremiah. "Justin mentioned that Lizzie

intends to renovate your family home in Maine. Is she headed there now?"

Jeremiah hesitated, and Simon said quietly, "We're on your cousin's side."

"Maybe so," Jeremiah said, "but that doesn't mean she won't throw *me* off the roof for telling you. I don't know for sure, but, yes, I think she's gone to Maine. She has her own place there. It's about as big as a butler's pantry, but she loves it." He dipped a hand into a trouser pocket and produced a set of keys. "Take my car." He nodded toward a side street at the end of the alley. "Go that way. You'll avoid the BPD."

Simon didn't argue or intervene as Will took the keys.

Jeremiah looked more worried, even afraid, than he likely would want to admit. "Lizzie's father trained her well. He gave the rest of us some pointers, but she had—I guess you'd call it an aptitude. She has a good sense of her limits. I hope she'll be safe in Maine. I hope this bastard Estabrook doesn't think she'll go along with him just because of her mother. I hope," he added, energized now, "she's not the key to finding him."

Simon plucked another dried geranium leaf and crunched it to bits between two big fingers. "What about her mother, Jeremiah?"

Jeremiah Rush obviously realized he was about to step into a bottomless pit, into dangerous layers of history, family, secrets, powerful men. Will could see Lizzie as she'd sipped brandy in Ireland and questioned the man who'd tried to kill Keira Sullivan. Lizzie had been born into this complicated world. She knew how to navigate it, just as Will knew how to navigate his world.

"From what I understand," Jeremiah said carefully, "Aunt Shauna was a daredevil with a keen sense of justice." He gave Simon a pointed look. "Just like Lizzie."

Simon studied the younger Rush a moment. His eyes were as

green as the Irish hills where the woman he loved was being protected. "Walk out to the street with Will and give him directions
to Lizzie's place in Maine. I'll see to the detectives." He turned to
Will. "Stay in touch."

Without waiting for a response or pressing for more information, Simon ascended the steps back into the hotel. Jeremiah did
as requested, and in ten minutes, Will was navigating a sleek, expensive sedan and the impossible Boston traffic as he found his
way north to Maine.

And, he hoped, to Lizzie.

# Chapter 22

*Boston, Massachusetts*
*7:15 p.m., EDT*
*August 26*

Fiona looked gaunt and stressed but also relieved to be back in her element. Bob watched as she and her friends set up in the bar of the Rush-owned boutique hotel on Charles Street. As far as he could tell, "boutique" meant small and expensive. He'd teased his daughter that he thought it meant a place that sold cute clothes, but she wasn't ready to be teased. Play music, yes. Music had been her escape as well as her passion since she'd first crawled up onto a piano stool as a tot.

Bob had peeled himself away from the crime scene up on Beacon, but it was in good hands. He needed to be here, nursing a glass of water at this same table where a killer had sat across from his daughter. Lucas Jones and Tom Yarborough had questioned Fiona thoroughly. Afterward, Lucas had told Bob, "I should have asked her when she'd last talked to Abigail," and Yarborough had told him, "She should have told us about seeing Abigail," which summed up the differences between the two detectives. Bob had felt their suspicion drift over him like a living thing. Yarborough had even said out loud that he thought Bob was holding back on them.

Which he was. He'd kept most of his chat with Lord Davenport to himself. While not a rule-breaker by nature or conviction, Bob had learned to rely on his instincts when it came to bending the rules to get things done. Right now, they had a mess on their hands, with no trace of Abigail or word—a single crumb of hope—from her kidnappers.

He had to stop himself from picturing her and Owen in their small backyard, teasing Scoop about his garden and compost pile. For seven years, Abigail had focused on her work and finding her husband's killer, living her life, a part of it always on hold. Then last summer, she and Owen fell for each other. They had some things to work out—houses, families, kids, careers—but they were the real thing, good together.

Now this.

Fiona's friends were all as young as she was, nervous about the murder and the fire but determined to play, to be there for her. "Can you guys sing 'Johnny, I Hardly Knew You'?" Bob called to them. "I used to sing that one as a kid."

"Sing it with us, Dad," Fiona said, her cheeks pinker now, even if only from the exertion of setting up.

Fiona had been after him to sing with her band since she'd discovered he had an okay voice. He hadn't hid it from her. He just wasn't that much for singing. He let them get through a few numbers on their own, then got up and sang with them. The upscale crowd seemed to enjoy themselves, like he was authentic or something—the Boston Irish cop singing an Irish tune.

When the band took a break, Fiona eased back toward him. "I'm sorry for all this, Dad."

"I'm putting a detail on you. Deal with it."

She nodded, not meek or acquiescent. Accepting. As if she knew he was making sense.

Relieved, Bob checked out one of the brochures she'd left on the table when she'd made her mad dash up Beacon Street, after her visit from Myles Fletcher. He hoped by their December trip things would be quieter in their lives, back to normal. They'd been magnets for trouble lately. Theresa was right, he thought. When Fiona was six, he'd had more control. His sister had told him he had to let his daughters grow up. Like he had any choice?

He noticed the brochure was of the Rush hotel in Dublin. "My grandmother used to make these little mince pies at Christmas. Melt in your mouth." He smiled at his daughter, probably his first real smile since the bomb had gone off yesterday afternoon. "Maybe they'll serve them at tea in Dublin."

"The Rush hotel there serves a Christmas Eve tea," Fiona said eagerly.

Great, he thought.

"It's within walking distance of Brown Thomas."

"What's that?"

"An upscale department store on Grafton Street."

"You've been memorizing maps of Dublin?"

She blushed. "You only live once, Dad."

He admired her resiliency but knew she had to process the ordeal of the past two days. And it wasn't over. They didn't have Abigail. Scoop was in shreds in the hospital but would be okay.

Keira was under police protection in Ireland. March's wife in D.C. Bob's own family here in Boston.

The bad guys were unidentified and at large.

"Have you identified the man who…" Fiona lost the color that had started back in her cheeks.

Bob understood what she was asking. "We're still working on a name."

"I saw the scratch on his arm, Dad. He helped kidnap Abigail, didn't he?" Fiona flinched as if she'd been struck. "Sorry. Lucas and Detective Yarborough said I shouldn't say that out loud."

"It's okay, kid."

"What if he left her tied up somewhere?"

"He didn't work alone. Almost certainly."

"I'm sorry I didn't say anything about seeing her here."

"Abigail didn't say anything, either, Fi. Whatever she was worried about, she probably didn't think it was that big a deal—nothing to make someone set a bomb on her porch."

But had Abigail come here specifically to tell his daughter to back off playing at the hotel?

If so, why?

He had about a million questions whose answers he suspected involved Lizzie Rush. She'd come to Jamaica Plain the afternoon before Abigail's evening visit here to the Whitcomb and Morrigan's. The next day, Lizzie Rush and Keira had called from Ireland about the bomb.

"If the man who was killed helped kidnap Abigail," Fiona said thoughtfully, dropping into a chair opposite Bob, "why did the Brit kill him? If he's a bad guy, too?"

"We can sit here and tick off all the possibilities. They had a spat. The Brit decided the other guy was reckless. The Brit got greedy and wanted the other guy's cut of whatever they're getting paid."

"Or he *didn't* kill him."

"My point is, we don't know. That's why we keep plugging away at the facts and evidence."

"Simon's friend Will must—"

"Do you know 'Whiskey in the Jar?'"

Fiona rolled her eyes in a way—not a bad way—that reminded him of her mother. "Of course, Dad. You've heard me play it a hundred times."

"I've never sung it with you."

But she wasn't giving up. "The Brit—Fletcher—could have killed that man in self-defense, couldn't he?"

"Yes. Whatever happened, Fi, you didn't cause it."

"I'm in the middle of it."

"That's ending now."

For once, she didn't argue. "How's Keira?"

"I only talked to her a few minutes before you called me. She's no happier about being under police protection than you are. She knows it has to be done. Simon has to concentrate on doing his job."

"Scoop...it was hard to see him this morning."

"You were brave to go to the hospital on your own like that. He's doing better. He'll make it." Bob tried to soften his voice, but heart-to-heart talks with his daughter—with anyone—made him squirm. "Fi, Scoop's a good guy. The best. But he's a lot older than you. In another five years, maybe it won't seem like so much, but right now—you should stick with guys closer to your own age. These losers here. The fiddle player. He's not bad, right?"

She made a face. "Dad, Scoop's just a friend."

"Yeah? What about the fiddle player?"

"Him, too. Besides, Scoop's got a thing for Keira."

"You see too much. Play your music."

She returned to her friends on the small stage and picked up her harp. They had a half-dozen different instruments among the three of them and would switch off depending on the number. They all could sing.

Bob walked up to the lobby to Lizzie Rush's cousin Jeremiah at the reception desk. Tom Yarborough and Lucas Jones had already interviewed him and said he was smart, clever and creative. Too creative, Yarborough had said, convinced the kid knew more than he was admitting. He wasn't lying, just parsing his answers—which Yarborough always took as a challenge.

"Talk to me about Abigail Browning," Bob said to the young Rush.

He scooped a few envelopes to stack. "She was here last week and again two nights ago."

"She? Not they?"

"Correct. She was alone both times."

"Irish music night?"

"Every night is Irish music night, but her first visit was in the afternoon. She had tea."

"Formal tea or like a tea bag hanging out of a cup?"

"Something in between."

"What about your cousin?"

"My cousin?"

Playing dumb. "Lizzie. The one who just found a dead guy up the street."

Jeremiah maintained his composure. "She's often in Boston. Our hotel offices are here."

"Right. So how much has she been in town since June?"

"On and off. Not so much in July. Almost constantly in August. She was working with our concierge services on new excursions. That's her area of expertise. But she spent time on her own."

"Spying on Abigail?"

He paled a little and gave up on his stack of envelopes. "I didn't say that."

"Okay, so back to Abigail. How did you recognize her?"

"Garrisons have stayed here. They book rooms at the hotel for their annual meeting and various functions for the Dorothy Garrison Foundation and Fast Rescue. Abigail's been here for those, but she's also John March's daughter." Jeremiah stopped himself, as if he knew he'd gone too far.

Bob tilted his head back. There was something about the way Jeremiah had said March's name. "You know Director March?"

"Not me. Not personally."

"But you've seen him," Bob said, getting now what Yarborough meant about dealing with Jeremiah Rush. If all the Rushes were like him, Yarborough would go crazy. "When?"

"He comes here once a year. It's a long-standing tradition."

"What, he got married at the Whitcomb or something? He and his wife have their anniversary dinner here every year?"

"No." The kid looked as if he wished he'd kept his mouth shut. "He has a drink at Morrigan's."

"He comes alone?"

"Yes, always."

"When?"

"Late August, so around now."

"Whoa. How long has this been going on?"

Jeremiah glanced at his desk. "I should get back to work. Reporters have been calling—"

"They'll keep calling, don't worry. So, how long?"

"I shouldn't have said anything."

"Well, you did. How long, Mr. Rush?"

The kid licked his lips. "At least thirty years. Since before I was born."

Thirty years ago, March was a BPD detective, and Bob was a twenty-year-old kid in South Boston, the son of a cop who wanted nothing more than to be a homicide detective. "What's this tradition about?"

"I don't know for a fact, but whatever it's about, it's always struck me as a private matter."

"Something to do with Lizzie or her dad?"

Jeremiah rubbed a smudge on his desk.

"You have an idea," Bob said, no intention of backing off.

"An idea," he said, "isn't fact."

"Do you Rushes ever tell the whole story about anything?"

"Fiona's excited about her trip to Ireland," Jeremiah said with a fake smile. "My dad wants to invite her and her party to something special at our hotel there—depending on what she wants to do."

"Shop, listen to music and have high tea. She talk to Lizzie about Ireland?"

"Some. Maybe. I don't know."

"When I was a kid, your pub downstairs was this WASP bastion. When did you decide to convert it to an Irish pub and call it Morrigan's?"

Jeremiah looked as if he wanted to melt into the woodwork. He gave up on the smudge. "It was after Lizzie's mother died. Her name was Morrigan."

"And what happened to her?"

This time, the kid didn't flinch. He seemed to know Bob had him now and he might as well give up the rest. "She tripped on a cobblestone in Dublin."

"Dublin," Bob said.

"It was an accident," Jeremiah Rush said.

Before Bob could drag the rest out of the kid, syllable by syllable if necessary, John March walked into the lobby, surrounded by FBI agents.

His teeth clenched, Bob kept his eyes on the young Rush. "You have a quiet room where Director March and I can talk?"

"Yes. The police watching your daughter—"

"Aren't moving. The rate things are going, people will like having a police presence. Won't hurt business."

"We all just want Fiona and her friends to be safe."

Jeremiah Rush seemed perfectly sincere. He pointed to the stairs that curved up to a balconied second floor. "Please feel free to use the Frost Room."

"Named after a relative or the weather?"

"The poet."

While March stood back, not saying a word, Bob suggested the FBI director's entourage go up and sweep for bombs, bugs, spies, God knew what. He took the half flight of stairs down to Fiona and told her and the officers on her detail where he'd be. He said on the mezzanine level with Director March. He didn't say he'd be prying the truth out of an old friend accustomed to keeping his mouth shut.

He returned to the lobby level, and he and March headed up to the elegant, wood-paneled Frost Room. Most of its furnishings looked as if they'd been carted up from the old bar. Musty books on shelves, dark oil paintings of dour men, pewter Paul Revere could have made. Somehow, the place managed not to be stuffy. But Bob didn't want to try to figure out the Rushes and their approach to hotel decorating.

He turned to his old friend, standing over by a coat of arms. "Ever think you'd be a knight in shining armor?"

March shook his head. "No."

"Me, neither," Bob sighed. "You haven't been straight with me, John."

"I've told you what I know."

"Nah. That's never the case with you. You've told me what you thought was relevant. You haven't asked too much about Will Davenport. Our Brit. You know him."

It wasn't a question, but March said, "I know that he and Simon are friends, but Davenport and I have never met."

A careful answer. "He's a lord. Son of a British noble—a *marquess* or something. Sounds like it should be a woman, doesn't it?"

March gave him the barest flicker of a smile, his dark eyes racked with emotional pain. "Bob, whatever I can do to find Abigail—whatever you think I can tell you—just say it."

"We're both on edge," Bob said with some sympathy. "Can Davenport find Abigail?"

"He'll do what he can to help. For her sake, and for Simon's."

"Not for yours," Bob said.

The FBI director kept his gaze steady. "No. I suspect he believes I withheld—personally withheld—information that ended in tragedy for his men."

"What do you believe about him?"

"The same."

"The other Brit?"

"I don't know who he is."

"Cagey answer, John. The fine print reads: you don't know but you have an idea."

"My speculation won't help you."

March abandoned the armor and walked over to a wall of books. Several were collections of Robert Frost poetry. Bob noticed that the FBI director's suit was expensive and neatly pressed, but the man inside it seemed to shrink into its folds.

"There are days I wish I'd become a poet," March said, turning away from the shelves. "You, Bob?"

"Nope. I like being a cop and asking tough questions. What do you know about Lizzie Rush?"

"We're putting the entire Rush family under FBI protection."

It was an indirect answer, yet filled with meaning. Bob saw it now. "How long has she been an informant for you?"

"I didn't know it was her until today."

"Because you didn't want to know. How long?"

"A year."

Bob gave a low whistle. "Anonymous?"

"She's good, and she didn't want to be found out. She created a story…persuaded me that pursuing her identity would put her at increased risk. Her help was critical but not asked for."

"Regular?"

"Intermittent. I thought she was a professional."

"Just not one of yours."

"I doubt we'd know about her now if she hadn't interceded with Keira and warned you yesterday."

"Abigail checked into Estabrook's Boston connections. She didn't like his threat against you and Simon." And Simon's relationship with her father had thrown her for a loop, even if she was trying to be big about it. Bob wasn't going there. March knew. "Lizzie Rush isn't here."

"I don't know where she went. She called me after she and your daughter—"

"Did you ask her where she was going, what her plan was?" Bob sighed, knowing the answer. "You people give me a headache. I'm going to find your daughter, John. I want to know why that thug who's now dead up on Beacon Street grabbed her instead of letting her get blown up. If your relationship with the Rush family has anything to do with what's going on, you need to tell me about it."

March ignored him. "Keep me informed."

"Go back to Washington. Stay out of my investigation."

"Get some rest, Bob. Where did you sleep last night?"

"Keira's apartment."

"Have you heard from her?"

"Yeah, sure. A little Irish fairy flew in my window last night and whispered in my ear."

March didn't so much as crack a smile.

Bob pointed a finger at him. "You keep too many secrets."

"Part of the job."

"Not all of them."

Bob kissed Fiona goodbye and left the Whitcomb as Theresa was arriving. She refused even to look at him, but he didn't care. She and the girls—all three daughters—were going back to her house in Lexington and staying there, under police protection, until they all had a better fix on what was going on. The rest didn't matter. Let Theresa blame him.

He helped himself to a handful of smoke-flavored nuts on his way out and went back to the hospital. Alone. No detail. No Yarborough with the suspicious looks.

Scoop still had his morphine clicker, but he seemed more alert.

"Your black-haired woman is named Lizzie Rush," Bob said. "While you were pulling weeds and talking compost, did Abigail mention her?"

Scoop thought a moment. "No."

"Fiona tell you about playing Irish music at the Rush hotel on Charles—the Whitcomb, Morrigan's Bar?"

"Yeah. Never occurred to me it was dangerous."

"No reason it should have. Why didn't I know? I could have gone to hear them play. I'm busy, but I'm not a total jerk. I like to keep track of what my kids are doing. Support them."

Scoop's puffy eyes narrowed. "You okay, Bob?"

"Yeah, sure. I just need to do something about my life. Same old, same old. Nothing to worry about. You just focus on getting better."

But Scoop was tuned in to people, and he said, "Fiona didn't mean to leave you out. She says she normally doesn't like family in the audience."

"Scoop, forget it. It's okay." Bob felt lousy for letting a guy in stitches, on morphine, see him crack, even a little. "Did Abigail say anything to you about Fiona, Morrigan's, the Rushes?"

"Not a word. Does she know, even? Fiona tells me things she doesn't tell you two."

"No kidding. Yeah, she knows."

"Abigail was onto something and not talking."

Bob grunted. "What else is new?"

"I can tell…Bob. Hell. What's going on?" Scoop shifted position, which seemed to be a major effort. "Let me out of here."

"The doctors'll spring you as soon as you can walk without spilling blood all over the floor. Until then—"

But Scoop had already drifted off. Bob sat there, watching him sleep. He was used to bouncing ideas off Scoop and Abigail, and now he didn't have either one of them.

Before he could get too pathetic, he drove to BPD headquarters in Roxbury. He'd pull himself together and work the investigations, see what his detectives had on Abigail, the bombs, the dead guy. The task force was set up in a conference room, with maps, computers, charts, timelines.

Nobody talked to him. He must have had that look.

He got Tom Yarborough over in a corner next to a table of stale coffee. "Don't start on me," Bob said. "Just listen. I need you to work on Norman Estabrook's Boston connections."

"The Rush family?"

Bob sighed. The guy was always a step ahead. "You've already started?"

"Just a toe in the water. I wonder what'd happen if we typed Harlan Rush into the system. He's Lizzie Rush's father. He's a reprobate gambler in Las Vegas—except when he's not."

"Think the feds would storm the building if we get too close to him?"

"Maybe not the FBI."

CIA. Terrific. More Washington types meddling in his investigation. "We'd get a visit by humorless spooks with big nasty handcuffs?"

"Cop or no cop, Lieutenant, I don't want to piss off this guy. Harlan Rush is a player. He's still in the game."

Harlan's daughter, Lizzie, was obviously a chip off the old block. "You've talked to him," Bob said.

Yarborough nodded.

"Good work."

"I'm not sure it gets us any closer to Abigail."

# Chapter 23

*Near Kennebunkport, Maine*
*8:19 p.m., EDT*
*August 26*

Lizzie took the stairs up to the wraparound deck of her small house built on the rocks near the mouth of the Kennebec River. The tide was going out, pleasure craft and working boats still making their way to the harbor. She let herself into her house—one main room with very little separation of space—and opened up the windows and doors, the evening breeze pouring in through the screens. She walked out to the deck and shut her eyes, listening to the sounds of the boats and the ocean at dusk.

The rambling house her grandfather Rush had built was two hundred yards up the rockbound shore. After an architect friend had walked through it with her, he'd sent her a book of matches in lieu of a plan for renovations. Lizzie loved Maine, but her father avoided it, just as he did Dublin and, to a lesser extent,

Boston. "The water's always too cold," he'd say. But memories haunted him here, too. Nostalgia not just for what had been but what might have been.

Lizzie was ten when she'd first fantasized her father was a spy and fifteen when she knew he was one. He always deflected her questions without giving a direct answer, even as he taught her how to defend herself, how to spot a tail, shake a tail, do a dead drop—how to *think* in such terms.

Only when she went to Ireland herself was Lizzie certain that her mother hadn't tripped on a cobblestone after all, and the circumstances of her death—his inability to stop it—were why her father had taught her how to jab her fingers into a man's throat. "Don't be bound by dogma," he'd say. "Never mind niceties or rules when you're in a fight for your life. Trust your instincts. Do what you have to do to get out alive."

Lizzie opened her eyes, noticing a cormorant swooping low over the calm water. Her grandmother, famous for her frugality, had spent as much time as she could in Maine during her last years. She liked her crumbling house the way it was, liked the memories it conjured up for her.

"Sitting here by myself, the memories are like a warm, fuzzy blanket," she'd told her only granddaughter. But that was a rare display of sentimentality for Edna Whitcomb Rush, and in the next breath, she'd said, "Tear this place down when I'm gone. It's the location I love."

Lizzie had smiled. "It's magical."

"Ah, you have your mother's romantic soul."

"Do you believe she tripped on a cobblestone, Gran?"

It was a question Lizzie had asked before, but her grandmother only answered it then, at the very end of her long, good life. "I'll ask her when I see her in heaven, Lizzie, but no. No, I never

believed your mother simply tripped and fell. But," her grandmother had continued, some of her old starch coming back into
her voice, "I do believe that whatever happened to her, justice
was rendered. Your father would have seen to that."

"What was she like?"

"She was very much like you, Lizzie."

The sound of a car pulled her out of her thoughts and drew
her attention to the gravel driveway down to her left. She walked
to the railing and leaned over as a familiar sedan pulled to a stop
behind the one she'd borrowed from Martha Prescott.

Jeremiah's car.

Jeremiah who now owed her, Lizzie thought as she watched
Will Davenport get out on the driver's side and look at the darkening horizon. She waited, but no one else appeared.

At least he'd come alone.

She remained on the deck, listening to his even footsteps on
the stairs. When he came around to her, she put both hands on
the back of an old Adirondack chair she'd collected from her
grandmother's house farther up the rocks. "You got here even
faster than I anticipated."

"Does that surprise you?"

"No. Not even a little." It was true, she realized. "You're more
rugged looking up close. I can picture you humping over remote
mountains with a heavy pack and a big gun."

He smiled, walking toward her. "I see your imagination and
flare for dramatics are at work again."

"Ha. SAS and MI6 equal heavy pack and big gun." She
frowned. "Jeremiah told you where to find me? I have blabber-
mouth cousins."

"Who adore you and whom you adore in return."

"Serves me right for using them to run interference."

But she saw the strain of the past day at the corners of his eyes as he squinted out at the Atlantic, seagulls crying in the distance, out of sight. "Is this your place, or does it belong to your family?"

"It's mine. My great-grandfather Rush was a Maine fisherman. His son did well and married a Whitcomb from Boston, and he came back here and built a big—but not *too* big—house. I own it, too. No one else in the family wanted it after my grandmother died two years ago."

Will turned and leaned against the railing, his back to the ocean, the evening breeze catching the ends of his hair. His eyes were more blue-green now, dark, observant. "Maybe they wanted you to have it."

Lizzie dropped her hands from the chair and stood next to him on the railing, facing the water. "I hadn't thought of it that way. My family—I love them all, Will." She watched a worn lobster boat cruise toward the river harbor. "My parents planned to raise me here. Then my mother died, and my father—well, things changed."

"Things always change."

She glanced sideways at him. "How much do you know about me?"

That slight smile again. "Not nearly enough."

She hadn't expected the spark of sexuality in his eyes, but it was there. And it pleased her even as it unnerved her. "I looked up your family in *Burke's Peerage and Gentry*."

"You were in London in July," he said.

"Josie's been busy following my trail?"

"Very. I spoke to her on my drive up here."

"I imagine the FBI will want to talk to her."

"I gave them her number."

"Supposedly you were in Scotland fishing when I was in

London. I was careful to stay off any spy radar. I met people at a hotel bar where you and Simon often meet for a drink, and I walked past your sister's wedding dress shop. I never saw her—I wouldn't do that." Lizzie shrugged, stood back from the deck railing. "I was just the hotelier on a London holiday."

"I never knew," Will said.

"That was the idea. I didn't get close enough for you to find out."

"You should have."

Lizzie turned and faced him. "Maybe you should go back to Boston and join forces with Simon and the rest of the FBI, do what you can from there to find Myles Fletcher."

"It's Abigail Browning we need to find. Myles isn't important compared to her safety."

"Will...this place is my refuge. I've never..." She paused, tried to smile. "I've had my cousins over for lobster rolls, but otherwise this is where I come to be alone."

"I get your meaning, Lizzie. I'm invading your space."

"'Invading' is too strong. I had ants once. Now, that was an invasion—"

He touched a finger to the corner of her mouth. "I can see you battling ants." He trailed his fingertip across her lower lip. "Are you all right, Lizzie?" he asked softly.

"Sure. Yes." Her heartbeat quickened, but she tried to ignore its meaning. That she was reacting to this man. That she'd lost all objectivity with him. "I'm not the one lying dead in an alley or recovering from shrapnel wounds or—" But she squeezed her eyes shut at sudden images of where Norman could have Abigail Browning, what he could be doing to her. She tried to block them as she opened her eyes. "I don't want him to hurt her."

Will tucked his fingers under her chin and raised it so that she was meeting his eye. "Whatever happens won't be your doing.

Guilt gets us nowhere." He lowered his mouth to hers and kissed her softly. "I've been thinking about doing that for some time now."

Lizzie smiled. "Long plane ride across the Atlantic."

"I started wondering what it would be like to kiss you when you pretended not to recognize my name at Eddie O'Shea's pub. When I saw you take on Michael Murphy—" Will kissed her again "—I knew it would be only a matter of time."

"Very bold of you."

This time, their kiss took on an urgency, nothing soft or tentative about it. She responded, putting a hand on his arm to steady herself. She was tired and raw emotionally, and all she wanted to do was to feel his arms around her, his mouth on hers.

"Kissing you is everything I imagined it would be," he said.

"I hope what you imagined was good."

He laughed. "Very good, just not sufficient." His eyes sparked as he stood back from her. "I want more than a kiss."

"Will—"

"Also only a matter of time, wouldn't you say, Lizzie?"

She hoped so. Every nerve ending she had wanted it to be so. But she said lightly, "You are very bold, indeed, Lord Davenport."

"A point to remember."

He turned to face the ocean, and Lizzie shook off the aftereffects of their kiss as best she could and reminded herself who was standing next to her. What did she know about this man and why was he really here? "Maybe being attracted to each other is inevitable after all the adrenaline of the past twenty-four hours. Heightened senses and all that."

Will seemed amused. "I was attracted to you before the adrenaline set in."

Now she felt warm. She looked out at the water. Lights were coming on at the inns and houses down toward the river.

"Does Estabrook know about this place?" Will asked, back to business.

"Yes."

"You think he'll come here."

"I think he knows *I'll* come here."

"Lizzie, you can't deal with Norman Estabrook on your own any longer. No one would ask that of you."

"What if I told you he kidnapped Abigail because of me? What would you say then?" She narrowed her gaze on him. "What would you ask me to do?"

He didn't hesitate. "The same. You're not a criminal, nor are you a law enforcement officer."

"Did John March tell you to keep an eye on me?"

His expression darkened slightly. "I don't work for March."

"Did the queen tell you? Your friend the prime minister?" Lizzie didn't wait for an answer. "You're after Myles Fletcher."

"I'm here because I want to help you."

She noticed the air was cool, almost chilly, with nightfall. Maine's too-short summer was coming to an end. "Thank you."

Will said nothing.

"I kayaked out here with Norman last summer. If only…"

"It's too easy to lose ourselves in regrets," Will said. "And not helpful."

"Maybe a drug cartel hired your friend Fletcher to deal with Norman—crash his plane, manipulate him, drag him out and shoot him. Whatever. Maybe yesterday and today weren't Norman's doing. If that's the case, we're clueless about who really does have Abigail." Lizzie watched seagulls perch on the tumble of barnacle-covered rocks below the tideline. She shook off any doubt. "No. It's Norman."

"You've become accustomed to keeping secrets. Not telling

anyone what you know. Not trusting anyone." Will eased his arms around her, locking his eyes with hers. "You're not alone, Lizzie."

She smiled at him before there was no turning back. "Fat chance of that with the feds, BPD and MI6 after me." She gave him a quick kiss. "Come on. I can at least make you dinner," she said, yanking open a screen door, and he followed her into her little house. He seemed as comfortable there as he probably did in London, Scotland, the home of his father, the marquess, or wherever else he happened to be at a given moment.

He walked over to a wall covered with family photographs she'd framed herself. "How did you get involved with Estabrook in the first place?" he asked, his back to her. "His other friends didn't know he had criminal dealings. Why did you?"

"Curiosity," she said, pulling open the refrigerator and frowning at the sparse contents. "For once I was responsible and tossed everything before I left. I don't even have a pint of wild blueberries to offer you."

"When were you here last?"

"A couple weeks ago. I don't need to be in an office every day. I did a little poking around—my trip to London, for example—but I figured I'd keep a low profile until Norman was tried and convicted. Once I realized he was about to make a deal…" She opened a cupboard, sighing as she glanced back at Will. "I have steel-cut oats, a couple of cans of kidney beans and salsa. Cooking's not exactly my long suit."

He pointed to the top photograph on the wall display and glanced back at her. "Your father?"

"Can you recognize a kindred spy soul?" She shut the cupboard and tried another. "Unopened spices and boxes of cornstarch aren't very helpful, now, are they? How do you suppose I ended up with two boxes of cornstarch?"

"One does," Will said with a smile, leaving the photos and taking a seat on a bar stool.

Lizzie shut that cupboard, too. "For a long time I didn't know who was good, bad, possible law enforcement, or if I was completely off base about Norman. But March stayed in touch. That was a clue. I didn't take crazy risks. I met a half dozen of Norman's drug-cartel friends, at least that I'm aware of…sexy, macho guys who like high living and adventures and are very, very violent. They prey on other people's weaknesses for their own pleasure and profit."

"When did you first run into them?"

"At a resort in Costa Rica. I took their pictures and e-mailed them to the FBI."

"To John March, you mean."

"Yes." She looked at Will and felt a rush of relief that she'd made the admission, even if he already knew and didn't need her confirmation. "For personal reasons. But we've never met. I've only seen him from a distance." It was the truth, if also a dodge. "I understand money, but I'm not in Norman's league. I latched onto bits and pieces of what he was up to."

"Did you tip off March in the first place?"

She shook her head, abandoning her efforts to muster together a dinner for two. "I wondered that myself, but no. He was already onto Norman. Simon took the big risks and got the most damning information against him. I did what I could to point whatever investigation might be going on in the right direction."

"Norman trusted both you and Simon," Will said.

"In different ways, but Norman has an unusual idea of trust. Relationships are entirely on his terms. He's the sun in his universe. Everyone else is a tiny planet that revolves around him. I was an especially tiny planet—but desirable to have around. That was helpful."

"Attractive, elegant, vivacious Lizzie Rush."

She gave a mock bow. "Compliment accepted with gratitude, especially considering you've now seen me in a knife fight and up to my knees in mud and manure."

"An image I shall never forget."

She managed a laugh, but she couldn't sustain it. "Norman's father was a police officer, just a regular guy. From what I've been able to put together, Norman felt inferior to him, vulnerable even as he was embarrassed that his father never rose up through the ranks."

"Going up against John March and the FBI makes him feel important. Why did you stay in, Lizzie? A year's a long time."

"I couldn't unring the bell. Once I knew, I knew. And I was in a position to help. I wasn't with Norman all the time. Not as much as Simon. I provided names, faces, numbers. I was careful. I didn't want March to know it was me. If something went wrong, I knew he'd blame himself."

"You never approached Simon or tried to find out if he was someone you could trust?"

"I couldn't let myself trust anyone."

But Will's changeable eyes narrowed on her, and she felt a surge of heat, as if he could see through her, straight to her secrets, her fears.

"There's more, Lizzie. Isn't there?"

She avoided his eyes as she came around the counter and sat upon a bar stool next to him. "How's Josie Goodwin? I figure she's MI6, too. Has she provided a complete dossier on me by now?"

"It's not complete."

"Does she know I love the smell of lavender?"

A chilly breeze blew through the little house. Will was very still next to her. "Do you?"

"I never knew why until I went to Ireland for the first time in college. I was on my own—my father would never go with me. I was standing in a lace shop and picked up a sachet filled with dried lavender, and I smiled and cried and laughed. I had an emotional meltdown there in the shop. I knew it was because of my mother. She loved lavender, too."

"Growing up without her must have been difficult," Will said.

"I didn't know any different. I'd watch other girls with their mothers…" Suddenly restless, Lizzie eased off the bar stool. "I love my family. My father's a mystery to us all. My uncle and aunt are kind and hardworking, totally dedicated to the hotels and to my cousins. And to me. But you know all this, don't you, from Josie?"

"Some." Will gave her a near-unreadable smile. "Josie is very thorough and dogged. I, on the other hand, am not."

"I don't know nearly enough about you. London, Scotland, lords and ladies. Made your own money, or at least that's what the U.K. government wants the rest of us to believe."

"Lizzie…"

She'd gone too far, and if he kissed her again, she was lost. "I could see what's in the freezer, or we could walk down to the river and have lobster rolls."

He got up from the bar stool, standing close to her, and tucked a few strands of her hair behind her ears. "I believe I've met my match," he said, a sadness coming into his eyes even as he smiled.

They sat at an outdoor table covered in red-checked vinyl. Tourists at nearby tables in the popular roadside diner glanced at Will as if they suspected he might be someone. Like British nobility, Lizzie thought, amused. "Forget cholesterol and calories," she said, "and order a cup of clam chowder, a lobster roll and wild blueberry pie—warm, with ice cream."

"With a salad?"

"Sure. You can order a salad."

He smiled. They resisted the lobster rolls and ordered clam chowder and salads.

Lizzie pushed back the fatigue from her long two days. "How did you and Simon become friends?"

"He saved my life two years ago."

"Because of Myles Fletcher," she said.

Will leaned back, tapped a finger on a white square of the tablecloth. "You see too much, Lizzie."

"My father taught me to be observant."

"I led a team into a remote area of Afghanistan. We—*I* trusted Myles. He betrayed us. Until yesterday, I had every reason to believe he'd been captured and executed by his terrorist friends."

"Your team," Lizzie said, feeling an overwhelming sense of dread. "What happened to them?"

Will leveled his gaze on her. "They were killed in action."

"What were their names?"

"David Mears and Philip Billings. They were the best men the U.K. has to offer. The best men I've ever known."

Lizzie was aware of a car passing on the street by their table and the smell of scallops as a waiter came out with a tray, but her mind was in Afghanistan, a place she'd never been, with men she'd never met. Finally she said, "I'm sorry."

"I'd have died in their place."

She knew he meant it. "People are loyal to you, aren't they? Josie Goodwin. Your men."

"Not Myles. I led Josie to him." Will spoke without bitterness, without flinching from the truth. "I led David and Philip to their deaths."

"You don't want to trust or be trusted anymore, do you, Will?

No one to disappoint or to owe." Lizzie leaned over the table, aware now only of the man across from her. He was emotionally self-contained and mission-oriented, but he was also, in his own way, tortured by the past. "I'd love to see you really laugh one day."

"Lizzie—"

"You need to know what Fletcher's been up to the past two years. And you need to find out what really happened in Afghanistan. The answers you thought you had are looking a little muddy right now. Am I right?"

"I like clarity," he said with a small smile.

A couple at another of the roadside tables laughed loudly, enjoying their late-summer vacation. Lizzie had pulled on a sweatshirt before leaving the house, but she still felt chilly. "Did John March have a role in what happened in Afghanistan?"

Will hesitated ever so slightly. "I suppose since I've told you this much, I might as well..." He sighed and looked away from her a moment. "Simon found me in the cave where I was trapped. I assume he was there because of March. David and Philip were already dead. Myles had already been captured. Simon had only an ax and a rope with him, but you've seen him."

"He's built like a bull. Do he and March know about Myles Fletcher?"

"Yes. Most certainly."

This time, Lizzie noticed a trace of bitterness in his tone. "Fletcher will try to kill you if he gets the chance, won't he?"

"He'll make the chance."

"Because you know he's alive," Lizzie said.

"Because if everything I've believed for the past two years is true, I know what he did." Will looked across the narrow street at a flower shop and a pretty gray-shingled inn. "In a way, I hope if Myles wants me dead it's because he can't tolerate having us know he's alive. Dead, he could still pretend he didn't betray us."

"It would say he still has something of a conscience." Lizzie reached across the table and took his hand briefly. "It would also say he knows you won't rest until you find him. You're handsome and elusive, Lord Davenport, and I do believe I'm falling for you. It's not just adrenaline and jetlag, either."

He smiled. "We'll see."

"Would your family be horrified?"

"Delighted. I've become something of a worry."

Their bowls of chowder arrived, thick, steaming. Lizzie tore open a packet of oyster crackers and dumped them into her soup. "My cousin Whit makes the best chowder of the lot of us. Are your MI6 and SAS comrades after Fletcher? The House of Lords? The prime minister? I hear you're mates."

Will managed to look something between exasperated and amused.

Lizzie shrugged. "Just trying to inject a touch of humor into a humorless situation. Are you a magnet for Fletcher?" She studied him. "You hope so. Do you suspect Norman has ties to some of the same people you ran into in Afghanistan?"

"Anything's possible."

"Ripple effects. Did you look for Fletcher after Simon saved your life?"

"Night and day for weeks."

"I guess he didn't want to be found. He's as dangerous as you say, isn't he?"

Will's expression didn't match their quaint, cheerful surroundings. "Myles can't have been in charge of every aspect of what happened yesterday in Boston and Ireland. Otherwise, the outcome would have been quite different."

"You mean he doesn't make mistakes. At least not that kind. He's a professional."

"You obviously have a sixth sense for…"

"Spies?"

This time, he smiled at her humor. "Eat your soup, Lizzie."

After dinner, they walked up to the rambling house her grandfather had built on the rocks above the Atlantic. There was no sign anyone was there now or had been since her last visit. Some days Lizzie wanted to renovate the house for the mother she'd never known and other days just to tear it down and start from scratch with a new house, fresh memories. Her aunt had asked her if Norman was in her sights and had been openly relieved when Lizzie had said no. Her aunt hadn't known then of his association with violent international criminals. She'd objected to him because of his personality. "He's self-absorbed, Lizzie. You wouldn't make a good trophy. You want a partnership, at the very least. You'd love to have a soulmate, but life doesn't always provide one. You might have to look under a few rocks and kiss a few toads."

Henrietta was as near to a mother as Lizzie had ever known, even more than her grandmother, but neither woman had ever tried to be something she wasn't. Successful, creative, not bound by clocks and routines, Henrietta Rush was a devoted wife and mother of four sons. The daughter of the Whitcomb's head maintenance man, she'd met Bradley Rush when she hand-delivered a list of a hundred things her father thought the hotel was doing wrong. The two of them still lived in the same drafty Victorian north of Boston. Lizzie considered it home as much as anywhere. When she was growing up, her father had maintained an apartment in Boston because it was convenient for him to leave her with his brother and wife when he had to be away for weeks at a time and couldn't take her with him.

When she left for college, he moved to Las Vegas.

"I was supposed to grow up here," Lizzie said, Will close to her in the dark. She could hear the wash of waves down on the rocks. "Then my mother died, and my father—I think that's when he gave up on leaving the CIA or whatever alphabet agency he works for."

"Do you believe your mother died because of his work?"

"I believe I don't have all the facts about her life or her death."

Will stayed close to her as they made their way back to her little house. The tide had shifted and was just starting to come in, bringing with it the cool night breeze and smells of the ocean.

Lizzie was intensely aware that Will would be sleeping close by again tonight. "I'm just enough on Irish time to be exhausted," she said.

"Taking on a killer and finding a man shot to death can't help."

"I didn't think. I just acted."

"You fight well." He nodded to her small living area. "Do you train here?"

"Sometimes. I almost took out a window in July with my kicking."

He stood in front of her, looking at her as if he wanted to push back all her defenses and see into her soul.

Which was just nonsense. She had to stay focused and couldn't indulge in romantic fantasies. But he took her hand into his and she leaned into him, letting herself sink against his chest.

He put his arms around her, and she lifted her head from his chest so that she could see his face. "When you walked into Eddie O'Shea's pub..." She wasn't sure she could explain. "There's something about that village. It's as if I was meant to be there, sitting by a fire reading Irish folktales. When I was in London, I thought you were just another spy. Of course, I didn't actually see you."

He smiled. "You didn't get this close."

"Too dangerous." She eased her hands up his arms, hard under the soft, light fabric of his sweater. "Way too dangerous."

"I don't know if I want to disabuse you of your romantic notions about me."

"You mean that you're as sexy—"

His kiss stopped her midsentence and took her breath away, a mix of tenderness and urgency. Lizzie tightened her grip on him just to keep herself on her feet. The ocean breeze gusted through the screens, hitting her already sensitized skin, and she let her arms go around him. There was nothing soft or easy about him.

"I'm breaking all my rules with you," he whispered.

"You're used to discipline and isolation."

"My father left broken hearts in his wake. I learned at an early age the dangers of romantic entanglements."

"*Entanglements.* Scary word."

He kissed her again, lifting her off her feet, and she gave herself up to the swirl of sensations—ocean, seagulls, wind, wanting— and relished the taste and feel of him, imagined him carrying her to her bedroom, and making love to her for the rest of the night. She knew it wouldn't happen. Not tonight.

Will pulled away, or she did, and they turned toward the water.

Lizzie cleared her throat and adjusted her shirt. "Our focus is rightly on Abigail, Norman, Fletcher and what we can do to help the situation."

Will pivoted around to her, his eyes dark and serious now. "Not *we,* Lizzie."

"You're a British citizen. You shouldn't be sneaking around southern Maine on your own, either."

"Lizzie—"

"I know what you're saying, but right now I'm here, and I'm

safe. I hope the FBI and BPD find Abigail and arrest Norman tonight. I'd love to wake up tomorrow morning with nothing more dangerous on my mind than a trip to the lobster pound."

"I'd like that, too, but whatever's happened by morning, you need to leave Myles and Estabrook to real professionals."

"And if I'm in the wrong place at the wrong time as I was with Norman and his friends in the drug cartels? Then what?" She smoothed the back of her hand along his rough jaw and didn't wait for an answer. "You've a job to do. I won't get in your way. But I really am falling for you. Tall, fair, handsome and loyal— and you can walk through an Irish pasture and hardly get a bit of manure on your shoes."

He grabbed her hand and pulled her to him and kissed her, nothing tentative or gentle about him now. He kept her close, smiled as he spoke. "You Rushes don't do anything by half measures, do you?"

This from a man who fought terrorists.

He kissed her on the forehead. "Hiking the Beara Way. One day…" He dropped his arms from her and stood back. "Go to bed, Lizzie. I'll stay out here. I'm not going anywhere, and I have no intention of taking advantage of a woman about to fall asleep on her feet."

"Will…"

"We have time."

"I hope so. You must be tired yourself."

"I slept on my flight. I didn't have a deck of cards to distract me, and I had the comforts of a private jet."

She gave a mock protest. "I was in coach with a toddler kicking the back of my seat, and you—"

He laughed softly. "Next time perhaps you'll think twice before you slip out on me."

# Chapter 24

Fiona had left her full-size, classic harp in the corner of the Garrison house first-floor drawing room, in front of Keira's sketch of the Christmas windowbox in Dublin. Bob plucked a string. Fiona had shown him how, but it made a twangy sound, nothing like the rich, full sound she could produce. He'd walked up from Charles Street. The joint task force was meeting at BPD headquarters in a little while. He'd be on his way there soon. They were making progress, but they still didn't have Abigail or her captors.

Yarborough materialized in the foyer door. "Lieutenant?"

Bob resisted biting the guy's head off and turned from the harp. "Yeah, what's up?" Even he could hear the fatigue in his voice.

Yarborough, who'd been glum all night, was almost perky. "We have an ID on the dead guy, a South Boston thug named Walter Bassette. Lucas and a couple precinct detectives are on their way over to his apartment."

Bassette. Bob liked having a name. It was something solid. "Good work, Yarborough."

"I didn't have anything to do with it. I'm just telling you."

Credit where credit was due. He was ambitious, but he was also fair.

"We're checking if Bassette was in Ireland recently, called there, met someone from there. Having a decent lead…" Yarborough shrugged, not getting himself too excited. "It helps."

"The bombs weren't sophisticated, but these bastards had to get the materials from somewhere and put them together somewhere." Bob looked at Keira's sketch of the Dublin window-box. "Someone had to hire Murphy, the guy in Ireland. If it was Bassette—" He broke off with a sigh and shifted back to Yarborough. "Who has Abigail now? What was Bassette doing in that alley?"

Yarborough rubbed the side of his nose and didn't answer. Bob recognized the tactic for what it was. The younger detective was giving him time.

Bob felt his stomach go south on him. "Bassette knew Fiona saw him. He'd talked to her. He came there to kill her."

"Don't think about it. He's out of the picture, and she's under protection. No one's getting near her." Yarborough walked into the empty room. "Abigail's spent a fair amount of time here this summer. I think she's trying this place on for size to see if it might work for her and Owen. Turn it back into a residence. She comes over and does paperwork while he does his thing. Sometimes Fiona and her friends are here practicing."

"Tom?"

He got a little red. "I don't know. Maybe there's something here we missed."

"I'll check it out," Bob said.

Bob saw past Yarborough's arrogance to his worry, but it wasn't a place either wanted to go. Bob liked being emotionally repressed and figured Yarborough was a fellow traveler on that score.

"I'll see you back at headquarters," Yarborough said.

"You getting any sleep?"

"There's time for that." He gave Bob a quick grin. "Us younger guys can go a few days without sleep."

"Go to hell, Yarborough."

"Do you need a ride? I can stay—"

"Nah. I'm all set. Go."

After Yarborough left, Bob paced, his footsteps echoing on the hardwood floor. Teams had gone through Abigail's desk at BPD headquarters, her computer, her car, the remnants of her apartment. They'd only swept the Garrison house for bombs. They hadn't searched it.

He walked up the stairs to the second-floor offices of the Dorothy Garrison Foundation. It focused on gardens and oceans—the things Owen's sister had loved most. Bob couldn't imagine losing one of his daughters at any age, but at fourteen?

He looked for any files or work Abigail might have left there and, tucked on a bookcase, found a laptop labeled with her name.

Yarborough wasn't easy, but he had good instincts. Bob took another flight of stairs up to Keira's apartment. She and Abigail were just getting to know each other. Simon had given her and Owen an early wedding present of one of Keira's paintings, which Abigail loved. Bob figured Owen didn't care one way or the other, provided she was happy.

And now they didn't know if she was even alive.

He forced back the thought before it could take hold and noticed Keira's apartment door was ajar.

Simon stood in the doorway with his Glock in one hand. "Hey, Bob."

"I'm glad I didn't have to shoot you," Bob said wryly, then sighed. "Too damn much time on a desk. I'm getting stale. Then again, I'm brains not brawn these days. You here alone?"

A twitch of his mouth. "I think so."

Meaning Simon had shaken his detail. "Bet your FBI friends aren't happy about that." Bob stepped past him into the little apartment. "A big target on your back—don't stand too close, okay?"

"I'm not staying."

"Anything from Owen?"

Simon holstered the Glock. "They've expanded the search for Norman's plane. Owen's focused on his mission."

Simon nodded to the laptop under Bob's arm. "What's that all about?"

Bob shrugged. "Probably wedding dress searches."

"Let's have a look."

They pushed aside books on fairies and folklore and a box of art supplies and opened up the laptop on Keira's table. Bob had taken a liking to Simon. His wanderlust niece wouldn't have trouble coping with an extended stay under the Irish guards. She'd have trouble being without him.

Even Bob, with his limited computer skills, had no trouble spotting a desktop file labeled "Rush hotels" on Abigail's laptop. He clicked on it, and up popped her notes, links and downloaded descriptions of each of the Rushes' fifteen boutique hotels.

Simon's eyes narrowed. "Looks as if Abigail was onto Lizzie Rush."

Bob kept clicking. Nothing was password-protected. He found a copy of an old *Boston Globe* article about the death of Harlan Rush's Irish wife, Shauna Morrigan, in Dublin when their daughter was a baby.

Simon leaned over and scanned the article. "John March flew to Dublin and consulted with Irish investigators about what happened. There's a quote from him about what a tragedy her death was."

"Ireland's a long way to go for an Irish citizen who tripped and fell, even if she was married to a rich Bostonian." Bob clicked on another file and gave a low whistle. It was another *Globe* article. "Simon, look at this."

He was all FBI agent as he read the article over Bob's shoulder about the deaths of Shauna Morrigan's parents and brother in a car accident on their way to identify her body. Apparently they were so distraught, they missed a curve and drove off a cliff.

"Another 'tragedy,'" Simon said under his breath.

Bob knew he had to take the laptop in. "Come with me to BPD headquarters," he told Simon. "We'll open up the files. I know this bastard Estabrook wants you dead, but you're hard to kill. I figure I'm safe with you."

"No," Simon said. "You go on."

Bob saw what Simon had in mind and shook his head. "You shouldn't do this."

"I haven't said what I'm going to do."

"Going solo *will* get you killed, Simon."

But Bob didn't argue with him and instead walked back down the two flights of stairs and out into the summer night. He looked up at the dark sky and thought of Abigail last summer, tearing up the journals she'd kept for the seven long years after her husband's death, burning them in the backyard charcoal grill.

When he arrived at BPD headquarters, Bob avoided everyone and went into his office and pulled up the file on Shauna Morrigan Rush. She'd died in August, two months after Deirdre McCarthy's body had finally washed ashore in Boston. It had been hard times in the city, particularly dark and violent days in South Boston. March's work with the BPD to bring down the mob had helped catapult him to the position he now held.

Where exactly did an Irishwoman married to a wealthy Boston Rush fit into March's rise?

Bob thought of his friend having a drink alone at Morrigan's every August.

He became aware of March in the doorway and looked up from his computer. "So, Johnny," Bob said, settling back in his chair. "It's time you told me all you know about Shauna Morrigan Rush and just how obsessed her daughter is with you."

Simon touched Keira's colored pencils, her paintbrushes, the Irish lace at her windows, allowing them to bring her closer to him.

But Owen called from Montana, breaking the spell. "We found Estabrook's plane. He didn't crash. He landed safely on a private airstrip on an isolated ranch owned by one of his hedge-fund investors."

"Where are you?"

"Standing on the airstrip. No one else is around. Looks as if someone met him and drove him out of here. The FBI's on the way. They can pick up the trail from here." Owen's voice was professional, but he took in a breath. "Estabrook had help, Simon. He had this thing planned. All he had to do was pull the trigger."

"That's the way he does everything. He doesn't tie his shoes in the morning without a plan."

"He could be anywhere by now. He has the money, the connections, apparently the will."

It wasn't exhaustion Simon heard in his friend but barely suppressed fear and anger. "We were mindful of that when we launched the investigation into his activities last summer. I went deep for that reason. Norman wants John and me, Owen. Abigail's his leverage."

"She's been preoccupied the past couple weeks. I thought it was the serial killer case, but I've been out of town a lot lately." He was silent a moment. "That can't continue. It won't continue."

"You and Ab will work that out when you're back together. You two are lifers." Simon wondered if it was Owen or himself he was trying to reassure. "None of us will rest until we find her."

After they hung up, Simon headed outside. The heat had gone out of the air with nightfall. Lucas Jones motioned to him from an unmarked car. Simon hesitated, then went over to the open window on the driver's side.

"Walter Bassette flew into Shannon Airport in Ireland two weeks ago," Lucas said. "Get in, Simon. I know what you're thinking, but taking off on your own right now won't help anyone. You can do more good working with us."

"If that changes, I'm gone."

"If that changes, you can take the keys to my car." Lucas managed a grin. "I made sure it's got a full tank of gas before I came over here."

Everyone was in the big conference room at BPD headquarters when the call came to March's personal cell phone a few minutes before 5:00 a.m.

Simon watched the FBI director—his friend—follow Norman Estabrook's orders and put the call on speakerphone.

"You'll never find her." Norman's voice was smug, but with

a hint of nervousness, too, as if he knew he was talking to men and women who were better than he'd ever be. "Not unless I decide to give her back to you."

"Tell us what we can do for you," March said, his voice clear, steady.

"You can listen. Listen to your daughter. Here, Detective. Say hi to your daddy."

There was a pause before another voice came on the line. "This is Abigail Browning—"

*"Daddy,"* Norman shouted in the background. "Say, 'Hi, Daddy.'"

As Simon stood across the table from March, listening to the exchange, he figured everyone in the room wanted to jump through the phone and kill Norman Estabrook. He knew he did.

"Hi, Daddy," Abigail said, toneless. "How—"

The sound of a hard slap—Norman hitting her—cut her off. She sucked in a breath. *"Bastard."*

Norman hit her again.

March's hands tightened into fists. "All right. You've made your point. What can we do for you? Let's talk."

Estabrook laughed. "What can you do for me? You can suffer, Director March. You can suffer and suffer and suffer."

He hit Abigail again, clearly a harder blow, and this time she screamed. "Beg him," Norman ordered. "Beg your daddy to come save you."

Farther down the table, Tom Yarborough got out his jackknife and worked on his nails, the muscles in his jaw visibly tight. Next to him, Lucas Jones had tears in his eyes.

Bob chewed gum. All of the dozen or so men and women in the room remained silent.

On the other end of the connection, Abigail complied with her captor's orders and sobbed and begged her father to come save her.

John March leaned forward to the phone. "I'll be there, sweetheart," he said. "I won't let you down. I'll come now. Let me trade myself for you—"

"There." Estabrook spoke again, sniffling as he caught his breath. "My hand hurts. I've never hit anyone that hard before. It was exhilarating."

March's eyes stayed focused on the telephone. "Tell us what you want."

"I want Simon Cahill. I want you." Estabrook was smug again, not as winded. "I want your source. I know you have one. Who is it?"

"I have no idea. Whoever it is wanted to remain anonymous."

"Liar. Lies, lies, lies. You tell so many you don't know when to stop. You'll want to hunt me to the ends of the earth by the time I've finished."

"How can we reach you?" March asked.

"I'll reach *you*."

March glanced at Simon, and he nodded, taking his cue, and spoke into the phone. "Hello, Norman. It's been a while. We should talk. You and me. Face to face."

Estabrook snorted. "I want March alive and suffering, thinking about me every minute of every day, but you, Simon. Nothing's changed. I want you dead. Dead, dead, dead."

He disconnected.

The room was quiet.

March said, "Abigail's alive. We have the call on tape."

"The screams were tactical," Lucas said. "Estabrook hurt her, but she played to it. She wanted him to think he'd gotten to her. Make him back off before he hit her harder, maybe keep his frustration from building to a breaking point."

Yarborough flipped his knife shut. "I heard a seagull in the background. Anyone else? It's not much. Damn seagulls are everywhere."

No one responded.

Simon went out into the hall. March followed. "Lizzie Rush is your source, John," Simon said. "You knew her mother. What the hell's going on? Does Lizzie think you covered up her mother's murder for your own ambition?"

"Did you?" Bob asked, coming out into the hall.

March looked at him. "No."

Bob shrugged. "Sorry, John. I had to—"

"I know you did." March's voice was tortured but controlled. "I don't know what Lizzie's personal feelings are toward me, but I believe she trusts me. We need to trust her."

"And we need to protect her," Simon added.

March gave a grim nod. "Unfortunately, she doesn't make that easy."

"She thinks she's one of us," Bob said.

"From what Will tells me," Simon said, "she has the skills and the instincts of a pro."

"That doesn't make her one." Bob looked from Simon to March before he spoke again. "If Estabrook finds out what she's done, he'll kill her."

There was nothing left to say. Simon remembered he had Lucas Jones's keys in his pocket. Without a word, he walked down the hall and out of the building.

No one stopped him.

# Chapter 25

*Near Kennebunkport, Maine*
*5:51 a.m., EDT*
*August 27*

Abigail could hear seagulls. She sank onto the cracked linoleum floor of the basement room where she was now being held. Her head ached, and she could feel blood trickling down her chin from where Norman had hit her on the mouth. Amateur. He had no idea how to hit a person.

She leaned her head against the wall, listening for more seagulls as she tried to stay focused and alert.

*Owen...*

Two of Estabrook's men had come for her in her stateroom on the yacht and taken her at gunpoint to a fast, rigid inflatable dinghy. She was alone with them in the Zodiac as they sped across choppy waves in the cold mist. She wasn't blindfolded, so she had seen the most beautiful dawn spill across the horizon in shades of pink, purple and red. Fog hovered over the western horizon. She'd sailed the New England coast with Owen and recognized the magnificent summer homes and inns of Kennebunkport, a popular tourist and fishing village in southern Maine. She and Owen had docked there a few weeks ago and wandered its attractive streets hand in hand. They'd had lobster rolls while watching the tide ebb from the mouth of the Kennebec River.

But even as she was allowing herself the comfort of that memory, her captors had shoved her down into the boat, and she'd vomited—flat-out seasickness, she'd told herself. Not fear or pain.

Thinking about Owen strengthened her, even as she felt tears hot in her eyes. Her face was bloody and swollen, and she was dehydrated. She had no energy left. Still, Estabrook's thugs had threatened to kill just about everyone she knew and cared about if she tried anything. They'd seemed agitated, even nervous, as if they understood they were working for someone whose tolerance for risk might exceed their own and lead them to disaster.

They'd tied the Zodiac to an ancient dock in a cove not easily seen from land or sea. Getting on either side of her, they escorted her at gunpoint up a steep trail to an abandoned house built onto the hillside overlooking the ocean.

They brought her down dusty stairs to a walk-out basement and shoved her into a room furnished with an old sofa and a folding card table and chairs. Tall shelves held board games, paperback novels and comics, and the walls were covered with posters of the Hulk, Batman and various other comic-book superheroes.

Kids had hung out here, Abigail thought now as she stayed still, pain pulsing through her. This had to be the Rush family home in Maine. Lizzie Rush owned it. Where was she now? Abigail resisted the urge to speculate and instead assessed her surroundings. The room had small eyebrow windows—she'd never get out that way. She'd have to get out into the hall somehow, where she'd noticed a door that exited onto the side of the house.

She shut her eyes against a flutter of nausea and a stab of pain. She could hear Bob telling her that one day the constant training they did would come in handy. "You'll be glad you know how to take a hit."

*Glad* wasn't the word she'd use, but tonight, on the phone with her father, with Norman Estabrook relishing his power over her, she'd acted with reasonable control and deliberation, falling back on her training to help get her through her ordeal. The agony and fear she'd experienced had been real, but she felt no sense of humiliation at having cried for her father. Whatever Estabrook believed about her, she knew what she'd done, and why.

Her father and anyone else listening would understand, as she would have in their place, that she'd been trying both to survive and provide them with as much information as possible about the man they were hunting.

At least now they knew she was alive, and they knew for sure who had her.

Estabrook and Fletcher entered the basement room. Fletcher had stood by while Estabrook hit her. But Abigail didn't think he'd liked it. If nothing else, the violence and the call to her father were reckless and unnecessary in the eyes of a professional. He slouched against the doorjamb, impassive while Estabrook massaged the hand he'd used to hit her. In the dim light, she saw that his knuckles were swollen.

He didn't speak to her right away as he paced in front of her, more agitated than she'd seen him in the long hours of her captivity.

"You can stop pacing, Mr. Estabrook," Fletcher said with a yawn. "Your man Bassette isn't coming back."

Estabrook spun around at him. "How do you know?"

"Because I killed him. It was necessary. He was dangerously incompetent."

"Who the hell do you think you are?"

"Sorry, mate. There was no time to ask your permission."

With a sharp breath, Estabrook splayed the fingers of his bruised hand, then opened and closed them into a fist two times before speaking again. "What about Fiona O'Reilly?" he asked, calmer.

Fletcher shrugged. "She's not a concern now that Bassette's gone."

"The police will know—"

"They'd know, regardless. They had Bassette's blood. He had a criminal record. He might as well have left a bread-crumb trail for them. Your two remaining men now understand the stakes if they get out of line." Fletcher never raised his voice or adjusted his position against the doorjamb. "I got you out of Montana, and I've kept the police away from you thus far, but I can't perform miracles. You have highly motivated law-enforcement personnel all over the world looking for you."

Estabrook nodded with satisfaction. "Good."

Fletcher's gray eyes narrowed slightly. "You must give up this quest for revenge. Cut your losses, Mr. Estabrook. Move on. I'll help you."

"I've never run from a fight."

"Simon Cahill and John March aren't fools. They're out of your reach, at least for the moment."

Estabrook sucked in another sharp breath and took a menacing step toward the Brit. "No one is out of my reach."

"Torment them from a distance if you must," Fletcher said, still impassive, "but it's my professional advice that you leave this place now. Let me get you out of here."

"I don't need your help." Estabrook bent down, peering at Abigail, her back against the wall, her legs stretched out in front of her. "I should have hit you harder."

A half-dozen retorts popped into her head. Being around Bob O'Reilly for eight years had taught her to be quick with remarks, but she knew that in this situation she had to choose her words carefully. "You hit me plenty hard enough."

Estabrook stretched his fingers and stood up straight again.

"It hurts, doesn't it?" Abigail nodded to his swollen hand. "Hitting someone. You don't expect how hard bones are. Scoop almost broke his hand once in a fight."

He ignored her. "Your new friend Keira Sullivan has the luck of the Irish. She escaped her serial killer in June and two nights ago in Ireland she escaped—well, she escaped an idiot, obviously."

"Bassette's work," Fletcher said from the doorway.

"Ah." Abigail tasted blood in her mouth but tried not to react to Estabrook's taunts. "Hired the wrong man in Ireland, did you?"

"Keira's luck will run out in due course," Estabrook said, completely calm now. "I'm patient. I didn't become a successful hedge-fund manager by being impatient. In a way, it's just as well my man failed. Simon was already in Boston."

"You didn't send one incompetent man to kill both him and Keira—"

"No. I didn't."

His smirk, the way he studied her, made Abigail sick to her stomach. "You wanted Simon to find Keira's body and know you'd killed her. Monster."

He smiled knowingly. "Simon was in the room with your father when we called. They're suffering right now. Both of them. That does please me. It's sufficient for the moment."

"You should listen to Fletcher and let me go."

Abigail felt her energy draining out of her, and she focused on a crack in the linoleum, aware of Estabrook watching her, enjoying her suffering.

He examined a Spider-Man poster, torn on the edges, slightly yellowed. "Tell me, Detective, why did your father leave the Boston Police Department after Deirdre McCarthy's murder?"

Estabrook's fascination with her father was unnerving, but she reminded herself it wasn't a surprise. What *was* a surprise was his willingness to risk his freedom and his millions to bloody his hands with revenge. But it definitely was more than that. She thought Fletcher had seen it, too. Her father was a fresh challenge. A new death-defying adventure, and an excuse to commit violence himself.

Abigail kept her voice matter-of-fact. "I don't know that my father's decision to leave the department had anything to do with Deirdre McCarthy's murder."

"He didn't like the blood. The violence of murder." Estabrook moved to another superhero poster and glanced down at her. "The suffering. He wanted to be at a distance."

"It was a career move," Abigail said, taking any drama out of her father's decision. Not that she had any real idea why he'd chosen to leave the police department thirty years ago. They'd never discussed his reasoning. "He earned a law degree and decided to join the FBI. He's not God. He's just a man doing a job."

"Was he just doing his job when Simon Cahill's father was executed?"

Abigail didn't answer. Estabrook was at a Batman poster now. Bob liked to tease Owen, calling him Batman and saying he probably had a Batmobile stowed away at the Fast Rescue headquarters in Austin. She pushed back thoughts of the two of them, how they'd react to her kidnapping, the call she'd been forced to make—her cries of pain and anguish. Bob would be tight-lipped and chew one piece of gum after another as he focused on his job. Owen would figure out what he could do. It wouldn't matter that he wasn't law enforcement.

Estabrook abandoned the posters and squatted in front of her. He seemed unaffected by the stress of the past two days—the past two months. "Was your father just doing his job when Shauna Morrigan was murdered the same summer that Deirdre McCarthy was kidnapped and tortured?"

Abigail's stomach lurched. "I don't know—"

"Shauna Morrigan was Lizzie Rush's Irish mother."

She tried to look confused. "The Rushes are in the hotel business. I've never met Lizzie, but she's got nothing to do with any of this." But Abigail didn't believe that. She ran the tip of her pinkie along her lower lip, feeling the cracks, the coagulating blood. "She's not in law enforcement. My father, Simon, Bob, Scoop. We're pros. Never mind anyone else. Deal with us."

"Lizzie loves Maine. This is her family's house. It's so simple compared to the luxury hotels they own. They pamper their guests, but not themselves." Estabrook smiled. "She's here, or she will be soon. She'll hope I've come."

"Why?"

"Lizzie knows, at least deep down, that I can help her find peace. She knows I can help her confront her anger through decisive action."

"You want her as your minion," Abigail said tiredly.

"Very good, Detective." Estabrook smiled nastily at her. "You do remember your lessons on evil. There's only one Lucifer. One devil." He turned abruptly to Fletcher. "See to Detective Browning. Then find Lizzie and bring her to me. She has a cottage farther down the rocks. She loves to spend time there alone. With all that's gone on—" He inhaled through his nose. "She'll be there."

Fletcher stood up from the door. "You should listen to me, mate. Vengeance is a temporary high. When it's over, you've nothing to show for it. You're left with an empty hand."

"I don't plan for it to end with this one flurry of activity. I'm looking to a new beginning. A new way of life." Estabrook started for the door, all business now. "Are you any closer to learning who informed on me to the FBI?"

Fletcher shrugged. "What difference does it make now? Because you couldn't resist making that call tonight, the FBI knows you have Detective Browning. They're not going to be diverted, thinking your friends in the drug cartels could be responsible."

"I could have been forced to hit her under duress."

"Perhaps, but it's not what you want. You want John March to know you're responsible for his daughter's predicament. You want him to know you have her and can do as you please with her. And that, mate," Fletcher said as he approached Abigail, "is what will get you killed or sentenced to a long stretch in prison."

Estabrook licked his injured knuckles. "You knew my arrest was imminent when you came to me in Las Vegas, didn't you? You said you'd get me out if I got into trouble. You already knew I couldn't trust Simon and didn't tell me."

Fletcher glanced back at him. "You're right. I didn't tell you. It would have made no difference. I was already too late to warn you properly. The FBI had you nailed."

"You wanted money."

"You didn't have to hire me. You did because you understood that our interests are aligned."

"Something you should keep in mind now," Estabrook said stonily.

Once Estabrook was gone, Fletcher handed Abigail a folded black bandanna. "You're dehydrated. Try to keep some water down."

She took the bandanna and dabbed it to her bloody face. She studied the pencil markings on the wall, names written next to them:

*Whit. Harlan. Lizzie. Jeremiah. Justin.*

Children's heights.

"I want children," Abigail whispered. "Do you, Mr. Fletcher?"

He didn't respond as he put a hand down to her.

She let him pull her to her feet, listening for seagulls and picturing herself with Owen on Mount Desert Island, farther up the Maine coast, walking on the rocks pregnant with their first child. Grief welled up inside her. After all this time, what if she didn't live to have babies? What if Owen...

"You'll be reunited with him soon, love. Your man, Owen, is searching for Mr. Estabrook's plane in Montana. He's not one to sit tight." Fletcher winked at her. "He'd be proud of you."

"Have you ever been in love?"

"Me?" He gave her a sexy grin. "Count on it."

As he turned from her, Abigail saw an ache in his gray eyes. She hadn't imagined it or wished it there. Whoever he was, whatever game he was playing, Myles Fletcher had his own secrets and regrets.

And he was more alone in the world than she was.

# Chapter 26

Will stood out on Lizzie's deck in the gray of the southern Maine early morning. Fog had overspread the coast and stolen away the expansive view of the water. He had endured an interminable night on her sofa, the doors and windows open to the breeze and the sounds of seabirds, boats, a nearby chattering red squirrel. He'd have enjoyed the atmosphere of the little ocean house more if he'd been in Lizzie's bed.

With her, of course.

She was down by an evergreen, gnarled from its exposure to the ocean winds and salt spray, clinging to the edge of the rocks above the water. She'd slipped outside while he was in the shower. A signal, he'd thought, that she'd slept as fitfully as he had—and that she was as worried about Abigail Browning as he was and hoping she'd made the right decision in coming to Maine. Lizzie was no more patient with feeling useless than he was.

She was an innocent civilian, he reminded himself. A hotelier, even if one who'd made sacrifices and taken dangerous risks to expose a criminal network and bring a wealthy, resourceful man to justice.

Josie Goodwin had texted him from Ireland asking him to call her. Will dialed her now as he watched Lizzie pick up a small rock and fling it into the fog.

"Our friends in the garda would prefer I not call you," Josie said when she picked up. "But I am ignoring their wisdom."

"Where are you?"

"At Aidan O'Shea's farmhouse. It's a delight. Two sheep just wandered up to me among the roses. I had tea with Keira this morning. The guards objected letting me see her at first, but I persuaded them."

Will smiled. "Of course you did. What have you learned?"

"Keira can draw scary pictures as well as beautiful ones, and Michael Murphy had helpers. He's cooperating. He led the guards to an isolated house near the old copper mines. He and two friends planned to take Simon there after he'd discovered Keira's body in the stone circle."

"They were to hold him for Estabrook," Will said.

"Yes. He wanted to witness Simon's grief and then kill him himself, with his own hands."

Will stared into the fog. He could hear a seagull, invisible in the distance. Lizzie had moved to the other side of her tree. "I want this bastard, Josie."

"So do I. We're not alone. The guards, Keira and I have become great friends. But there's more, Will. Before her death, Shauna Morrigan Rush tipped off the Americans to an FBI agent working with the Boston Irish mob...." When Will didn't respond, Josie added, "That would be Lizzie Rush's mother, Will."

"Who tripped on a cobblestone on Temple Bar."

"And whose family died in a tragic car accident when they rushed to Dublin after hearing the news of her death. The Boston police sent a detective to Ireland to look into Shauna's death."

Will gripped his phone. "John March."

"Indeed," Josie said. "Shortly after he returned from Dublin, he exposed the identity of an FBI agent who had dealings— imagine this—with the Boston Irish mob. The Irish ruled the deaths of Shauna and her family accidents."

"Undoubtedly March didn't tell them all he knew."

"Does he ever tell anyone all he knows?"

It wasn't a question Will was meant to answer. Below him, Lizzie's hair seemed as black as the rocks that ran up and down the immediate coastline. The famous beaches of southern Maine were farther to the north and south. He envisioned exploring tide pools with her in some vague and no doubt unrealizable future.

"Will? Are you there?"

He understood the concern he heard in Josie's voice. He wasn't one for a wandering mind, in part because he was so disciplined about avoiding romantic entanglements, particularly on the job.

But was he, really, on the job right now?

"March attracts tragedy," Will said.

"No one goes through life without facing tragedy, but a man with *his* life is bound to face more than his share. Director March is a complex and honest man," Josie said, unusually thoughtful and introspective. "He's had to make difficult choices, and he has secrets. They come with the work he does, and he's been at it a long time."

"What do you suppose we'll be doing in thirty years, Josie?"

Her bright laugh broke through their somber mood. "I'll be having tea with other toothless old women and telling tales about my days working with a handsome nobleman. They'll think I've gone daft and won't believe a word." She quickly returned to the serious matters at hand. "Will, if Shauna Morrigan was killed because she was an informant for March, then your Lizzie Rush has reason to hate him."

"Estabrook must know. Her past could be the reason he befriended her in the first place. He could have been drawn to the drama of it initially, and as his obsession with March grew—"

"He could want Lizzie as his ally in fighting March," Josie interjected, "or perhaps as a prize of some sort—the motherless child wronged by a powerful and ambitious man. Estabrook's a very twisted human being, Will. It's not easy to get inside his thinking."

"Lizzie knows, or at least suspects, what he's up to," Will said. "That's why she's here. She hopes he'll come to her."

Josie didn't respond at once. "From what I've managed to get out of our Irish friends, Shauna Morrigan was very good. Regardless of how she died. Sometimes, despite our best efforts, things don't work out the way we mean them to."

Will stiffened as he noticed two men emerge from the trees and fog on the path along the edge of the rocks and approach Lizzie.

A dark-haired man touched her arm, and she turned to him.

Will peered through the gloom, recognizing the man's movements, his posture. "Josie, I have to go."

"He's there, isn't he?"

But Will had disconnected.

Lizzie called up to him on the deck. "I'll be back soon."

She went with the two men.

With Myles Fletcher.

They ducked behind the evergreen and disappeared up the path, in the thick fog.

Will bolted for the stairs, but Simon was on the top step, blocking the way. "Hold on, Will," he said, putting up a hand. "Think."

"Simon, it's Myles. I can't let him—"

"We won't let anything happen to Lizzie. You, me, we're here for her."

"You're an FBI agent. You have procedures you need to follow."

"Listen to me, Will. Norman doesn't know Lizzie is March's source. March didn't even know until yesterday. I sure as hell didn't have a clue." Simon came up onto the deck, its wood shiny and wet from the damp air. "She's been playing this game for months."

"Not with Myles she hasn't."

"Norman forced Abigail to talk to her father last night." Simon turned to Will as he stood in front of the railing. "It was bad."

Will understood what his friend was saying and didn't need him to describe the call in detail. "I'm sorry, Simon. I can only imagine how painful that must have been for March—for you." He walked over to the railing. A red squirrel scampered up the tree where only moments ago Lizzie had been throwing rocks into the water. Had she seen the men on the path? Could she have called for his help sooner, run back to the house—kept them from taking her? "I know how Myles thinks. I know his tactics."

"And you want him," Simon said.

"Simon, we must do this my way or Lizzie and Abigail Browning are almost certainly dead."

"What about Fletcher? Is there a chance—"

"Is there a chance we can trust him? It makes no difference.

Whether Myles is with us or against us—or only looking after himself—doesn't affect what we must do now."

"All right." Simon gave a grim smile. "Lucky I came armed."

"Simon," Will said, "you don't have to do this."

"Does Lizzie have a weapon?"

Will pictured her lithe, small body in jeans and a sweatshirt down on the rocks. He wished he'd shut her up in the fog with him and left Norman Estabrook, Myles Fletcher and their violence to the Americans.

Simon frowned. "Will…"

"No. No weapon. She has her wits, and her father trained her well. She's managed to keep her secrets for months from you, John March and a brilliant, wealthy risk-taker." Will looked down at the rocks and water. The squirrel chattered, out of sight. A seagull landed on a large boulder and stared up at the deck as if he had answers, knew all the secrets of his coastline. "Lizzie guessed Estabrook would come here."

"Maybe she hoped he would." Simon pulled open a door. "I'll alert SWAT and get them moving."

"On our direction. Not a moment sooner."

"Sure, Will. We'll make sure they get here in time to save our asses or put us in body bags."

# Chapter 27

*Boston, Massachusetts*
*7:02 a.m., EDT*
*August 27*

Bob sat across from John March at a table under a window in Morrigan's. It was very early, and the bar was closed, the liquor bottles still put away for the night. Jeremiah Rush, who seemed to be perpetually on duty, hadn't stopped the FBI director—or Bob—from going downstairs. March was alone. He'd shaken his protective detail, told them to go to hell, threatened to shoot them—Bob didn't know what.

None of them had slept. Him, March, Lucas Jones, Tom Yarborough. Who knew where Simon was. Hearing Abigail tortured on the line with her father didn't sit well with any of them.

"It's too early to drink," Bob said. "You should at least have a cup of coffee."

"I just wanted to be alone for a few minutes. Here, where…" March cleared his throat without finishing his thought.

"We're never alone, John. Our ghosts are always with us."

March's eyes showed a fear no man should know. "Lizzie Rush. Abigail…" He sighed heavily and nodded to the empty bar. "It all started here thirty years ago."

Bob didn't know what good drifting into the past would do. "We've made progress in the past few hours. Not much. Some."

"You shouldn't have come here, Bob." March abruptly snapped up to his feet. "Don't follow me," he said, making it an order, and started for the half flight of stairs.

Bob's head throbbed. John March had never made anyone's life easy. It wasn't why he was on the planet. Resisting the temptation to sit there and wait for the bar to open, order Irish whiskey and not move for the rest of the day, Bob forced himself to get to his feet.

If he wasn't breaking federal laws, March had no authority over him.

Bob headed up the stairs after the FBI director. Given what she knew about her mother's death—what any of them knew except March himself—Lizzie Rush had good reason to hate him, at least to be a little or a lot obsessed with him. She was up on the board as a person of interest, potentially in cahoots with Norman Estabrook and guilty as hell.

Except no one really believed that.

Jeremiah Rush was standing behind his desk, directing a middle-aged couple to the Freedom Trail. Without breaking eye contact with them, he gave a subtle nod toward a hall behind him.

Two minutes later, Bob took the hotel's back steps to a narrow alley, one of the countless nooks and crannies he was always surprised to find on Beacon Hill.

March was eyeing a shiny dark blue BMW.

Bob motioned to the expensive car. "Going to steal it, John?"

"I want to trade my life for hers." March didn't meet Bob's eye, the only indication—other than being there in the first place—that the strain of his daughter's kidnapping had gotten to him. "Let Estabrook torture me instead."

"Come on, will you?" Bob said, nearly knocking a pot of geraniums off the bottom step. "Cut me a break. I lose the FBI director in Boston, and they'll zap my pension for sure."

March's shoulders slumped, but only for a second before he straightened again. Even now, after hearing his kidnapped daughter scream in agony, cry for her daddy, he didn't have a thread or a hair out of place. But anyone who thought he was unaffected would, Bob knew, be making a mistake.

March blew out a breath at the overcast sky. "It was hard enough to shake my detail, but you, O'Reilly. Hell." He looked over at his longtime friend. "Fill me in."

Bob was relieved to have the emotions out of the way. "The dead guy, Bassette, was local. You know that. He hired a couple of guys from Chicago—Estabrook's old stomping grounds. One of them must have sneaked into our yard and planted the bomb on Abigail's porch. Cops. You'd think we'd sew up the place, but only so much you can do. They could have thrown the bomb over the fence and killed Scoop and Fiona outright."

"Bob—"

"You don't need Estabrook to torture you. You're torturing yourself. I know. I've been doing the same thing, blaming myself for Fiona having to sit there with Scoop bleeding all over her. For what she saw yesterday in that alley." Bob bent over and righted the flowerpot. He had no idea why. He sighed. "It gets us nowhere. The blame."

"I'm sorry, Bob. For Fiona. She's a good kid. She—"

"Why are you sorry? What did you do to her?"

The FBI director barely cracked a smile, and Bob suddenly remembered them standing on a South Boston street years ago. March, ten years older, handsome, had been on the move, and Bob, just a kid, had been a cop's son who didn't want his friend up the street to be dead. Every night, he'd prayed for Deirdre McCarthy to come home to her mother. Things hadn't worked out that way, and now, thirty years later, he could feel that awful, hot, violent summer reaching out to him and the man a few yards from him, sucking them back into a time and a world they both had tried to forget.

Bob felt ragged and out of control, even as he was determined to get through the day. Do his job. Find Abigail. Arrest her kidnappers.

March looked as if he'd crumble if anyone touched him.

"You know Abigail wants a wedding?" Bob dug out another pack of gum. "She's not waiting anymore. She's marrying her rich Garrison. I'll be invited. Who knows where it'll be."

"Owen's a good man," March said, choking back his emotion.

"He didn't grow up like we did. None of them did." Bob worked a piece of gum out of the pack. "Then there's Keira. Ten to one she and Simon will be getting married. She's already dragging me on that Christmas trip to Ireland. Hell, John. These women are going to break my bank."

March had tears now in his dark eyes. "Are you at peace with your past, Bob?"

Bob grinned at him. "Never."

"I keep hearing her scream."

"I know. We all do, but it's worse for you. Be glad her mother didn't get that call." Bob peeled off the wrapper and stuck the gum in his mouth. "Because I'm your friend, John, I'm going to tell you this. Kathryn wants to take you to a spa retreat."

"A spa—Bob, what are you talking about?"

He chewed his gum. "She told Abigail on her last trip to Boston. I was up on my porch, and I overheard them talking down by Scoop's garden. I can see you in a bathrobe, drinking herbal tea, waiting for your massage—"

"All right, enough." March sighed up at the sky again. "We're not as young as we used to be."

"So? Who cares? We know what we're doing now. Right?"

"Does anyone ever—"

"You're giving me a headache, John. I figure we have ten minutes, tops, before that prick Yarborough lands on us. You know damn well he's on our trail. He's not going to let us off Beacon Hill."

March managed a weak grin. "Whose job does he get first, yours or mine?"

"He can have mine. I'm moving to Ireland to sing in pubs." Bob saw now what he and March had to do. Maybe March had already seen it, and he'd just been letting the younger police lieutenant come to the same conclusion on his own. Or maybe Bob was taking the lead this time. It didn't matter. "Lizzie Rush's old man taught her well, but let's go find her and her new Brit friend, Lord Davenport. You and me."

The back door to the hotel opened, and a tawny-haired, middle-aged man in wrinkled khakis walked down the steps. Clearly a Rush, he looked at the two men in the alley as if he knew exactly who they were. "Lizzie's her mother's daughter." The newcomer was tanned and leathery, his tone cool, controlled—but he radiated an intensity that told Bob that this man, too, had a loved one in harm's way. "I took the red-eye from Vegas. I hate flying. Fill me in, or do I need to kidnap Boston's chief homicide detective and the director of the FBI?"

Harlan Rush, Lizzie Rush's father, could do it, too. Bob balled up his gum wrapper and shoved it in his pocket as he looked to March. "John?"

March didn't hesitate. "We go."

Harlan dangled a set of keys from his hand. "My nephew said we could borrow his dad's car. It's that one right there. Lucky, huh? You don't need to steal it after all."

"Licensed to carry concealed?" Bob asked him.

Harlan headed past Bob for the BMW. "I'm licensed to carry a cruise missile to shove up Norman Estabrook's flabby butt."

Bob figured, who was he to argue?

He climbed into the leather backseat of Bradley Rush's sedan, Harlan Rush at the wheel, next to him, the former BPD detective who'd investigated his Irish wife's death.

"I hope by the time we get to Maine," Bob said as Rush started the car, "we find out Abigail is safe and sound here in Boston, and we can all have fried clams."

The two men in front made no comment.

"Yeah," Bob said on a breath. "Let's go."

# Chapter 28

*Near Kennebunkport, Maine*
*7:45 a.m., EDT*
*August 27*

"I love cormorants," Lizzie said as she ambled along the narrow path above the rocks. "I can watch them endlessly."

Neither of the two men with her responded. Myles Fletcher had stayed next to her, even if it meant he had to veer off the path, into pine needles or onto the rocks. The second man, silent and obviously less fit, walked a few steps ahead of them. Both men were armed with nine-millimeter pistols, Fletcher's holstered at his waist, his partner's in his right hand.

Lizzie hadn't left her house with so much as a butter knife. She'd tried reaching for a fist-size rock, but Fletcher had calmly touched her shoulder and shaken his head, effectively changing her mind.

She nodded to the ocean, calm and gray in the fog. "It's a beautiful spot, isn't it? I know you can't see much today. I used to walk this path with my grandmother." She tried to adopt the breezy style she'd had with Norman—oblivious, personable, as if she had no concerns about being escorted to him by armed guards and wasn't a woman who'd send information anonymously to the FBI. "She'd tell me if she had her way, she'd die out here, watching a cormorant dive for food."

Fletcher stepped over an exposed spruce root. "Did she?"

"No. She died in the hospital."

Fletcher eased back onto the path. His manner was detached, but he was clearly on high alert. "You miss her."

"I do, but it's okay. You'd want someone to miss you if you died, wouldn't you?"

"I don't know that I would, love."

He and his partner must have seen Will on the deck and Simon's arrival. Fletcher, at least, would know he had an SAS officer and FBI agent after him. Lizzie would concentrate on finding Abigail Browning and giving them a chance to act. Her father had lectured on being tentative. "Be bold. Be decisive. Especially if lives are at stake."

She noticed the man ahead of them had picked up his pace. She looked up at Fletcher. "Quite a difference between here and Las Vegas, isn't there?"

He glanced down at her. "Quite."

"What did you do, look up Norman in Las Vegas and offer your services? Did you know he was about to be arrested?"

"Keep up," Fletcher said.

"No problem. Is Norman here or on a boat? He came here last summer in a yacht he'd leased. Gorgeous. I had dinner with him on it, a real step up from my sit-on-top ocean kayak." She tripped on a sharp, exposed rock but righted herself before

Fletcher could take her arm. "How much is Norman paying you to create the mayhem of the past couple days?"

"He's a wealthy man."

Lizzie resisted a smart remark and kept to her role. "Norman knew I'd come, and I have. We should hurry." She gestured back toward her little house. "I gather you and Will go way back."

A glint of humor came into Fletcher's gray eyes. "That's why I'm staying out of his line of fire."

"He's not armed."

Fletcher laughed outright. "He's a man of many talents, our Lord Davenport."

The path curved uphill along the edge of a steep cliff. Seagulls swarmed onto the rocks below, their familiar cries and the rhythmic wash of the tide helping Lizzie to control her breathing. If she hyperventilated, Norman and his men would see through her. She'd walked this route hundreds of times since she was a child. Her grandmother would point out landmarks, plants, birds, the occasional seal, dolphin or whale. Edna Whitcomb Rush hadn't been a demonstrative woman—no hugs and kisses from her—but she'd been loving in her own way.

"Estabrook will leave us to hold off the FBI and whoever else turns up," Fletcher called to his partner. "Are you okay with that, mate?"

The thug paused and shrugged. "I don't plan to stick around for a tactical team to get here, but we do what we have to." He was American, in his early thirties. He gestured at Lizzie with his gun. "I say we kill this one and the detective and clear out. They'll only slow us down."

Lizzie was careful not to react, but now she knew. Abigail Browning was here and she was alive.

Fletcher didn't look as if he cared one way or the other what happened to her or to Lizzie. "Do you suppose Estabrook has an escape route for himself?" he asked his colleague. "One that doesn't include us?"

"He pays me before he leaves. That's it. I don't care what he does after that."

"All right, then," Fletcher said, impassive. "We're on the same wavelength."

The other man increased his lead over them. They veered off the path onto the overgrown yard of the shingled house that the first Harlan Rush, Lizzie's grandfather, had built. He'd died when she was small, but she had a vague memory of his taking her out in a rowboat, staying close to the shore as he told her stories. He'd loved the sea. "Take everything else away from him," her grandmother had said, "and if Harlan could still get to the ocean, he'd be a happy man."

It had mystified her that their older son, his father's namesake, preferred the dry desert of Las Vegas. But there were reasons for that, Lizzie thought.

She angled a look up at Fletcher. "Will believed in you, didn't he?"

The ex-SAS officer didn't meet her eye. "Will believes in honor, duty and country."

"And you don't?"

They continued through tall, wet grass on the soft ground, past a dense row of beach roses, entangled with wild blackberry vines, but he didn't answer.

"I know what I'm doing and why," Lizzie said, falling a few steps behind him. "Do you know the same about yourself?"

"Listen, love." Fletcher waited for her to catch up. He draped an arm over her shoulders and leaned in close to her. He was self-confident, amused. "I'd enjoy a nice chat with you, but not now. All right?"

"Why did you kill that man in Boston?"

His eyes held hers an instant longer than was comfortable. "Necessity."

Lizzie took a breath. "He was about to kill Fiona O'Reilly, wasn't he?"

Fletcher kept his arm around her as they crossed the lawn to stone steps that led up the hill to the front of the house. His partner had gone on ahead. "You don't give up, do you?" He spoke without humor now. "I had no other choice. Whatever side I'm on, that's a fact."

"Norman hired him. He got him working on his hit list without your knowledge."

"Mr. Estabrook is a very independent man, love. As you know."

"You scared the hell out of Fiona."

"All right, then. I scared her. She's agreed to police protection, now, though, hasn't she?" He dropped her arm from Lizzie's shoulders. "How is Lord Davenport these days?"

"Handsome. Those changeable eyes of his." Lizzie went ahead of Fletcher and started up the steps, but he met her pace. "I think he might be my Prince Charming."

Fletcher's mouth twitched. "He'll find you, love." He smiled, enigmatic, a man very much in control. "I think Will's been looking for you his entire life."

Her heart jumped. "You're—"

"If you want to get Abigail Browning and yourself out of here alive, you must do exactly as I say." His gray eyes leveled on her, but he maintained the same detached manner she'd first noticed back at the bar in Las Vegas. "Do you understand?"

"You want me to trust you."

"I don't give a damn if you trust me. I want you to follow my lead."

Lizzie hesitated, imagining this man and Will on a secret mission together. She understood now how Will had trusted Fletcher—how shocking it must have been to believe that trust had been betrayed. How devastating. Right now, standing in the fog above the oncoming tide, she wanted to put her life in Myles Fletcher's hands.

"I'll do as you say," she said, "but if I'm making a mistake and you're not—"

"It won't matter. You and Abigail will be dead." He grinned and winked at her. "You're good, love, but I'm better."

"I came with you because I can help."

His gaze narrowed on her. "I know."

Lizzie felt a coolness in the small of her back as they followed a walkway around to a side entrance. "How long have you known?"

"You're Harlan Rush's daughter."

"So," she said carefully, "since Las Vegas. You tried to warn me."

"And you paid no attention." Fletcher wasn't one to be distracted by the past. He stayed next to her, close, serious. "Estabrook wants the identity of John March's source. I've pointed him in the direction of someone in his financial empire. Right now, he's still completely fascinated with you."

"Because of my mother," Lizzie said half to herself.

"You and Detective Browning mustn't leave with him. Whatever else happens, that can't. Clear?"

Lizzie nodded. "Where's Abigail now?"

"Locked in a room in the basement—"

"Put me down there," she said, then gave him a quick smile. "There isn't a room in this house my cousins and I can't get out of."

"You were an incorrigible child?"

"We're a resourceful family."

His eyes were half-closed. "You are still to take my lead."

"Norman has a backup plan. He always does. I can find out what it is."

"You can get Abigail Browning and hide while I do my job."

"Let Will and Simon help you—"

"Off we go, love." Without waiting for a response, he grabbed her by the elbow and shoved her up the steps. "Mr. Estabrook, get yourself together. We need to leave. Now. Simon Cahill and Will Davenport are here." Fletcher kept his grip on Lizzie as they entered the mudroom. "I have your rich-girl landlady."

Norman appeared in the doorway, rubbing his thumb on the swollen knuckles of his right hand. "Good," he said, pleased, without even glancing at Lizzie. "We make our stand now."

Maintaining his grip on Lizzie's arm, Fletcher shook his head. "They'll have called in a tactical team."

"Then we'll just have to deal with Simon and Davenport before SWAT can get here. I want them both. Special Agent Cahill and his princely friend."

"These men know what they're doing. They won't let us see them, much less get off a shot at them." Fletcher's tone was professional, still somewhat deferential to Norman's authority. "My advice is to leave Miss Rush and Detective Browning and get out of here."

"I know what I'm doing, too," Norman said, petulant. He shifted his attention to Lizzie, finally acknowledging her presence. "It's good to see you, Lizzie. I knew you'd come to Maine. This house..." His gesture seemed to take in the entire property. "The very walls cry out with what might have been if John March hadn't caused your mother's death."

"Where's his daughter now?" Lizzie asked. She wriggled in

Fletcher's grasp, and he let her go. "I can't help it, Norman. She had the life I didn't. A father *and* a mother."

"We have her now, Lizzie."

She noticed a flicker of distaste—of *hatred*—in Fletcher's eyes before his detached manner took hold again.

"I want to see her," Lizzie said.

"I'll take Miss Rush downstairs," Fletcher said. "She and Detective Browning can chat about her father while we deal with Cahill and Davenport. No argument, Mr. Estabrook. We do this my way here on out or I walk now."

"All right. Lock Lizzie in with our detective." Norman smiled and brushed his fingertips across her cheek. "Detective Browning needs to know the impact her father's had on your life. Tell her. Make her understand it's his fault she's in this predicament."

"I thought I hid it from you…how much I hate John March."

Norman gave her a supercilious little laugh. "You could never hide anything from me. You're refreshingly transparent. I'll come for you." He tucked a strand of hair behind her ear in a possessive but asexual manner. "You're special to me, Lizzie. You have been right from the start."

"Same here, Norman. You're special to me." She ignored the sudden dryness in her mouth. "You've transformed my life."

Fletcher took her by the arm and led her down the basement stairs. The man who'd helped him collect her in the first place unlocked the door to the old rec room. He waited in the hall while Fletcher brought her inside.

Abigail was sitting on the floor with her back against the wall, her face, especially her mouth and left cheek, swollen and bloody, scabs forming on the deeper cuts. Lizzie stifled a gasp and turned to Fletcher, grabbed his wrist. "Tell Norman he's proved his point," she said in a low voice. "There's nothing unique about killing Abigail now. If he leaves her, he'll have even more power over her father. March will know what Norman could have done, that it was in his power to do more."

"Power through restraint."

"Exactly."

"Will do, love." Fletcher winked at her. "I'm thinking more in terms of putting a bullet in the bloody bastard's head at the first opportunity."

"But you need him," Lizzie said. "Why? If you're MI6—"

"A fiction."

"Colloquial expression. The Secret Intelligence Service isn't a fiction. Neither is the Special Air Service. Even if you're free-lancing, you're on a mission. You disappeared in Afghanistan. Are you after some drug lord-terrorist connection?"

His eyes darkened to a hard slate color. "I have to go. A boat's on the way to the old dock here. I need it not to be scared off by shots. I'll try to keep Simon and Will from coming to your rescue too soon. In the meantime, find a nice hiding place." He glanced at Abigail and then winked again at Lizzie. "Be good, love."

At the click of the lock in the door after he left, Abigail let out a low moan of pain and sat up straighter. "I look worse than I feel."

"I hope so."

"You're Lizzie Rush." Abigail struggled to focus, one eye markedly less swollen than the other. "My father looked into your mother's death in Ireland. It was ruled an accident."

"It wasn't," Lizzie said.

Abigail nodded. "No, it wasn't."

Following Fletcher's lead, Lizzie concentrated on the imme-diate problem, quickly explaining the situation to the detective. "I told Myles I can get us out of here."

"Myles…" Abigail swallowed visibly. "Fletcher. He's an interesting character. There are at least two other men in addition to him and Estabrook. A third—I think he's dead."

"Yes. Fiona O'Reilly and I found him yesterday. It's a long story. Let's focus on getting out of here before Norman pays us a visit. Can you stand?"

She nodded, allowing Lizzie to help her to her feet. "You obviously have something in mind."

Lizzie smiled. "My cousins and I used to pretend we were prisoners on a pirate ship."

"And this room was the ship? There's an exit?"

"Sort of." She pulled the ratty couch away from the wall and pointed to a knee-high door. "It goes under the stairs to the laundry room. My cousins and I would…well, we liked our adventures. You'll have to crawl."

"I can do it. I should have found this myself. The laundry room—there's an exit just outside the door, isn't there?"

"It leads right into my grandmother's hydrangeas."

"If Estabrook or his men catch us—"

"We end up back here playing cards," Lizzie said lightly.

Abigail tried to smile. "My optimism took a hit along with my face." She studied the door a moment. "I'll go first. If I run into problems, get back here and blame me."

Lizzie didn't argue with her and squatted to unlatch the door. "I wonder if the adults in our lives realized the door was here and wanted to encourage a certain amount of creativity and rebellion in my cousins and me." She looked up at Abigail. "I'm not promising we won't happen upon mice, dead or alive."

"I heard mice running in the walls." Abigail got down low and peered into the pitch-dark crawl space. She gave Lizzie a beleaguered smile. "I figured they were better company than the rats upstairs."

She got on all fours and went through the small opening. Lizzie pulled the couch back as close to the wall as she could, but it wasn't enough—Norman and his men would know exactly what had happened the minute they entered the room. She shut the door behind her, anyway, as she ducked into the crawl space. She breathed in dust and in the darkness, thought she really did hear a mouse scurrying. But she moved fast, making her way to another small door, which Abigail had left open.

Lizzie emerged in the laundry room. It was equipped with an old washer and dryer, a freezer and a wall of hooks and shelves. Abigail, panting and ashen, held a pair of large, rusted garden shears. "I'd rather have my Glock. Stay behind me, Lizzie. Let me—" Abigail frowned as Lizzie grabbed her grandmother's old walking stick. "What are you doing?"

Lizzie held the stick at her side, felt its worn, smooth wood as her eyes misted. "My gran...I can see her now, walking in her garden. She was so proud of her delphiniums." She shook off the memories. "I'm pretty good with a *bo*."

"You know martial arts?"

"Harlan Rush arts," Lizzie said with an attempt at a smile.

"We can do some damage with garden shears and a walking stick, but they've got automatics." Even bruised, Abigail looked like the experienced homicide detective she was. "Nothing crazy, okay?"

They eased out into the hall. Lizzie pulled open the door, wincing at every noisy creak it made, and they slipped outside, into the fog, squeezing along the edge of the six-foot hydrangeas that grew on the hillside. She shut the door tightly behind her.

Abigail was clearly done in, fresh blood oozing from a cut on her cheek. Lizzie smelled the hydrangeas in the damp air and fought an urge to hide under their low, thick branches. But she knew what she had to do. "You're hurt, and you've been through hell," she said softly. "Let me do this, Abigail. Norman thinks I'm on his side—"

"No. We stay together."

She touched Abigail's shoulder. "Fletcher needs something from Norman. It's important, and I can get it. If he gets away now, we'll never find him. He'll win. He *will* be your father's nemesis."

"I can't let you—"

"I'll at least buy you all time. I won't take unnecessary risks. Here." Lizzie pointed Abigail to an old wood bench hidden among the hydrangeas. "I knew I didn't have these bushes cut back for a reason. They'll hide you."

Abigail sank onto the bench. "Stay here with me."

"There's no way Fletcher can do this alone. Norman trusts me. If I don't do what I can now—" Lizzie didn't finish. "Make sure Will and Simon know Fletcher's one of the good guys. Another reason for you to stay behind. We don't want a friendly-fire incident."

"No, but—"

Lizzie straightened with her walking stick and smiled. "Don't make me knock you out. I'm trusting you and our fairy prince, Prince Charming and dark lord to come save me."

"Simon, Davenport and Fletcher." Abigail smiled weakly. "Very amusing. You can take my garden shears."

"Take a look around at all the overgrown stuff. Do you think I'm any good with garden shears?"

Lizzie didn't wait for an answer and walked out from the cover of the hydrangeas toward the stone steps. She couldn't see anyone through the fog and continued down the sloping yard. She debated calling out for Norman, but she spotted him by himself next to the wild blackberries and roses above the rocks.

She waved and ran toward him. "Norman! Abigail just almost killed me! She used me as a hostage—I'm sorry. I took off. I didn't know what else to do."

"Where is she now?"

"She's gone upstairs. She's looking for you. She thinks she can take on your men."

"She'll learn otherwise."

"Norman…" Lizzie caught her breath. "This is for real, isn't it?"

His eyes were cold, and beads of sweat glistened on his upper lip. "Very real," he said. "And whether or not you're lying, Lizzie, you're mine now."

Fog enveloped the coastline in its shroud of gray. Abigail shivered as she crept toward the sounds of the ocean, staying in the cover of overgrown shrubs and gnarled, drooping evergreens. She ached and she was sick, but she would do what she could to distract and divert Estabrook and his men—anything to back up Lizzie Rush.

Her teeth chattered now.

Simon materialized through the fog as he came up from the rocks. He lowered his pistol when he saw her. A tall, light-haired man, also armed, came up beside him. Simon's British friend, Will Davenport.

Lizzie's Prince Charming.

Abigail fought back a surge of emotion. "Estabrook has Lizzie Rush."

Simon took in her injuries with a quick scan. "We'll take care of her, Ab."

Her cut, swollen lip cracked painfully as she gave him the barest of smiles. "Ab. Hell, Simon." She focused and described the situation to the two men. "Lizzie's trying to stall Estabrook. She thinks

Fletcher needs information from him. He's—I don't know what he's doing. Estabrook has two other men. Hired guns."

Will squinted toward the water, into the gray, then turned to Abigail. "Myles has been alone long enough." He seemed to struggle a moment. "Lizzie's as stubborn and independent as he is."

Abigail hugged her arms to her chest, the damp air making her ache even more. "I'm sorry I couldn't stop her," she whispered.

"No one's been able to stop her for a year," Simon said.

Will looked at him. "I have to go."

Simon straightened, a federal agent taking charge. "Will—hell. Fletcher's a British agent, isn't he?"

"Now. Yes. I didn't know."

"You two can at least try not to kill anyone else on U.S. soil."

Without comment, Will headed back past the evergreen and down toward the water, disappearing in the fog.

Abigail put a hand out to Simon. "Give me a gun. I'm not going after these bastards with garden shears," she said, tossing them to the ground.

He smiled grimly as he handed her his pistol, retrieving another from his holster.

Abigail felt marginally better having a gun in her hand. "We need to hold off on firing as long as we can. If Norman thinks he's lost…" She knew she didn't need to finish. She glanced toward the water, almost invisible now in the fog. "Simon…can you at least clue me in?"

"Afghanistan," he said.

It was enough. Drugs, terrorism. Whatever the specifics, the Brits were on the case.

So, undoubtedly, was her father.

And Lizzie Rush.

# Chapter 29

A fine mist was falling now, collecting on Lizzie's hair and shoulders. She saw a Zodiac tied to the ancient dock her grandmother had meant to have removed. But her husband had built it with their two sons, and it had stayed.

Norman walked behind her with a nine-millimeter pistol pointed at her back. He'd pulled it from under his lightweight jacket. As far as Lizzie knew, none of his exploits over the past year had included guns, but how much did he need to know about shooting? He just had to pull the trigger.

He hadn't taken her walking stick from her. She used it now to navigate a steep, eroded section of the familiar path down to the dock. "Where are we going?" she asked.

"Trust me, Lizzie." When they reached the bottom of the path, he moved in front of her and steadied his gaze on her. "You do trust me, don't you?"

"Sure, Norman, I trust you, which I'd say even if you didn't have a gun in my face. Will you put that thing away?"

He lowered the pistol but didn't holster it. He was breathing rapidly, almost panting as he peered up toward the house, invisible in the gray. "I can't see through this fog."

"Going on a boat probably doesn't make much sense in these conditions."

Irritation sparked in his eyes as he focused back on her. "You're not to worry."

"I can't help it." Lizzie hoped she was striking the right note— not too combative but not too meek, either of which Norman would hate. "Where are your men? The Brit and the other two?"

"They'll meet us here. Again, you're not to worry. I'll deal with them."

Lizzie tried not to show any reaction, but she'd never experienced such cold hatred. It was even worse than what she'd seen in him when he'd called Simon from Montana and threatened to kill him and John March. Norman had clearly nursed his anger and sense of betrayal in the two months since his arrest, holding on to that moment when he'd learned Simon Cahill wasn't a former FBI agent and didn't despise John March.

"What happened?" she asked. "Did Abigail Browning come after you the second you were set free because you dared to threaten her father?"

"*I* came after *her.*"

"Oh. I see. You meant what you said when you told Simon you wanted to kill him and her father."

"I always mean what I say."

"You want them to suffer first," Lizzie said.

Norman smiled. "Yes."

Lizzie realized she hadn't needed Fletcher to have told her not to get into a boat with Norman. She leaned on her grandmother's walking stick at her side and tried to keep him talking. "You know I was supposed to be raised here, don't you?"

"Of course. I know everything about you. You don't have to pretend anymore, Lizzie." Mist glistened on his hair and made his pasty skin shine. "It will be ironic, poetic even, for March's daughter to die here."

His eyes were so frigid, his hatred so deep, that Lizzie could only manage a nod as she heard a boat close by in the fog.

Norman's gaze was still on her. "It will be just as poetic for you to die here if you've betrayed me."

"How would I betray you? Have your bed at one of our hotels short-sheeted?"

He almost smiled. "I've always loved your sense of humor. I have had so little to laugh about this summer, but that's about to change."

Lizzie ignored the chill she felt and pointed to his bruised hand. "Did you do that defending yourself against March's daughter? I saw how beat up she looked—"

"Lizzie, Lizzie. She didn't attack *me*. I attacked *her*." He stepped onto the dock. "Everything changed in June when I realized what had been done to me. John March went from being an amusing challenge to figure out—to thwart—to..." He paused, inhaled through his nose. "It's a deadly battle we're in now."

"You didn't just come up with this plan in June," she said, pretending to be impressed—a small planet circling his brighter, smarter-than-everyone sun. "Did a part of you hope March was investigating you?"

"He's a compelling adversary, and I plan for everything."

"Those friends of yours the feds were after...well... It's not for me to say, but why didn't you tell me what you were up to?"

"Reasons of operational security."

"Fletcher came to you in Las Vegas. I saw him—"

"He helped me get out of Montana," Norman said curtly.

Lizzie glanced at the gun in his hand. It was a pricey Sig Sauer. He didn't have his finger on the trigger. "When we became friends, was it because of my personal history with March?"

"You tell me, Lizzie. Was it?"

She felt an involuntary shiver. "My mother..."

"Help me. Be at my side. That's what I want and need from you now. Do you for a moment believe the FBI has everything on me? That I..." He spoke with an intensity that reminded her he had made billions for himself and his investors. He was focused, driven and very intelligent. "My work in hedge funds taught me the value of secrecy and discretion. You want John March to suffer, don't you, Lizzie? For what he did to your mother."

Ignoring how cold she felt, she nodded. "Yes."

"That's good. None of this is personal for me. My motives are more pure—more interesting—than hatred and revenge. I need you to have those simpler emotions. I have a powerful, secretive man obsessed with me, Lizzie. An equal. A man who will know I have killed people he cared about. I refuse to submit to his authority. I'll be out here forever."

The silhouette of a small speedboat materialized in the fog beyond the dock, and he glanced out to the water. "We must hurry."

"I'm not the risk-taker you are, Norman." Lizzie added a note of uncertainty to her voice, as if she needed his strength, cleverness and certainty. "Tell me where we're going. Please."

"A yacht's waiting to take us away from here." He shrugged and added, almost as an afterthought, "I have powerful allies."

"What yacht? I gather you came here by boat. Is this a different—"

"I assume that yacht's compromised. This one is registered to a company of mine that no one knows about. You're her inspiration." He looked back at Lizzie and raised his free hand to her. "You're my ally. My number-one helper."

Lizzie caught her breath as she realized that Myles Fletcher had to be after the yacht. "I want to help you…but…I'm nervous. This yacht. What's it like? Where—"

"Your mother loved lavender. You told me. Think of her out there waiting for you. *Lavender Lady.*" Norman was gentle with her now, reassuring and yet still smug. "Don't be afraid. We'll win. March. Simon. I'll be an enemy like they've never had."

The speedboat slowed as it approached the dock. Lizzie could see a man at the wheel and another seated in the stern, armed with an assault rifle.

She pretended to be confused. "We're not going in the Zodiac?"

"Don't be afraid, Lizzie," Norman whispered.

"What about your men at the house? The Brit and the other two—"

"They'll deal with Simon and his friend Will Davenport. I told them they'll receive bonuses if Simon finds Abigail dead." Norman wiped his brow with the back of his gun hand, wistful. "I thought I wanted to take her with me, but I'm bored with her. I should have killed her myself so that I could tell her father what it was like to feel her blood dripping down my arms."

"Simon and your three men and you and me…" Managing to ignore the shiver in her back at Norman's words, Lizzie frowned as if she were still trying to understand his plans. "We won't all fit in the boat, will we?"

The change in Norman's expression gave her his answer.

"You're having them killed. The men in the boat will do it."

"I need a fresh team."

If she got into the boat with these men, Lizzie knew, she'd be lost. Will, Simon, Fletcher, March—they'd never find her.

And they'd never find *Lavender Lady.*

The rocks, trees, fog and steep hillside all offered cover and concealment, but only if she could get away from Norman before he and the thugs in the boats figured out she wasn't on their side.

"I'm not going with you," she said.

Her words startled him, and in that split second, Lizzie acted, smashing the walking stick onto his hand with the gun. He dropped the weapon and cried out in pain and shock.

The gun skittered across the dock and into the tide.

Norman lunged for her, but Lizzie leaped out of his path onto the rocks. She knew every tide pool, boulder and stone in the cove.

The man in the back of the boat jumped out onto the dock with his rifle pointed in her direction. She ducked for cover behind a large, square boulder, just as she heard a movement on the hill in the thick fog above her.

Myles Fletcher dropped down from behind a windswept spruce tree and leveled an assault rifle of his own at the man on the dock. "Drop your weapon now."

The man didn't obey and tried to get off a shot, but Fletcher was faster and fired. Norman yelled, a squeal of rage and terror as he tried to get his footing on the wet rocks. Fletcher ignored him. At that moment, billionaire, thrill-seeking Norman Estabrook might as well have been a tiny hermit crab.

In the next instant, Will burst out from the spruce tree and bounded onto the dock, pistol pointed at the second man in the speedboat. "You. Hands in the air."

The man complied and raised both his hands above him.

A three-shot burst rang out farther up on the hill, but neither Fletcher nor Will seemed concerned that it was anything but friendly fire.

Will addressed Fletcher but kept his eyes—and gun—on the man in the boat. "Do you need him on the boat or off?"

"Off. You're bloody relentless, Lord Will." Fletcher sighed, rifle pointed at Norman, who was still thrashing for balance on the rocks. "I've been trying to stay a step ahead of you for two years."

"Myles. My God." Will stepped onto the dock and spared a half glance toward the rocks. "Lizzie?"

"I'm okay. I think I stepped on a starfish." She climbed over the tumble of rocks to Norman, still thrashing for his balance. "Don't move or one of the Brits will shoot you." She checked him for additional weapons but found none. "You had everything, Norman. Money, adventure. Friends. But they weren't enough. Now you're alone in this world, and it's your own doing."

He hissed at her. "A hotelier. A Rush. You're one of John March's people. You betrayed me. I will kill you one day, Lizzie." He spoke coldly, as if he hadn't lost. "Slowly. With my own hands."

Lizzie stood on a dry boulder. "John March is a good man, and you're exactly what you're afraid you are."

"Not one of the big boys," Abigail said, appearing at the bottom of the steep path.

Norman breathed in with a snarl and started to charge for her, but she leveled a pistol at him. "Don't," she said.

He stopped, debated a fraction of a second and dived for her and her gun.

Simon was right behind her on the path and fired at the same time Abigail did.

If Norman made a sound as he fell, Lizzie didn't hear it over the echo of the gunfire, the whoosh of the tide moving on and off the rocks behind her.

Abigail collapsed onto her knees and vomited among the rocks. Fletcher stepped off and put an arm around her, helping her to her feet. "Might not just be seasickness, love," he said. "Ever think of that?"

She stared at him. "What?"

He winked. "You'll make a hell of a mum." He walked past Norman's body to Lizzie, no humor in his gray eyes now. "Don't look at him. He's gone. A pity, in a way. He'd rather be off to hell than in prison."

"You're right. He…" Lizzie shivered in the cool, damp air. "I did what I could."

"I know, love. I wouldn't have let him shoot you." Fletcher grinned suddenly. "Not with Lord Davenport on the premises. He's besotted with you."

Down the dock, the man on the boat refused Will's order to disembark and scoffed. "You won't shoot an unarmed man."

"Watch this," Fletcher said, amused, beside Lizzie.

In the next instant, Will leaped onto the boat, nailed the man with the butt of his gun and sent him sprawling into the cold Maine water.

Fletcher smiled at Lizzie. "Now he's off the boat. You're just as handy with your walking stick." His eyes matched the color of the fog as he nodded toward the water. "Estabrook has a yacht waiting for him offshore. It's not the same one he took here from Boston."

"I know," Lizzie said.

Simon took charge of the man in the water, and Will approached his fellow Brit. "Its name?" he asked.

Fletcher looked at him. "I'd kill for its name."

The dripping thug walked down the dock, his hands held high, Simon behind him. He glanced down at the body of his partner. "We were just transportation. We didn't know where we were headed from here."

"And killers," Simon added.

"You've been onto a terrorist plot," Will said to Fletcher.

"For two years. It's a bad one. The name of the yacht gets me closer to stopping it." Fletcher settled his gaze on his friend. "I couldn't prevent what happened in Afghanistan. David and Philip. You. There was nothing I could do except carry on. It was necessary for you to think I was dead. A traitor."

"You latched on to a drug-terrorism connection. It led you to Estabrook."

"I tipped off March. Anonymously, but I think he sensed it was me. He didn't ask."

Abigail glanced at them from the dock. "My father won't ask a question if he doesn't want to know the answer."

Fletcher nodded. "Smart man." He turned back to Lizzie and Will. "Afghanistan wasn't March's fault, either. Or yours, Will. I found out about the attacks in Boston too late to do anything but try to mitigate the damage. I didn't know about the attack in Ireland."

"You were there," Will said.

"I'd contemplated talking to Simon myself, but he wasn't in the village. I came to my senses." Fletcher's gray eyes sparked with amusement. "If I wasn't talking to Special Branch, I wasn't talking to the bloody FBI."

"You had to remain a ghost. Whatever I can do," Will said, "I am at your disposal. You're not alone."

Fletcher grinned. "As if I have a choice."

Lizzie contained her emotions. "You were right. Norman was headed to a yacht. He had it all planned. I was to be his…" She took a breath, not looking at his body. "The boat's name is *Lavender Lady.*"

*"Lavender—"*

"My mother loved lavender," Lizzie whispered.

"The man was a manipulative, controlling bastard who relished the thought of being John March's nemesis, with you at his side," Fletcher said. "You've helped this past year more than you know. I promise you. We'll catch the rest of these bloody bastards."

"I'll do what I can—"

"What you can do is keep Lord Will busy and off my tail." He turned to his friend. "Take care of Josie."

"She'll hate the idea," Will said, but his humor didn't reach his eyes. "She's been muttering about killing you for two years even when she thought you were dead. She said we should find your body, dig you up and kill you again."

Fletcher's grin broadened. "That's my girl."

He ran onto the dock, jumped in the speedboat and took off into the fog.

Lizzie began to shake. Will turned to her, easing his arms around her, and they held each other as the last sounds of the boat carrying his friend faded in the distance.

# Chapter 30

*Near Kennebunkport, Maine*
*10:45 a.m., EDT*
*August 27*

When Bob saw Lizzie Rush for the first time, standing on a rock with the tide swirling at her feet and Will Davenport not taking his eyes off her, he decided he might as well give up. Things had happened in his city in the past thirty years that he didn't know about and never would, and most of them involved John March.

He, March and Harlan Rush had arrived just as the Maine SWAT guys were sweeping the property for bombs, bodies, thugs and weapons, but Lizzie, Simon, the two Brits and a beat-up Abigail had the situation under control.

All the Maine guys found was a .22 revolver in a sugar canister.

The old lady who'd lived her last years here had been as self-reliant as her offspring.

Paramedics were still trying to talk Abigail into letting them strap her to a stretcher. She'd collapsed in her father's arms when she saw him, but she was back on her feet now, reenergized, ready to argue with anyone or anything.

And puking. Bob could take her fat lip better than the vomit.

He watched Davenport walk up the hill from the water. The fog was burning off, creating a glare. The investigation was just getting started. Two thugs dead and two thugs captured. One dead billionaire.

One missing Brit.

"I used to wonder what kind of people lived in these big old houses on the ocean," Bob said to Davenport as he walked up the hill. "Now I know. You meet Harlan yet? Lizzie's pop?"

"Briefly," the Brit said.

"He's one of you. American, but a spook."

Davenport's hazel eyes settled on Bob. "He says he's a semiretired hotelier."

Bob held up a hand. "Don't start with me." He nodded to the horizon as the sun burned white through the last of the gray. "I gather your Brit friend got away."

"So he did."

"He's one of you, too."

"British, you mean," Davenport said.

Bob knew the drill. They were all supposed to pretend the missing Brit was one of the bad guys.

Myles Fletcher was another damn spy.

"He killed Walter Bassette," Bob said.

"In self-defense, after he discovered Bassette planned to kill your daughter and confronted him." Davenport shrugged as he, too, stared out at the water. "She stopped quarreling about being under police protection, didn't she?"

"Hell of a wake-up call."

"Myles isn't subtle, but he's effective."

Bob saw Davenport's expression change, soften—if that was possible—as he lowered his gaze down to a knot of Maine state troopers and feds. At first, Bob didn't get it. Then he saw Lizzie Rush break off from the law enforcement types and head up the hill in their direction, her black hair shining in the mist-filtered sunlight. She was soaked up to her knees in seawater, but Bob had no doubt she was up to handling a British lord, spy and SAS officer who was falling in love with her.

"If you'll excuse me," Davenport said.

As he started to her, John March and Harlan Rush eased in next to Bob, and none of them spoke for a moment as they watched the two young people embrace.

"You know," Harlan said finally, "when I taught Lizzie how to fight, I wasn't thinking she'd be defending herself against a gun-toting billionaire out here on the damn rocks."

"What were you thinking?" Bob asked him.

His eyes, the shape of his daughter's if not their light green, shone with the mix of pain and happiness that, Bob had decided, was memory. "I was thinking I didn't want to lose her."

"She's as brave and as beautiful as her mother, Harlan," March said.

Rush didn't argue. "She doesn't like secrets."

"Neither does Abigail."

"A different generation."

Bob frowned at the two men. "Who the hell has secrets anymore these days? My kids know everything."

March shrugged and seemed almost to manage a smile. "We all have our wars to fight." Lizzie and Will joined them, and March went on briskly. "We boarded *Lavender Lady* a few minutes ago. We didn't find Fletcher or any sign he'd been there."

Bob spoke up. "He got what he needed and disappeared. A ghost."

Harlan Rush and Davenport—two bona fide spooks—didn't say anything. Neither did March, who, Bob figured, knew when a lizard crawled out from under a rock anywhere in the world.

Lizzie stayed close to her Brit as she addressed John March. "I could have done things differently this past year."

But before March could respond, her father rolled his eyes. "Lizzie. Damn. What did I teach you?"

She smiled at him. "How to block a punch from Cousin Whit."

"After that."

She sighed. "Don't look back with regret."

"Right. Look back to learn, but since you're never doing this again, spying on some lunatic billionaire, there's nothing to learn. So there's no need to look back at all."

But Bob knew she would. They all would. Abigail, terrorized by a man obsessed with her father. Scoop, bloodied. Fiona and Keira, traumatized.

They'd recover. What other choice did they have?

Lizzie turned her pale green eyes to the FBI director. "Norman believed you destroyed the life I could have had."

"Maybe I did," March said.

"Do you think you'd be the FBI director today if you had?"

"Doubtful. Your father would have arranged an accident for me. Payback." But March's rare display of humor didn't take. "Lizzie, your father was prepared to trade himself for you and Abigail. I was, too."

"Two of us for one of you?"

"Two for two."

Harlan Rush's eyes misted. "Whatever it took."

Bob decided he'd had enough and scoffed at Lizzie. "Shin splints. What crap. You should have knocked on our door and talked to Scoop, Abigail and me. Leveled with Scoop when he caught you."

She didn't look the least bit intimidated by him. "I didn't have any information you didn't have. You might have prevented me from going to Ireland. Then what?"

"Keira would have had to rely on her Irish fairies."

"Maybe she did," Lizzie said.

"Don't start with me."

She grinned at him and Bob was pretty sure he saw her Brit kiss the top of her head. Maybe it was just a brush of his lips.

Who the hell knew anymore.

But Bob saw Owen Garrison walking across the yard and said, "Batman arrives."

Owen spotted Abigail sitting on the stretcher down by the dock and broke into a run. No one tried to stop him.

Bob glanced at March and quickly averted his eyes. It wasn't that he didn't want to see the director of the FBI was crying. It was that the man deserved a moment.

Harlan Rush crossed his arms on his chest, looking as at home on the Maine rocks as he probably did at a poker table in Las Vegas. He nodded toward Davenport, still with an arm around Lizzie as they walked back toward the water, and said to Bob, "His grandfather was a good man. I ran into him during the Cold War from time to time in my misspent youth. Funny how things work out. Does our Lord Davenport spend a lot of time fishing in Scotland?"

"Apparently," Bob said.

"That's what his grandfather used to do, too." The old spook sighed. "I don't know if it's occurred to Lizzie, but we Rushes don't have a hotel in London or Scotland."

"You should open one," Bob said. "It'd give her something to do while she and Davenport think up how to get into trouble again."

# Chapter 31

*Boston, Massachusetts*
*6:30 p.m., EDT*
*August 27*

Owen took Abigail's hand and led her into a large, spacious apartment in the renovated building on the South Boston waterfront that was to be the new headquarters for Fast Rescue. She stood at the tall windows overlooking the harbor. Jeremiah Rush had set aside rooms for everyone at the Whitcomb on Charles Street, and the E.R. doctor had told her to rest. But she'd wanted to come here.

"There are two apartments here that we can choose from," Owen said, staying close to her, "or we can renovate the house on Beacon Street. I don't care where we live. I just want to be with you."

She leaned against him. "We're lucky. We have each other. We have friends, families…"

Owen seemed to understand what she meant. "Norman Estabrook made his choices, Abigail. So did the men with him."

She thought of Myles Fletcher coming to her on the yacht that first time and had to fight back tears. Was he safe now? Was he safe ever?

"Abigail…"

"I'm not going to feel sorry for myself over what happened. It wasn't good, but…" She smiled at this man she loved. "I'm here with you now, and that's enough. I knew you were there for me. With me. The whole time."

"I'd have traded places with you in a heartbeat."

"Maybe things worked out the way they were meant to." She watched a large yacht sailing out into the harbor. "I was so sick on that damn boat. I tried not to let myself think I might be pregnant. But when Fletcher said it, I knew."

She felt Owen's arm tighten around her, but he didn't speak. The doctor in the E.R. had confirmed that she was pregnant. Four weeks. They'd have a spring baby.

"I loved Chris with all my heart. If he'd lived…" Abigail thought of the man she'd married and lost so long ago. "The memory of him is good. He'll be a part of my life forever."

"I know, babe," Owen said. "I'm glad for that."

She turned to him. "I love you."

"Then let's have a wedding."

"Will Davenport offered us the use of his house in Scotland. Anytime. Owen, I don't want to wait another second, never mind months…even days…"

Owen smiled. "Good, because I told Will to cut the grass. We're coming. I can't wait any longer, either."

She touched his mouth with her fingertips. "My cuts and bruises are superficial. I'll be fine…"

He kissed her on the forehead. "Just being with you is enough." He held her and smiled again. "Bob's going to Ireland with his daughters and Keira for Christmas. Telling him he's invited to a wedding in Scotland—"

"Oh." Abigail's face hurt, but it felt good to laugh. "This'll be fun."

Will spoke to Josie from the Garrison house on Beacon Hill. Simon was pacing in the near-empty drawing room, periodically pausing to stare at Keira's sketches of the Dublin windowbox and her Celtic stone angel.

"Did he die a clean death this time?" Josie asked.

"He's a phoenix, our Myles."

"Our?"

Silence. She knew now. There was no more doubt.

"I'm still in Ireland," she said, her voice cracking, "but Arabella and I are having tea upon my return to London. Your baby sister is quite worried about you."

"Tell her to get her needle and thread ready."

"You and Lizzie Rush?"

His heart almost stopped, but he said, "Abigail Browning and Owen Garrison are having their wedding at my house in Scotland in a few days."

"Ah. Well, then."

Simon obviously couldn't stand it any longer and took the phone. "Hello, Moneypenny. Any chance you can get me to Ireland? I want to leave in the next ten seconds."

Will smiled. Knowing Josie Goodwin, she had a plane already waiting at the Boston airport for him.

# Chapter 32

The doctors had sprung Scoop sooner than they'd expected, and Bob found him at their burned-out triple-decker, out back inspecting his garden. He was bandaged and clearly in pain, but he stood up with a squished tomato. "Bastard firefighters trampled my tomatoes. That was uncalled for."

"They were dragging your sorry butt out from behind the compost bin."

Scoop sighed. "My apartment's got so much smoke and water damage, they're going to have to gut it."

"Whole building."

"You can supervise. Where are you going to live?"

"Keira's apartment for now," Bob said. "The lace curtains have to go. I don't care if it's Irish lace."

"What about her?"

"She has plans."

Scoop was silent a moment. "Simon."

Bob winced inwardly. What a dope he'd been. Fiona had tried to tell him it wasn't her. It was his niece. "Scoop..."

"They're good together."

Scoop wasn't exactly up to it, but nothing would stop him from heading with Bob to Morrigan's Bar at the Whitcomb Hotel on Charles Street. Simon had left for Ireland. Jeremiah Rush and a couple other Rushes were there, including Jeremiah's father, Bradley, and his uncle, Harlan, the spook.

Lizzie showed up late. Nobody knew where her Brit was, or at least no one was saying.

Fiona was pink cheeked and happily playing Irish tunes with three of her musician friends. She saw Scoop and blushed, and Bob's heart broke, but he knew she'd be okay.

John March appeared on the steps for a few seconds before turning around and heading back toward the lobby. Lizzie got up and quietly followed him. Her father stayed put.

Making peace with the past, Bob knew from experience, wasn't the easiest thing to do.

Theresa arrived with Maddie and Jayne. "We got through this one," his ex-wife said and gave Bob's hand a little squeeze. "Thank you."

"I didn't do much."

"You didn't get killed."

"All in a day's work."

They sat at a booth together, and Bob was off his guard for that split second that put him back in the past, and he saw what he could have had if he hadn't been such a jerk. But Theresa and their daughters looked happy, and he figured the least he could do was not to saddle them with his regrets.

At a break, Fiona joined them with more Ireland brochures and printouts. "The Rush hotel in Dublin is now officially on our Christmas itinerary. I made reservations for us to have Christmas Eve tea there. It's expensive."

"What a surprise," Bob said.

"Jeremiah has a brother in Dublin. His name's Justin. He's just twenty-two."

"So long as they serve those little buttery mince pies my grandmother used to make, I'm good. And sing Christmas carols." Bob smiled as Jayne crawled onto his lap. "I like Christmas carols."

Lizzie found John March alone at a quiet table in the Whitcomb's elegant second-floor restaurant. He had a bottle of good Irish whiskey. He poured her a glass as she sat across from him. "I met your mother here before you were born. Before she'd met your father. I was a young cop. She was a pretty Irish girl who happened to know some very bad people. She stayed here."

"Good taste," Lizzie said, but her mouth was dry, her hands trembling. She'd stood up to Norman Estabrook and his killers, but this, she thought—talking to a tortured man about the mother she never knew—was almost too much for her.

"She was in Irish tourism development," March said. "Except, of course, she wasn't."

"It was a good cover for her intelligence work."

"She knew what she was doing, Lizzie. She went up against very dedicated, very bad people." He looked away. "I wish I could have saved her. If you hate me…"

"I don't. I never have, even when I suspected that I didn't know everything about her death. I'd have loved to have known my mother. I'd love to have her at my side if I ever get married and have babies of my own—"

"Lizzie." His dark eyes, so like his own daughter's, filled with tears. "I'm so sorry."

"I had a wonderful, interesting upbringing, with a truly loving family. My mother has remained unreal to me, but the choices I faced this past year, the decisions I made, dealing with someone like Norman, have brought me closer to her, helped me to understand her better."

"She loved you and your father with all her heart."

"And you, Director March?"

He didn't flinch at her question. "I could have fallen in love with her. Maybe I did. We met just before Kathryn and I started dating. But then pretty, black-haired, green-eyed Shauna Morrigan ran into Harlan Rush here at the Whitcomb, and that was that."

"My father knew she was a spy?"

"He wasn't a part of what she did. She had IRA contacts in Boston. That's how I hooked up with her. After you were born, she quit. But it was too late."

"Who killed her and her family?"

"An FBI agent with ties to the Boston Irish mob was responsible. I'd been on his trail. She got me closer to him. He found out. He thought killing her would keep me from him. He gave her up to her enemies in Ireland. It didn't matter that she'd retired. They killed her and her family." March drank more of his whiskey. "We cooperated with the Irish in order to save lives."

"So that's why their deaths were ruled an accident. What happened to this corrupt FBI agent?"

"He died in a South Boston gunfight. The shooter was never

found." March polished off his whiskey and set the glass down firmly. "Rough justice. They were violent, turbulent times, Lizzie. We got those mobsters, but others took their place."

"Do you think she knew she'd been murdered?" Lizzie looked down at the amber liquid in her glass. "Or did she believe she fell?"

"I think she loved you and your father, and the rest of it isn't where I would dwell."

"I wanted you to have answers."

"People do. You're not alone. The older I get, the fewer answers I have. I wish I'd known your mother was in danger. I wish I'd saved her. After she died, everyone just wanted to save you, her little baby she loved so much."

"I knew I didn't have the whole story." Lizzie tried to smile through her tears. "Tripped on a cobblestone outside an Irish pub and fell to her death. Ha. What about Simon's father?"

"Brendan Cahill was a friend. He was killed ten years after your mother."

"Ripple effects," Lizzie said, giving the man across from her a long look. "You have a lot of secrets, Director March."

"So I do."

"Thank you for being there for me this past year."

"Lizzie…" He sighed, less tortured. "Abigail and Owen want you at their wedding. It's in Scotland in five days. The Davenport castle."

"Will says it's a house."

"You can tell me what you think when you see it. In my world, it's a castle."

"You mean you've been there?"

He shrugged. Another secret. "You should get your father talking sometime. He has tales to tell about British lords and ladies."

She laughed. "I'll bet he does."

"He loved your mother, and she loved him. Most of all they both loved you. Maybe the rest doesn't matter anymore. Live your life, Lizzie. Don't put it on hold because of the past." He leaned back, eyeing her as she rose. "And stay in touch."

On her way out of the restaurant, she noticed a framed photograph she'd never seen before of her parents hand in hand on the rocks in Maine, her mother visibly pregnant, both of them smiling as they looked out toward the ocean.

"Your father hung it there this morning," Jeremiah said next to her.

"Where is he now?"

"It's Uncle Harlan. Who knows?"

# Chapter 33

Lizzie sat at what she now considered her table by the fire in Eddie O'Shea's pub. She had Keira's book of Irish folktales opened to an illustartion of trooping fairies. She sighed. "I wish I could draw."

"You have other talents," Eddie said, sitting across from her. His dog, settled on the hearth, kept staring at her as if he knew she'd been kissed a by British lord and didn't approve.

"This place feels different than it did the night I was here," Lizzie said.

Eddie reached down and patted the dog. "I'd hope so. Simon's returned. He'll be here soon to start up an argument." The barman seemed to relish the idea. "Have you heard his Irish accent?"

"I understand it's very good."

"Not to a real Irishman."

Lizzie laughed. "Keira will be happy to see him, now that the guards are satisfied she's safe." She turned to another illustration, one of a beautiful fairy princess and a handsome fairy prince. "Imagine loving someone that much. Having someone love you that much."

"There are rules about weddings in Ireland, but I have a feeling Keira and Simon will figure them out." Eddie sat up straight, and the dog rolled onto his side close to the fire. "Your mum was Irish."

"Yes, she was. When I lived in Ireland, I found the cottage where she was born. It's been abandoned, but it's structurally sound, tucked in a quiet, isolated valley not that far from here."

"A magical valley?"

Lizzie smiled at the Irishman across from her and decided he wasn't as skeptical about the wee folk as he liked to pretend. "I have an open mind. I'd like to take Keira there. Maybe it'll inspire a painting. We can find old stories."

"You've a new friend in Keira."

"I hope so. I'm also good at wishful thinking."

Eddie kept his eyes on her. "You've fallen for your Brit, haven't you? Well, your mother fell for a Yank."

"You like Will. My Irish ancestors—"

"They'd want you to be happy. I hear there's no Rush hotel in London."

"Imagine that."

"Convenient, wouldn't you say?"

Josie Goodwin entered the pub and walked behind the bar, helping herself to a bottle of expensive whiskey. She collected a glass and headed to Lizzie's table. Eddie rose and gave her his seat.

"I've become very fond of the Beara Peninsula," Josie said, setting down her glass and opening the bottle. "Should I have brought you a glass?"

Lizzie shook her head. "I've a weakness for Eddie's black-berry crumble."

"Ah. Who doesn't."

Josie poured her whiskey and, after taking a sip, produced a handwritten invitation to Abigail and Owen's wedding in Scotland, along with arrangements for transportation. "And I wasn't sure if you'd have time to shop, so I've a dress for you, too. I've had it sent to Scotland. It's pale blue, flowing, I'm sure just the right size. Your auntie's a dear. Your cousin Justin in Dublin put me in touch with her." Josie took a breath and another swallow of her drink. "How are you? It's all a bit of a crush, I know, but that's how these people are. Will and his American friends. I expect you'll fit right in."

"I love weddings," Lizzie said.

"I expect you do. Will's delayed, but he plans to arrive in time for the ceremony. Whatever's between you is more than the heat of the moment." She pursed her lips, as if debating how much to say. "His family's complicated."

Simon had come into the pub. The local men moaned but were obviously delighted to see him. They exchanged a few good-natured barbs as he dragged a chair over to Lizzie's table and joined her and Josie by the fire. "All families are complicated, Josie." It seemed to be a familiar exchange between them, but he was serious as he addressed Lizzie. "March should have told me about his connection to you. I should have found out on my own. I shouldn't have left you out there alone for so long."

"I was never alone," Lizzie said. "I'd only to give Director March my name, and I'd have had help. I knew that, even when I was most convinced I was on my own."

"This was a tough mission from start to finish. Norman was manipulative and deceptive, but even he didn't have all the pieces."

"Did John March?"

It was Josie who answered. "One never knows."

Simon reached over and tapped the wedding invitation. "Time to sing and dance." His deep green eyes sparked with mischief. "I haven't a clue whether Will knows how to do either."

"As a matter of fact," Josie said, "I don't, either."

Simon smiled. "You'll have to find out, Lizzie, and tell us."

She felt a surge of heat that, she knew, had nothing to do with the fire and everything to do with the thought of dancing in Scotland with Will Davenport. "Is that a challenge, Special Agent Cahill?"

He got to his feet. He truly was a bruiser of a man. "Designed to appeal to the daredevil in you." His eyes were warm now, a promise in them. "You'll be among friends in Scotland."

The local men teased him, and he them back. He was affable and well liked, but he didn't linger. He headed out, and Lizzie rose, restless, uncertain, suddenly, why she'd even come here.

She thanked Josie, who'd given up on her whiskey and was providing Eddie O'Shea with precise instructions about the blackberry crumble she was ordering.

Lizzie followed Eddie's dog out to the pretty village street. The spaniel trotted ahead of her and turned, tail wagging. Hugging her Irish sweater close to her, she let him lead her onto the lane along the ancient wall above the harbor.

As they turned onto the dirt track, she saw a woman running across the field from the stone circle, and recognized Keira Sullivan.

Simon was by the fence, the barren hills quiet except for the intermittent bleating of sheep. Lizzie stopped, and the springer spaniel wandered back down to her in the fine, gray mist. To-gether they watched as Simon climbed over the fence. Keira cried out as she spotted him and started to run, and he scooped her up into his arms.

They held on to each other as if they'd never let go.

"Soulmates," Lizzie whispered, and she and the dog headed back down the lane.

When she reached the village, she had a panicked text message from Justin in Dublin.

Help. Uncle Harlan is here.

She called her cousin. "Lizzie," Justin said, still worked up, "Uncle Harlan's taking me to the Irish village where your family's from. I'm touched, I swear I am, but I have a feeling he's going to teach me how to survive a night in an Irish ruin. And he wants to drive."

"Maintain situational awareness, and you'll be fine."

"Situational—Lizzie!"

She laughed. "I'm going to a wedding."

# Chapter 34

Will Davenport's "house" was a stunning Regency period mansion in the Scottish highlands. Lizzie found Abigail Browning on a path that meandered through the extensive gardens. The detective, more or less healed from her ordeal, was in her element. "I'm so glad you're here," she said. "The Davenports have been so generous. Will's sister, Arabella, had a rack dress that fits me. Will arranged for a private plane so that Scoop could make it. I don't know how he did it. Josie Goodwin said she'll have an ambulance on call. He looks awful, but he says it's because he spent hours trapped on a plane with Bob complaining about another cross-Atlantic trip. My folks are here. The Garrisons. I don't know how a small wedding got so big so fast." She caught herself. "I'm talking a mile a minute."

Lizzie smiled. "It's a special day. Your family and friends are all delighted to see you happy and well."

"It's perfect. And I've never..." Her dark eyes, no longer filled with pain and fatigue, settled on Lizzie. "Thank you for saving my life."

"Myles Fletcher wouldn't have let you be killed."

"He'd have done what he could, but you had instincts and information and doggedness. They're what made the difference. Without you, Estabrook..." She made a face. "Never mind. Let's not ruin a perfect day by mentioning him."

"Your father—"

"He arrived last night. And here comes my mother. She's so nervous, she's making me nervous."

"She's had a rough time."

Abigail grimaced. "I love her, and I don't take her for granted—"

"No, it's all right. Go let her fuss over you. Be a mum and daughter."

Lizzie wandered the grounds until a few minutes before the ceremony started in a large, airy room with tapestries on the walls and giant urns of hydrangeas. She was seated next to Arabella Davenport, who had her brother's hazel eyes. She whispered to Lizzie, "Will is due back any moment."

He arrived in time for the ceremony and stood in back, elegant, reserved, well mannered and thoroughly sexy. Their days apart hadn't changed anything, not for her. She was as attracted to him as ever. It hadn't been a passing fancy fueled by the danger and fears they'd faced together.

And he couldn't dance. Neither could Lizzie.

"Your family, Will. They're proud of what you do?" She stumbled in his arms, righted herself. "Or don't they know?"

"My sister...but the rest...no."

An answer without answering.

Out of the corner of her eye, Lizzie saw Simon dancing with Keira, keeping her off her feet most of the time. "Now, Simon can dance."

"He can, indeed. Philip Billings could, too. David and Myles and I were always surprised...." Will smiled at her, holding her close. "They were right, Billings and Mears. About you. I've met my match."

"Will—"

But he spun her toward glass doors that led to the gardens. "Tell me what you want, Lizzie."

"I want to live in a castle with a handsome prince and grow hollyhocks and lavender."

"With the occasional holiday to save someone?"

"I suppose I'll have to work, too. I have to find somewhere in the U.K. to locate a hotel."

"An adventure in its own right." He bent down to whisper in her ear. "Let's skip the dancing. I've two left feet, as you can see."

"You're faking it. You can dance as well as any Jane Austen hero."

He walked with her onto a cool terrace, fragrant with roses. "I've told everyone I'll be fishing here for the next few weeks. I thought you might like to see where."

"I don't fish."

"You don't fish and you don't dance. Just what will we do to amuse ourselves?"

He took her to a small stone cottage on a stream amid fir trees.

Sweeping her into his arms, he carried her into the bedroom and lowered her to the soft sheets and undressed her to the sounds of the stream. He worked slowly, patiently, or at least deliberately.

Lizzie shivered at the feel of his breath, his hands, on her bare skin. "Can you fall in love with someone in such a short time?"

"I can," he said, his hands warm on her bare skin. "I've been waiting for you my whole life."

"My Prince Charming."

He smiled, smoothing his palms over her hips. "You're not going to turn into a Sleeping Beauty, are you?"

She sank deeper into the soft bed. "Not for a while."

A breeze floated over her, adding to the sensations of his touch, his kisses. She slipped her hands under his warm sweater and spread her fingers over the muscles of his back, felt his shudder of pleasure.

He shed his clothes and came to her again. She sank into the soft bed and lost herself in the feel of him. Touching him, caressing him, kissing him, until she was quivering and hot. She led him into her, their eyes locking as he whispered her name. He moved inside her, and she was gone, pulling him deep, crying out for him as his own urgency mounted.

Days they had ahead of them...

He seemed to read her mind and held her tight. "We're just beginning," he said, and that was the last either spoke for a long time.

Later, they dressed warmly and walked along the stream, holding hands in the cool late-summer air. Lizzie leaned against him, and suddenly the pressures of the past year—its secrets and dangers—seemed far away.

When they returned to the cottage, they found a basket on the doorstep, with a bottle of champagne...and a sprig of lavender.

Lizzie looked at Will and squeezed his hand.

*Myles Fletcher.*

Will took the basket inside without a word. He opened the

champagne and filled two glasses, handing one to her as he slipped one arm around her.

"To friends in harm's way," he said.

They touched their glasses together, and Lizzie whispered, "May they always know they're not alone."

★ ★ ★ ★ ★

# Acknowledgments

For sharing their knowledge and expertise with me, many thanks to Gregory Harrell, my detective cousin; to Fire Chief Stephen Locke of the Hartford (VT) Fire Department; to Hilda Neggers Stilwell, my nurse sister; to Paul Hudson; and to Dave and Margie Carley (ah, Maine!). Any mistakes and liberties are my doing.

A special thanks to Denis Burke in Cleveland for the Irish stories!

There's nothing like visiting Ireland—it's an amazing place. I brought home several books that have helped me better understand what I saw on our trips. For more information on the Beara Peninsula, I recommend *Beara: The Unexplored Peninsula* by Francis Twomey and Tony McGettigan (Woodpark Publications); the Ordnance Survey's *The Beara Way* (Wayfarer Series); *The Stone Circles of Cork & Kerry* by Jack Roberts (Bandia Publishing). Among my favorites of the countless books on Irish folktales is *Irish Folktales,* edited by Henry Glassie (Pantheon Books).

Finally, many thanks to thank my editor, Margaret Marbury, and to everyone at MIRA Books for their support, patience, creativity and thoughtfulness.

Thank you!